THE BLACKFORD OAKES NOVELS
BY WILLIAM F. BUCKLEY, JR.

Tucker's Last Stand

Mongoose, R.I.P.

High Jinx

See You Later Alligator

The Story of Henri Tod

Marco Polo, If You Can

Who's On First

Stained Glass

Saving the Queen

★ ★ ★ ★ ★ ★ ★ ★ ★ ★

Tucker's Last Stand

★ ★ ★ ★ ★ ★ ★ ★ ★ ★ ★ ★ ★ ★ ★ ★

TUCKER'S LAST STAND

A Blackford Oakes Novel

WILLIAM F. BUCKLEY, JR.

Random House Large Print

★ ★ ★ ★ ★ ★ ★ ★ ★ ★ ★ ★ ★ ★ ★

Copyright © 1990 by William F. Buckley, Jr. All rights reserved under
International and Pan-American Copyright Conventions. Published in the
United States by Random House, Inc., New York, and simultaneously in
Canada by Random House of Canada Limited, Toronto.

Library of Congress Cataloging-in-Publication Data
Buckley, William F. (William Frank)
Tucker's last stand / by William F. Buckley, Jr.—Large-print ed.
p. cm.
ISBN 0–394–58858–4
1. Large type books. I. Title.
PS3552.U344T8 1990 813'.54—dc20 90–53341
Manufactured in the United States of America
24689753
First Large Print Edition

Map © 1990 by Anita Karl/Jim Kemp

THIS LARGE PRINT BOOK CARRIES
THE SEAL OF APPROVAL OF N.A.V.H.

FOR JAMES P. MCFADDEN
DEVOTEDLY (AND WITH APOLOGIES)

BOOK ONE

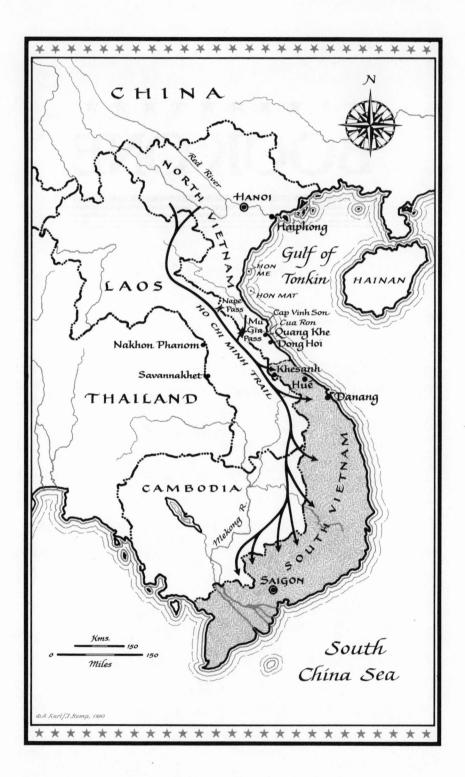

★ ★ ★ ★ ★ ★

Chapter One

Blackford Oakes tried to remember: Had he ever been hotter?

There had been that stifling cottage on the beach in Havana where he spent those miserable weeks waiting on the caprices of Che Guevara. How hot had it got there? he tried to remember, on one of those endless summer afternoons. One of his professors at Yale in the mechanical engineering school had said airily to his class that engineers *always* know the temperature of the air, even as pilots always know in which direction north is, and navigators can tell you within millibars what the barometer is reading: part instinct, part the need, every little while, to consult the thermometer, the compass, the glass. . . . Yes, Professor Schmidt, the students would nod, mutely. God, what an iceberg; you always knew what *his* temperature was. He'd have sunk the *Titanic* in tropical waters.

Blackford brightened, as he stepped around the manure on the ground. A wonderful, creative thought had just occurred. Only a few years ago, when in October 1957 the Soviets had launched their dazzling satellite, striking dumb the great superpower of the West with this display of advanced technology, President Eisenhower had rushed through Congress a bill to help pay the college tuition of engineers and scientists, citing the critical scarcity of them. Could it be that Professor Schmidt had something to do with generating that shortage? Had the deadly word gone out from Yale to the whole of the Ivy League, to the state colleges, reaching even to California? *Study engineering and you'll spend four years with the likes of Professor Schmidt.* Well, Blackford could not remember exactly what the temperature had been in Havana, but it couldn't have been this bad—or was he suffering the normal biological decomposition of the thirty-eight-year-old?

"Shit," said Tucker Montana, as he removed

from his massive left forearm what looked like a baby tarantula. Using thumbs and forefingers, he spread the little creature apart and examined it. "It's only a *Tarantulus virgo*," he said, tossing it at Blackford, who stepped deftly to one side, letting it fall into the steaming bush-nettle that reached up toward them, sometimes a foot high, sometimes three feet and more.

"If you want to make pets out of your tarantulas, make pets out of them. I don't collect them."

He realized suddenly that he had sounded more acidulous than he intended. He was feeling the heat, and now he was making Montana feel the heat—not a good idea at all; very unprofessional in tight, oppressive circumstances. He hadn't worked with Montana before, knew about him only that he came from a purposefully obscure unit in the Army, designed to take on special projects. And Montana knew only that Blackford was CIA. Blackford permitted himself to reflect that, really, Major Montana didn't know him quite well enough to toss tarantulas his way.

He forced himself to smile. "On the other hand, I might save it and send one to Mother. She loves nature."

Montana grinned and with his long ferule beat

the bush directly ahead of him, calling out to Ma Van Binh, their sun-grizzled Laotian guide. "Binh, we getting a little too high? Yes? I mean, the trail is now a couple of hundred meters over"—he pointed to his right. Ma Van Binh said it was necessary to watch for "bayno"—booby traps—planted close to the trail. Montana interrupted. He knew all about booby traps. Hell, he even knew the specialist who had gone over to Hanoi to teach them the latest models. "I almost got the son of a bitch one time." He opened up to Blackford as he continued beating his way behind Ma Van Binh toward Point Easy, where the helicopter would meet them. "Former Huk. His name, I kid you not, is Jesus Joseph Sacred—Jesús José Sagrado, graduate of a fine little Catholic school in Luzon. Far as I can make out, all they graduated was Huks." With his hand he swatted the mosquito on his nose.

"I'm exaggerating, obviously; sure there were a couple of others besides Jesus the Boobytrapper came out of that missionary school. The Huks gave ol' Jesús a little portable laboratory all his own, and didn't like it if he didn't come up with a new trick every day. He got a chicken to swallow explosives before we walked into Miramar: that chicken stayed alive until one of the

Huks turned him over to the cook for dinner—one less cook in the Philippines. Then there was the case of beer—not a trace of rust, no holes, nothing. Beer came out like a TV commercial, only when you drank it you had about three minutes to live, three unpleasant minutes.

"Jesús liked most of all gravity, though. Some of those trails, hunting down those man-eating bastards, some of those trails got so you didn't want to walk over any surface of any kind, didn't matter what it looked like, didn't matter if it was a slab of concrete, because old Jesús Sagrado had a way of covering his boobies so no geologist could tell that it wasn't a good solid stretch ahead of you. But every now and then it was just a wafer-thin layer of earth, and just under that a nice deep hole with maybe three punji stakes, almost always got their guy right in the crotch. One of those boobies was worth a hundred casualties, if you counted the morale; got so you couldn't get the Filipinos to tread over freshly laid concrete."

Blackford confessed he had never heard about Jesús Sagrado.

"We never caught the bastard, but after the surrender in 1954 Colonel Lansdale's scouts discovered he had been scooted out to Hanoi and given some medal or other by the great Ho himself, and reestablished with a new and better laboratory so he could do something to diminish the frog population."

The conversation had the effect of sharpening Blackford's vision. Granted, he was walking directly behind Montana, who was walking directly behind Binh: he had, in effect, without planning or even desiring it, two forward scouts to step into any of Jesús's booby traps, plenty of warning. Still, the heat and the fetid air seemed to magnify all ugly possibilities, including the bizarre possibility that either man could walk safely right over a booby trap without setting it off, yet it would go off under Blackford. Time for a drink of water. And yet one more photograph.

He gave word to stop the column of five men and snapped what must have been his five-hundredth picture, yet another view of the jungly bramble that all but covered the trail that was serving the North Vietnamese as the vital, if narrow, difficult, and treacherous supply line into the southern part of the country they were determined to conquer. It was Blackford's responsibility to specify, and then design, with his own engineering background and especially with the help of the wizards at Aberdeen Proving Ground, means by which traffic on the Ho Chi Minh Trail could be detected, so that something might be done to interdict the materiel and men beginning to travel over it in greater and greater volume. Down the Trail they came: guerrillas, of course—members of the North Vietnamese army—and weapons, weapons, weapons, everything from .22 pistols to bazookas, the latest kind, made in the Soviet Union.

They had walked almost eight miles that day, the fifth day of Blackford's exploration, and he was habituated now to the redundancy of the Trail's surrounding features—the hanging Spanish-moss-like vegetation, the sprouts of sharp underbrush, the varicose little ditches engraved by the spring floods. He was to isolate one hundred miles of the Trail, in pursuit of the Grand Design to block it, and he needed to come up with specifications for whatever mechanisms might transform this otherwise unseeable, impenetrable bush-jungle "road" into a highway as visible as a stretch of highway laid over Arizona desert.

A hell of an assignment, but then President Johnson was a big man and he thought big and the word to the CIA was: *Find out a way to block*

*the trail those mothers are using, what the hell
we got all that technological know-how for, if we
cain't stop a few half-armed yellow savages
from supplyin' a major revolution in South Vietnam?* When the Director called Rufus and
Blackford in and told them what he wanted, he
paraphrased the President's instructions, running them through that verbal laundry he and so
many others in direct contact with the Commander in Chief used when relaying instructions
to subordinates. But when the President, in his
impulsive way, had said he wanted to see this
Tucker Montana in person, plus the two CIA
officials he'd be guiding to do the necessary
surveying of the Trail, it was only left to make the
appointment and the arrangements. So that at
10:30 at night, Appointments Secretary Jack
Valenti took all three of them to the White
House, where they had a personal taste of the
presidential vernacular. They were not shown
into the Oval Office, or even to the private quarters, but were taken directly to the swimming
pool. Five minutes before they arrived, the President had decided he wanted to go for a swim.
When Rufus, Tucker Montana, and Blackford
were led to the indoor pool the water was dimly
lit, but it was easy to see the President, lying on

his back, his nose and his penis projecting just above the water, his paunch like a mountain protecting the artillery pieces on either side from each other.

The water's fine, come on in, the Commander in Chief said, more an order than an invitation. Blackford was unhesitating. Montana looked at him, then followed his lead. They stripped, an attendant taking their clothes, and dove in. Rufus simply turned away, tilted one of the canvas chairs to one side so that his eyes did not fall on the pool, and said nothing. The President was gurgling in the water and chatting away with great spirit about the magnificent resources at Aberdeen with which he intended to meet the yellow bastards who were doing everything they could do to ruin his administration and maybe even turn the country over to that maniac Goldwater, if he ever got nominated, and elected, "though I myself like the dumb son of a bitch, except maybe he would get us into a third world war, and that would be bad for my spread down on the Pedernales." He sank his head a final time and waddled to the stairs, climbing out of the pool into the bathrobe held stretched out for him. Towels were given to the other two men as they climbed up the ladder and sat on the marble bench while dressing. One was still tying his tie, the other lacing his shoes, when President Johnson walked out fully clothed and motioned them all to follow him.

Seated in the Oval Office, he talked about the report he had had from "Secretary McNamara—back only a few days from 'Nam, you know, and he says we going to lose all fucking Indochina unless we stop them at the Trail." The President then paid the legendary Rufus a handsome compliment, stroking him as if he were a long-lost brother, and was clearly distracted by Rufus's failure to purr: Rufus was that way, laconic, formal. Everybody who had ever worked with him knew that, and Blackford permitted himself a smile as President Johnson worked, like Jimmy Durante on a reluctant nightclub audience, trying to get it to swing with him, Durante lifting his chair and bashing it down on the piano. LBJ soon gave up on Rufus, and turned now to Tucker Montana. "Montana," he said, "you got one Medal of Honor already. I'm prepared to give you another one, but I want you here alive for that, so don't take any of those crazy risks you're famous for." Tucker Montana was not displeased that his name was known in the White House. Blackford, who knew nothing about Major Montana's past, except what he had just heard, did know that it was one of Jack Valenti's jobs to give the President useful biographical data about the men and women who came to see him. Addressing Blackford now, the President said simply that he knew the esteem in which Blackford had been held by "my predecessor." Blackford bowed his head ever so slightly. "One of these days I'm gong to bring you in and hear you tell me yourself about the time you spent with Che Guevara. Son of a bitch is takin' Castro's revolution to South America; hope they catch the bastard, string him up."

LBJ lifted his right index finger ever so slightly, and Valenti, looking out for the signal, rose, followed quickly by the three men he had brought in to the White House. The President rose too. "McCone says you'll be in the field within a week. I've told him to report to me *directly* what recommendations you come up with." He extended his right hand to each of them. With his left he opened a drawer and pulled out a fistful of presidential tie pins, money clips, and cuff links, dropped them in Valenti's open hand and said, "Jack, you give these distinguished genelmen some of these souvenirs." He nodded his big head, and walked out of the office ahead of his guests.

The sun was directly overhead and the little scouting party huddled under the shade of a tamarind tree. Ma Van Binh sat at one side of the tree trunk with his two Vietnamese porters, who put down the radio and photographic equipment and laid their rifles alongside his. They ate the rice from their moist sacks silently, taking sips from their water gourds and exchanging only at long intervals a few words in Vietnamese. Behind them Blackford was thinking over the question. Montana wanted to know why we hadn't raised hell with North Vietnam for violating the two-year-old treaty guaranteeing the neutrality of Laos.

"Because they know we have no means of enforcing it. I mean, we have no means of enforcing it that we're willing to use."

Montana was silent for a minute. Then, "Why don't we make them?"

Blackford swallowed a draft of water and leaned back on the tree trunk, removing his large-visored sun hat and using it as a fan. "Well, that reminds me of something that hap-

pened when I was at college. There was a professor there, political science, bright as hell and
ornery as hell, loved to twit his colleagues,
ACLU types. A faculty meeting was called to
protest the prosecution in New York of the Communists rounded up under the Smith Act, the
Foley Square trial—you remember that?"

"Yup. I was in Japan. Just before the Korean
War, right?"

"Nineteen forty-eight, I think. Anyway, for an
hour or so it went around the big table in the
faculty room, all the professors talking about the
unconstitutionality of the Smith Act and so on,
and then they came to my mad professor, Will-
moore Kendall, asked him what he thought
about it. And he said, 'You know, there's an
elderly Negro lady who cleans up my Fellow's
suite every day and this morning just before I
came over here she said, "Professor, is it true
that there are people in New York who want to
overthrow the government by force and violence?" And I said, "Yes, that's true, Mary." And
she said, "Why don't we run them out of town?"
'Now, that lady' "—Blackford was imitating the
Oklahoman–Rhodes scholar accent of his old
tutor—" 'that lady knows more about politics
than any full professor in this room.' "

Montana laughed. And then he paused. "What's the equivalent? How would you run the North Vietnamese out of town?"

Blackford changed the subject. "The President wants to control the traffic on this highway, that's true. The North Vietnamese shouldn't be on it in the first place, but then they shouldn't be in South Vietnam, the way I figure it—"

They were distracted by the sound of the helicopter approaching. The rotors were deafening as the large OH-13 Sioux began to squat down. It had reached a hovering station only a few feet above the ground when they heard the shot coming from the bushy ravine below. One of the pilots slumped in the cockpit. Montana snapped orders even as his own rifle began to spit fire into the densest bush to the right of the plane.

"Cover cover cover move your ass Binh!"

The three natives were on their stomachs firing. Blackford had only his pistol. He leaned over and shouted to Montana.

"We'll have to run for it." Montana needed no instructions in guerrilla technique. He slapped Binh on the shoulder. "Tell your men to continue firing, you run into the chopper with Mr. Oakes. Resume firing when you get there. Tell the other

guys to begin running when we pick up your covering fire."

Montana, Binh, and Oakes ran the fifty yards, then crouched beside the helicopter, firing into the ravine. The two guides rushed forward. The second one was stopped by a bullet a dozen yards before reaching the chopper. Blackford started back to fetch him and was floored by Tucker Montana's heavy fist. "You mind your business goddamnit, Oakes. Get in the chopper." Montana himself, crouching his huge frame, went back and dragged the wounded guide back, as if he were light as a child. Binh was firing now from the open window of the helicopter. Blackford fired, and then pulled up the wounded guide as Montana shouted to the pilot to take off. The helicopter rose quickly and Blackford reached over the cockpit seat to help the copilot, whose head was far over, the chin thrust down, the flying helmet on his lap, where the man had put it just before a bullet entered his right temple. Blackford turned to the pilot on the left. "You want me on the controls, Jeff?"

"Nahr," he said. "I can handle it. Just check the radio signals for me." He handed Blackford his clipboard. Blackford studied it. He stretched over the copilot to adjust the radio to the frequency for Checkpoint Alpha at Savannakhet. Then he took a knife from his belt and cut away his rolled-up sleeve. With the strip of cloth he bound the wound of the dead flyer. The bullet had entered one temple and come out the other. He found himself thinking, oddly, sadly, Well, at least we were firing in the right direction. After binding the wound he leaned back in the second row of seats. In the rear cabin, Binh tended to the shattered knee of his guide. Suddenly, at two thousand feet of altitude, the air was cool. "Welcome to Vietnam, Mr. Oakes," said Tucker Montana.

★ ★ ★ ★ ★ ★

Chapter Two

APRIL 5, 1964
ABOARD THE YAI-BI-KIH
EN ROUTE TO CINCINNATI, OHIO

The senator stretched his legs and set his heels on the edge of the empty seat opposite him in his chartered 727 jet. He rested his sunburned hands on the table as he read over the text of the speech he would give that night in Cincinnati. The airplane had passed through the turbulence and now no motion was felt, except for the quiet purring of the engines. His young speech writer, Fred Anderson, sat on his right, making notes on the carbon copy where the senator indicated, as he read out loud, minor changes he wanted—"Not 'President LBJ.' President Johnson."

"How about, 'My predecessor, President Johnson'?" Freddy asked with a smile.

Goldwater released a quick grin, going back to the text. Goldwater continued reading in a monotone, interrupting himself from time to time to comment on the speech, or on something a passage he was reading reminded him of, and Fred Anderson knew through experience when such interruptions were an invitation to counter-remarks by him or when he was simply supposed to listen. Or when, catching the eye of Bill Baroody across the aisle, it was especially appropriate for him to say nothing, on issues or ideas the campaign manager did not want commentary on.

"What does Lodge think he's going to accomplish, leaving Saigon suddenly? I've knocked out Rockefeller, he's gone. All the liberals can come up with is Scranton. The city of Scranton, Pee Aye is, I suppose, named after the first Scranton? When did that happen, about the time of the Pilgrims?"

"About then," Baroody grinned, drawing lightly on his pipe.

"But I mean, why Bill Scranton? I'm not sure he'd set even Scranton, Pennsylvania, on fire."

"He did pretty well when he ran for governor of Pennsylvania."

"He reminds me of Adlai. Freddy? Does he remind you of Adlai? I wish you'd give up that pipe, Bill—smells like a war chief's teepee in here."

"I see what you mean, Barry." Baroody ignored, as always, the repeated protests over his pipe. "Yeah, he reminds me of Adlai."

"But"—Goldwater laid down the speech and was asking the question now directly—"that does *not* tell us why Lodge quit Saigon. It isn't as though he had settled our problems there. It's a goddamn mess and it's going to get worse."

Baroody leaned over and faced the candidate diagonally. "Don't you see, Barry, he's coming back here to help Scranton. Rockefeller will finance the whole thing. And they have exactly one objective in mind, and that's what we've got to keep our eyes on. They want Ike to come out for Scranton. That's about the only thing that would keep us from getting the nomination."

"Eisenhower said he was going to stay neutral, didn't he? Didn't he say that twice?"

"Yes," Baroody said. "Ike said that twice. But

he also said exactly—" He looked at his watch a full second before reminding himself that it was hardly necessary to do so in order to say, "—exactly six days ago he said that as far as he was concerned, the race for the nomination was open until the day the Republican Convention named a candidate. You hardly overlooked that snub, Barry. You hammed it up for the picnic crowd in Phoenix, let them stick an arrow out behind you. Made a fine photo, looked as though it was coming right from your back, not from your armpit. Shot in the back by Ike—the message got through."

"Yes," Goldwater said. He turned to his right. "Freddy, have we got anything nice in the speech here"—he shuffled vaguely through the pages he hadn't yet read—"about Ike? Maybe you can work in something about how he won the Second World War single-handed. Or maybe something about how he anticipated the Indochina problem at the Geneva conference in 1954 which is why we have no problem in Vietnam today."

"Quiet, Barry! Where Ike is concerned, We Are Not Sarcastic Ever." Baroody turned his head to Anderson, to make certain that the injunction had got home to the blond young speech writer with the horn-rimmed glasses and the slightly cheeky expression on his face, even when working at highest tempo. Goldwater looked up again from the manuscript.

"Say, Bill. Did you see in the last issue of *National Review* where Buckley proposes I tap Ike as my Vice President? Kinda cute, that."

"If you think so, you and Buckley are the only people who think it's such an interesting idea. For one thing, it's unconstitutional. The Twenty-third Amendment says no one can be President more than twice, and since a Vice President is directly in line to become a President, then that's unconstitutional. It's that simple."

"Bill"—Fred Anderson interrupted, stooping over to reach into his briefcase—"actually, I think you could be wrong about that. By the way, it's the Twenty-second Amendment"—he flipped open his well-worn 1964 *World Almanac*—"and what it says"—he turned the pages—"is . . . No person shall be *elected* to the office of President more than twice, et cetera. Hell, a Vice President who becomes President because the President is shot—excuse me, Senator, just making a theoretical point—hasn't been *elected* President. Suppose the President *and* the Vice President were shot and the

Speaker of the House was next in line, but he had already been President twice—are you saying he wouldn't qualify? Or are you saying that he wouldn't qualify to serve as Speaker because he might just end up being President, and that's against the Twenty-second Amendment?"

"Goddamnit, Freddy, you sound like a Harvard debater."

"Bill, I *was* a Harvard debater. But does that make my constitutional reasoning wrong?"

"Well," Goldwater interrupted, "it's not a crazy idea, let's face it. I'm not sure I'd want to be the person to suggest it to Ike, that he come back into government as a second lieutenant. But it would take care of the inexperience bit, and the Goldwater-wants-to-go-to-war—you've got to agree on that, don't you?"

Baroody drew on his pipe, and his dark, puffy Lebanese-inherited features contracted as he communicated an urgent wish to stay on the point. "The point is, Barry, that's an out of-this-world suggestion. But it is true we've got to keep Ike neutral, and there's one thing Lodge said in Saigon yesterday that helps."

"What did he say that helps? I don't remem-

TUCKER'S LAST STAND 25

ber ever hearing Cabot Lodge say anything that helped anything. Except maybe Cabot.''

Baroody pulled the clip from the folder at his side. "He said, he said, let's see . . . 'I cannot see how Vietnam could possibly be a presidential campaign issue. It involves the Eisenhower administration and the Kennedy and Johnson administrations and the Truman administration.' "

"Goddamn—he said that?"

Baroody handed over the clipping. Goldwater turned to Fred Anderson. "You got anything about that in the speech?"

"No sir."

"Well, take this down." Goldwater leaned back, closed his eyes, and spoke slowly, as he did when dictating to his secretary. "I hope Ambassador Lodge will not . . . be a . . . lone Republican voice crying . . . excuses or evasions in the—er, confusion, er . . . ."

"Wilderness, maybe?"

"Yes . . . in the wilderness of this Administration's Vietnamese policy."

"Here's something you might add. How do you like this''—Baroody had been scribbling while Barry Goldwater dictated. " 'I find it difficult for me to believe that anyone could leave such a post at such a critical time, simply to pursue a personal political course.' "

Fred Anderson looked up from his pad. "You don't want, 'I find it difficult for me . . .' "

"What's the matter with that?" Baroody's pipe tilted up truculently.

"Just, 'I find it difficult.' Not, 'I find it difficult for me,' " Freddy said, his pencil tapping the air in front of him. The schoolboy, making a minor correction. Then he smiled. "Old debaters' stylebook." Baroody nodded, and looked up at Goldwater.

"Okay?"

"Okay. What's the *matter* with those Eastern Establishment types? Leaving Saigon just when things there are getting really hot. . . . Scranton for President and Lodge for Vice President. Who will they want for Secretary of State? Billy Graham?"

Baroody picked up his copy of *Time* magazine. Goldwater went back to his manuscript. Fred Anderson lifted his portable typewriter from under the seat and began to transcribe the notes he had made. The steward came in, did anybody want anything? Baroody nodded, "Coffee." Goldwater, engrossed in the manuscript, did not answer. "Coke, please," said Fred Anderson. Baroody pointed at Senator Goldwater. "He'll have the same. Coke." The steward nodded, and left through the door of the private compartment.

★ ★ ★ ★ ★ ★

Chapter Three

APRIL 11, 1964
ST. PAUL'S EPISCOPAL CHURCH
NORFOLK, VIRGINIA

Once again, he reflected from his righthand-most position in the front pew, he was the principal male figure among mourners. Then—as now—the widow was of course the emotional center of attention. He thought back to November twenty-fifth: Jackie had never looked more beautiful than on that awful day; more gravely, stoically dignified. Oh God what a nightmare that was, and just seventy-two hours earlier he had been alive, President of the United States, the most glamorous political figure since—combine Roosevelt, *both* Roosevelts, with some of Lincoln and some of Jefferson, and that came close. His eyes felt full, but there was no sign of tears. Bobby Kennedy did not shed tears—"He cries on the inside," he had heard Ethel say about him once over the telephone when he was playing with the kids and she thought he couldn't hear him.

And now yes, the newest widow, Jean MacArthur—tiny woman, maybe four feet ten? he wondered, glancing across the aisle to appraise the general's wife, her fine features barely visible through the black lace.

Yes, he had been the primary male figure at St. Matthew's Cathedral in Washington only (he counted on his fingers: December, January, February, March, April) five months ago, even though that great big loutish Texan, now President of the United States, thanks to the stupidity of the Secret Service and the maniacal marksmanship of a young madman thankfully dead—President Freckle-Belly had occupied the principal position by the aisle on the left, while Bobby had stood, and knelt, next to his—their—mother, and Jackie. Today he had no emotional standing. He had met General MacArthur only two or three times, ceremonial occasions. MacArthur had managed to look him over as he might have inspected a cadet newly arrived at West Point. Well, no one who knew him for five

minutes confused him with a cadet—ask Jimmy
Hoffa; I'll have him in jail before summer. But
Dugout Doug was a commanding figure, no
doubt about it. Jack had thought him godly during the war and after, but had been smart to stay
out of the way when Truman fired him. Jack had
that *great* sense of when to stay out of the
way—look how he'd handled Joe McCarthy!
Managed to stay out of McCarthy's firing line,
treat him as a pal, and yet say all those ACLU
things.

And then trust MacArthur to raise a stir even
after he died, with those two ten-year-old inter-
views released by Lucas and Considine—good
journalists, diggers—about how MacArthur
would have won the war in Korea if Truman had
only let him. . . . Interesting idea, actually, to
detonate a string of atom bombs along the Yalu
River, sealing off North Korea from any access
to the Communist Chinese. Be nice to do that
across the Ho Chi Minh Trail. Lucas also quoted
MacArthur on Truman: "The little bastard hon-
estly believes he is a patriot." But he had said,
according to Lucas, that Truman had—what
was that, exactly? Yes. "Raw courage and
guts." Wonder what MacArthur thought about

Lyndon Baines Johnson? Interesting, Johnson deputizing me to come here to Norfolk to represent him instead of coming himself, though he made quite a fuss over the corpse when it was in Washington for a couple of days on the way down here. But half the world's cameras are in Norfolk, and LBJ doesn't run away from cameras. Funny. Why didn't he deputize Rusk, or McNamara? McNamara would have made more sense—Secretary of Defense Goes to Funeral of a Five-Star General. One thing for sure: We'll never know why he picked me. And we're all here like sardines. Couldn't squeeze in an extra altar boy.

. . . LBJ likes to ask you what *you* think, but he doesn't often tell you what *he* thinks, old Freckle-Belly—nice, Pierre Salinger coming up with that description, just right somehow. An express secretary's coup, putting that phrase in circulation. And the whole world thinks he's a real decisive type. Huh. He's danced with every position on Vietnam since he took Jack's place. Mac comes back a few weeks ago and puts it to him: blockade Haiphong . . . bomb the airports . . . bomb the railways . . . stiffen the Khanh government. . . . Yeah, he tells McNamara—his

Secretary of Defense!—he'll think about it. What he's thinking about is the election, as if he could lose it.

The eulogist, with one final reference to duty, honor, country, sat down, crossed in front of the altar, bowed his head to the bishop, turned, bowed to Mrs. MacArthur, and then turned another few degrees and bowed to Robert Kennedy, who returned the gesture with a small nod.

Magic. It's magic. What we *do* to people. Sure, there are Kennedy-bashers out there, mostly right-wing nuts and a few snobs. Mostly, they get shaky in the knees when they spot a Kennedy. . . . Some of his people are telling LBJ that with me on the ticket with him, Goldwater would sew up the Southern vote because the rednecks hate me. A lot of people hate me. One reason why so many people like me. As Jack said to his old pal Charlie Bartlett, Look Charlie, some people have it, and some people don't. . . . What are we supposed to do about it?

Max Taylor has done his work, really got the word around, the perfect Democratic ticket: *Johnson-Kennedy in 1964.* Speaking of magic. *That's* the way to make it up for Jack, make up for Dallas. Might lose a few redneck states—

Mississippi, Louisiana; maybe more than a few—Georgia, Alabama, probably Florida, I suppose Arizona. But everywhere else? In my pocket. And it won't hurt my feelings if the pollsters rub it in that more people are drawn to the ticket on account of me than on account of Ol' Big-Belly. He'll run again in '68, sure. But in '72 I'll be only forty-seven years old. . . .

The Catholics in the congregation discreetly crossed themselves as the bishop gave the blessing. The organ blared out "America the Beautiful." Mrs. MacArthur looked across the aisle at the Attorney General, who nodded and gestured that she and her son should proceed down the aisle first. Bobby and Ethel followed, and then Prime Minister Choi Doo Sun of South Korea, General Carlos Romulo of the Philippines, and the former Prime Minister of Japan Shigeru Yoshida, paying final tribute to the memory of the man who had served their countries with such distinction.

Outside the church the cameras and the newsmen formed an arc, leaving only enough room for the flag-draped coffin to enter the hearse, and for Mrs. MacArthur to disappear into the limousine directly behind. The moment her door had been shut by the attendant they tried to descend on the tousle-haired, bright-eyed Attorney General. Bobby Kennedy was used to reporters, but there was an unusual intensity in their struggle now to come within speaking distance. The two cordons of Marines leading to the cathedral held them back, as did the solemnity of the circumstances—the organ music sounding right up to the curbside. Attendants carrying what seemed to be cratefuls of floral wreaths were pressing their way, parallel to the official mourners, to hasten to the burial site at the courthouse. Then the voice broke out. A youngish woman, her hand-held microphone held high over the cordon:

"Mr. Attorney General! Mr. Attorney General! What is your comment on what President Johnson said?"

Two aides thrust themselves between him and the reporter, and Robert Kennedy gently but firmly pushed his wife into the limousine, whose door was quickly slammed shut. The thick bulletproof glass blocked out the voices of the reporters, who had come around the cordon and were crowding now on both sides of the Cadillac. Kennedy's brow furrowed. He stared intently ahead. But the limousine could not move until Mrs. MacArthur's car began the solemn vehicular procession toward the burial site. He hissed to his aide in the jump seat, "Goddamn the press. What in the hell is going on?"

The car ahead began to move forward. The Attorney General barked at his driver to move and the car lurched forward, scraping past cameras snatched back out of the way. In a moment the caravan was moving forward at a ceremonial fifteen miles per hour.

"What's going on?" he asked his aide again.

"Don't know, sir. We were in the church."

"Turn on the radio."

The Attorney General then reached to his side to do it himself and take over the controls. He fiddled with the dial. He slid by the stations of country music and then by what his son Bobby called "the Beatles channels." He stopped the dial when he heard a voice giving the news. He knew immediately that he had tuned to someone broadcasting live from the crowd of reporters they had just left behind.

"—the funeral procession is on its way now to the old courthouse, where General MacArthur will be buried. Attempts to get a comment from Attorney General Robert Kennedy when he left the church were unsuccessful. He and Mrs.

Kennedy entered their limousine before the reporters could get him to comment on President Johnson's statement this afternoon when asked if he had decided who to tap as his running mate for the election. 'I haven't made my choice yet,' President Johnson said. And then added, 'All I can say at this time is, it won't be anybody who is serving in my Cabinet.' . . ."

The Attorney General felt genuine pain in his chest. He didn't hear what else was coming in over the radio. Ethel gripped his hand, that special grip he had got used to when she knew he was crying on the inside.

★ ★ ★ ★ ★ ★

Chapter Four

On Tuesday, two days after the attack on Pearl Harbor, the line outside the army recruiting station at the corner of 7th Street and East Avenue went almost around the entire block. The next day the *Austin American,* in its story on the rush to enlist in the armed forces, remarked that it was the longest line seen in Austin since the opening night of *Gone With the Wind* two years earlier. The difference in the composition of the two lines was obvious enough: today's line was composed of very young men, though there was a scattering of thirty-five- and thirty-six-year-olds, the paper reported. The recruiting station had broadcast repeatedly that thirty-six was the oldest eligible age—the youngest, of course, being seventeen, but to enlist at that early age required the acquiescence of the applicant's father or, if dead, his mother.

Tucker Montana's father was dead. He had been run over by a taxi while hailing a bus in a rainstorm to make a delivery of an electric fan he had repaired for a parishioner who operated a souvenir factory near the Alamo. Tucker was six and his father had struggled to feed wife and son, doing odd jobs at St. Eustace Church during the day. Faraday Montana, who traced his background to General Sam Houston and one of his Indian concubines, during the year the general left Tennessee en route to Texas, was proud that he could offer his services as an electrician, as a carpenter, as a plumber, as a mason, or for that matter as a janitor: there wasn't anything, really, he could not do with his hands. Fr. Enrique would almost always find something in the large church that needed fixing, and on good weeks, when Fr. Enrique would give a particularly galvanizing sermon at all six masses, he would manage to count out enough nickels and dimes to pay Faraday fifteen, every now and again twenty dollars. Although the elderly priest and the twenty-eight-year-old jack-of-all-trades got on wonderfully well, Fr. Enrique knew that Faraday was looking about, always, for more lucrative work. Far from resenting this, Fr. Enrique kept his own eyes open and it was he who had told Faraday about the opening at the Alamo.

Fr. Enrique had stopped by the little factory-shop on a summer day to chat with his parishioner, Al Espinoso. Sweating profusely in his Roman collar, the priest had looked wistfully at the idle electric fan behind the counter. Why wasn't it turned on, on so hot a day? Al Espinoso said it was broken and he hadn't found anybody who could fix it. Moreover, the only one of his workers who knew anything about electricity had left the factory the week before to join a brother in Houston.

Fr. Enrique pounced. He would have the fan fixed by a young man of extraordinary talents as a craftsman if Al would agree to interview him for the opening. It was agreed, and the exciting news was given to Faraday that if he landed the job, he would be paid thirty dollars every week. Whereupon Faraday (Fr. Enrique would tell and retell this to young Tucker in the months and years ahead) "took that old fan, it was in pieces in about"—he snapped his fingers—"maybe four minutes, then said, the trouble is in the armature, and in about eighteen more minutes the copper was stretching right from there"—Fr. Enrique pointed to the door into the sacristy—"to the main altar. But five minutes after *that,* he had it all rewound. Then what really impressed me about your father happened. He said he was ready to take the fan to Señor Espinoso, and I said to him, 'Faraday, what you *mean* you ready to take the fan to Señor Espinoso—you don't even know if it *works!*' And he said to me, he said, 'Father, of course it works. I just fixed it.' So I said, I said, 'Now look here, Faraday Montana, you plug that fan into that socket right now and we'll just *see* if you fixed it.' Well, he did that—and the fan began to turn, and in a couple of seconds it was shooting out a fountain of air.

"You know what your father made me feel like? He made me feel like St. Thomas! You know about Doubting Thomas, yes, Tucker?"

When he first heard the story at age six Tucker hadn't read about Thomas, who had doubted the resurrection of Jesus until Jesus asked him to probe His wounds, and then Thomas knew. Because Tucker didn't know, that first time, about Doubting Thomas, and because he didn't want to lie to Fr. Enrique or confess his ignorance, he managed to change the subject. As soon as he got home he asked his mother, who told him that when he wanted an answer to a question like that he should consult their little library, in which there were two— not one—copies of the Bible. Tucker, with his mother's help, found the reference, and afterward it seemed as though a month didn't go by without Fr. Enrique talking about Faraday's tragic last afternoon on earth, and about how, just before the end, he had made a Doubting Thomas out of Fr. Enrique.

His mother took a job as a receptionist-bookkeeper-telephone operator at a small hotel, coming back to the little apartment late at night but always with a fresh book for him from the library. She would stop there on her way to work—the library wouldn't let children under twelve take books home. When Tucker ran out of reading matter, often on Sunday afternoons, he would leave the apartment and go to the drugstore, which was never closed, and read through one magazine after another. Mr. Eggleston let him do this, but only on the understanding that he would wash his hands at the sink in the back of the drugstore first, so as not to leave any marks on a magazine that might be sold to a customer. Tucker liked especially *Life* magazine, whose pictures he would stare at with hungry curiosity, and *Popular Mechanics,* and *National Geographic.* There was only one copy of the *National Geographic,* to which the store subscribed, and it was earmarked for a professor at St. Mary's University, but the professor never got around to picking it up until after a week or so, giving Tucker time to come in, even during weekdays, to make sure he hadn't missed anything.

Tucker attended the parochial school at St. Eustace's and during the afternoons stayed on after classes to help Fr. Enrique. By the time he was thirteen, Fr. Enrique would discreetly confide to anyone conceivably interested in the point, Tucker Montana could perform any job his father had been able to perform. "I don't know where he picked up the knowledge," he told Tucker's mother one Sunday after Mass on Tucker's eleventh birthday, "but he did." He pointed to the cathedral-shaped wooden Victor radio. "That stopped working on Friday. I thought it needed a new tube and I told Tucker to take it to a radio shop. He said he would have a look. He took it apart. I mean, all apart. In a half hour he had it working. Wasn't a tube, your boy said. Some kind of short circuit. He is some kind of a kid!"

By the time Tucker was fourteen, Fr. Enrique knew that he had to do something about him. So one afternoon, after making an appointment over the phone, he went over to St. Mary's, the Marianist men's university at San Antonio, and was told where he could find Mr. Galen, the professor of physics. He explained the problem and Mr. Galen agreed to see the boy, and the following afternoon, at the designated hour, Tucker arrived in Mr. Galen's study, which was also his classroom.

Tucker was tall for his age. His hair was cropped close but not mercilessly short. A "bean shave" meant fewer quarters spent at the barber. (Tucker had begun, at age seven, restricting himself to four haircuts every year, explaining to his mother that hair grew at the rate of a half inch per month, and that if cropped close enough, once every three months was all he really needed to spend at the barber's—exactly one dollar per year.) He had lately taken to asking Antonio if there was anything in the barber shop that needed to be fixed—one day he said, to his own and the barber's astonishment, "malfunctioning"—and as often as not there was: a chipped mirror, dull shaving blade, whatever. Tucker would fix it, sharpen it, clean it, paint it, and Antonio would remit the price of the haircut. Antonio took to cutting Tucker's hair less drastically than directed because Antonio didn't want to go a full three months without seeing him. So that although Tucker, entering the physics professor's domain, had had his hair cut the day before, he didn't look as spare as he would have a year earlier.

He was tall, but somehow not ungainly. His arms and legs seemed fully developed, and Mr. Galen found himself wondering whether the boy was full-grown at fourteen. At five feet six or seven inches his body seemed mature, though his face was that of a prepubescent boy. His brown eyes were oddly adult, penetrating but not obtrusive, and his ears lifted slightly when he was spoken to (though perhaps this would not have been noticeable if his hair had been a little longer). Tucker's chin was slightly pointed, and since he did not smile, one saw only a trace of his white, regular teeth. He was beardless of course but there was the peach fuzz, lighter in color than the light-brown hair on his head. His manner was direct—polite, obliging, but not in the least intimidated or obsequious.

Mr. Galen told him to sit down. He turned then, and pointed to the blackboard. He asked Tucker whether what was written there meant anything to him. Tucker looked up and said Yes, of course, those were the basic propositions of calculus. Mr. Galen then asked him if he knew anything about the subject of physics, and Tucker said only what he had read in a textbook. Which textbook? Tucker pointed to the book by Hatteras and Guy sitting on top of one of the desks in the classroom. Mr. Galen, who used that book for his introductory physics course, asked if Tucker had experienced any difficulty with the subjects covered in that book, and Tucker looked up at him with quite evident dismay.

"Difficulty? What do you mean, sir?"

"What do I mean? I mean just that. Some students have a problem with spatial mechanics, some with the introduction to electricity, some with theories of motion—did you have any problem with these?"

Tucker still found it difficult to answer. He was obviously thinking about the social consequences of the fix he found himself in. He did not wish to appear boastful. He found the solution. He said brightly, "Sometimes I have a problem with Latin. For instance: I can never absolutely remember whether *pre, in,* and *post* take the ablative or the accusative case. I just forget."

Mr. Galen said nothing. Then he stood up and went to the bookcase behind his desk and reached for a large volume bound in maroon-colored cloth. He pulled it out and brought it to the boy, who obediently looked at its title and pronounced the title out loud: "*Theories in Advanced Physics.* By"—he looked up at Mr. Galen. "Did you want me to read the names of all the authors? There must be ten, fifteen maybe."

"Those authors," said Mr. Galen, "twelve men and one woman, are at the frontiers of the study of physics. Do you want to have a look at the book?"

"Oh, yes. Yes, sir. I promise to take very good care of it."

Mr. Galen, who stood six feet one inch tall, looked down at the fourteen-year-old boy. "Take it. And come back here next Tuesday, same time. We'll see how you get on with it."

Tucker said thank you, extended his hand, and left the room, his heart pounding with excitement at the treasure carried under his arm. He remembered, on the way down the staircase, to recite a quick Hail Mary of gratitude in thanks for his good luck.

The recruiting sergeant scanned the application.

"This your mother's signature?"

"Yes, sir."

"You might as well begin your training. I am not a 'sir.' I am a sergeant."

"Yes, Sergeant."

"And this is your birth certificate?"

"Yes . . . Sergeant."

Sergeant Brisco looked at it. He then looked up at Tucker. "You were seventeen day before yesterday. On Pearl Harbor Day?"

"Yes, Sergeant."

Sergeant Brisco looked at him. "And you entered the University of Texas as a freshman last September?"

"Yes, Sergeant."

"That means you were only sixteen when you came to Austin."

"Yes, Sergeant."

At this point Brisco took the heavy lead ashtray on his desk, raised it and with all his strength struck it down over Tucker's application form. "You know something, kid," he said, his lips parting into something between a smile and a snarl. "I don't think you are seventeen. I don't think that '1924' on your birth certificate was written by the registrar of public records in San Antonio. And I flatly doubt that your mother signed this piece of paper.

"Now I'll tell you where we go from here. One possibility is we go to the police, and they call the registrar in San Antonio and verify your birth certificate. Then we call your mother and ask if she signed this certificate. Then we take you to the juvenile court and suggest thirty days in the juvenile lockup for forgery. That's one alternative."

Tucker stood, almost as if at attention.

"You want to hear the other alternative?"

"Yes, Sergeant," he whispered.

"Get your baby ass out of this office before I light my next cigarette"—he reached for a pack of Luckies—"and go back to your freshman class and let us big boys fight the war." He searched theatrically for his matches. When he looked up, Tucker was gone.

One year later Tucker *was* seventeen, and he knew that if he really worked on her, he could get his mother to sign the application form listing his true date of birth, December 7, 1925. But he had been told informally by the major in charge of the V-12 program on the campus that on the recommendation of the chairman of the department of physics, no application of Tucker Montana for early enlistment in the Army would be accepted. Moreover, said the major—he had come to Tucker's little room at the Zeta fraternity house, a most flattering gesture—he had already written, at the request of the dean, to the local draft board, flagging Montana's name and registration number. "You're not going to be seeing any trenches in this war, Tucker, as far as I can figure out. They'll probably scoop you up and put you in an Army lab." He smiled. "There you can design radios or bombsights, to help us win the war more quickly."

Tucker didn't reply. He didn't smile either. On the other hand he didn't want to appear rude, so finally he said, "Okay, Major. We'll see how it goes."

The major smiled and started out the door. Suddenly he turned around. "Listen, Montana. If you want so badly to serve your country, don't be so fucking stupid about how you can do that best. Every now and then—not often, just every now and then—the Army does the smart thing, and the smart thing is to keep you in physics. If you don't like that idea, go over and join the Japs or the Nazis, because you might as well be on their side as to refuse to use what you've got for us." He looked Tucker directly in the face, and then shut the door quietly. Two years later, Tucker was working under very strict Army supervision at an installation called Los Alamos in New Mexico. He was helping Professor Seth Neddermeyer with the infernal problem of developing a trigger mechanism that would detonate what they referred to as an atomic bomb.

Fifteen months later, Division C, as Professor Neddermeyer's department was called, was confident the thing would work. There was no such thing as a fully reliable laboratory test. Tucker Montana thought briefly of Fr. Enrique recounting the story of his father, so confident he had fixed the electric fan that he didn't think it necessary even to plug it in. Well, this was very different. Those frontiers of knowledge about which he had first heard from Mr. Galen, those frontiers had been pushed a long mile forward, if that was the right word for it. And no one doubted that he, nineteen-year-old Tucker Montana, had done some heavy rowing against that current of physical stasis that kept saying No, you can't get there from here, nature won't permit it. Day after day, month after month, he had worked out the implications of this and the other tiny alteration in the known sequence. And when Professor Neddermeyer had seen that last schedule of Tucker's he had gone right to Dr. Oppenheimer who one hour later said, "We'll build this one."

And then those fateful decisions, in two stages.

He was to join the professional Los Alamos crew who would first disassemble Little Boy, as the bomb was called, for shipment to San Francisco where it would board the *Indianapolis* for Tinian, in the Marianas. Tucker would fly to Tinian with the other Los Alamos scientists to reassemble Little Boy and prepare it for its mission. At Tinian the technical crew would check, check, check, every hour, to record any electronic movement, impulse, vagary. No human patient, Tucker thought one night after making the routine tests with his meters and noting the results, had ever been subjected to more intense stethoscopic scrutiny. And then the time came, D–1. He was present at the briefing of the airplane crew as they were told for the first time about the special aspects of the bomb they were to drop the following day over the city of Hiroshima, Japan.

And then, the next morning, he was called in by the deputy mission commander, General Groves's representative, and told that he was to be the twelfth member of the large crew—for the purpose of applying, four times an hour during the five-hour-thirty-minute flight, his instruments to the nerve ends of the bomb, carefully recording every registration. "We want a log on Little Boy just like the kind we've kept since we left New Mexico right up to when she leaves the bomb bay. You're one of the six people on this island who know what to do, and the other five are old enough to be your father. So I've decided it will be you."

Tucker was glad, as he was being fitted up with a pilot's suit, that he hadn't been told the night before. The large crew was led to the runway for pictures. It hadn't yet been decided in Washington when or whether to release the pictures (much would depend on reaction to the bomb). It occurred fleetingly to Tucker as the photographer adjusted a bandana around Tucker's neck to give him a little of the fly-boy look that, not inconceivably, he might have been selected to go on this mission instead of one of the older men because of his youth, yes, but also because of his poster-boy-innocent good looks—a young Gregory Peck—not easily linked to an apocalyptic episode. And it was true: Tucker, at six feet one inch, his hair—longer than Antonio used to leave it—framing a thoughtful and animated face, permitted himself these days a more frequent smile, associated with the tension relief needed by scientists who work in close quarters almost around the clock.

Sleep would not have been possible. He could not believe his good fortune. With his own eyes he would see it—happen. The fruit of many men of genius, but the fruit, also, of his own efforts and imagination. He had heard it said at Los Alamos that if this thing worked the Japanese would sue for surrender. Surrender! That could mean saving half a million American lives. Half a million American lives! Among them maybe—Harry Evans. Joe Savage. Helicio Espinoso. Stowie Cleaver. Johnny Galliher. They marched through his imagination one at a time, his fraternity brothers at Zeta Psi; his fellow students in the physics classes and in the history and Spanish classes. The barber's son. Mr. Galen's son. They had all gone off to war and, he hoped, most of them were still alive. Now, if this—thing—worked, they would stay alive, instead of dying on Japanese beaches. And he would actually see the breakthrough happen.

Since the test explosion at Los Alamos, no communication of any sort had been permitted, even to friends or relatives, except routine messages done through the official clerk reporting nothing more than that the writer was in good health. But he felt he *had* to write a letter. He would leave the letter in a sealed envelope, and mail it after the embargo was declared ended, at the finish of the mission. There was the possibility they would not return, in which case at some point the adjutant would see the letter, accompanied by the note asking that it be mailed, posthumously. He wrote:

Dearest Mother: One hour from now I will be flying very high over the Pacific Ocean. I will be in direct charge of an instrument that may mean the end of the war. I have been with that instrument *pre partum, in partu, post partum* (ask Fr. Enrique what that means). If it works for the best, we have God to thank for letting us come up with a response to people who set out to advance themselves by visiting Pearl Harbor early on a Sunday morning with dive bombers. If I do

not live through it, know that you were in my thoughts
at the last moment when I was free to think about those
I love, instead of those I must help to kill.

Your devoted,

Tucker.

They wanted him to stay on at Los Alamos. Professor Neddermeyer told him that he possessed singular theoretical talents and that he must continue to put them to the use of his country, and also of science. Tucker wished above all not to intimate that what was troubling him was a moral question that simply hadn't afflicted his colleagues, so far as he could see. He would say only that his mother was ailing and he absolutely needed to be with her as soon as possible, that perhaps the next season, the next year. . . .

By January of 1946 he had accumulated enough points of service to qualify for discharge. One final effort was made to persuade him to stay on at least until the atomic tests of that summer at Eniwetok. He smiled and said that if there was a turn in his mother's health, in one direction or the other, he would be in touch.

There was the final dinner, only six or seven people, but Tucker felt that he knew them as well as he would ever know anyone, given the close intellectual and emotional company he had kept with them for over two years. (There was no talk of what it was that had held these men together during these frantically busy months: Tucker had noticed that. They never spoke of the bomb, except in the laboratory.) A soft-spoken toast was given by the commander of Division C, and it was clear that these men, four of them scientists, two of them professional Army, would miss the energetic, focused, and brilliant mind of their young associate, missing also that conduit to the innocent world which he uniquely provided to two men who had commanded battalions and the four others who for years had been separated from students who once upon a time had been the center of their professional lives. Tucker responded to the toast only by saying that he would never forget their joint experience, which was a safe thing to say, and true.

Two months later, after visiting with his mother, whose health was robust as ever, and spending four weeks at St. Luke's, where the attempt was made to diagnose his depression, he took a taxi from Providence, Rhode Island, to Portsmouth to the rendezvous he had arranged, after the long exchange of letters, with the Benedictine abbot at Portsmouth Priory. Arriving just before five in the afternoon, he was taken from the office of the abbot a few minutes later by a novitiate to the small spare cubicle with the bed, the modest hanging locker, the table-desk, the straight-backed chair, and the empty bookcase. The novitiate told him there would be vespers at 5:30 in the chapel, followed by supper in the refectory. The monks would be silent at supper, while they listened to a reading from St. Benedict, but directly after supper the Benedictine habit was to gather in the adjacent reading room with their coffee, where general conversation was engaged in for thirty minutes. After that, conversation was rare, save for those monks whose job it was to supervise the activity of the boys. A preparatory school was an administrative function of the monastery. The other monks and the novitiates maintained silence throughout a day spent in prayer, in reading, and in physical work on the 150-acre farm. Every novitiate had a sponsor, a monk with whom he could converse at any time during the two-year period, after which vows were taken and you were then a Benedictine monk, from that moment until you died.

He would from now on be Brother Leo. And his sponsor was Brother Hildred, the elderly monk to whom the abbot had communicated, at the urging of Fr. Enrique, everything he knew about Tucker's background. On the afternoon of the following day the older monk invited the novitiate to walk with him. "We'll go past the orchard, then alongside the Sound. You will enjoy the view of Narragansett Bay." A half hour into the walk, Brother Hildred, who taught physics, asked "Leo"—the monks called themselves by their sacerdotal first names—if he would like to visit the school's physics laboratory that afternoon. Tucker replied that he would not like to visit it this afternoon, tomorrow, next month, or next year. But quickly he recoiled from his apparent asperity, and said simply that he did not wish to revisit any aspect of his past professional life. He went on to say that at Austin he had studied history and Spanish as well as physics, and that there was much reading he wished to catch up on in history, so he would not be idle. Brother Hildred understood, and changed the subject quickly.

Fr. Enrique had sent Tucker's troubled letters, written from Los Alamos, to Brother Martin. What Tucker had written to his old patron was not formally confessional in character, so that Fr. Enrique felt free to send the anguished letters to Brother Martin for his own appraisal. Fr. Martin had gone on to select Brother Hildred as an appropriate sponsor for young Tucker because he was, in a way, the St. Augustine of the Benedictine community. He had lived, up until just after his fortieth year, a robust sensual life, in America and in Europe, using up most of the toothsome legacy he had been left by his parents. When he decided to enter the monastery, he gave the remainder to the Benedictines and decided, as a novitiate, to impose upon himself the intellectual mortification of learning physics, which he had never studied during his school days, and to which he had never been attracted. Five years later, only a year or so after taking his final vows, he exchanged his dissertation for a doctorate in physics from Harvard. Brother Hildred's perspectives were cosmopolitan and at times earthy, and at one point, a week or so after their first walk, he counseled Brother Leo in gentle but grave tones. "Don't try to excrete it all at once, as if it were one large spiritual bowel movement. It doesn't work that way. It takes time."

And it did. But nine months later, Tucker was a well-integrated novitiate in the Benedictine community. He had decided to study Spanish intensively, and did well enough over time to undertake with confidence to teach the introductory course in Spanish to the eighteen students who signed up for it at the beginning of the fall semester. The abbot, who prided himself on his own fluency, achieved during his missionary work in Mexico, enjoyed their conversations in Spanish. Indeed, it was on that account that Brother Leo was given another assignment. He was designated as the appropriate monk to drive to Newport to visit with Doña Alicia, the ailing widow whose wealthy husband, sometime ambassador from Spain to the United States, had made a critical contribution to the monastery. Indeed, the ambassador's money was much of the fund raised to construct the impressive modern chapel in which the monks worshipped, as well as the 180 schoolboys (or in any event, they pretended to do so). When Don Luis Alargo knew that he was in his final days he asked the abbot to keep an eye on Doña Alicia, so helpless in her resolute ignorance of English.

The abbot had made the promise, and frequently called upon her himself. But now that it was clear that she would need regular attention and instruction, he thought it appropriate to introduce her to the newest brother.

When Leo rang the bell at the mansion, he came face to face with Josefina, Doña Alicia's beloved niece. She had, it turned out, lost both parents during the Spanish Civil War. Luis Alargo had paid the cost of Josefina's schooling while she lived with a maiden sister near Barcelona. Now the closely knit Spanish family thought it right that Josefina should repay her debt to the Alargo family by being with her aunt during her illness.

Josefina had arrived in New York on the *Queen Mary,* traveling in tourist class. Traveling in first class was the ravishing Ava Gardner, returning from making a movie in Europe in order (that, at any rate, was the rumor) to pursue her romance with Frank Sinatra. When Josefina, dressed in a bright red cloth coat, descended the tourist gangway, a paparazzo, one of many guarding the first-class gangway, spotted her. So! *Ava Gardner was attempting a hidden exit down the tourist gangway, dressed in a simple cloth coat!* He rushed toward her, his large camera in hand, and began to flash bulbs at the startled Josefina. Other reporters and photographers quickly joined him and there was a large commotion until suddenly it settled on the press corps that the young lady who was saying in sentences that she was not Ava Gardner, acting out her lines in fractured English as she might have done for a Hollywood director, really was *not* Ava Gardner. She was someone called Josefina Delafuente.

A month later Brother Leo in his monastic cell consulted the diary he kept of his activities, and counted nine visits to the Alargo mansion. He stood up and pulled at his hair by the roots with both hands until he felt genuine physical pain. He went, then, to the chapel, and on his knees prayed most earnestly. He tried to distract himself. He forced his mind back on those five hours and thirty minutes from Tinian to Hiroshima and back; forced himself to re-create in his mind the memory of the huge mushroom cloud that rose behind the *Enola Gay* as she flew back to the sanctuary of the island; he thought of his father, run over by a taxi on his way to a bus with a big electric fan in his hand; thought back to his humiliation at the hands of the recruiting sergeant in Austin.

But the daemon would not detumesce, so that when, during the social hour immediately after the monks' dinner, he was called to the telephone, as he knew that he would be by prearrangement with Josefina, he took the call in the office of the abbot, said the prearranged words, and went back to the sitting room where he whispered in Spanish to the abbot that Doña Alicia had taken a turn for the worse and had asked her niece to bring Brother Leo to console her. The abbot nodded. *"Por supuesto. Véte, cuídale bien"*—Of course. Get on with it. Take good care of her.

Josefina was there in the car, radiant, the smell of her intoxicating. It was raining. She didn't speak, nor did he. She drove toward Newport while Tucker reached over to the back seat, opened the suitcase, and pulled out the gray flannel pants, the shirt and tie, and the blue blazer. He slid into his pants without difficulty, as he had been wearing a monk's surplice. This he pulled over his head, putting on the shirt and then the tie. And, finally, the jacket. Josefina now spoke, attempting a gaiety of spirit as she stared in concentration through the windshield, making her way in the driving rain. "Too bad," she said, "taking so much trouble getting

dressed. It is so much faster getting undressed." She reached for his hand and slid it
through the cleavage of her silk blouse under
her breast. Tucker nestled her and then moved
his hand to her other breast as she made the
sharp right turn to the motel with the bright red
light flashing VACANCY, under the incandescent
NEWPORT ARMS MOTEL. She parked the car.
"Vamos corriendo. No olvides la petaca"—
Let's make a dash for it. Don't forget the suitcase. They ran and in a few seconds were
protected by the portico. In the lobby, he signed
the register for himself and his wife. The receptionist asked for the twenty dollars and suddenly
Tucker was dumb. He had no money. But
Josefina spoke: "Dahrling, you leaves your wal-
let in my *bolso,* don' you remember? Here," she
pulled out a twenty-dollar bill and handed it to
the clerk.

"Do you need any help with your baggage, Mr.
Engaño?"

"No no, thank you. We have just this . . . one
bag."

They were shown the direction in which to go,
and he fumbled with the key to Room 219. He
closed the door behind her. She opened the
suitcase and brought out a bottle of chilled

wine, the cork unstopped. Then she turned off the overhead light. "I get glasses from the bathroom." She emerged three minutes later, with two bathroom glasses filled with wine. She was nude.

★ ★ ★ ★ ★ ★

Chapter Five

Lyndon Johnson depressed the button and answered the operator with the phrase the White House operators had got used to any time between seven in the morning and ten at night: "Tell Valenti to come in."

Jack Valenti was there within minutes, energetic as if it had been twelve hours earlier, attentive, devoted, formally dressed in a gray suit, with a tie of just the currently fashionable width.

And Valenti knew—always—which attitude would appropriately complement the President's disposition: indignant; defensive; aggressive; inquisitive; astonished.

"This morning, as I tol' you, Mac Bundy volunteers to go to Saigon as ambassador to replace Lodge. This afternoon Bob McNamara offers—himself. You know this, because I tol' you that too, an' I hope you didn't hear it from anyone else, or I'll have *that* asshole's ass. First, trade off National Security Adviser for Ambassador to South Vietnam, for Chrissake. Does that make sense to you? Maybe that's why Mac's advice hasn't exactly been—consistent on Vietnam, though McNamara isn't any better. Get that! He wants to give up Secretary of Defense for Ambassador to Vietnam! But *now*—"

The President stood up behind his big walnut desk in the Oval Office. "Look at this!"—he slid forward a sheet of paper. It was only a sentence or two. From Robert Kennedy. Offering to go to Vietnam as ambassador, replacing Henry Cabot Lodge.

LBJ was thundering. "What the shit's he want to do in Vietnam, run for President? Threaten to prosecute Ho Chi Minh? Bring Diem back from the grave he an'—" LBJ was careful to observe presidential protocol, whatever his fever; he paused slightly, "President Kennedy sent him to—you remember, Jack, I was agaiynst that coup—no more coup shit, I've said ever since, much good it does, whatever I say, the way those gooks go in for changin' government in Saigon. What does Kennedy 'spect to do? I tell you what he 'spects to do, he 'spects to make a big impression over there and cash in on it here. But how? Doing what? So I send him to Saigon. So he does what *I* tell him to do, period, end, over, out. There's talk—you've heard this, I've heard this, John-John's heard this—he's pullin' out of the Cabinet and runnin' for the Senate—from New York." Lyndon Johnson put his hands before him, preacher-fashion, half-closed his eyes, and peered slightly up, in the general direction of heaven.

"We all know how Bobby is *reel*-ly a Noo Yorker, only accidentally raised in Boston, schooled in Rhode Island an' Boston an' Virginia, but he's *really* a Noo Yorker, down deep. 'Deep in the heart of—*Nyew* York,' his favorite song. Whass he up to, sayin' he wants to go to Saigon as ambassador? Maybe I'll juss say yes. Yes." Dramatic pause. "Yes, Bobby. That's a real good idea. Wish I'd of thought of that, Saigon is just where you belong; all your trainin' as Attorney General makes you juss *ahdeal* for ambassador in Vietnam. Where they're tryin' to skin our ass. Yes. Now, Bobby, what you think it's a good idea to do, once you get to Vietnam?

Hunh?" He leaned over and grabbed Jack Valenti by the lapels, the President's large nose one inch away from his aide's. "Hunh?" the President began to shake him, demanding an answer.

Jack Valenti drew his head back in very slow motion and said, "Yes, sir, it is certainly confusing, virtually our whole first team deciding they all want to volunteer as ambassador to Vietnam. I guess they think that is where the action is—is going to be. And your report, the one you showed me this morning from that agent, Oakes, on the Trail, seems to say that's what's coming down at us. But you're right, it doesn't make any sense, not for any of them, not Mac, not McNamara, not Bobby—"

"You know what!" Valenti's pacification program had not worked on LBJ. "They think I'm a great big"—he slowed his words to give them extra emphasis—"*asshole. That is exakly what they think. Especially Bobby. He's still mad about my X-ing him out of the vice-presidential business. What do you think of this—"

He reached down and picked up a legal pad on which he had scrawled in pencil. Drawing the chair back with his left hand and sitting down on it, leaning, he began to read, aloud. "Dear

Bobby: I have your communication in which you offer to serve the Administration as ambassador to South Vietnam. I'll certainly take your offer into consideration, on'y it would help me come to a conclusion if you tol' me what you think you could do when you got there. Like, settle the dispute between Khanh and Minh? Mebbe something on the village pacification problem that Genral Lansdale hasn't thought about? Give the CIA team hep on our Trail project? Come up with something that will keep the Russians an' China from stuffin' North Vietnam with weapons?" He looked up at his aide. His left eyebrow stretched up, a hint of tentativeness. "What do you think?"

Valenti knew that his reaction needed to come in stages. 1) "That would certainly take care of Bobby, Mr. President." Pause. Then, 2) "Of course, there are other considerations." Pause. 3) "There's the—uh, election coming up. You don't absolutely need Bobby, and half the Camelot crowd is already working for you. But on the other hand, I guess it doesn't make sense to have Bobby sulking all the way through the Atlantic City convention scene and until November." Pause. 4) "Maybe you should think some more about it. But it is a hell of a letter, no doubt about that."

Lyndon Johnson looked up at Valenti, and let his eyeglasses slip down toward the end of his nose. He depressed a buzzer by his desk. "Bring me a Sprite." He looked up questioningly. Valenti nodded. "Two Sprites."

"Whaddayathink I ought to say to him."

"Well, sir, there's two ways to handle a gesture like the one he's just made. One way is what you did. Another way is to be sort of, you know—terribly pleased, honored, that kind of thing."

"Lahk what?"

"Well, like, er, 'Dear Bobby: I've always known you have a great capacity to give everything to your country. But I think your country needs you right here at home, and I would not want to miss your advice and counsel here in Washington.'—Something like that."

The President looked down.

"Think there's enough piss in that?"

"I would think so. He'll see it."

"I want him to *feel* it, not jes' *see* it. . . . Waal, go ahead. Draft your letter for me. I'll want it in the morning. An' I'll want to meet here, nine o'clock. McNamara, Bundy—both Bundys—Rusk an' Rostow. Tell them we'll discuss that paper came in from the CIA boys on the Trail."

"Yes, sir."

★ ★ ★ ★ ★ ★

Chapter Six

Bui Tin was only thirty-eight but he was entirely relaxed in the presence of the maximum leader, President Ho Chi Minh. In part this ease of manner was owing to, first, his background. Bui Tin was the oldest son of an aristocratic family in Hué, the second-largest city in South Vietnam. The Bui clan had for generations lived well, very well, off their great tract of farmland. They had to pay taxes to the French, but Bui Tin's father was never apparently concerned about this: what he had always feared, he told his son in the late 1930s when Bui Tin was a teenager in the French-run Haute École, was the Japanese; and of course the Japanese had come and for four frightening years, beginning soon after the military strike against Singapore a few weeks after Pearl Harbor, life at Hué had been very hard. The father and mother had been moved to a peasants' cottage that sat on their own property, quickly confiscated in the name of the Japanese emperor. Tin had been permitted to continue to attend his school, run now by a harsh Japanese academic who doubled the work of the students and tripled the discipline. When Tin reached seventeen, he would be conscripted and used for the imperial purposes of the Co-Prosperity Sphere of the Japanese. His fluent French and schoolboy knowledge of English and Japanese suggested a clerical career, which never eventuated because a few months after his seventeenth birthday the Japanese surrendered. The fate of Hiroshima at the hands of something called *la bombe atomique* was the cause of much celebration in Hué, and by Christmas of 1945 the harshly aged father had begun the reconstitution of his properties and was again reporting to the very same French deputy who had escaped the scene just in time, and was lately sent back to Hué as overlord of what was to be, in turn, the reconstitution of the French Empire.

It had been a source of great dismay when, on Christmas Day, young Bui Tin announced to his father that he intended to go north to join the forces of Ho Chi Minh, consecrated to ending French colonialism in Indochina. He was eighteen years old when he first presented himself to Ho Chi Minh.

Tin knew, as indeed everyone in Vietnam knew and, increasingly, the whole world knew, that Ho Chi Minh was a man of commanding presence. He was the supreme ascetic, and dozens of interviewers went to him to behold the man who had undertaken to outwit, militarily and psychologically, the mighty French. Asked about his genius in mobilizing an effective army from peasants who had needed to break from their long docility first to the French, then to the Japanese, Ho had merely given his benign smile and answered that he had learned the principle of the class struggle from his reading of Marx and Lenin, but that all other impulses were the result of his immersion in poetry. Poetry, he had announced ("Ho closed his eyes when he spoke these words," the French reporter had written in *Le Monde*), was his daily bread, and nothing was more beautiful than the alignment of poetry and the class struggle designed to eliminate the base instincts of man, corrupted under the bourgeois order. His pointed features and wispy beard, Tin thought when first he was presented to him, might have been modeled by a great artist molding the face of a Spartan poet pained by the sounds of war, warmed by the peals of beauty that rang out of men's verbal inventions. But Tin had no reason to doubt that Ho was also a highly organized commander in chief—and Ho did not hesitate in deciding what to do with his latest volunteer.

Ho told Tin to go out to the field where his partisans were engaging the French, to learn guerrilla warfare. Tin was stationed in Saigon, close to French headquarters, and before long Ho Chi Minh grew to rely on the young, re-sourceful patrician to undertake intricate assign-ments. After the fall of Dien Bien Phu and the division of Vietnam, Ho Chi Minh made it known, quite simply, that the war against colonialism would continue; that the so-called government of South Vietnam was in fact an ad hoc aggrega-tion of lackeys of foreign imperialists, primarily American this time around; and that the struggle for the people's communism would go on until accomplished. Bui Tin never gave Ho reason to doubt that he would stay with him until that struggle had ended and all of Indochina was liberated.

It was in 1963 that Ho Chi Minh reasoned that his South Vietnamese partisans would never alone achieve the strength necessary to over- throw the southern republic, backed by the Americans. The only means of supplying Viet- cong allies in South Vietnam was through the great Trail of which he would soon become the eponym. Bui Tin, thirty-six years old, small like most of his countrymen, tough, sinewy, in- novative, single-minded, had been put in charge of an exploratory group whose job would be to go down the Trail and determine what would be needed to make it a more effective conveyor belt for Northern supplies and personnel sent to benefit Southern allies.

Tin worked his way down that complex of hot jungle paths and ice-cold mountain streams, the ancient route that passed through the habita- tions of aboriginal tribes, where tigers and ele- phants had been hunted down, making way for migrants who brought gold and spice from China to the cities of Southeast Asia. He spent more than five months fighting leeches and mosquitoes and hunger, living mostly from food deposits laid down at stipulated points by the

Vietcong cadre. And he had come back to make his report.

It was, in brief, that the Trail was useless unless a gargantuan effort was made to make it possible for substantial traffic to move down to effect the infiltration of South Vietnam. Bui Tin had informed Ho and his generals that, relying only on partisans in the South, they would need to wait until the end of the century before the Vietcong movement succeeded in overthrowing the South Vietnamese government. The revolutionary action would need to be staffed and supplied from North Vietnam, and in order to do this, it would be necessary, first, to tame the Trail.

After much consultation and the exploration of alternatives, Ho and General Giap concluded that Tin was correct, and what then began was the Vietnamese equivalent of building the Chinese wall.

They were meeting, this afternoon, several months after the critical decision had been made to modernize the Trail, in the old French colonial courthouse used by Ho as his headquarters. They needed to confront the implications of two developments. The first, the discovery by the South Vietnamese military of their Grand Plan for the Trail.

This had happened when, a week earlier, a detachment of North Vietnamese construction workers were ambushed by the enemy. Most of them had got away, fading into the jungle they had come to know so well. But not the chief engineer, and he was carrying in his satchel the blueprints, so to speak, for the Ho Chi Minh Trail. Late on the evening of the ambush two of the unit's military guards had worked their way back to the site. They had had no difficulty in finding their engineer and identifying him, even though his head had been severed from the body. But what they were after—the satchel—was gone. And now Ho Chi Minh and General Giap and Bui Tin were thumbing through other copies of the seventy-two-page document that had been assembled by Colonel Dong Si Nguyen, the large, weatherbeaten architect of the great Trail, who had been named minister in charge of constructing it.

It was all there, they gloomily conceded. A description of the Soviet and Chinese machinery that the Trail would need to be able to handle, specifications of the necessary width of the Trail, the essential built-in detours to cope with the unbridgeable, with weather contingencies, with bombs. Colonel Nguyen had anticipated in due course heavy American bombs and intended to be prepared with adequate antiaircraft defenses. There would be underground barracks, workshops, hospitals, storage facilities, fuel depots. He anticipated platoons of drivers, mechanics, radio operators, ordnance experts, traffic managers, doctors, nurses. It was the intention of the architect of this Trail, a full description of which the enemy surely had in hand, to expedite the passage of 20,000 North Vietnamese soldiers per month upon the Trail's completion. And yes, that detail too, 20,000 North Vietnamese soldiers per month, appeared on the document.

Ho Chi Minh turned to Frédéric Gruyère, the archaeologist who had defected from the French and served now as principal monitor of the news as it came in from the French press and from his myriad contacts in the French intelligence community. How would President Johnson react on seeing the Trail document?

Gruyère said that, after all, the Americans had already begun surveying the area, obviously in anticipation of infiltration through a much heavier use of it than at present, but 20,000 troops per month could only sound like an invading army.

Ho nodded. He had always done so ceremoniously. Bui Tin found himself wondering whether he nodded in that way when receiving ultimatums from the French. (Would he nod in that way to someone who ordered him executed? Probably.) But Ho also kept his own counsel. Instead of replying to Gruyère, he asked for his current estimate of the political situation in the United States. Gruyère replied that it had not changed, in respect of Vietnam. There was solid support from both parties for continued aid to the enemy, and President Johnson regularly went on with his stream of public pronouncements to the effect that the United States would stand by its "allies" to "curb Communist expansion." The party of Republicans would almost surely nominate a senator named Barry Goldwater, a most bellicose man who would look for the least provocation to move in the direction of converting the American military cadre now in South Vietnam into a full fighting force.

General Giap said that it was his impression that President Johnson would move in the same direction.

Gruyère said that yes, this was so, but President Johnson—he looked over at Ho, pausing very briefly—was not as decisive as the senator from Arizona, and had many conflicting concerns.

Once again, Ho bowed his head. "It will be a long war," he said, his lips parted in a half smile. He turned first to General Giap, then to Colonel Nguyen, then to Colonel Tin, with just the faintest tilt of his head. They rose. Ho Chi Minh had dismissed them.

Ho told Gruyère to summon Xuan Thuy, who acted as his foreign minister. He was there immediately, coming in from his office next door. Ho asked his foreign minister whether he had told the Canadian member of the International Control Commission that the government of North Vietnam would reply to the American overture on a given date.

"I didn't say when we would reply, Excellency. I just listened." Xuan Thuy looked up at Gruyère and back to Ho. Did the President wish him to repeat what he had been told? In front of Gruyère? Ho blinked an assent.

"President Johnson made an advance through Canada. If you will stop the war against South Vietnam he promises you a vast program of economic aid to rebuild the entire country, to restore it after all the damage done in the current conflict and in the conflict with the French."

Ho looked over at Gruyère. "Is there any public knowledge of this initiative?"

Gruyère shook his head. "None."

Ho turned back to Xuan Thuy. "You will almost certainly be hearing again from the Canadian ambassador. Do not approach him. Wait until he comes again to you. When he comes, which I think will be very soon, he will no doubt tell you that U.S. Intelligence has picked up a document that suggests we are preparing to move as many as 20,000 soldiers per month down the Trail when it is built up."

Xuan Thuy nodded. Yes, he said. He knew about the captured document.

"You are to tell him the document is a forgery. The work of provocateurs in the South. When the Southern patriots take over the country from the colonialist stooges, the forgers will be sought out and specially punished."

Xuan Thuy bowed. There was a trace of a smile. He had been ordered to say just the kind of thing he enjoyed saying when negotiating with representatives of the imperialist world.

★ ★ ★ ★ ★ ★ ★ ★ ★

Chapter Seven

The first part of their mission completed, Black-ford Oakes and Tucker Montana were back in sticky, crowded, volatile Saigon. It was late in the afternoon when they checked in at the hotel, going directly to the restaurant, where they ate, drank, and agreed that they looked forward to sleep in air-conditioned quarters before the meeting the next day with Rufus and Colonel Strauss.

In the late spring of 1964 Saigon seemed to be attacked more heavily by domestic than foreign problems. The assassination of the leader, Diem, had been followed by civil turmoil, with one general or junta replacing another at dizzying speed. A determined war initiated by the North was a strategic concern worth worrying about, but it was hardly the dominating concern of the day to the South Vietnamese: a domestic insurrectionary movement was not gaining ground, the South Vietnamese army, the ARVN, was in the field, doing its business. And Saigon was profiting as the center of geopolitical attention. Security within Saigon was not a problem of any magnitude. Yes, of course there would be spies in Saigon, just as there were spies in Berlin and Singapore and Hong Kong. But nothing to warrant elaborate disciplinary procedures, let alone curfews, let alone curtailment of the kind of life appropriate to besieged cities. The restaurants and hotels and nightclubs and brothels were prospering, and life for many Vietnamese and foreigners could be sweet, if only the Westerners could get used to the heat, and stop worrying about the never-ending anarchy within the government. But surely that too would go away, perhaps under the latest general, who spoke frequently over the radio, though to a half-hearted listenership more intent on workaday concerns, on inflation, schooling, food, lodging, entertainment, than security. Saigon was an informal, loose, open city. If a visitor had arrived there knowing nothing of politics, he might spend months there before discovering that a civil war made possible by foreign aggression was going on.

Leaving the hotel restaurant, Blackford depressed the elevator button, sleepily staring at the floor indicator. Montana said he thought he would take a walk before turning in. "Maybe just say a quick hello to a girl I met last time I was in town, nice little thing, pretty, and very, very hospitable."

"You just said a half hour ago you couldn't wait to go to bed."

"Didn't say whose bed."

Blackford smiled. "I understand a lot of nice women in Saigon are good at quick hellos. Even at protracted hellos. . . . By the way, Tucker"— he addressed Major Montana for the first time by his Christian name—"you did me a favor on the field today. Thanks."

Montana waved his hand dismissively. "It was your expedition, but I was in charge of getting you in and out; couldn't very well bring you back dead." He lowered his head for a moment. "Bad, the copilot. At least he was unmarried, I found out."

"Yes," Blackford said.

The elevator door opened. Blackford gave his companion a lazy mini-salute, went into the elevator and on reaching his bedroom made a quick decision: He would go instantly to sleep rather than fight the fatigue; set the alarm for six and then work on his notes. Shortly, he was bouncing about lazily and happily in the green pastures of heavy slumber when the little tinkle began. His light and carefree gamboling was infinitely pleasurable—he found that he could jump about as though there were hardly such a thing as gravity, bounding from this little oasis of trees and flowers to that one a half mile away, as fleetfootedly as a ballerina and with the powers of Superman.

What *was* that little tinkling bell? It was beginning to annoy him. He ignored it in exchange for leaping over to explore another green corner in the vast garden. . . . And then suddenly the fairyland disappeared, evaporated. He woke up. It was the telephone.

The *telephone.*

He looked at his watch. It was not quite midnight. He reached out for the receiver, brought it down to pillow level and said, "Yes?"

"Are you Mr. Greyburn?"

Mr. Greyburn! Sally! "Yes." He jolted up to a

sitting position. In a few seconds she was there, loud and clear, only the slightest background feel of over-come-in-please button-pushing somewhere along the line, perhaps a short-wave radio operator in the picture.

"Darling, were you asleep?"

"No. No, not at all, darling." The connection was perfect.

"You are an unaccomplished liar. I don't know how you succeed, given your line of work. You evidently forget that I have heard you speak when you wake up and I am seven inches away, not seven thousand miles away. I *know* that sound."

"Yes, I remember," Blackford said. "And I don't like it when you keep yourself seven inches away. I find that extremely snotty. How do you say snotty in Spanish?"

"Er . . . *desinclinado.*"

"I don't believe you. You are an unaccomplished fake. An academic sciolist."

"Oh? You're talking to a Ph.D. It is I—not you—who lectures in Spanish at the University of Mexico on Jane Austen; who, by the way, got on very well in her novels without having to use the word *snot*—"

"I bet she didn't get very far without using the word 'disinclined,' because my guess is that *desinclinado* translates to 'disinclined' in English."

"Oh Blacky, I do miss you."

"I miss you, love. How is the little monster?"

"He had his second birthday yesterday: He is two months old. He is quite beautiful. Just like his father. . . ." There was the moment's silence. Blackford quickly broke in.

"Have any trouble getting through to me?"

"Yes, actually. I put in the call two hours ago thinking that was a pretty safe time to find you still awake. And then when I got through to the operator and asked for 'Mr. Greyburn' she said there wasn't anybody there with that name, and of course I remembered, and had to go to your telegram to get the right room number. You are back from the bush, as you put it?"

"Yes—I'll have to be a little vague about that."

"So what now?"

"I'm not absolutely sure. But just possibly I'll be going to Washington for this reason and that, and when I do I'm going to put in for a little Frito-time south of the border."

"That would be so nice. I want you to meet your future stepson. Do you remember his name—Daddy?"

Blackford panicked. She had told it to him first in the letter announcing his birth, then in the second letter, which he got just before he left Washington. CIA agents are not supposed to forget important details. He would try to bluff his way out of it.

"I do think you might have named him after our Director. John McCone Partridge Morales. That would have been very nice. Or, to show that people don't necessarily just fade away when they leave us, Allen Dulles Partridge Morales."

"That is very funny. Maybe you'd have liked Anthony Strangelove Partridge Morales."

"You always think we people want war, when what we want is peace."—He blessed himself that his ruse had worked. "Anthony" was the kid's name. Antonio, he supposed, named after his father.

"We won't go into that old subject again, not on my nickel."

"How much does it cost, phoning from Mexico City?"

"Since this is Sunday, the day on which when

you were younger you used to worship, the rates are only fifty percent."

"Fifty percent of what?—and no cracks about my religion."

"Of a hundred and fifty pesos. Seventy-five pesos is six, just over six dollars."

"I will send you a money order."

"You forget. I am wealthy."

Blackford paused for a moment. He decided to be serious. "Antonio's will probated already?"

"Yes. I knew it would be substantial. I didn't know how substantial it would be."

"I'm very glad for that, darling, I truly am. That means you can look after me in my old age."

"My problem has been looking after you in your young age."

He laughed, as did she, and they cuddled together, over a distance of seven thousand miles, as a growing number of Americans were now doing, from one place or another, talking over the telephone to wives, husbands, lovers, and when he put down the phone and eased back to sleep, there were no green pastures there waiting for him, just Professor Sally Partridge.

. . .

They were to meet in a safe house. In Saigon, June 1964, Blackford reckoned, if you knocked on the wrong door you would probably be admitted into a CIA safe house. A young man in khakis, a pistol on his hip, asked Blackford and Montana for a password. He then took them upstairs where Rufus and Colonel Abraham Strauss were waiting for them. More properly, they were expecting them. (In the CIA world nobody waits because everyone is on time, or has been kidnapped.) Blackford had been told that the appointment was for eight minutes past ten, and it was now nine minutes past ten.

Laying eyes on Rufus was always a restorative. As usual, he was formally dressed, though not, Blackford was glad to notice, in blue-black. Although the rural Vietnamese wore black pajamas, that costume was now regularly associated with the Vietcong. The garb made them inconspicuous in the dark as they traveled the countryside, threatening and then murdering uncooperative South Vietnamese village chiefs, magistrates, small landholders, teachers. He greeted Rufus with the closest you could come, with Rufus, to a bear hug, which he would endure from his most intimate friends, always provided there was no substantial body contact.

Rufus said, "Mr. Montana," and then introduced them: "Colonel Strauss, from the Aberdeen Proving Ground."

"Abe," the colonel said.

Rufus brought the meeting quickly to order and Blackford began, here and there consulting his notes.

He described the dismaying problem. From the point northwest of Khesanh, where it crossed over into Laos, to Tayninh, fifty miles northwest of Saigon, the Trail stretches over four hundred miles. "We've surveyed only about eighty miles. Obviously there's no way to close the entire Trail. All we can hope to do is interdict traffic coming down it. The point will be to select a section long enough to make a detour by the North Vietnamese effectively impossible, but short enough to give us the kind of concentrated target we'll need if we're going to keep those"— in deference to Rufus, Blackford sanitized the language he would ordinarily have used at this juncture—"gentlemen and their supplies back in the Communist world."

They devoted an hour to studying aerial photographs—which proved all but useless: the planes saw only the green carapace that sheltered the entire area like an endless awning.

The photographs Blackford had taken, and had then developed and blown up at Savannakhet, suggested the nature of the problem. The twists and the turns of the Trail, the offshoots to the target areas in the east, the difficulty of access from the air . . . Staring at the photographs, Rufus and Colonel Strauss could almost feel the asphyxiating heat, the dampness, the awful luxuriant growth of myriad trees, vines, shrubs which they needed to penetrate.

"Well," Blackford said, "are you here, Abe, to design what we need?"

"Here to help," said Colonel Strauss, looking once again through his thick glasses at one of the pictures.

Rufus said, "Colonel Strauss—Abe—is an electrical engineer by training. He helped design the South Korean barrier at the 38th parallel. . . . You should know, Abe, that Blackford here is a graduate engineer." He looked up at Tucker Montana. "Major Montana is with us from Army Special Forces. He is an expert on antiterrorist operations. Fought the Huks. I'm sorry, I don't know whether you have a technical background, Major."

"Tucker, please. My background is in Spanish and history."

Abe Strauss suggested that they should lunch, then disperse and meet again late in the afternoon. It would take him, he said, several hours to assemble his thoughts on the kind of facilities the military needed. Rufus suggested "about five o'clock," which meant five o'clock. Tucker said that under the circumstances, unless he was needed, he could usefully take the time to visit someone he had promised the day before to spend a little time with. Blackford was glad for the opportunity to go off with Rufus. He wanted to catch up on the home front.

They walked down the Rue Pensif, away from the broad boulevards with their grinding noises from the motorbikes and the honking of the taxis and jeeps. The little street, which took them to the family owned and operated restaurant Blackford had heard about, was calm. Old trees—when might they have been planted? By the French, surely: a hundred years ago? Blackford noticed that they gave signs of evanescence—did they miss their Gallic patrons? Still, they gave some shelter from the sun, and approaching the restaurant you could smell the fresh bread fifty yards away, and admire the sweetness of the neat arrangements of geraniums and poinsettias and the orange nasturtiums.

The home front, he learned as they set out on their French fixed four-course menu beginning with the onion soup and ending with the blueberry tart, was confused, and confusing. "The President's moods," Rufus said, "evidently oscillate from high belligerence to heavy reliance on diplomatic negotiation."

"Is he afraid of Goldwater?"

"The polls last week report that one half of the people who voted for Nixon in 1960 will nevertheless vote for LBJ in 1964."

Blackford whistled. "Landslide stuff. Why, I wonder?"

"Goldwater's campaign hasn't been very reassuring. Plus he's being undermined by the liberal wing of the Republican Party. Plus the American people—conservative Americans, in this one sense, regardless of party—don't much welcome the thought of a third President in twelve months. Assassinate JFK in early November and then a year later assassinate his successor at the polls—in order to bring in someone who's being painted as a renegade Republican, a quick-triggered conservative fundamentalist."

"But Goldwater does have some strength as a candidate, doesn't he?"

"Great strength. In Houston last week, a few miles from the district that first sent LBJ to Congress, he was mobbed by enthusiasts. And his book has sold over a million copies."

"*The Conscience of a Conservative*?"

"Yes. Have you read it?"

"No. I intend to."

"It is entirely unambiguous, among other things, about the nature of our responsibilities in Vietnam."

"But that's no different, is it, from JFK and Johnson? Their commitments are unambiguous."

"The difference is that Goldwater is hammering home the kind of thing the Democrats don't like to hear discussed."

"Such as?"

"One: The assassination of Diem and Nhu in November—clearly an operation sanctioned by the White House, three weeks before JFK was assassinated. And look at the mess—I am quoting Goldwater now"—Rufus was always careful to detach himself from political analysis done by others, which he was merely reporting—"in Vietnam since then, with governments that go in and out as in the so-called banana republics. Two: Whatever happened to Laotian neutrality?

That deal, made in 1962 by JFK, is being blatantly violated. We wouldn't be here worrying about the Trail if the independence of Laos, guaranteed under the treaty, were being respected. Three: Democrats are lousy at preventing wars (you know the line—World War One, World War Two, Korea, now Vietnam, all happen when a Democrat is in the White House); and four: Democrats are lousy, once the wars begin, at concluding them successfully (and you know *that* line—Versailles, Yalta, Potsdam, Cuba, the Berlin Wall, the loss of China, the ambiguous victory in Korea leaving us with the necessity of maintaining two divisions there).

"Put it this way: Goldwater is scoring and, more and more, what happens in Vietnam is the yardstick by which the competence of LBJ is being judged. I don't see how the President can lose the election, but there is every reason to assume, from the Richter-scale meters in the White House, that Lyndon Johnson is acting as if he might actually lose."

"Lose Vietnam?"

Rufus returned Blackford's smile.

"I think you are right, basically LBJ is ambiguous on Vietnam. But I don't think he would let Indochina go without a major struggle."

"When LBJ makes major struggles he sets out to win, doesn't he?"

Rufus replied. "He sets out to win, but he doesn't always win. He wanted the presidential nomination in 1960, after all."

"But this time he is Commander in Chief of the delegates—he virtually owns the U.S. Army, Navy, Air Force, and, incidentally, you and me."

"I am not saying he could not win in Indochina," Rufus said, rising from the table. "We both have work to do. I'll see you at five."

★ ★ ★ ★ ★ ★

Chapter Eight

Tucker had no problem in getting a taxi. He was driven toward 17 Henri Brevard and reminded himself for the twenty-seventh time that normal people should carry earplugs in Saigon, where you would think that car mufflers were a federal offense. The noise from the cars, motor scooters and bikes was deafening, and of course the hot, awful air made it necessary to keep windows open. Happily, Lao Dai's apartment had an electric fan. When he was first there, a few days before he met Blackford and flew with him to Savannakhet to begin their survey, he had found the fan—not working. He was delighted! A nonworking electric fan! While she looked on, after pouring the two glasses of wine, he impatiently opened this drawer and that one, trying to find tools or, if not, kitchen instruments that would do the work of tools. Lao Dai finally caught his attention, raised her hand gently to indicate that he should stop his frenetic search, and then glided off.

She always glided. Tucker studied her: there could not be a centimeter's difference in the high-low elevation of her head when she walked, though perhaps he was taken in by the whole of Lao Dai, that regal air that had caught his eye from the first, the night he spotted her at La Tambourine, the dark hair so neatly coiffed, the delicate gold earrings, the calm, enticing smile, the animated breasts that seemed to accompany her vibrant conversation. She came back from the bedroom, a little tool kit in hand, which she unzipped. The fan's problem was slightly more complicated than expected, but he had rewired the rotor to eliminate the short circuit, screwed everything back together, and smiled up at her. It is fixed, he said. He liked it that she frowned skeptically as she took the electrical cord to press the plug into the socket. And her smile had been radiant when the current of air began.

He had promised to get away from his "meetings" as soon as he could, unhappily not always
in time for dinner. But at whatever time in the
evening, he would take her to La Tambourine,
and they would talk and drink champagne and
listen to the music and to the singer. Tucker had
said that if she did not hear from him over the
telephone, she could expect him between 9 and
9:30—"My companions," he said, "like to dine
early." Tonight he was there at 9:30, and when
she opened the door she overwhelmed him—
the scent, yes, but also the arresting poise of
that beautiful face and figure, from her ankles to
her eyebrows a model of Asian delicacy, everything about her dainty and fine, though her
breasts were more pronounced than those of
some of the scarecrow beauties who were mod-
eling the latest French fashions in the shops. He
had never seen in any other woman eyes that
communicated such tender intelligence, and her
lips were warm, softly framing her special, private smile. His impulse was to kiss her deeply,
but instead he gave himself almost equal pleasure by bowing slightly, taking her hand and
touching it to his lips.

"Hello, Mr. Tucker. It has been lonely without
you since this afternoon. But"—she pointed to

the desk at the end of the room—"there were all those papers to correct. I must return them to-morrow to my students."

The taxi had been kept waiting. At La Tam-bourine, the recessed little table was reserved and Toi, the grandfatherly sommelier, had their champagne waiting. The nightclub had once been turn-of-the-century gilt and the velvet was still there, though badly worn, and only one chandelier hung where obviously three had once decorated the room with its thirty-odd ta-bles. The air was heavy with cigar smoke against which two standing fans and a ceiling fan vainly contended. The piano played, await-ing the singer, a middle-aged misty-eyed Frenchwoman who sang songs first heard in French movies made during the thirties.

They spoke as if it had been months, not hours, since their last meeting. And yet they had been together only a half-dozen times, three of them within the last twenty-four hours, but these communions, as Tucker thought of them, at first physical and then something more, had gener-ated a mutual excitement about every detail of their lives, their interests, their ambitions. She told him a great deal. Lao Dai was twenty-two. Her husband, a captain in the South Vietnamese army, had left her pregnant when he went off on a mission to Khesanh, where—Lao Dai had lowered her head on telling Tucker this—he was killed the day of his arrival by a sniper bullet. Her eyes were moist, but Lao Dai was not a woman to weep, at least not with strangers. She departed suddenly from her narrative. "You *are* a stranger. Yet you don't seem to me a stranger. Very odd—what is the word?—unprecedented."

Tucker held her hand. "So you went back to teaching?"

Oh no, she hadn't *gone back* to teaching. She had never missed a single day at the school, "not even when Nguyen and I were married. Our honeymoon was from ten P.M., when the guests left here"—she pointed in the direction of the private dining room of La Tambourine—"to eight the next morning, when he reported to his regiment and I reported to the Lycée." Tucker winked. "Did that give you time to become pregnant?" She smiled: "As a matter of fact, yes. Or—it might have been the following weekend, when he came back for two days, after maneuvers. But I never saw him again after that. It is not very safe, in Vietnam today, to be married to someone in the army. It is not very safe in Vietnam to do anything, never mind Saigon. That is why I—had the abortion." The little smile was gone.

Of course she had wanted to know about him. He wasn't certain of how much to say. Tucker had had similar experiences of instant attraction. With Rosita in Manila, Aleka in Seoul, and—well, back to that night at the motel in Newport when that dormant hunger had been so irrevocably awakened. That appetite, so long . . . *sublimated* was the word he wanted to use, but couldn't bring himself to do so—it didn't fit well with his preoccupation, which had been to build a nuclear weapon—had been satisfied often enough that now he could count more readily the brief intervals when he had not been in love with a woman than the women he had loved. He was, quite simply, never happy except when in the company of a woman, and although he loved, deliriously, the sexual exchanges, he loved his women as much after as before; and his women in turn found that his nearly unique postcoital exuberance—in conversation, in the sharing of workaday tasks and pleasures— made him especially exciting. "What I do not understand," Lao Dai was saying, "is why you stay in the Army. You say you are thirty-eight years old. Even in South Vietnam, with full conscription, you do not have to serve in the military if you are more than thirty-five."

That same question had been asked before, and as with the narrative of his life, he had a packaged answer which was honest, even if it left certain things untouched. Lao Dai knew by now that Tucker had been raised by his mother, that he had gone to the University of Texas, that after that, in the later stages of the World War, he had had some training in what he called "the Signal Corps" but that he had never seen action in World War Two. That after a year or so during which he had had several jobs, including grounds supervisor at a monastery and Spanish teacher in a parochial school in Hartford, Connecticut, he had been called up to serve again, this time in Korea. When that war was over he was asked to volunteer for service in the Philippines as a military adviser to the army of President Magsaysay, who was fighting to put down the insurrection of the Huks, which had begun as a kind of anarchist-terrorist operation "until our friends the Commies got involved, and then it became serious." It had not been intended that Colonel Lansdale's specialists, of whom he was one, would themselves engage in combat, but there had been no way of avoiding combat on that day in May of 1954.

"Tell me about it."

Tucker turned his head away, as though to listen more intently to the chanteuse, who was singing—it was inevitable, at least once during each of her three forty-minute sessions—"La Vie en Rose."

"Tucker. I mean it. I want to hear about it. If you don't tell me, that—special thing between us will, maybe, go away." Her eyes expressed at once command and entreaty.

Tucker took a little sip from his drink.

"By early May 1954—we're talking about almost exactly ten years ago—we had the Huks pretty well in a corner. Their hold on countryside Philippine peasants was slipping. Magsaysay—he was president—had done a lot to restore confidence in the Philippine economy, and the results were being felt. For instance the anti-Huk farmers in Mindanao were really beginning to pitch in. That, plus the kind of physical protection we were providing under Colonel Lansdale. One day at breakfast Lansdale's bodyguard brought a sealed envelope into his tent—we were operating in the field. The colonel had taken it from a campesino who said he had been paid 100 pesetas to deliver the envelope to the colonel. It was a message from the big Huk honcho, Luis Taruc. It said he was willing to negotiate an end to the hostilities, but would only do so in conversation with one man. And—he named me."

"Why?"

"We gave that a lot of thought. I was twenty-eight years old, but I had been used on radio a lot because I speak Spanish, and the Huk leaders were brought up on Spanish—everybody in the Philippines who went to school knew Spanish in those days. But because of my broadcasts, which went out as 'Don Libertad'—Mr. Freedom—I had become a spokesman of the anti-Huk forces, and in ten months my voice had become as well known in Mindanao Province as El Gallinero's. He was the Philippine's Frank Sinatra."

"The folk singer, balladeer? I've heard his records."

Tucker nodded.

"So?"

"So, Lansdale called me in and asked if I would play along. I said"—he shrugged his shoulders—"sure. Now: That letter was very specific about the proposed meeting. Taruc said that his conditions for ending the civil war would be given to me in three stages, and Stage Two wouldn't be divulged unless he had got an okay on Stage One. And he would need to get that okay within twelve hours because, he said, he was taking great risks. He was acting without the knowledge of the Soviet agent in his head-quarters, a guy called Compañero José, who, if he smelled out what was going on, would have Taruc assassinated. If Colonel Lansdale would go along with Stage One, Taruc would take the initiative and 'dispose' of Compañero José and proceed to the next stage in the negotiations. Total secrecy was critical, and there could be no use of radios, since one of Compañero José's staff always monitored radio transmissions from Huk territory.

"So Colonel Lansdale would need to be situated at a specified point, where 'Don Libertad' could go directly from the conference, spell out the terms, and get back a yes or no. If the answer was yes, then my regular eight A.M. broadcast would begin, 'Good morning, Filipino friends of liberty, this is Don Libertad bringing you your morning report. First the weather: Sunny and clear.' If the answer was no, I'd use the same opening words, and then say about the weather, 'Local storms expected.' Now if Lansdale agreed to go ahead with the meeting, I was to say on my evening broadcast at six P.M., 'Good evening, Filipino friends of liberty. This is Don Libertad bringing you your nightly report. Are you listening? I hope so.' If Colonel Lansdale would not agree, then I would leave out the phrase, 'I hope so.' Complicated, Lao?"

"No, not really. But I, do you say, smell a rat?"

"Yes. So did I. Which is why I spent most of that night working on my jeep. I didn't tell you that if we agreed, he also required that I would set out alone in a jeep beginning at a designated crossroads about 150 kilometers from our headquarters (they knew our general location) at exactly seven P.M. Head south on Camino 83, and a 'vehicle'—they didn't specify what kind— would come down from one of the many roads that feed into 83. It would have a three-star-general's badge next to the license plate. I was to follow it. It would take me to Taruc."

Lao Dai's nervousness was not simulated. She was a shade paler. "Yes," she said apprehensively.

"Okay. I go through all the motions. It took almost three hours to get to the crossroads, and

Colonel Lansdale took off to a rendezvous point nearby where I would meet him later. Past the crossroads, a couple of miles down the road, a battered old van, looked like a school bus, comes barreling down a hill from my right, hitting the road directly in front of me. I spotted the three-star badge. A few miles farther, it turns left. I follow. There is a lot of twisting and turning, up and down that hilly stuff in Mindanao. We come finally to a small village, maybe a dozen houses, a little square, and, at the end, a church. The truck stops behind the church, out of sight of any of the houses, and the driver and his companion walk toward me, both wearing fatigues, and you could see the bulge where their pistols were. The lead guy—he must have been all of twenty years old, never mind the beard—says, 'Don Libertad?'

" '*Sí.*'

"They said in Spanish they would need to search me and the jeep. I said okay and they frisked me, then looked carefully inside the jeep, then opened the hood, gave a quick look, slammed it shut and motioned me to follow them. I did, right into the church, using the rear entrance. Luis Taruc was all alone, sitting in the sacristy with a newspaper. I'd have recognized him, but he introduced himself anyway. Ever seen a picture of him?"

"No."

"No beard, but a Pancho Villa–style mustache almost as wide as the hat he was wearing, never mind that we were inside a church. Big bastard, maybe two hundred pounds, two front teeth missing. Under one eye is a scar—splotchy scar, as though the doctor that patched him up wanted to leave a big fingerprint. He spoke in rapid Spanish snatches, then paused, then another splash. Like, 'I'm-glad-you-agreed-to-come-Don-Libertad. Pause. I-have-listened-to-your-broadcasts-and-you-are-a-very-persua-sive-fellow-so-many-fascists-are. That kind of thing, for maybe a half hour. I said as little as I could get away with without being rude." Tucker paused. "Interesting point, Lao, don't you think? It's okay to act hostile, that's expected. But you mustn't be rude—that's different. After all, this was a negotiating session. It was getting dark, and he used up maybe one half hour. He said, 'We've always known you weren't a Filipino, though your Spanish accent's pretty good. But I wanted to deal with someone who worked for Lansdale, not Magsaysay. Don't ask me why; I have my reasons.' "

Tucker paused to refill his glass.

"What Stage One amounted to was: Amnesty for him and for six other Huk leaders—he gave me their names on a slip of paper. I tried to get from him some idea of what Stages Two and Three would amount to. Nothing doing. No further discussions until he had an affirmative on the amnesty question. Now, Taruc said, he knew that Colonel Lansdale didn't have the authority to grant amnesty on his own. That would have to come after a conference with President Magsaysay back in Manila. What Taruc wanted, before he would agree to reconvene on Stages Two and Three, was a signal from Lansdale that he would *recommend* amnesty. Did I understand? Yes, I said, I understood. And Lansdale could reach that decision in the field; he did not have to go back to Manila to make up his own mind. I told Taruc I was acting only as a messenger, and that, as agreed, if Lansdale was willing to make the recommendation, I would use the agreed all-clear signal on my eight A.M. broadcast. Taruc nodded, got up, went to the door and called his guards. 'Take Don Libertad back to his car.'

"It was very dark, and I needed to be guided back to Route 83. When I got there, my guide stuck out his hand, indicating the direction back to the crossroads. At the crossroads, I turned right and looked at the odometer. At exactly two-point-three miles, I would find the left turn down the dusky road; after that, three and a half miles to the traveling headquarters Lansdale and his little staff had come to, over a hundred miles from the field headquarters.

"I made my turn and looked back. No lights, nothing. But I had two radios stitched into the side seat and had them both on, one set to Channel A, the other to Channel B. And I heard the voice. *'Ha volteado. Izquierda. Camino cuatro.'* 'He's turned left, on Road Number Four.' Oh shit. I drove fast, looking for something I could hide behind—the right kind of tree, a stone wall. I spotted something, not perfect but I was in a hurry. I turned off my lights and opened the hood. With a flashlight in my mouth it took me only a couple of minutes to assemble the machine gun I had hidden in the engine compartment. I had its parts tucked in here and there—the barrel looked like a lug-nut wrench for changing tires. Under the chassis I had more than a thousand rounds of .30-caliber ammunition and the flare. I ran to the low stone wall— took me three trips to haul my equipment—

grabbed a couple of loose boulders and piled them up to elevate the wall a foot or so. I waited.

"Not long—maybe six, seven minutes. The big van stopped behind my car. I was maybe fifty yards away from the road, and I couldn't hear what was being said. But then someone came out from behind the truck. I could see his rifle in the headlights of the truck as he walked slowly up to my jeep. He opened the door—and that triggered my parachute flare.

"Goddamn, those things can be beautiful. The whole fucking area lit up like the stage of Radio City. And out of the truck—one miserable truck—a whole goddamn *platoon* of armed men. Forty-four that we know of. I began firing. I fired—man, did I fire, almost without pausing, maybe four, five minutes. Then there was no sign of life. But I wasn't going to take a chance. So I waited—until dawn. Then I cradled the machine gun in my arms and crawled over there on hands and knees. I could hear some moaning. A couple of them were still alive. But nothing else. If there was a survivor, he had taken off. I got into my jeep. Nothing doing. Bullet holes had pierced the gas tank. So—I walked. Took me just over an hour. Got there while Colonel Lansdale was having breakfast. I went into his tent and sat down and said, 'Any more messages this morning from Taruc, Colonel?' "

Lao Dai looked up at him. "What—what had Taruc planned to do?"

"Kill Colonel Lansdale and his immediate staff. Only way to do this was to lure him to a point outside his headquarters. By following me, they'd know for sure Lansdale was where he was supposed to be."

"I hope the colonel was . . . grateful."

"I got a medal."

"Let's go home. I'm scared."

"Not of me?"

"No. Just scared. It is the opposite. I want—you. I want to feel your life, deep inside me." In the taxi she said nothing, but clutched his hand. In bed she embraced him as if she alone stood between him and the surrounding enemy.

★ ★ ★ ★ ★ ★

Chapter Nine

Barry Goldwater was by nature a friendly man, and those of his aides in charge of scheduling despaired over his inclination to interrupt a scheduled walking tour in order to engage almost anyone in discussion. He made, instantaneously, distinctions in his dealings with people who wanted to question him. Those who accosted him simply to adore—and there were many of these—got the friendly handshake, nothing more. Granted, it "feels good," as one woman told a reporter who was following the candidate, "to shake his hand. Like a movie star," she went on. "Is there anybody better-looking than he is? Not John Wayne, not Gary

Cooper, not anybody. If Fort Apache were being attacked, I'd like General Goldwater there—and you can quote me if you want," she told the reporter testily. "You and your types would surrender, first thing."

Those who came to him to ask questions-on-the-run got back answers-on-the-run. Most questions asked of a candidate, he had explained to Fred Anderson over a drink of bourbon a few days after his young speechwriter came to work for him, almost have to be answered by clichés. "Look, somebody stops you, Freddy, and says, 'Senator Goldwater, if you become President, will you protect Quemoy and Matsu?' I mean, the Quemoy and Matsu islands are protected by Taiwan, and we have a commitment to protect Taiwan. But if I say, 'Of course. We're already committed,' that person thinks you're not really leveling with him, so you have to say, 'I've always thought Quemoy and Matsu have been symbols of Free China. Dick Nixon thought the same thing four years ago, I agreed with him then, and I agree with him now.' What have I actually said? Nothing." He shrugged his shoulders. "But that's politics, and politics is my profession, so I'm not going to criticize it, am I?"

Then there was the questioner who was antagonistic. Here Goldwater would immediately distinguish between the two varieties of opposition. The first was inquisitively antagonistic. With them he would linger as long as he could, in particular if they were students. Fred Anderson, in his weekly letter to his mother, told of the young man in Tallahassee who had asked Goldwater why he had opposed the civil rights bill.

He delivered a little sermonette distinguishing between opposition to civil rights and opposition to a particular civil rights bill. "Hell," he said, "I'm in favor of a lot of things I couldn't vote for. I'd like to make the head of the Ku Kluxers go live with a Negro family—I know the family I have in mind—and wait on table and learn some manners. I'd like to sentence a dozen congressmen I can think of to spending thirty days filling out some of the forms issued by the regulatory agencies. I'd like to vote for a law requiring every ambassador from East Germany, Bulgaria, Czechoslovakia, Rumania, and Hungary to dress in red suits when they are more than one block away from the United Nations. But—see—I don't have the right to do that and I don't have the right to tell Mrs. Jones she has to rent her room to a Negro if she doesn't want to. I've opposed segregation since I was twenty years old."

—It doesn't always work, of course, but those people get answers they can think about, and they like the
guy they talked to.

What makes him really sore isn't the people who
wave signs saying things like, "Goldwater Wants
World War. He Thinks It Would Be Fun!" What gets
him is the guy at the press conference—a reporter,
maybe, or the local ADA type—who begins his question, "You said in your speech at Milwaukee last week
that you were in favor of giving NATO commanders
the right to use nuclear weapons whenever they feel
like it—" Yesterday one guy said almost exactly that,
and Goldwater answered, "If that's what the reporter
wrote, then he can't report and ought to be in another
business. If he didn't say that, then it's your problem,
you can't read, and you ought to learn to read before
you waste my time." Baroody practically fainted. After
the press conference, Baroody went after him about it,
and Goldwater just said—excuse me, Ma—he said,
"Fuck 'em!"

The speech that night in Toledo was to be on
Vietnam. Goldwater's principal military informant, well hidden in the catacombs of the Pentagon, had briefed him from a pay phone. Told
him that William Bundy had drafted a congressional resolution that would put it to Congress:
Do you, or do you not, want me, the President

of the United States, to use American military resources as required in order to protect American interests in Southeast Asia? President Johnson, the hidden general told him, was *thirsting* for explicit congressional backing for more aggressive action in the deteriorating situation. A U.S.-backed naval operation, Goldwater was told, was already in action in Tonkin Bay, its design to provoke North Vietnamese radar installations freshly planted by Soviet technicians to send out signals which U.S. receivers could log, giving the exact location and range of enemy radar. That whole secret operation was going on under the cover code "34-A." Johnson, the general kept repeating, desperately wanted blanket congressional approval for this *kind* of cautionary military action without being forced to reveal exactly what he *was* doing. But, the general reported, Johnson after a week of going this way then the other way had finally said no to Bundy's draft resolution, on the grounds that it would provoke an outcry from the pacifist left. "LBJ wants a united Democratic party behind him at the convention in Atlantic City." The general had spiced his report by telling Goldwater that at the Christmas Eve party at the White House, President Johnson had said to the Chairman of the Joint Chiefs, "Tell you what. You help get me elected in November, and you can have your war after that."

Senator Goldwater's meeting with his principal aides that night had been protracted and tense. It was agreed, of course, that no exact detail of the general's covert package of information could be revealed. But the speech must communicate to its primary audience—Lyndon Baines Johnson—that Goldwater had the inside story, and that Johnson would need to act decisively on Vietnam, even if that meant he'd run the risk of losing the enthusiasm of fifteen and one half Democratic delegates.

"Either that," Baroody put his pipe right down on the table and, suggesting the actual text, "or else say it: That political and military events in Vietnam point to the collapse of the Western doctrine of containment, and I, President Lyndon Johnson, candidate for reelection, don't intend to do anything about it."

How to word that speech was Fred Anderson's responsibility and he went to it. He was glad the hotel had a pool and a sauna open twenty-four hours. He took his first cup of coffee from the thermos. "Ladies and gentlemen. Toledo is in the heart of America, and this is a

good place to speak from the heart. / / / / /
/ / / / / / / / Toledo is the heart of America,
and a good place for a presidential candidate to
speak from the heart. . . ."

When he finished a draft, the sun was up. At
ten, Goldwater and his four top aides sat in the
spacious hotel suite in Columbus. There were
just the two copies, the original and the carbon—Baroody had forbidden the use of the
Xerox machine until the approved draft was
completed.

And, departing from the usual procedure this
time, press copies would not be distributed until
after Goldwater had begun speaking. Word had
got out that the speech would be challenging,
and, accordingly, President Johnson had directed that discreet cable connections bring the
speech live on television into the Oval Office,
where he sat with his principal aides.

"Handsome bugger," somebody said.

Johnson stared at him. He might as well have
said it: You queer or something?

Goldwater's ovation was prolonged. He made
the necessary remarks about being in Toledo,
told the famous story about Toledo, Spain: during the Civil War, he said he had been sent a
souvenir from Toledo, Spain, a little steel letter

opener, and was able to discern the fine print on the blade, "Hecho en Toledo, Ohio." Made in Toledo, Ohio. Roars.

There was a lot of steel traveling across the oceans these days, he said—unfortunately, not all of it being used to make letter openers. There was a lot of Soviet steel going into the radar and antiaircraft devices being installed along the coast of North Vietnam. What did they intend to do with those installations? Whose airplanes were they planning to shoot down? India's? Sweden's? What was the United States doing about those installations, so clearly aggressive in character and so clearly designed to hinder any attempt by the United States to help South Vietnam maintain its sovereignty? . . . When President Kennedy died there were sixteen thousand U.S. military advisers in South Vietnam. What has been their mandate? To do nothing? . . . Nothing is a lot better than what has been done, when you count five military coups in about as many months. And that happened while a Republican served as ambassador to South Vietnam. How many more coups can we expect—

Goldwater looked up, as though addressing

his question to a remote authority—to President Lyndon Johnson:

—when a Democrat succeeds him? . . . If the Ho Chi Minh Trail is being groomed as a super-highway for the infiltration of South Vietnam, what exactly are we doing about it? Hadn't Ambassador Averell Harriman, on behalf of President Kennedy, concluded a treaty with Laos—to which the Soviet Union was a signatory, along with thirteen other nations including North Vietnam—guaranteeing the sovereignty of Laos? And how do you reconcile the sovereignty of Laos with the use of Laos by the North Vietnamese to wage a war of aggression against the South? . . . Hadn't the Tonkin Gulf become a North Vietnamese lake under our do-nothing Administration? . . . President Johnson talks a very good line about resisting the forces of aggression, but how is he doing? . . . Fidel Castro continues to try to undermine countries in Latin America, and he is absolutely secure under Lyndon Johnson. The only Cubans the government is prosecuting are the Cuban-American members of the Alpha Cuban liberation team in Miami. . . . Lyndon Johnson is a nice man and means well, but he tries to please too many people. He wants to appeal to isolationists who want no responsibility for containing communism. . . . He wants to appease the Harvard professor types who spend a lot of time studying but never quite enough to learn the differences between Ho Chi Minh and George Washington. They have a lot to learn, but there isn't anything Lyndon Johnson can teach them! . . .

Et cetera.

Standing ovation.

LBJ used the little remote control on his desk to silence the television set. There was silence in the room. Finally he spoke up. "Some son of a bitch is talkin'." To Valenti he said, "Get me J. Edgar Hoover." To Bundy he said, "Let's have another look at the draft of that congressional resolution." To McNamara: "Work up a plan—a contingency plan—for the South Vietnamese to get the kind of ships necessary to stop the Gulf traffic south and also to knock out those radar installations." He inclined his head in the general direction of the television set, murmured again, "Somebody's talkin'," and left the room.

★ ★ ★ ★ ★ ★

Chapter Ten

JUNE 15, 1964
SAIGON, SOUTH VIETNAM

Abe Strauss shook his head as Blackford came around with the large coffeepot, and came to the conclusion of his analysis: There was no alternative to a land operation. "I've looked carefully at your report and your photos and sketches," he pointed to Blackford, "and what you have, any way you look at it, is a trail over four hundred miles long reaching into the Mekong Delta in the south, and then you have six hundred miles of offshooting trails into South Vietnam's northern sectors. And all these are being used."

"Are there operative bottlenecks? Points, or

passages, through which they need to go before they reach the offshoots?'' Rufus asked.

''Yes,'' Colonel Strauss said. Again he turned to Blackford: ''It seems to me that the Nape Pass and the Mu Gia Pass don't permit detours. We're going to need more intensive photography of the Nape Pass—''

''You're not going to get it, Abe,'' Rufus said. ''There's no way to penetrate the overhead cover. If we send photographers by land, think in terms of a fighting battalion because there's no way to anticipate the strength of the North Vietnamese army columns headed south. Besides that, your photographer, shooting from the ground, isn't going to give you the perspective you're looking for.''

Colonel Strauss paused. ''I get the point. Still, we know we're talking about a canyon. They have got to go down over Nape, unless they go airborne, and that's a narrow stretch of land. And then, about . . . sixty miles south of there is Mu Gia, which stretches twenty-two miles and isn't going to let anybody around unless they're prepared to scale this''—he pointed to the rugged mountain on the east, ''or that''—another such mountain, on the west. ''You could get *individuals* to scale those mountains—they'd better be Swiss, and maybe they'd get through with a pack on their back—but they're never going to get supplies into South Vietnam of any quantity, certainly not the heavy stuff, unless they transport it. And if they transport it, they've got to go over Nape first."

Colonel Strauss leaned forward and read aloud its coordinates, as if to infuse it with reality: "Eighteen degrees 18 minutes North, 105 degrees 6 minutes East—that's my deduction, Blackford, from the coordinates you gave on either side. Mu Gia is at 17.4 North and 105.47 East. We have to put these passes out of action. But I don't see how we can keep them out of action without sending people there to set up a Maginot Line. Those two places are perfect for Maginot Line strategy. But that kind of operation has got to be done by human beings on the ground."

Blackford agreed. "There's no other way."

Tucker Montana slouched, puffing on a small cigar, as he liked to do when the air was very still and he could blow his smoke rings, at which he was proficient. "Trouble is," he commented, "that means an on-the-ground war, which LBJ ain't about to authorize, and you can't just keep bombing blindly, can you? They can go right back to moving the stuff when you're not there."

"There's another problem," Rufus said. "The Geneva Accords. The passes are in Laos, and Laos is supposed to be neutral—never mind that it isn't, but it's supposed to be. Which, after all, is why all our aerial work is being done by Army aircraft coming in from Thailand, or naval aircraft coming in from the Gulf, disguised as South Vietnamese—"

Blackford half-laughed. "That's what we call being neutral?"

Rufus accepted the jibe. "Your point is obvious, Blackford. But after the pact was executed, the North Vietnamese, a party to the agreement, withdrew exactly *forty* men. The South Vietnamese pulled out *nine thousand.* The whole purpose of the Geneva Accords was to end the war in South Vietnam. In fact it is proceeding *exactly* as before, but with greater intensity, through Laotian territory." He recovered the line of thought in which he had been interrupted and gave its conclusion. "The kind of sustained operation you would need would first require Washington to rescind the treaty, or simply to declare it null and void—on the grounds that all parties are not respecting it."

"Well, Rufus," Blackford said, "that's Washington's problem, no? Our job is to figure out how it *could* be done, theirs to decide whether they want to do it and what diplomatic or military means are appropriate to the realization of that end."

"Yes. But we must recommend something we think can work, and simply to recommend the bombing of the two passes seems to me to leave unanswered, as Tucker says, such questions as just how to bomb. That is: How to know where and when to bomb; how to strike targets, not mountains; how to develop an intensity of aerial coverage that would really make the difference."

It was at this point that Tucker, finally aroused, spoke up. "Rufus, can I have the floor a minute? Abe?"

He opened his briefcase and took out a large sketch pad. From his pocket he fished out a small metal container. He lifted its cap off and plucked out two large thumbtacks. He ripped the first sketch from the pad and fastened it on the wooden wall behind them.

"That's a Sonobuoy. We use these to keep track of Soviet submarines. Up here," he pointed to the upper end of what looked like a slim bomb, "you have this little detachable buoy, corklike material. Its function is to keep that little ten-inch antenna up there on top of the water and to maintain the capsule with its microphone at the desired depth. So: The reconn plane drops the Sonobuoy. The little bomblike thing here sinks just deep enough to provide equilibrium for the antenna.

"The Sonobuoy is a sensor, very sensitive. When a submarine passes within a dozen miles of it, the sub's sound registers and a signal is sent to the antenna. That antenna has the power to transmit its signal fifty miles. Nondirectional, so you can pick it up over an area of maybe 175 miles. Now, the crystal on that Sonobuoy is, let's say, Radio Frequency A. The crystal on the Sonobuoy five miles south is B. The crystal on the Sonobuoy five miles west is Frequency C. As those signals come up, the reconn planes can triangulate in and figure out pretty close where the submarine is, what its heading is, and how fast it's traveling. Or, they can project from the passage of the sub and the progressive alerts sent out what direction it's going and at what speed.

"Now, I don't see any argument against tak-

ing that technology and adapting it to our problem—"

"What kind of a sound or vibration is made by
men making their way over a trail?"

"Hold it, Abe! Hold that for a minute. What do
we know in 1964 that we didn't know twenty
years ago? Well, *we have computers,* and they
will do the triangulation work for you in maybe
one second. But we also have acoustic devices
that are a hundred times as sensitive as the
Sonobuoy's. Human voices, yes, and not only
the buzz and hum of human voices: what they
are actually *saying.*

"We want sound," he said reflectively, "and
we want sound waves. We need to build a ver-
sion of the Sonobuoy—an acoustical buoy,
'Acoubuoy,' if you like—that will come down all
over those two passes and will transmit—
sound. The actual noises will include conversations by NVA foot soldiers, though that would be
incidental. Primarily the aim is sounds of vehi-
cles, and our ability to particularize will tell us
whether we're dealing with jeeps or trucks or
tanks. Now, those signals could go up to orbiting
aircraft and be relayed to our proposed facility at
Nakhon Phanom. Over there we would need
analysts to sort out what the noises all mean. If

they add up to an opportunity for aerial attack, we shoot that information over to the airfield, or to the reconn planes.

"Now, if Rufus is right—that we aren't going to be allowed to use our stuff to drop down on these gentlemen—we might as well go home. But we do have the technology to take those two passes and convert them into electronic highways. Wherever we have Acoubuoys we would see their registrations on a huge situation display—to light up the locations where the sound is being picked up. And the instrumentation in those sensors"—Blackford was staring at Tucker Montana in amazement; he had heard nothing before from him that suggested he had any background in science—"shouldn't have any problem in giving out signals that will show up in different colors on our screen, depending on whether it's infantrymen or tanks, jeeps, trucks, whatever. And then we send out the right kind of signal to the right kind of airplane, which drops the right kind of stuff in the right place."

"How would you get those sensors where you want them?" Strauss asked.

"You'd drop them from airplanes or helicopters. And they can be dropped in daylight—at least they can do that up until the NVA sets up radar and antiaircraft stuff, which can't be long delayed, Black and I figure."

He took the second page from his scratch pad and fastened it alongside the first. "Here is my idea of a cross section of a revised Sonobuoy. I call it, for the hell of it, a Spikebuoy. You need to protect the delicate acoustic and seismic sensor from the impact of striking the ground. I calculate," he pointed at the second drawing, "a 2.5-foot average penetration, with the sensor then sitting, camouflaged, right on the ground with its little antenna. Now, keeping equipment from being destroyed after a drop is something the parachute people have been working on for years. Our Spikebuoys should be of two kinds. One would come down by parachute and hang from the upper branches of trees where they'd be hard to notice. But most of them we'd want to come right down near and parallel to the Trail. Impact could be absorbed by collapsible cushioning elements in the Spikebuoy. What the paratroop guys do is make adjustments that depend on the weight of the object and the distribution of that weight. They spread about collapsible material which, on impact, itself crushes, absorbing the impact energy. It's very carefully done, so that the force of the crash is almost entirely absorbed by the collapse of the cushioning layers, which are variously tiered.

"So that work has been done, and done well after the war. It was done, interestingly enough, under the guidance of a foundation sustained by people—family, sons—who mourned a race car driver who died because his crash helmet didn't protect him. Safety helmets lined with sponge rubber are deadly. What happens is the foam collapses under impact, allowing the strike force to hit the head or even to transmit right through the collapsed rubber a jolt that reaches the head and then—the rubber having absorbed the incoming energy—release it back as the outside force disappears. The rubber then kicks back in the opposite direction and delivers a whiplash blow that, at the right frequencies, can create a bad nerve-tissue problem."

"You are talking about helmets already developed?" Rufus wanted to know.

"Oh yes. The helmet that works we can borrow from, borrow the basic design to shield a Spikebuoy. It's lined with a rigid but collapsible foam which, on taking an incoming blow, absorbs the energy by collapsing its own rigid structure. The structure, now disintegrated, can't deliver the energy backward. The force is dead.

"It takes careful engineering, but that's what created the Snell Foundation–approved safety helmet."

"Wouldn't that suggest the need of a very large circumference in the Spikebuoy?" Blackford asked.

"Good question. Depends on the weight. But the weight of the sensors is always diminishing, just as the size of the batteries is down to about one tenth of what it used to be. The Spikebuoy could have just that amount of protection it needs. We could very quickly establish how much. An aspect of how high off the ground the plane is when it's dropped, among other factors. With a few thousand of those peppering those passes, on the ground, on trees and vines, and replenished every month or so—that's how long the batteries would last—and besides, we'd be blowing them up along with the stuff in between them—we'd have a pretty good chance, seems to me, to find the best places to block that Trail . . ." he paused, for the first time ". . . without senseless, random bombing."

There was silence for a minute. Colonel

Strauss spoke: "You believe you could design the Spikebuoy, and also the other receiver—the acoustic buoy that would transmit sounds of Trail activity and yield exact targets to appropriate receiving stations?"

Tucker Montana said, "Give me a lab and a few assistants who speak science, and the answer is, sure. Only thing I'd need to brush up on is the size and weight of components and the latest computer capabilities. And I'd need to know something about our aircraft and aerial ordnance capabilities as they stand these days, to recommend the right kind of airplane—that kind of thing. It can't be done overnight. But there just isn't any problem about designing something. We got to design it, then we got to manufacture it, then we got to build up that Nakhon place, then we get some sound analysts, then we get permission from Lyndon Johnson or from God or whoever is in charge to use the Spikes, preferably before the South is inundated with the stuff that's going down that crazy Trail. Blackford and I saw enough of it getting by as it is. Unless we block them, that's only the beginning."

Rufus spoke slowly. "Gentlemen, I have reflected on what Tucker has said and on our other conversations. We must meet very soon again. But in Washington. Blackford will arrange the details and inform you of flight schedules. We should try to leave on the eleven P.M. flight to Honolulu." He looked over at Blackford, who nodded.

Tucker spoke. "Gee, Rufus, sorry, but not tonight for me. Just plain can't. Absolutely unbreakable engagement, a matter of personal honor." He looked up at Blackford. "Make my flight tomorrow, okay?"

Blackford nodded. And suppressed a smile. He'd as likely have denied a request by Thomas Alva Edison.

Riding in the Army sedan with Rufus, Blackford turned to him. "Why in the hell wasn't I told about that guy's background?"

"For the very good reason that I knew nothing about it. Special Forces sent him over to us as an expert fieldman with an antiterrorist background."

"I'm surprised our friend Tucker hasn't invented a bomb that aims only at terrorists."

"Or a bomb that eliminates dumb personnel in Special Forces who send Wernher von Braun types out to the field to do guard duty." Rufus was annoyed. Blackford wondered: Was Rufus *angry*? Could that ever happen to a man so professional?

Only, Blackford, concluded, when provoked by highly unprofessional behavior. He knew that not much time would go by before Rufus had the full biography of Major Tucker Montana.

★ ★ ★ ★ ★ ★ ★ ★ ★

Chapter Eleven

JULY 9, 1964
MEXICO CITY

Tucker Montana caught up with Rufus and Blackford in Hawaii, where Rufus spent a day in consultation with CINCPAC, the Commander in Chief, Pacific. In conversations with Washington, Rufus established that the officials critical to a decisive meeting on the proposed operation could not assemble until ten days later. He would use that period to explore and refine Tucker's proposals. And he was now free to yield to Blackford's request for a week's vacation.

In San Francisco, Rufus and Tucker caught the connecting flight to Washington. Blackford flew south to Los Angeles, changing there for a flight to Mexico City.

Why didn't Compañía Mexicana de Aviación offer their tourist-class passengers Mexican food? He'd have exchanged the entire menu—tasteless shrimp, mystery meat, mashed potatoes, unclassified beans, the kind of pudding that reminded him of Greyburn, his old school in England—for one hot enchilada, one tamale, a half-dozen tortillas. Never mind, he would make up for it in Mexico, though it is hard, he had discovered, to find good Mexican food in the city of Mexico—at least hard to find it in restaurants where you'd want to eat.

After the events of the past year, he had thought so much about their next encounter that he decided finally he would not speculate any further on how it would be, exactly, to see Sally again, for the first time since she had been married. They had, after all, always tended to extemporaneity with each other; yes, ever since that crazy afternoon at the college fraternity cocktail party when they had first met. He (in the Air Corps books a senior), a minor hero (he had knocked down three Messerschmitts in hand-to-hand encounters), studying—and playing—in a large undergraduate class that had a dozen such heroes, uniformly unrecognized as such. She, a graduate student, stunning, smart, scholarly, and in no particular need of young heroes. She outshone him, he remembered, in every way that mattered. And when, on the fateful night only ten days after their first meeting, lying together, she had told him in the matter-of-fact tones she used in describing her academic work that he was the most beautiful young man she had ever laid eyes on, he remembered what she had said more because it amused him than because it appealed to his vanity: his vague, outspoken, irrepressible mother had repeatedly embarrassed him in public with such references to him ("Oh, my beautiful Blacky!") ever since he was fourteen years old. Theirs had been a volatile romance, but Blackford had never doubted that in the truly providential sense of it they were meant for each other, and when she suddenly married Antonio a year earlier, he had known what it meant to go about, for weeks on end, with an empty heart.

In due course he came to know the works of Jane Austen, of necessity, that author being Sally's specialty, and he had to remind himself that what had happened to him that afternoon after the football game was not insane or unique: it happened several times in Miss Austen's six novels, genuine struck-dead, love-at-first-sight situations. Sally was slightly withdrawn, indomitably independent in spirit, dazzling to look at if you began by discarding as irrelevant most of the competition in icons of the day—she didn't look like Rita Hayworth or Marilyn Monroe. In fact, she didn't look like anybody else, and every now and then he wondered whether he alone found her so beautiful, and then one day he asked the question, rather shyly, of his closest friend, Anthony Trust, who had answered: "Is Sally beautiful? Is Mona Lisa beautiful? Is Venice beautiful? Is that Grecian Urn beautiful that Keats wrote about? What's the matter— Ah! You are thinking maybe of Doucette? She was very beautiful too. I wonder what she looked like with clothes on."

Blackford had smiled at this reference to a joint "date" Anthony had engineered in Paris with two quite unusual ladies of the night. Blackford had had numerous engagements in the sportive mode during the fifteen years since he had met Sally. In an unconcentrated sort of way he vaguely disapproved of his own casual sexual behavior, but excused himself on the grounds that Sally had put off a wedding date, pending the completion of her dissertation; and then it was he who had (twice) put off fixing a date because he had been preoccupied with two successive time-consuming appointments for the Agency, the result of all of which had been frequent separations over extended periods of time. And then there was the summer when they were both in Washington and it was the season of her maximum irritability, the locus of which was Blackford's continuing service in the Agency, which, more or less flippantly, she held responsible for the prolongation of the Cold War. He remembered one expression of it.

"Darling," she had said, "do you agree with the sociological generality that people tend to be very anxious about holding on to their jobs?"

"Of course I do—is this the right turn?" They were headed for a little inn they visited from time to time in Virginia, where they were always welcomed as Mr. and Mrs. Rhodes, "the handsomest young couple in the state," the old lady behind the desk would beam.

"No. Next one. Well, wouldn't it then be fair to say that people who work in the . . . Agency" (she always went along, if a little playfully, with the protocol never to refer to the CIA as the CIA.

She flatly declined to refer to it as the "firm," never mind that it had become quite universal, but went along with "the Agency") "would be out of a job if the Cold War ended?"

"Yes, sure. And doctors would be out of a job if illness ended."

"You know," she said in quick exasperation, "you are *always* doing that kind of thing when we talk about these subjects, just sheer outrageous point evasion. When you study engineering, I forget, do you have to take a course in logic? Obviously if you did, you failed it. So let me just say, Blackford—yes, that's the right one. Turn and go about two miles, it's on the left— that illness is a part of the human condition; the Cold War isn't."

"You're only half right. The Cold War is a part of the human condition for so long as you have two social phenomena which we can pretty safely denominate as constants. The first is a society that accepts what it sees as the historical mandate to dominate other societies—at least as persistently as microbes seek out human organisms to infect. And the second phenomenon, of course, is the coexistence of a society that is determined *not* to be dominated or have its friends dominated. Now, when the setting I have just so nicely described takes place in a world in which both the aggressor society and the independent society have got hold of nuclear weapons, you are going to have a Cold War, or whatever you'll call it, and if you have a Cold War you don't want to get hot you are going to need to know what are the enemy's resources, number one, and that is relatively easy, and then you are going to need to know, number two, and that is relatively hard, what are the enemy's *intentions.*"

"So, you are saying that there is no prospect of a CIA agent losing his job?"

"Sure there is. We don't get tenure, the way hard-driven Austen scholars do. We can screw up and get fired. Or get dead. There can be a Reduction in Force—remember that? Under Eisenhower? Federal employees got 'RIFed.' That lasted about six months. After that, dear Ike kept on hiring people, at just about the same rate as FDR and Truman."

"Well, what would you do if *you* were 'RIFed'?"

They had the inn in sight.

"Hadn't actually thought about it. I have a degree in mechanical engineering, and I suppose I could brush up on what's been discov-

ered in that line in the past fifteen years. Hmm.
I suppose I could teach people how to fly . . ."

"What you could do," Sally said, in one of
those rapid changes in mood of which she was
capable, "is model clothes, and teach people
how to make love, you gorgeous thing"—she let
her hand touch him.

"Hey. Not here! Yes, we're here! Later."

Not *much* later, he remembered; the porter
had only just brought up their bags and closed
the door and got out just in time.

He had asked her not to meet him at the
airport. "I don't want to see you, for the first time
in a year, at a crowded airport, with everybody
there. Send that chauffeur of yours. Tell him I'll
be carrying a copy of *National Review* in my
hand. That ought to eliminate any confusion. Or,
God knows, duplication."

In the big Buick he confessed to himself that
he was apprehensive. As recently as a week
before, over the telephone from Saigon, they
had spoken as if they would, in fact, marry. Two
years earlier, weekending in Taxco, she had
abruptly said: Let us get married on June 1,
1964, and he had said, Yes, let's; and as the
months went by he thought of that date with

almost superstitious anticipation, like an oasis at first dismissed as ephemeral, which on approaching begins to take life: real trees, real water, a real garden and house. . . . She hadn't mentioned the date at their rendezvous in Acapulco in January 1963, the last time he had seen her, eighteen months ago. He had thought it a blissful three days, and six weeks later he learned that she had married a man named Antonio Morales.

The residence was in Coyoacán, very old Mexico City and still an enclave of old-family houses, many of them dating back to colonial days. The stone wall surrounded the residence, the garden, a small plot where flowers and vegetables grew, two or three buildings for servants, one for equipment. . . . She had described all of this to him, in fact had sent him a picture—a picture, as it happened, taken on the day of her wedding reception. It was not a huge house, but it was a proud house which had been in the Morales family for several generations and belonged to Antonio briefly, between the day his parents died in an airplane crash in Venezuela and the day he had been shot dead sitting at a picnic table at Tres Marías, ten thousand feet high, halfway between Mexico and Cuernavaca. He had died on that cold damp day during the rainy season in August because he sought to advance the prospects of human freedom in Cuba. He had risked his life, and then given it.

From that day on, the Casa Serena had become the house of little Anthony Morales de Guzmán—Jr., he'd have become, in America— who, lying in the womb of his mother, was twelve weeks old. The will stipulated, pursuant to Spanish custom, that the Casa Serena would pass to the heir effective on the day he was married. Until then, the matrona of the Casa was the widow, Señora Sally Morales de Partridge.

Raúl guided the car slowly up the circular drive toward the portico with the tiled tableaux on either side. She was standing there, waiting for him.

★ ★ ★ ★ ★ ★ ★ ★ ★

Chapter Twelve

The meeting this time was at the residence of Rufus, the farmhouse an hour and a half from Washington. Allen Dulles, when he had served as Director, enjoyed going there to meet with Rufus when certain Great & Serious plans needed to be made, and had passed along to his successor, John McCone, word of the suitability of the relatively isolated small house by the woods, twenty-five miles southeast of Gettysburg, where Rufus spent his spare time tending to his rose garden, living alone now since the death of his wife. "Nobody ever interrupts you there, and there's something about getting away from the air of Washington that allows you not only to breathe better, but to think better." CIA Director McCone had made the trip out there twice and this time persuaded the Chairman of the Joint Chiefs of Staff, Maxwell Taylor, who would be succeeding Henry Cabot Lodge as Ambassador to South Vietnam, to join him there for a critical meeting.

Tucker and Blackford arrived earlier in a rented car, had coffee, admired Rufus's flowers and the pharmacy of chemicals from which he selected just the right blend of nourishment for just the right rose. They didn't speak about the war, but the public crossfire the night before between President Johnson and candidate Goldwater suggested that there was little else on the mind of official Washington than the Vietnam question.

At 10:45 the chauffeured limousine drove in, and out of it stepped the studious, affluent, pious Californian, sometime Chairman of the Atomic Energy Commission under Eisenhower, successor to Allen Dulles after the disgrace of the Bay of Pigs, in charge of the second-largest intelligence agency in the world. One would have said of him as he approached the house on the flagstone walkway that he was erect in his bearing, except that he'd have needed to be

compared on this occasion with General Maxwell Taylor, who was ramrod-straight and yet
somehow springy, flexible in posture: a nice
combination, Blackford thought, as he prepared
to meet the general for the first time, and the
Director for the second.

Rufus's penchant for using as few words as
possible extended to introductions. He accomplished this now by vaguely pointing at Blackford, who stepped forward and extended his
hand, "I am Blackford Oakes, sir," to the general, to whom Rufus vaguely pointed, turning
then to Tucker Montana who also stepped forward and identified himself. The younger men
shook hands with the Director, who said something about how they had both had a fruitful
experience in Laos, exploring the Trail; and they
went off to the terrace where the table had been
simply prepared: yellow note pads and iced tea.

McCone began. He turned to Tucker and said,
"Major, we have run a more thorough check on
your background—that is, a check on what you
did during the war years. We were satisfied,
before sending you on the current mission, to
know what you have done—have accomplished—in the Army, and then in the Special
Forces, since 1949, in what turns out to have

been your second hitch in the Army. There is no need at this point to explore the reasons why you have so assiduously disguised your first hitch. Even though we can hardly pass without notice that none of the several forms you have filled out during the past decade and a half lists accurately what you did in the years 1944 and 1945."

Blackford cocked his head. He was curious. He had become fond of Tucker, and was of course grateful to him for helping to save his life. But he was uneasy about Tucker's well-concealed past. What was the point in concealing the extensive training he had obviously had in science? And what was it that had caused him, so suddenly, to reveal that training, on that hot, humid day in Saigon, by an exposition that marked him as not only skilled in science, but inventive? On the night they both were brought together by Rufus to be taken to the White House to meet the President, Blackford had been told only that he was a member of an Army Special Forces unit. No biographical details were given out, any more than details of Blackford's background had been given to Tucker Montana. "I don't know myself what his background is," Rufus had said. "Special Forces is that way. But who are we to complain?"

"The command decision on this one," General Taylor interrupted, "is to take you out of our Special Forces and assign you to the CIA. You'll maintain your Army rank and all the benefits. But from now on, you take your orders from—" he pointed in the direction first of John McCone, then Rufus.

McCone resumed: "And clearly your first responsibility is to superintend technology at Nakhon Phanom. The interdiction of enemy movement down the Ho Chi Minh Trail is now the *first* priority of this Administration. I do not mean by this that it is the first priority in *that* theater. I mean that it is the first priority, period. Nothing needed that can be obtained will be denied to you. Every scientist we need to consult, conscript, kidnap"—this was a conscious levity by serious John McCone, and his subordinates smiled appropriately even as, twenty-five years earlier, they'd have done for their headmasters—"will be at your beck and call. We *absolutely need to staunch* that flow of trained guerrilla fighters to the south projected by Hanoi. The volume right now, even though it's

only a small fraction of what's intended, is causing a lot of damage in the countryside. The
North Vietnamese feed the legend that what's
going on in the South is a civil war. Hell, the
Vietcong operating within the South would be
subdued in a fortnight except for the reinforce-
ments from the North. You are to confer with
Colonel Strauss during the next few days,
before returning to Saigon, to select a staff,
pass on their qualifications, and submit a general plan the realization of which will receive, as
I say, top priority."

While Tucker was dipping his head slightly,
just enough to communicate that he agreed to
go along, Blackford was wondering whether he
was now expected to accept a reversal of roles,
to work on the Trail as Tucker's subordinate—
an assignment he did not relish because of the
nature of the work, but which he would not have
resented, given the clear superiority in Tucker's
scientific qualifications. But—

"And you, Mr. Oakes," General Taylor was
speaking now. "You will leave the area—leave
the Trail, but not the theater. We are placing you
in charge of Operation 34-A."

Blackford's eyebrow went up inquisitively.

"It's a top-secret operation. Has to do with the

east coast. There's a lot going on in the Gulf of Tonkin. We need to know more than we do. We're picking up a lot from 34-A, need to pick up a lot more, and to refine procedures, which is where you'll come in. There's sophisticated Soviet-supplied military technology going in there, right along the coast of North Vietnam, all the way to China. What we want is an effective blockade against the movement of men and materiel by sea into South Vietnam. Most of them disguised as fishermen. You," he pointed to Tucker, "and you," he pointed to Blackford, "are our pincers on Vietnam. Except that your function is not to close in on South Vietnam, but to protect it. To close in on the arteries from the North. The objective is to begin immediately to diminish the flow of troops and supplies—even as you, Montana, work through the Nakhon Phanom facility to stop the traffic on the Trail.

"The enemy's objective is to transport X numbers of men and Y tons of materiel to South Vietnam. Short of truly difficult infiltration right across the frontier—the DMZ—which is heavily observed and easily protected, there is no way to do this except through the Trail or by sea. To the extent pressure mounts on *you*"—once again he pointed at Tucker—"it will diminish on you"—he pointed to Blackford. "And vice versa. And just as they will need to coordinate *their* efforts, we will need to coordinate ours, which is why we think of Montana's operation—Nakhon Phanom—and yours—34-A—as a joint enterprise. We will need to be constantly informed on what you find and what you're doing, and *you* will need to inform each other. You should plan to come back in from the field regularly to Saigon, maybe even once a week. And in about one month, I will be there myself, as ambassador. That's it."

That, really, was it. Granted, Blackford thought as the brass got up from the table ready for the light lunch Rufus had prepared for them, there were problems. Exactly how was Admiral Oakes supposed to stop commerce coming in from a country with which we maintained, formally, nonbelligerent status? The hypocrisies in the whole Vietnam situation were very nearly asphyxiating.

The younger men had been excused. Rufus and Blackford confirmed their rendezvous for the following day. Tucker was expected early in the afternoon at the Aberdeen Proving Ground by Colonel Strauss and, in his rental car, would drop Blackford off in Baltimore. Blackford had accepted an invitation to spend the evening with his oldest friend, Anthony Trust, at some exotic restaurant Anthony had spoken of over the telephone.

"Why Baltimore?" Blackford had asked over the phone.

"Don't ask questions of the man who recruited you to serve your country."

"None of *that,* Anthony"—Blackford sensed the old roué plotting.

"None of *that,* Blackford. We'll just talk about Sally."

Blackford reflected in silence—the only (prayerful) state appropriate when sitting in a car being driven by Tucker Montana—that Anthony Trust was the one living human being Blackford would permit to propose such an agenda.

At thirty-nine, Trust was one year older than Blackford. He had developed hedonistic habits, and managed with skills not readily matched to combine duty to the Agency he had worked for since leaving college with hard concentration on earthly delights: wine, women, and song, of course, but also relaxed and relaxing reading usually having no bearing on the problems that consumed most of his working day. His mother having left him a considerable legacy, he had no problem in financing his extravagances. He did not begrudge those of them that had to do with the opposite sex; indeed, he was capable of clinical examination of relative costs. One of his themes was that sexual romance was never really "free" because when it was nonprofessional, the maintenance cost, so to speak, was every bit as high, over the long term, as a succession of pleasant evenings with pleasing women who did that kind of thing for a living. He would never marry, he had told Blackford years before, because—well, because he feared that his nature would not make possible what he considered the serious monogamous obligations of marriage. Anthony Trust really did not approve of adulterous behavior. He saw enough of it, both among his companions and among those he was being paid to observe, and he understood that the call of the flesh often overrides moral commandments.

True, Blackford could remember three times when Anthony, blissfully content with his latest companion, in a relationship of several days, even weeks, had said he was reconsidering the question of marriage; but after a while Blackford would smile, and wait until the inevitable happened: Anthony Trust with a new friend.

On the other hand, he reflected, Anthony had every reason to think the same thing about Blackford, whose unrealized betrothal to Sally almost justified the assumption that it was unrealizable. It was Anthony who had broken the news to Blackford, a year ago, that Sally had married in Mexico, and even over the telephone Blackford's dismayed reaction had made Anthony worry for his health: that total desolation on hearing the most unexpected news imaginable. But Anthony knew also that Blackford's reserves of strength were considerable, as was his dogged determination, at times of crisis, to have his own way. As praepostor at the British public school it had fallen to Anthony Trust to help hold down young Blackford, age fifteen, over one end of a sofa as he received a serious flogging from the headmaster. After which Blackford had calmly asked Anthony to order him a taxi: and he left the school. It had been a very long friendship, begun a few months before Pearl Harbor when Blackford went to Greyburn College, and now, twenty-three years later, they were closest friends.

"Why Baltimore?" Blackford said as Anthony, tall and slim, his brown eyes lit with fun and curiosity, his hair straight and ample, dressed in a polo shirt and white ducks, opened the door of the apartment.

"You ass!" Anthony took Blackford's briefcase from him and motioned to him to remove his jacket. "Why Baltimore indeed! First, some of the best beer on the East Coast is made here. Second, much of the best seafood in the East is found here. Third, there is pulchritude at hand here second to none. Fourth, because Baltimore is exactly thirty-five miles away from Aberdeen, which is where administrative action has already begun to bring together the 'Jason Summer Study Group' to create your facility at Nakhon Phanom. I've been made head of the recruiting cadre. I've got a staff of six, and we'll spend all tomorrow with your pal Tucker Montana and start rounding up anybody who has skills we don't already have at Aberdeen. So how you like that, Black: we're working on the same project again!"

"Well," Blackford accepted the glass of beer, "not exactly. I've been moved. To the Gulf." He waited instinctively, to feel out whether Anthony knew about 34-A. The rules on the subject were so often stressed that they became instinctive: You did not tell another agent something that other agent did not need to know.

Anthony, seated in an armchair, looked up. "Ah. The business on the Gulf. I've run across the trail of that operation, but am not formally briefed. So let's be proper and drop the subject. Leave it that we're both working on projects designed to help the same country."

"Designed to help the Western alliance, is how it's been put to me."

Anthony shrugged his shoulders as he stretched out his legs on the coffee table. "Yeah. And I think that's right, by the way. Only the subject is so mixed up in presidential politics, let's face it, it would require a polygraph expert to tell you whether to believe anything you hear from the White House these days. And," Anthony sighed rather dramatically, "the same goes for the Pentagon, to tell you the truth. But sure I think it has to do with the Western alliance. The doctrine of containment is exactly what we fought for in Korea. Not the most popular war in the history of the U.S. No war in the Pacific ever would be. America needs a little more time for the memory of our Oriental Exclusion Acts to fade away. But there isn't any difference, Korea–Vietnam, except that the North Vietnamese have succeeded in persuading the persuadable that it's a civil war within the South. Well, it isn't. It isn't another Greece 1946, either, or even another Huk rebellion. This one, if I read it right, and you can correct me, is sustained as directly by current flowing in from North Vietnam as that air conditioner over there is by this electrical outlet. Yank that cord and the air conditioner stops. Takes a gulp or two going out, but that's all. . . . So. Tell me. How is she?"

"She's fine," Blackford began. He stretched back in the deep armchair, and allowed his eyes to look up toward the ceiling. Easier that way, actually, than to look Anthony straight in the face as he spoke.

"First: There has never in the world been a more glorious-looking woman than Sally Morales. I don't know, but becoming a mother did something to her. That little tension we ran into every now and then? Gone. She is mistress of that household as if she had grown up there. Her spoken Spanish is—perfect: alongside the average Berlitz Spanish teacher, she sounds like Unamuno. When I drove in there were maybe seven or eight people in sight: gardeners, a butler, the chauffeur of course, and a couple of maids and the nurse with the baby. Sally really embraced me. Well, not quite the way she might have done it say in the moonlight, under the Yale Bowl. But it was obviously more than a cousinly greeting, and she planted the message right there, in front of everybody: *This is one of my dearest friends,* was her greeting. And it probably conveyed the thought: This is someone with whom I might well have had a romantic attachment—and may someday again have one. It gave me instant standing at the Casa Serena, which is what the spread is called, about four acres in the middle of Coyoacán, probably worth a couple of million dollars."

"And then," Anthony poured him a fresh beer.

"Funny—though maybe not, come to think of it—we didn't talk about ourselves, not at all. And though she made a few routine references to Antonio, she didn't even hint at the part the Agency and I played in his getting killed. Not a trace of it. She wanted to know, naturally, what I was up to, and I told her about Vietnam, with the usual circumlocutions, which of course she spotted, but which she let go.

"The baby? A cute little guy—it would help, I guess, if I could tell one two-month-old baby from another—and he is the light of her life. She has a routine which didn't vary during the three weekdays I was there: breakfast at seven, a half hour with the baby, then hard work on her lecture, departs for the university, which isn't far, you remember—on the road to Cuernavaca. On the road to Tres Marías." Blackford's voice changed slightly; he spoke the words more slowly. "She is back in time for lunch except on the day she has office hours. After lunch we walked around the property, the first afternoon. Then we drove around the city, saw the new anthropology museum—gorgeous!—shopped in Sanborn's. Back at five, and she spends an hour with the baby and another hour or two correcting student papers, then at eight we meet, and she serves dinner at nine-thirty."

"Any guests?"

"She asked me, Did I want any old friends to come in? I said, 'At this point I don't know one other living soul in Mexico City, don't want to know anyone but you and your child. I don't even know the name of the CIA official here.' But then I asked if *she* wanted to have some people in. Indeed she did. She wanted Antonio's uncle—he's only about sixty, a lawyer, like Antonio, and part of the firm; sort of the reigning behind-the-scenes Morales, though the bulk of the estate, I gather, is in the name of the child, with plenty of income for Sally for the rest of her life, though she has to give up Casa Serena when little Anthony gets married.

"Anyway, she wanted the uncle, Don Álvaro. She wanted Antonio's best man, Pedrito Alzada, and his wife; and a cousin of Antonio, a god-damn Spanish goddess, I am telling you—I didn't know until after she had left that she is in the movies under the name María Estada: she is the Mexicans' Rita Hayworth, but she behaves more as one would expect Katharine Hepburn to behave: a little withdrawn, beady intelligence, captivating charm. Speaks good English, by the way, and I caught her speaking French to Don Álvaro. She has been married and divorced, not a popular thing to do in Mexico, not among that class, but everybody apparently agreed that her husband was a drunken bounder. She has gone back to her maiden name, just plain María Morales."

Anthony didn't want Blackford to go on other than at his own gait, but still was ready to press him just slightly. "How were you introduced? Other than merely as a—former friend?"

"Oh yes. It was not the kind of thing I expected, not at all. They all came promptly, nine

P.M., and champagne was served after formal
greetings. She raised her glass and said, 'I am
so glad that you, my best friends in Mexico, are
here to meet my best and oldest American
friend. In fact over the years it often seemed that
we would end by being husband and wife. But
we had a few competitors.' She let the suspense grow before she went on. 'Mine was Jane
Austen. Blackford's was his country's diplo-
macy'—I had been introduced as a professional
diplomat—'and then, of course, there was the
main entry in my life.' She turned to Don Álvaro:
'Your nephew.' She turned to María Morales:
'Your cousin.' She turned to Pedrito: 'Your best
friend.' And then she looked up at the eighteen-
foot ceiling and blew a little kiss up in the direction of the nursery with her left hand, brought the
champagne glass to her lips, and said softly,
'Your father.' ''

"Well," said Anthony, putting aside his half-
consumed drink, "now *that's* what I call an ice-
breaker! Did it work?"

"It worked like a charm. I was treated from
that moment on as Sally's brother."

"Is that what you were looking for?"

Blackford smiled, got up and walked over to
the bar and, this time around, poured himself a

scotch. "No. Not exactly what I was looking for, though it increased my admiration of her."

"Your *admiration* of her?"

"Yes. That and the love I feel for her."

"Does she feel the same thing for you?"

"She says she does. Says it very convincingly."

"Did she, er, demonstrate that love?"

"Don't be coy. No. I made an advance, two nights before leaving, and she said no. And the worst of it is, I understood. I mean, in that environment. It would have been like making love in church, I really mean it. She just said—'Later. I mean, in other circumstances.' "

"When you're married?"

"When we're married."

"Will that happen?"

"I don't know for sure. I hope so. We have, as usual, a tentative date. By the way, it would be out of the question, in the Spanish tradition, to remarry less than a year after Antonio's death."

"So you're talking the end of the year?"

"Yes. And I think she means it. And I know that I mean it."

"Meanwhile?"

"Meanwhile," Blackford downed his scotch and smiled. "Meanwhile, I guess I'm free to act as I've been used to acting, and I know she knows this, expects it to be that way. She said something interesting about Antonio at one point when the subject came up; she said that when he died, he had been the center of her life. And then she said, I quote her, 'I can't reasonably expect, Black, that he was ever the center of *your* life—why should he be; it wouldn't be natural.' There wasn't much I could say, and then she said, 'And I don't think I can reasonably ask you to co-mourn his death along with me.' What do you mean, 'co-mourn,' I said? She smiled. 'I don't expect you to take a vow of celibacy. But when we marry—if we do, and I hope we will—it has got to be very different, and I want you to tell me you understand that.' "

"And you said?" Anthony asked.

"I said I understood that. She changed the subject."

It was after dinner that Anthony told Blackford he had invited two girls to come in "for a nightcap." He paused. Would Blackford veto the idea? He looked at him. His old friend looked up, and Anthony spotted that distinctive smile he had seen on other joint adventures.

"A nightcap?"

Anthony shrugged his shoulders. "I know that ten days ago you were hacking your way up the Ho Chi Minh Trail, and I gather that ten days from now you'll be facing the sharks in the Asian waters of Tonkin. There ought to be something in between to lift your . . . spirits!" He didn't give Blackford another opening. Instead he dialed a number, looked at his watch, and Blackford heard him say, "Nine-fifteen will be just fine, Alice." And then, to Blackford, "Alice is a very old friend, and Mayday is one of Alice's oldest friends—they're both twenty-two—and they'll be right along."

"How can you be 'old friends' when you say they are only twenty-two?"

"Some girls—I don't mean Alice and Mayday; you will see that they are different—consider anyone an old friend whom they've known for more than thirty days. But actually, Alice and Mayday went to college together."

"College?"

"Yup, U of Maryland, majored in sociology. They just want a very good time before they make wonderful, monastic mothers, and at their rates they will be rich by the time they go to the altar. I don't know what they studied in their sociology course, but it must have been principally Samoan." Anthony was exuberantly recalling a joint experience he and Blackford had had in Paris when the doorbell rang, and he let the girls in.

They were in light summer wear, Alice in yellow with flecks of white like a light snowstorm against the sunlight. She was short, fair, pretty, full-bodied, and had a twinkle in her lively eye. Mayday was taller and more nearly beautiful, with pale cheeks, aquiline nose, and soft black hair. She wore pearls over her light blue chiffon V-necked dress. They were both offered, and accepted, champagne. The talk was animated. Mayday was especially excited by the action of the Supreme Court, which the day before had reversed a ban on the French movie *The Lovers.*

"I mean, Alice and I have seen the movie— have you?"

Both men shook their heads.

"I mean, there isn't anything there a Boy Scout doesn't know, age, oh, fifteen. One of my professors, Dr. Moore, predicted the Supreme Court would reverse. I mean, the lower court's ruling on *The Lovers.* The furthest it goes is when the girl undresses the guy. Slowly, lots of music. He's finally down to just his shorts. Then as she goes on, he turns his back to the audience, you know, and she draws down his shorts, but all the audience sees is just, well, his backside, then the lights dim and they make it to bed—I mean, that's it."

Alice was equally pleased by the decision, but she thought the companion decisions of the Court were just as interesting. The Court would review the ban on Henry Miller's novel *Tropic of Cancer*—"Granted, I haven't read it. I did try to, but in fact you can't get it in Baltimore, though a friend of mine who is going to be in France said she'd bring me back a copy. Anyway that, and the Court's overturning the Florida ban on *Pleasure Was My Business,* by the madam in Miami—she doesn't give her name—and *that* book I've read, a straight-out account of the life of a modern madam—what she does, what the girls do, what johns expect, that kind of thing. Straight-out information, right, Anthony?" Alice reached over and kissed him. Mayday would not be delinquent and said, mock-teasingly to Alice, "That's not the way they do it in *The Lovers.* Look, more like this." She moved forward and put her lips on Blackford's—and lingered. Before she was done, Alice felt contrition over her peremptory handling of Anthony, and now used lips and hands to express her feeling for him. Blackford, when Mayday retrieved her tongue, said to her a little hoarsely, "Just how does it go, in *The Lovers,* when she takes his clothes off?" Mayday smiled exultantly, got up and led Blackford to the bedroom to which Anthony pointed her. She dimmed the lights, closed the door, and took off his shirt. He lowered his trousers, which maneuver required gentle circumnavigation, while she undressed. Then she said to him, "In the movie, it goes just like this. Here," her hands went to his hips and with her two thumbs she engaged the boxer shorts. "She does it like this . . . very slowly. When the shorts are halfway down," she said, "he begins to turn"—she moved him gently— "like that, exactly, so that your back is now all they can see." Her hands had moved the shorts down now to his ankles. "Whereas the girl can see *everything.* Just like me, Mayday. I can see everything, and it's all very beautiful," she said.

★ ★ ★ ★ ★ ★ ★ ★ ★

Chapter Thirteen

JULY 18, 1964
THE OVAL OFFICE
WASHINGTON, D.C.

When Lyndon Johnson wanted legal advice, he wanted Abe. He had known Abe Fortas a good many years; thought of him, as he had several times put it sensitively to close associates, as "one of the smartest Jews in the United States." And he intended to put him on the United States Supreme Court the first chance he got. Meanwhile Fortas was always good for a little legal or constitutional advice, and not at all bad at giving political advice.

"Abe," said the President to the cosmopolitan attorney-musician-intellectual with the dark, handsome face of an elderly Valentino, "I want you to tell me: Is it conceivable that Ike would run for Vice President on a ticket with Barry Goldwater?"

"You asking me a political question or a constitutional question, Mr. President?"

"Both. But before that, listen to this." From his drawer he got out the clippings. "Alexander Wiley, former Chairman of the Judiciary Committee, the man—get this, Abe—who *actually wrote* the Twenty-second Amendment and shepherded it through Congress in 1947. He is quoted in the *Baltimore Post* as saying that the drafters of the Twenty-second Amendment 'never meant it to prohibit a man from running for Vice President even if he had served two terms as President.' "

"Wiley said that?" Abe Fortas wrinkled his brow.

"Wait. Wait . . . here's another one. Joe Martin was Speaker of the House when the amendment was passed. And now *he* writes, 'I never thought the Constitution stood in President Eisenhower's way.' And so now having given Ike a constitutional okay, he goes on with stuff might as well be a nominatin' speech: 'If he would take this new prospective assignment, there's no question he would be elected. It would chase away any doubts that some people now seem to entertain concerning our coming national ticket. If Ike went on the ticket, he would bring to it that stability, confidence, and security we all want. He well might have to face up to a personal sacrifice' "—President Johnson was standing now, imitating the gestures and the inflections of a nominating speaker at a national convention—" *'He well might have to face up to a personal sacrifice, but I have no doubt it would be a winning sacrifice.'* "

"I hope you're through, Mr. President."

"Nope. George Aiken. *George Aiken!* Votes half the time with *us.* 'I am happy to go along in suggesting former President Eisenhower as Vice President at this critical period in world history!' Now watch, Abe: He's putting it to Ike here to save the GOP from Goldwater. Careful now. Watch how he does it: '. . . It will *undoubtedly* be a *great* sacrifice for the former President to re-enter the national political arena. However' "— at this point the voice of Lyndon Johnson was sheer molasses. His erstwhile colleagues in the Senate knew that voice well, and it was generally good for ten extra votes—" 'for one who has so ardently preached party unity, it is up to *him* to decide. If he wants it he undoubtedly will get it.' "

Lyndon Johnson sat down. He looked at the clippings. "I won't bother you, Abe, to hear what other senators and congressmen said. Jack Miller, Leslie Arends, Paul Findley, Karl Mundt. No. I'll read you just the *las'* sentence of what Mundt said. 'I would consider it an honor to nominate Ike for the Vice Presidency.'" He banged his wrist down on the table. "Have none of these people *heard* of the Constitution of the United States?"

"Well, Mr. President, presumably Alec Wiley has, since as you point out he wrote that part of the Constitution you're talking about."

"Well goddamnit, it says right there that no person who has—er . . ."

"What it says, Mr. President, is 'No person shall be elected to the office of President more than twice.' They're not proposing to elect him President."

"Do you mean to sit there and tell me, Abe Fortas, you who I have always respected, do you mean to say that this shit they're thinkin' of would get by the Supreme Court?"

"Lyndon"—it was almost inevitable, hard though he tried, but when matters got tense it was still and always would be, "Lyndon." "I think you could make a very good constitutional argument saying that any man you can't elect as President, you can't elect as Vice President. You could use all kinds of arguments. If you're less than thirty-five you can't serve as President; could you elect a thirty-four-year-old as Vice President? If you're foreign-born, you can't serve as President; could you elect someone born in Jamaica as Vice President? You can carry those arguments forward and say that having served two terms is as much of a dis-qualification as being under thirty-five years old, or being foreign-born. But look at it as a practical matter."

"Lookin' at things as a practical matter is mah *specialty,* Abe."

"I know it is, I know it is. As a practical matter, what happens? Ike gets nominated, say. The Attorney General files a suit asking the Supreme Court to invalidate that nomination. But the Supreme Court can't hold that the Twenty-second Amendment has been violated until it has been violated. And that wouldn't be until Ike was sworn in as President—if Goldwater died, or was killed.

"But here's where it helps to be practical. And I expect, Mr. President, that you know exactly what I know, which is that the Justice of the

Supreme Court never existed who would step in and say, *The man you just swore in as President can't serve.* It's just that simple. If they nominate him, no matter what the Philadelphia lawyers say, or the columnists, or the editorial writers, or the deans of the law schools: If Goldwater wins with Ike on the ticket, he'll be sworn in as President, and Ike will be sworn in as Vice President. . . . What you got to do, Lyndon, is make it so Ike won't be tempted."

Johnson looked up. "How'm I going to do that?"

"You know Ike better than I do."

"What you sayin', Abe?"

"Ike loves to be above the conflict. And he likes to be thought of as pure of heart. Father-of-his-country type. What you got to do is two things. First, give it out that the Goldwater boys are trying to manipulate him. Get that into Jock Whitney's *Herald Tribune*—Ike reads it every day. Quote some of the stuff Goldwater and his cronies have said about the Eisenhower years—they have been pretty careful not to mention *him,* but there isn't anything he did or didn't do that they didn't blast him for. Hell, he appointed Earl Warren! He's the guy who didn't go save the Hungarians! The guy who invited

Khrushchev over here! The guy who got caught lying over the U-2 incident! The guy who broke up the summit! Who's had a budget deficit every year except the first, and that was on account of the Korean War ending. Get him to get mad at the people who are courting him with this idea."

Lyndon Johnson was attentive. He removed his glasses. "What's your second point?"

"Stick it to Goldwater. The attacks on him have been pretty tough—and well earned, needless to say. But I mean really *stick* it to him. Get his name associated with American mud. Link his name to—the people Ike led the war against."

"You mean . . . ?"

Abe Fortas looked right back at the President. "I mean . . ."

In the cramped working quarters of the LBJ Ranch in Texas President Johnson was serene, as he generally was when outside the heat of Washington. But he was made even more serene by the collection of clippings that had been gathered together for him by his press secretary. They were there in chronological order.

The *New York Herald Tribune:* "The Republican Party now does face a clear and present threat from the Know-nothings and purveyors of hate and the apostles of bigotry."

"That's a beauty," said Lyndon Johnson. "Jock Whitney is one good, responsible, patriotic Republican. I thought the publisher would come through. I think I *will* have a scotch, haven't had one all week." Jack Valenti nodded. "Keep going, Mr. President."

He read the lines from the editorial in the *New York Times:* "Barry Goldwater is a man with an incredibly bad, short-sighted, simplistic voting and speaking record. He is unfit, on the basis of his views and his votes, to be President of the United States."

"I always like the *die-rectness* of the *New York Times,* don't you, Jack? I mean, I cain't always *agree* with them. But you just have a feeling they're . . . incorruptible. Right?"

"Right, Mr. President. Go on."

"Okay. *St. Louis Post-Dispatch:* 'The Goldwater coalition is a coalition of Southern racists, county-seat conservatives, desert rightist radicals and suburban backlashers.' Don' much like that Southern-racist business, but that's really giving it to him." He had a deep swallow of scotch.

"Oh man! Jee-zus! This one must have been

written by Abe Fortas! Only it's by Jackie Robinson, fust colored ballplayer in baseball, and God bless him. He says, 'I would say that I now believe I know how it felt to be a Jew in Hitler's Germany.' That is telling it, eh? And what about Martin Luther King? Here he is: 'Goldwater articulates a philosophy which gives aid and comfort to the fascists.'—Now, can Drew Pearson beat that? Here's what *he* says: 'The smell of fascism has been in the air—' Get that? *Smell of fascism?*

"And, oh-ho, and Pat Brown. The Governor of the Great State of California says that speech by Goldwater 'had the stench of fascism. All we needed to hear was *Heil Hitler.*' "

"That's a pretty good collection. They've all gone to Ike?"

"Jock Whitney volunteered to do that, Mr. President. With a covering letter on the Vice Presidential business."

Lyndon Johnson looked out at the setting sun and said, "Do you know, Jack, you get down here in Texas, and the whole world smells clean."

"Yes, sir," Valenti said.

★ ★ ★ ★ ★ ★ ★ ★ ★

Chapter Fourteen

JULY 20, 1964
DANANG, SOUTH VIETNAM

Blackford flatly disbelieved that the port of Danang had once been, among other things, a beach resort used by the French for pleasure. But Alphonse Juilland, his balding, ascetic, fifty-one-year-old guide, who had taught French to the same young Vietnamese who now scorned the language and disdained anyone who would stoop to learn it, assured him that it was so. "It is very full of shipping here now, I grant you"—he spoke in French, which Blackford managed without much difficulty (when stuck he would resort to German, in which Juilland was shakily fluent)—"with all that shipping, it is difficult to visualize the scene here before Dien Bien Phu."

That had been the critical battle, lost by the French, won by Ho Chi Minh, that had ended the French colony of Indochina. "But there are old photographs, and even a few paintings. On some days, may God save me if I mislead you, the scene there"—he pointed to the north end of the deep harbor—"might have been the beach at Cannes or at Nice.

"You know, M. Oakes, I have been at Cannes and at Nice. My father was also a school-teacher, at Lyons, and when I was a boy, before he decided to come here, just before the war, we often went to those places to vacation, so that what I tell you is the truth. Danang was a very beautiful resort facility."

Blackford wanted to grumble something to the effect that it was certainly making up now for all the imperialist pleasure it had given in the past. But he only shook his head, which he frequently did in replying to the tall, thin, talkative bachelor, an amiable outcast who was without relatives in France, Blackford was quickly advised. The only skill he could merchandise, now that he could no longer teach French to the Vietnamese, was that bilingualism on which he traded. He would translate any instructions Blackford directed at the leaders of the flotilla of little fishing ships, 95 percent of which came in and out of Danang to sell fish, 5 percent of which came in and out of Danang to report to Central Intelligence.

The 5 percent fished for information during their innocent little forays into waters close to North Vietnam, when by their movements they triggered radio signals and well-concealed radar devices that beamed out reciprocal attention from the mainland. They regularly provoked defensive bursts from the batteries of North Vietnamese radar installations, the characteristics of whose short-range signals the South Vietnamese military technicians would carefully transcribe, leaving to the offshore American naval vessels attached to the Seventh Fleet the job of tracking and fingerprinting the character and location of the heavier radar installations.

On that first day Blackford was briefing the captain of one of the larger fishing boats equipped with the new 34-A radar gear. Alphonse Juilland relayed a question by the captain.

"He wants to know whether he isn't violating North Vietnamese territorial rights by advancing to within eight miles of Quang Khe, which is in North Vietnam."

Blackford replied succinctly. "Tell the captain that the United States acknowledges North Vietnamese territorial rights over only three miles offshore, just as the United States claims for itself only three miles offshore."

Juilland came back. "The captain says that the Chinese have always insisted on twelve miles' jurisdiction, and that when the French were defeated he assumed that the Chinese, not the French tradition, was adopted."

"Tell the captain, Alphonse"—Blackford attempted to communicate his conclusion that no more needed to be said on this thorny subject, which so greatly concerned diplomatic nail-biters in Washington—"that the North Vietnamese have entered no such claims before any relevant authority and that therefore any interference with any boat observing the three-mile limit is interference with the freedom of the seas."

"How'd he take it, Alphonse?" Blackford asked as they walked down the wharf, looking for the next boatman they needed to brief and rationing their intake of air in a vain attempt to limit their intake of the fetid-fish odor.

"If you want to know, M. Oakes, he was quite skeptical. I took the liberty of adding to what you said that if the captain did not wish to take this assignment, there were others who would be glad to substitute for him.

"How close do you intend to maneuver your private navy, if I may ask, M. Oakes. Right up to the three-mile limit?"

"The answer to that is easy, Alphonse. You may not ask."

Alphonse smiled, and then stopped. "Here is the *Mau Cao.*" They were alongside the scruffy-looking 44-foot fishing boat with its single, stubby mast and coarse, furled mainsail to give it stability in a heavy wind. Blackford looked at the boat with intense concentration to ascertain at what distance its large concealed radar set would be discernible by the enemy as such. He could readily make it out to be what it was, but then he was alongside it at eye level. The North Vietnamese would be training powerful telescopes on the fishing fleet. Would they be able to make it out as radar? Probably not, he concluded. But if one of their little NVA patrol boats ambled up and made its observations from the edge of the three-mile limit focusing 10 × 7 lenses on a boat idling at, say, four miles offshore, what then?

Still safe, he decided.

What would not be in the least safe was any

situation in which a North Vietnamese patrol boat advanced *beyond* its own territorial waters to within two or three hundred yards of the 34-A boats. And they had every right to do so, under the law of the seas, provided they did not interfere with the right of the fishing boats to do as they liked. And it was not illegal to have radar, even hidden radar, trained on the coastline of a foreign country. To do such a thing—Blackford recalled the briefing in Washington by the British specialist on the law of the seas—"may be provocative, but it is not illegal. A boat may approach the three-mile limit off Coney Island and snap pictures of a honeymoon couple having at it in a hotel room on the beach and there isn't anything illegal about it, though we will all agree that that is offensive behavior. But then we're not talking about prurient activity. We are engaged in examining the resources of the enemy."

"Of the *potential* enemy." The colonel had interrupted him.

"Of the potential enemy," the expert said, correcting himself.

Summoned by Rufus to Saigon, Blackford landed at the Tan Son Nhut airport at four on that steaming hot afternoon and went to the Naval Officers Quarters, where he was expected in a suite reserved for a "technical consultant." A half hour later he flagged a taxi and took it to a corner two blocks from the safe house. Five minutes later he was in Rufus's company. Beginning at 5:12, they spent an enjoyable two hours together.

"You're going to want me to go through all this again when Tucker comes in, right?" Blackford said.

"I would think he would be as eager to know what is going on on your front as you will be to discover what is going on in planning on the Trail. Since we now have the cross-clearances, you can tell him everything you told me. The objective of your weekly visits, after all, is to coordinate your operations. But on this first trip he'll be bringing us news from Aberdeen—he left yesterday."

"Which reminds me, where in the hell *is* Tucker?"

Rufus looked at his watch. "The dispatch said his plane was due in a half hour after yours. He said he would be here at the same time as you, five-twelve." Rufus went to the telephone. He stood motionless for just a moment. Blackford knew that Rufus was engaged in recalling Air America flights (an unlisted carrier) coming in from Honolulu—arriving, given that the carrier was an arm of the Central Intelligence Agency, at unpublished times—and doing calculations. He dialed and spoke a few words, then put down the telephone.

"The plane landed as expected. At three-thirty-five."

Blackford said nothing.

Rufus also paused. And then said, "I rule out foul play."

Rufus looked up at Blackford.

They had known each other now for . . . it was London, September 1951, his first assignment . . . The search for the highly sheltered person leaking nuclear secrets to the Soviet Union. An assignment so delicate as to warrant overseeing by the legendary—"Rufus" was his entire name, for all that Blackford knew. Blackford remembered sensing, after fifteen minutes with Rufus, that the older man knew exactly what was going on in Blackford's mind, which spooky knowledge Rufus sometimes gave away by answering a question before it was asked, even a question Blackford had never intended to pose. And now, after a moment, Rufus said:

"I think you're right." That was all. Quickly followed by, "In which case we may as well go ahead with dinner." He reached for his brief-case and umbrella.

★ ★ ★ ★ ★ ★ ★ ★ ★

Chapter Fifteen

JULY 22, 1964
ABOARD MR. FORTAS'S CHARTERED YACHT,
POTOMAC RIVER

Abe Fortas was well known for his hospitality. His tastes were refined in all matters, food (French), music (he played the violin), and the law (he was a distinguished practitioner). And he didn't mind it that *tout Washington,* as the gossip columnists like to put it, knew of his singular intimacy with the President of the United States. Abe Fortas enjoyed the relationship with a sitting American President, quite apart from his growing certainty that it would bear fruit with a seat on the Supreme Court. He was not in a great hurry for that lofty distinction because his habits required high-octane cash flow, and, of course, acceptance of a seat in the Court meant goodbye to those clients who maintained him in a lifestyle he found entirely comfortable. His income, in combination with the power he was known to exercise by his access to the President and the President's known confidence in his judgment, permitted him to see whom he chose, pretty much under such conditions as he chose.

It was hardly remarkable, then, that Abe Fortas should be having dinner with the Director of the Central Intelligence Agency on a Friday in July. The Director had frequent contact with the President, of course, but that was a formal relationship. Dining with Abe Fortas was like dining with the President with his hair down.

The setting, as always with Fortas, was: just right. It was a chartered boat . . . a little cruise on the Potomac, just the four of them, the two couples. The social understanding, as ever, was effortlessly suggested: there were burdens of government to be shouldered, so that the wives, congenial, made it plain that they were content to sit in the sheltered aft cockpit, sip at a cocktail or two, and watch the evening's television news, or the shoreline, while Abe Fortas and the Director shared a corner of the walnut-stained saloon, nicely air-conditioned, from which the

500-horsepower motors were a mere purr in the background, Washington a passing aesthetic gratification. And so they sat with their highballs, viewing the profile of the Athens of the modern world sliding by serenely at the relaxing 7-knot pace Abe Fortas had specified to the captain. Abe found his memory going back twenty-five years to a ride he had taken at the New York World's Fair. Seated on a moving platform, he had glided past visions of the world of the future. It was so very comfortable, so relaxing, so—right.

Abe Fortas led the Director on. The news from Vietnam was persistently bad, was it not?

It certainly was.

Just conceivably—conceivably even the Director did not know of this particular event, because, uh, the President had told it to Abe Fortas in *supreme* confidence—but of course that confidence could hardly exclude the Director of the Central Intelligence Agency! Still, just as a *matter of precaution,* please—please!—never let it be known that he now knew about it, if in fact he didn't already know about it.

Know about what? The Director leaned forward just slightly.

"The Canadian overture."

The Director hesitated. On the one hand he did not in fact know anything about any "Canadian overture." On the other hand, he did not wish to admit ignorance of something that obviously touched directly on his concerns as Director of the Central Intelligence Agency. He thought for a moment to give an ambiguous answer, but then decided he had better not try that kind of evasion with this . . . particular . . . person.

"I don't know about it."

Ah. Well, Abe Fortas was not entirely surprised, because they both knew the President's habits. He would not be surprised to discover that Mrs. Johnson knew nothing about it or, for that matter, the Chairman of the Joint Chiefs. Ho-ho-ho.

The Director smiled, and then waited.

What it proves, said Abe Fortas, concentrating the features of his face on what he was saying and rubbing his thumb on his highball glass, is *the extent* to which the President is willing to go in dealing with Vietnam.

What had he done?

Well, what he did was send a *personal* emissary—it doesn't matter who that emissary was, does it?—to the Canadian member of the International Control Commission, which, let's face it, is just about the *only* way to get private word to Ho Chi Minh, unless you want to use the Soviet Ambassador, which avenue we do not want to use, obviously—

The Director caught the "we."

—to put it on the line. If Ho Chi Minh will just cut it out in South Vietnam, if he will simply let the South develop its own democratic system, in its own way—let it loose, in the fashion of South Korea being loose—if Ho Chi Minh would just agree to that, the President would stake *his very office* on his ability to reconstitute the economy of North Vietnam. Abe Fortas used the figure—it was a whisper now—*ten billion dollars.*

The Director said nothing, though he inclined his head, as if to acknowledge that ten billion dollars was a great deal of money.

Abe Fortas leaned back and sipped at his highball.

That was *three weeks ago.* Ho Chi Minh had not even *acknowledged* receipt of the message! In Hanoi, he had just nodded at the Canadian representative, and said nothing.

The President is not the most patient man in the world, and after two weeks he instructed the Canadians to *go back* to Ho and ask him to *reply* to the offer.

Do you know what Ho said?

The Director did not know what Ho said.

He said, "What offer?" Abe Fortas rang for another round of drinks.

The President believes that there is only one way to curb the appetite of the North Vietnamese, and that is to show them that it hurts *them* more than they can endure to pursue their present policies. But what he does *not* want— and Abe Fortas certainly saw his point of view, and he hoped the Director did too—what he does *not* want is a plain, all-out, Korean-style war. There are 17,000 U.S. troops and technicians in South Vietnam now. He doesn't want that number to grow to 170,000, let alone a quarter of a million. In order to exert force on the North but avoid triggering a formal, Korean-style encounter, Lyndon Johnson has to have *flexibility.* We all know how Truman got that: through a U.N. resolution that authorized a "police action"—Hah! Some *police action:* 33,000 killed, 103,000 wounded! But the fact of the matter was, Truman could do anything he wanted. He could send in fifty divisions or no divisions. He could have used the nuclear bomb if he had wanted to.

And then, of course, the Director knew of the more recent parallel?

"Quemoy, Matsu?"

"That was exactly what the President had in mind," said Abe Fortas. When Quemoy and Matsu were threatened by mainland China, which, as we all remember, began to bomb the two little islands situated only a few miles from the Chinese coast—islands governed, however, by Taiwan—Eisenhower asked Congress, which readily granted it, permission to react as he thought "advisable" to "protect U.S. interests."

The result? The threat to Quemoy and Matsu diminishes. There was a great deal of rhetoric spilled over the question when Jack Kennedy ran against Nixon. That was phony: Nixon knew and every student of the question knew that the congressional authority given to Eisenhower to react as he saw fit in his role as Commander in Chief would carry over to his successor, whether it was President Nixon or President Kennedy. But it was critically important that Eisenhower *had* that instrument.

"President Johnson wants something like it?"

"President Johnson wants something like it,"

Abe Fortas confirmed. *"But,"* and here was a big *but,* "he doesn't want to step right up and go to Congress just like that and ask for it. Bill Bundy—and this I know you are aware of— drafted a resolution in the spring that he thought would be appropriate, and Walt Rostow worked on it, and for a while it looked as though the President was willing to go right to Congress and ask for it. But there is a lot of inertia out there, and with Goldwater screaming his head off about Vietnam, the President on the one hand wishes to distinguish between America under his leadership—cool, reflective, but strong and energetic—and America under the leadership of a senator who is pretty much of a fundamentalist in all his political reasoning. So what he needs is—"

"A *casus belli?*"

That, said Abe Fortas, was probably too strong a way to put it. A *casus belli,* a cause of war. "We don't want something to happen that simply requires war. But if the North Vietnamese were to"—Abe Fortas chose to be specific here—"if they were to attack one of our ships, say a unit of the Seventh Fleet, while that ship was cruising in international waters, that would be"—sure, the Director was free to call it a *casus belli* if he chose to do so. But it would *certainly* be a military provocation. With such a thing in hand the President could go to Congress and say: "Enough is enough! Not only do we have a nation engaged in a war of aggression against a southern neighbor, which neighbor we are, by codicil to the Geneva Accords, and SEATO, bound to assist, we face now a nation which has violated the freedom of the seas, and this is intolerable. Accordingly, I request of Congress a resolution that authorizes—enjoins me—instructs me . . ."

"We," Mr. Fortas paused, "have cautioned against the President's using the word 'empower,' since we take the position that he *has* that power, as Commander in Chief, under the Constitution." Anyway, with such a resolution, or even in anticipation of its passage, he could retaliate and give Ho Chi Minh a taste of grapeshot, Abe Fortas said with just a hint of apology at using a cliché in the presence of so discriminating a listener.

"God knows we have accumulated a pretty exact knowledge of exactly where the targets are along the coast," said the Director. "The

Navy would know exactly where to go, exactly where to drop the bombs. Take out months of Soviet mischief."

Exactly! said Abe Fortas; exactly. And with that hard pill to swallow, who knows? Before you know it, it will be Ho Chi Minh calling in the Canadian representative to the Control Commission, not the other way around. Everything would change. The whole balance of forces.

The Director smiled. "The correlation of forces."

Ah, said Abe Fortas, the Director knew his Lenin. Yes indeed. To be sure, there was always the possibility that the North Vietnamese would simply decline to take any aggressive step against a unit of our fleet. Abe Fortas wanted to be reminded—just exactly how close had any unit of the Seventh Fleet ever come to North Vietnamese territory?

"Eight miles."

And of course, Abe Fortas mused, we have always taken the position that three miles is all the distance we need to respect. So perhaps the best way of testing the North Vietnamese would be to instruct one of our naval units to edge right up there, right up to four miles. See if they will stomach that. Abe Fortas wanted to know whether the Director thought the North Vietnamese *would* strike out against a U.S. unit that came in that close.

The Director only the day before had the report. Oakes had filed it in the telegraphese in which he was so uncomfortable, but which he could manage in his sleep now, after thirteen years. The Director reached for his briefcase and pulled it out. "You'd better read it yourself, easier to understand."

WENT 7/22 0600 WITH COMPANY FISH BOAT PROBE GOOK REACTION TO 4 REPEAT 4 MILE APPROACH. AT LAT 19–42 LONG 105–21 RADAR SPOTTED PATROL NVA GUNNING USWARD. FEIGNED FISHNET SNAFU ATTEMPT DISTRACTION. NO SOAP PATROL BOAT STEAMED IN LET FLY 3-INCHER AT APPROX 900 METERS. DROPPED NET HEADED S.E. AT MAX PLAUSIBLE VELOCITY, HIT RADIO WITH VN RAPID VOICE PROTEST, LOST VALUABLE FISHNET ACCT THREATS IN INTERNATIONAL WATERS. NO ACKNOWLEDGMENT BUT INTERCEPT RADIO NVA TO HQ REPORTING INCIDENT BUT EXAGGERATE OUR VESSEL PROXIMITY TO SHORE, SAID 2.8 MILES ACTUALLY 4.1. WILL STAY TUNED. OAKES.

When Abe Fortas finished reading, the Director gave an account of Blackford Oakes's probe the day before in relatively lyrical translation.

And he summed up, "No way of telling, in a word. Our 34-A project has got the NVA mad as hell, we know from intelligence, as you can tell from Oakes's sortie."

Abe Fortas agreed.

The thing to do was to get on with it, and the Joint Chiefs, who had been eager for months simply to bomb the hell out of North Vietnam, would be given the word that aggressive behavior against South Vietnamese fishing boats *requires* us to advance one of our destroyers or cruisers closer to the coastline, to be some kind of a *presence* there to affirm the freedom of the seas. At the Director's end, Abe Fortas said, the 34-A operation should be instructed to get the fishing boats in very close to the coast, beginning approximately on the day that U.S. naval forces dispatch their own vessel to come in closer to the coast, the idea being that the mere presence of the U.S. boat will provide protection to the fishing boats.

The Director said he would alert his unit in Danang. All he needed was to be informed of the day when the U.S. naval vessel would begin patrolling in close quarters.

Abe Fortas said that, after all, he was not an official member of the government, that all he was trying to do was to advance the situation in line with the thinking of the President. He was certain that the appropriate word could be got to the Chief of Naval Operations to act aggressively in defense of the freedom of the seas, but perhaps, under the circumstances, that word ought not to go out directly from the Oval Office—the Director surely would have no difficulty in getting this done? And after all, the Seventh Fleet had been patrolling the waters of the Gulf of Tonkin since the fifties, and our concern to defend the freedom of the seas was internationally acknowledged. Had the Director ever seen, anywhere, a lovelier combination—Abe Fortas pointed out the yacht's picture window—a lovelier combination of colors than those caused by the red descending on the white-marble profile of the City of Washington?

The Director said no, he had never seen a lovelier combination.

★ ★ ★ ★ ★ ★ ★ ★ ★

Chapter Sixteen

MAY, 1964
SAIGON–HUÉ–HANOI
VIETNAM

Lao Dai performed a little ritual before leaving her apartment for the school. She pulled up the glass on her makeup table and slipped out a photograph of Le Duc Sy. She closed her eyes and brought the print to her lips, paused for a moment and then replaced it. It had been almost three months since she had seen him. Two months since she had had any word from him, but for this hardship she had been prepared. "It will be weeks. Maybe months, even. We have our duties to do. The revolution comes first." She understood. And, of course, officially Le Duc Sy was—dead.

.   .   .

Le Duc Sy never denied it. He just had been born a hot-blooded human being. He had been a hot-blooded boy, in point of fact. During all those years at the Lycée in Hué where he and Bui Tin had been best friends during the years of the Japanese occupation he had been unruly. Le Duc Sy was fifteen years old, impudent, engaging, lithe, when the Japanese arrived, and when the Japanese headmaster came in to replace the French headmaster he found Sy recalcitrant beyond the point of toleration. The boy mimicked him, answered before the question was asked, refused to obey simple orders. He was sent home to his father, who thrashed him soundly. The Japanese authorities at the school quite naturally assumed that Sy was expressing a precocious resentment against the foreign occupation. In fact, although Le Duc Sy resented the Japanese authorities, he had acted not very differently before they came. He had often been punished by his father, at the specific recommendation of the French schoolmaster and, before that, of the nuns at the little Catholic primary school.

But those who knew Le Duc Sy—and most of the members of the aristocratic Vietnamese enclave did know him—tended to be indulgent of the ungovernable son of Le Duc Ton. For one thing, he was wonderfully attractive. Handsome, smart, a star athlete, a wonderful mimic who had only to listen to the radio in order to duplicate exactly the voice of the person he had heard speak, whether it was General Tojo addressing his troops in Japanese or Tokyo Rose speaking her voluptuous subversions to the Americans in her Sunday-suited English. Le Duc Sy would at the least urging become General Tojo, or Tokyo Rose or, for that matter, his headmaster, his father, or his classmate Bui Tin. On one occasion he managed to deepen his soprano voice sufficiently to persuade a local merchant who dealt frequently with his father that it was Le Duc Ton himself on the phone, and that he desired not one, but two of the Swiss movie cameras displayed in the window. That got him another thrashing, but Le Duc Ton was secretly amused, and told all his friends about the Great Imposture.

Surely he would grow out of it, they all said, and become, like his father, the exemplary citizen: worldly, affluent, a man of commerce and civic-mindedness who had maintained perfect relations with the French, managed to endure the humiliations and the privations imposed on

him and his family by the Japanese with forbear-
ance, knowing that the nightmare would someday end. When that happened, surely Le Duc Sy
would grow up, stop getting into scrapes, stop
provoking his teachers. In any event, if liberation
did not come sooner, he would need to be
tamed before reaching the age of seventeen,
when the Japanese would conscript him for military duty—which day never came.

The Vietnamese–French community quickly
changed their opinion of Le Duc Sy when he
announced one day that he would depart for the
North to join his friend Bui Tin and the forces of
Ho Chi Minh to fight the French. This time his
father closed the door on his son, indeed would
not let him into the house even to bid his mother
and two sisters goodbye. Loud enough for Le
Duc Sy to hear through the closed door, Le Duc
Ton said that he was finally convinced that Le
Duc Sy's teachers had been right, that he was
a disorganized, disrespectful, disloyal boy—indeed, no longer a boy but, at age eighteen, a
young man; that he could leave and do what he
wished in the way of treachery to old and benev-
olent gentlefolk like the French, who had
brought peace and industry to Indochina; that
he was ungrateful for everything he, Le Duc

Ton, his father, had done for him, ungrateful to his mother who had cared for him, to his sisters who had been loyal to him during his delinquent youth; that he could reenter the family home only after he had renounced treason and gone to church and confessed his sin. Until that moment, Le Duc Ton hoped not to hear uttered in his presence the name of Le Duc Sy.

Like his friend Bui Tin, Sy fought hard for Ho Chi Minh. But unlike the calm, measured, reflective Bui Tin, Sy was always his own unruly self. This resulted in bizarre acts of bravery. He thought nothing of taking on French patrols that overwhelmingly outnumbered the platoon he was in charge of. He was several times wounded, several times reprimanded, several times rewarded for bravery, and never—because of his eccentricity—seriously promoted; so that after Dien Bien Phu and the temporary halt in the fighting, it hadn't been known exactly what to do with him. Given his background and qualities and quirks, and of course his continued friendship with Bui Tin, the matter of his future was brought before Ho Chi Minh himself.

Ho brought in Bui Tin, who had become something of a confidant, and asked his advice on how best to use the talents of his old schoolmate. Bui Tin answered immediately: intelligence work in the South, he said. Le Duc Sy generates the right kind of attention. No woman can turn him away, and men are instantly taken by his charm. He is handsome, laughs easily, can imitate any pompous ass. There is always the risk, Bui Tin admitted, of Sy's doing something reckless. But then—Bui Tin smiled at Ho Chi Minh—"you are hardly equipped, Bac Ho"—he had instructions to call him Uncle Ho—"to criticize those who are bold. First you challenge the French Empire, now you challenge the American superpower. There are those who would judge you to be a reckless man." Ho Chi Minh with a small smile gave orders to an adjutant to train and send Le Duc Sy to Saigon as an agent. The chief of intelligence would design an appropriate cover for him in Saigon and assign him appropriate duties.

The chief of intelligence (he was the nephew of army chief General Giap) was hungry for well-qualified agents. He had been observing for over one year the increased military preparations in the South, actively subsidized by President Kennedy and now by President Johnson, all hustle and bustle centered in Saigon. And Danang, although admittedly the center of commercial fishing in South Vietnam, had become in effect an American naval base. In short order, young Le Duc Sy was affiliated as a salesman for the Perkins Company, a worldwide distributor of British marine engines ranging from 50 to 1500 horsepower. In Saigon, commercial headquarters of the fishing industry, Le Duc Sy would make contacts, pressing the advantages of the British engines over those of German and U.S. competitors. And he would travel frequently to Danang, there to do business with individual clients and entrepreneurs—fishing captains and large and small fleet owners. He was encouraged by his superiors to advertise his wares directly to U.S. purchasing agents who, if they were not getting exactly what they wanted from the United States, had deep pockets to purchase foreign-made goods that suited their purposes, as these famous engines almost always did.

Within ninety days, Le Duc Sy had gained access to almost everybody in Saigon and Danang who was concerned with the sea. And in less than one half that time, Le Duc Sy had penetrated the gestating plans of an operation called 34-A. He observed with impatience the quiet transformation of the little fleet of boats. His fury when first he discovered the deception was very nearly uncontained. Le Duc Sy's ears had picked up a careless remark, overheard at a bar, made by a fishing captain who spoke obliquely about his "new mission." This led the agent to make a fresh, inquisitive visit to Danang. Within a few days he spotted the same captain he had seen in Saigon and followed him stealthily to his fishing boat. Thereafter he watched. When one day it left the line of wharves where the boats were docked, he was behind it, moving carefully in a 34-tender he used to demonstrate one of the smaller Perkins engines. He kept the boat in sight. Instead of leaving the harbor to enter the Gulf, it darted to the left, into the area that housed U.S. naval units from the Seventh Fleet. He berthed at a discreet distance and walked up a hill from which, with his binoculars, he could soon see the radar installation being done on the fishing boat. Further inquiries made plain the nature of the "new mission" of such boats. His rage flamed. His first inclination was to set fire to the whole fleet of fake fishing boats. But he restrained himself, for once. The resources of the United States were extravagant. The Americans would simply build more boats. He knew the purpose of the altered fleet: to discover just how the Great Ho, with Soviet aid, was preparing to protect the coastline from any attack by the U.S. Navy and Marines. Torching the little armada would mean one less effective intelligence agent studying the work being done, and reporting it diligently to Hanoi.

He distracted himself by wooing and easily winning the betrothal of the most beautiful young woman he had ever seen—and at the same time, he was prepared to aver after his first night with her, the most satisfying sexual partner he had ever engaged. With this woman, he said in a letter to Bui Tin, he must settle for nothing less than marriage. He described her graces and beauty, giving a leisurely and genial account of her background and making no effort to conceal that she was an experienced woman of the world, given her profession; indeed, Le Duc Sy had written without any trace of resentment, she had had a considerable number of experiences of an intimate nature with both Vietnamese and American men, but had not on that account been coarsened in any way. And anyway, this was all in the past. Their future as man and wife would bring on a total change in her habits, and significant differences in his own.

He sent this letter, as was his practice, to a

name and address in Singapore, whence it was redirected to Hanoi. Bui Tin was sufficiently intrigued by it to cross the hall to the office of the chief of intelligence. There he asked Colonel Giap to check in the copious files of that department for possible information on this singular woman.

Giap proceeded to do so; no request by Bui Tin was denied in Hanoi. The following day he called Bui Tin back to his office to advise him that the woman, under another name, "Lao Dai," was a covert agent doing duty in his own department. On being told by Bui Tin that she had plans to marry another of his agents, one Le Duc Sy, Colonel Giap expressed his astonished disapproval in unmistakable language. He would instantly communicate to Le Duc Sy, by mail through the usual channels, that under *no circumstances* was Sy to marry someone so useful to the cause of Vietnam independence. That letter arrived three days after the discreet private wedding had taken place (Lao Dai had wished it so, inviting only two or three friends) and on reading it, Le Duc Sy discerned silently, sadly, that his wife and he were engaged in identical activities, she using different methods, lures, and techniques.

That night, after a wonderfully satisfying meal and a bottle of rare French white burgundy, he took unhurried delights with his bride. In due course he disengaged slowly and, his body illuminated by a shaft of light that streamed through the window from the half moon, walked to the bathroom, while Lao Dai observed briefly the perfect torso of her thirty-five-year-old husband who might have been an eighteen-year-old boy. She lay back on her pillow, deeply satisfied by her overwhelming experience, so different from those others so trivial by contrast, with all those other men, in all those other bedrooms. She was beginning to dream when suddenly the voice caused her to shoot up in bed.

"Do you know that the man who just finished fucking you is a spy?"

It was unmistakably the voice of Colonel Giap.

"Are you aware that he is the foreign agent of another country?"

She thrust the sheet in front of her. *What was this nightmare?* What was Colonel Giap doing in Saigon? What was he doing in *her bedroom*? Where was Le Duc Sy? What had happened to him!

"Have you told your lover the nature of your

mission in Saigon? Have you told him that you too are an agent of a foreign power?"

She could stand it no longer. Lao Dai screamed.

The overhead light flashed on. In front of her stood Le Duc Sy, the mimic, whose talent she had not known. He began to roar with laughter. He was still naked—except that in his hand he held what appeared to be an envelope.

Le Duc Sy turned off the light. "It will be more fun," he said in his own low, musical voice, "to read you this letter in the light of the moon." He moved her tenderly to one side. His left hand fondling in feather touch her breasts as he did so, he read from the letter in his right hand: firm orders from Colonel Giap *not to marry Lao Dai.* She was too valuable to the independence movement.

"That," Colonel Giap had written, "is an order."

Le Duc Sy dropped the letter on the floor and let his right hand travel down the body of his fellow agent. He whispered, "My sweet little spy. Let us explore our secrets together."

Five days later he was ordered back to Hanoi.

. . .

At first, Le Duc Sy considered simply defying the order. Obviously he did not welcome a separation, however brief, from Lao Dai. But then he reflected on the possibility that he might be ordered to another theater, effecting an even longer separation, but only until Lao Dai could settle her affairs (in a manner of speaking) in Saigon and join him. Perhaps he should cooperate with Hanoi, and they could then live together, faithful to their common anticolonialist cause. Apprehensive, she wondered whether he might be punished. Le Duc Sy scoffed at this. "After all, the letter arrived three days after we were married. And when we *were* married, you didn't know I was taking orders from Hanoi, and I didn't know you were taking orders from Hanoi. So—" He shrugged his shoulders. It was not in his nature to fear punishment. He had never been afraid of punishment by his headmaster, his father, the Japanese army, or his superior officers.

He decided to go. He informed the division manager at Perkins that he would need to visit an ailing sister in Singapore but would return quickly.

From Singapore he flew to Hanoi. He was met by one of those anonymous-looking but physically fit clerks who worked in the office of Colonel Giap. In the car he was told that he was being driven to the apartment of Colonel Bui Tin, on orders of Colonel Giap. Le Duc Sy experienced a certain relief that whatever administrative action was in store for him, it would be administered by his old friend; or in any event, his friend would leaven the news by informing him in advance of what lay ahead.

Though by nature Bui Tin was solemn and Le Duc Sy buoyant, the two men were linked with that complementarity of spirit that had attracted them to each other at school. Young Bui Tin thoughtful, docile, seemingly reclusive; young Le Duc Sy extravagantly enthusiastic, defiant, exhibitionistic. What was especially strange, but satisfying, was that they had arrived independently at their decision to fight against the French resettlement after the war. Bui Tin would never have revealed to his friends at the Lycée, or to his family, the direction his thoughts were taking. Not until his mind had been finally made up. Le Duc Sy typically did. But the particular daemon that drove him to the movement for national independence, animated by Communist universalism, he did keep buried within him. Moreover he did not trace his decision to any particular resentment of the French. It was more that he was uplifted by the notion of independence from old ties, stirred by the challenge of national unification under the Marxist aegis. Bui Tin once said to him, after a long and vinous meal, that Le Duc Sy's mutinous inclinations were really undifferentiated: He had not got on with the Reverend Mother, nor with the principal at their primary school; he had not got on with either the French headmaster or his Japanese successor; had not, really, got on with his father, with whom he was continually quarreling.

"So it may be, Sy, that your renunciation of the French is more an aspect of your temperament than of any patriotic aversion to imperialist practices."

Le Duc Sy had countered casually that he was not given to psychological self-examinations of this kind, but that if ever his enthusiasm for the independence movement of Ho Chi Minh had flagged, it was revived with the gradual appearance of Mighty America on the Indochinese scene. "I always enjoy a little icon-smashing, the bigger the better."

"Ho Chi Minh is an icon," Bui Tin had said gravely.

"Yes. True. And I confess it—sometimes I

feel it would be great sport to pull on his wispy beard."

Bui Tin put down his wineglass, his eyes widening.

"But—I never have, and I never intend to. I recognize that there has got to be some structure in organizational life. Even though I liked to subvert the designs of the headmaster, I always knew there had to be one. There has to be a supreme leader of our movement. And I have been very faithful to Bac Ho."

As they began to talk now in Bui Tin's apartment, the sun going down, two bottles of beer on the table, Bui Tin recalled that earlier conversation. "You told me once that you have been very faithful to Ho Chi Minh—"

"Yes," Le Duc Sy interrupted. "And I have also been very faithful to Colonel Giap."

"Up until now."

"What do you mean, up until now? Are you aware that I did not receive his letter until after Lao Dai and I were in fact married?"

"I was not aware of that. But I am aware that as a member of the corps of which you *are* a member, marriage is not permitted except by special permission."

Le Duc Sy shrugged his shoulders. "That is a

silly rule. I have never believed in observing silly rules."

Bui Tin got up and began to pace the floor. He said nothing for a few minutes. Then he began.

He spoke of the accelerating pace of events on critical fronts. He told Sy of the American mission to the Ho Chi Minh Trail, concerning which much was known in Hanoi inasmuch as one of the two surviving native guides on that mission was an agent.

"Clearly the decision of the Americans is to try to interdict our passage down the Trail. Passage down the Trail is at the heart of the strategy of the Independence Movement. It is *my* responsibility to see to it that the traffic moves. Men, materiel, guns, food—everything needed for what will probably seem to the Americans a very long struggle. The President of the United States," Bui Tin spoke pensively, "is to some extent an unknown quantity. Ho has said to me that the portrait of Mr. Johnson is not finally fixed in his mind. Only recently, Johnson sued once again for peace. He approached Ho through the Canadian member of the International Control Commission. Giving terms that are entirely unacceptable, of course—independence for South Vietnam. Ho treated this initiative by simply ignoring it. But he did ask Melkow-ski to check with Moscow for any recent intelligence gathered in Washington, and last Wednesday the good and faithful Soviet Ambassador came in with a very full report."

Le Duc Sy found the developing story engrossing. He put down his glass. "Are you permitted to tell me?"

To the extent that Bui Tin could laugh, he now did so. "It would hardly be possible to instruct you on your next mission *without* telling you. The CIA and the Pentagon, on instructions from the President, are planning a major, innovative program. They call it 'Igloo White.' It is, no less, a program to implant a great technologically devised barrier at the choke points of two critical passes, Nape and Mu Gia, in an attempt to seal off the Trail *I am in charge of keeping open.*"

Bui Tin paused to light a cigarette. "We know the identity of the official who is in charge of that operation. His name is Mon-tana. Tucker Montana. He has the rank of a major in the army. We assume that his training is in engineering or physics. Apparently he has contributed novel ideas that involve the use of sensors of various kinds designed to pinpoint movement through those passes, the purpose being to alert bombers and fighter planes to the means to stop our traffic. The scientific work, under the general guidance of Montana, is being done at Aberdeen Proving Ground, the center of clandestine technology. It will take we do not know how long to develop. But we must learn everything that can be learned about the Igloo enterprise. And the man who knows it in every detail—this Montana—spends his time in Nakhon Phanom in Thailand, which is the U.S. headquarters for the Igloo operation. And he travels regularly to Saigon where he meets with another CIA operative, one Blackford Oates." Bui Tin reached for a scratch pad and wrote out the names of the two men. "Oates—no. O-A-K-E-S—was the other official who conducted the exploration of the Trail I have mentioned."

"So. What is my mission?"

"Your mission is very indirect. Very . . . personal."

"And?"

Bui Tin paused. "When your letter to me arrived, I took it to Colonel Giap. I don't mean the letter, merely the name of your—wife. His reaction was explosive."

"What are you talking about?"

"Your wife, Lao Dai, is our most important—" he paused. Was there another word for it? Bui Tin was not given to euphemisms. "Our most important—seductress. She has performed important work for us, very important work for us. And," Bui Tin got up, and turned his head away, "she had been selected, though not yet informed of the fact that her mission would be—to seduce Mr. Tucker."

Now Le Duc Sy stood up. "But now she is my wife!"

"That she is your wife," Bui Tin spoke solemnly now, "is entirely subordinate to the Independence Movement. That you react this way is one reason why agents are not supposed to marry."

Le Duc Sy's imagination had always been vivid. Suddenly he was able, as the soldier in a movement, to shift perspectives. He paused, and found himself saying, "There is no doubt in heaven itself that she is the most alluring woman in Saigon. What is it proposed that / should do?"

"You are to be 'conscripted' by the South Vietnamese army. This is very easy for us to effect, through our contacts within that army.

You will be sent on maneuvers. And, on a night patrol, you will meet with a most unfortunate fate."

"Like what?" Le Duc Sy's professional curiosity was now dominant.

"You will be killed. Killed in action."

"Are you suggesting that Lao Dai will think me dead?"

"No. We cannot expect a sacrifice of that character. She will be told what duty requires. You will be reported as having been killed, she will publicly mourn the event. And privately she will be confident that, at the correct moment in the future, you will be reunited. Meanwhile, your own operations will be transferred to Dong Hoi. Our naval facilities there are, after all, the true center of the objectives of Operation 34-A, concerning which you have already performed commendable work. Instead of surveying the work being done by the enemy in Danang through Operation 34-A, you will survey the effects of that work at Dong Hoi. We are almost certainly approaching a period when something will need to be done to obstruct the work of 34-A. All the more vital, this, as I devote myself to the work of keeping the Trail open. Our only other avenue to the South is by sea, in the Gulf. After your 'death' at the hands of our soldiers, you will go to Dong Hoi.''

Le Duc Sy sat down. "I will need to consider your plan."

Bui Tin, finally relaxed, sipped the last of his beer. "My dear Sy, you are not given to 'considering' anything. Not even"—this was risky, Bui Tin thought hastily, but worth it—"impetuous marriages."

Le Duc Sy spoke gravely. "If you mean that I married Lao Dai after a very brief courtship, I acknowledge this. If you are suggesting that she is other than the woman I desire as my wife, you misunderstand our marriage."

"No, no. I am suggesting nothing of the sort. I honor your devotion to her. Even as I honor the devotion you have to our movement. But this is not merely *my* plan. It is *the* plan. You have no alternatives."

Le Duc Sy laughed. His laughter came in two volleys: the first, general merriment at the maneuvering of his old friend. The second reflected his sudden understanding of the "alternatives."

"Otherwise, I don't get shot in the battlefield with a dummy bullet. I get shot with live ammunition here in Hanoi. Correct?"

"Correct."

They finished their beer. Bui Tin leaned over to his desk and pressed a button. In short order an elderly clerk knocked on the door and an orderly brought in two trays with hot meals and a bottle of wine.

"Notice the vintage, Sy—1954. The year of Dien Bien Phu. Amazing, what the French left behind."

★ ★ ★ ★ ★ ★ ★ ★ ★ ★ ★

Chapter Seventeen

Senator Goldwater and those three of his inti-
mates who knew about "the general" who was
supplying information clandestinely permitted
themselves to laugh about it all, the helpful, sin-
cere, anonymous "face" they called General X.
It was late at night and they had talked at melan-
choly, frustrated length about the new vote-for-
Johnson commercial. Drinks were passed
about, and the drinks brought on organic,
locker-room laughter. Barry Goldwater loved
good company and good talk and he had a nice
facility for taking a comic situation and carrying
it to surrealistic lengths.

"I mean, do you suppose his wife is called *Mrs.* X?"

"Of *course*! And his oldest son is X major, the second boy is X minor, the third, X tertius," Baroody said, never reluctant to exhibit his knowledge of classical constructions.

"What about his daughter?" Clif White, the political intimate and consultant, insisted on knowing.

There was hesitation. How to feminize "X"? Senator Goldwater said he supposed there was no alternative than to refer to her as "Little Miss X."

Goldwater had won at the convention the preceding week with 228 more votes than the 655 needed to nominate him as Republican candidate for President. He leaned back in his chair and took a drink of bourbon. To Baroody: "Do you know, Bill, here we are receiving information from a general in the Defense Department and *we* do not know who he is! Our General X. I'm trying to think. In the last ninety days, has he misled us?"

No one could come up with any example, though several pieces of information he had passed on to Goldwater, Goldwater did not have the resources to verify. For instance, he had not been able himself to investigate the existence or the scope of Operation 34-A, which General X stressed was doing heavy work in the Gulf of Tonkin, virtually fingerprinting the locations and the characteristics of North Vietnamese installations. And now, tomorrow, Goldwater was scheduled to meet General X face to face.

Their only conversations had been over the telephone. Clif White or Bill Baroody would get the call—from which telephone, where situated, they did not know. General X would announce that he had information he thought the senator would want to have. Baroody or White, both authorized to make binding commitments on behalf of the candidate, would give an exact time and a private telephone number. At exactly that time, Senator Goldwater would himself answer the private telephone and converse with the general, making notes of the information he was being given.

The relationship could not have been initiated by the senator, and would not have been countenanced by him except for the odd way in which it had begun. It was at the funeral of General MacArthur in Norfolk. At the reception Mrs. MacArthur, the minute widow with the beautiful, stricken face who spoke in those comforting

Southern accents one associates with loving aunts tending to the cares of helpless little children, signaled to him after her duties in the receiving line had been completed. A Coca-Cola and ham sandwich in hand, Goldwater went quickly to her side and she nudged him to the corner of the room. He leaned down in order to make out her quiet words.

What she said was that there was a general in the Pentagon who had been an admirer of her husband, whom he had served as a lieutenant colonel in the Korean campaign. That general was critically situated in the Pentagon and despaired over the developing situation in South Vietnam. The anonymous general was a great admirer of Senator Goldwater and wished to give him information that would enable him to affect public policy during the forthcoming campaign.

"Now heah, Senator, is the thing about it, and that's that the general wohn't under *any circumstances* let you know what his name is, an' I guess I can understand that, when I remember all the intriguin' done to mah general," she tipped her head in obeisance in the direction of the crypt where her general had only just now been put to rest. So, she whispered, all she

could say to the senator was that he must accept any telephone call he got from General X.
And he was kindly to tell her—if he was willing
to enter into this relationship—which single
member of his staff would be advised of this
"telephone pahtnaship, is how I think of it"—
someone to whom the senator would say, Accept any calls from a man who announces
himself as General Eggs. That was so that operators who received the call in the first place
wouldn't be tempted to make fun of someone
calling himself General X. If a new operator
asked how he spelled his name, he would say,
"E-G-G-S." Whenever the widow had looked up
at him for a reaction, Senator Goldwater simply
blinked. Now he said, "Tell him to ask for Bill
Baroody."

"Is that B-a-r-o-o-d-y?"

He nodded.

She took his hand and gave it a warm little
squeeze and said she now had to get back to
her other guests.

There had been, since April, six conversations with General X, and in the conversations
he had given Goldwater the information about
Operation 34-A and about captured North Vietnamese plans to transport as many as 20,000

men per month down the Ho Chi Minh Trail, with supporting materiel. But in the exchange yesterday, General X had said that there was simply no alternative to arranging a personal meeting. What he now had to say to the candidate could not be said over the telephone and in any event might require a half hour's common probing.

"It's not easy for me to move around these days, General. It's easy enough for me to tell my own security to bug off, but there's usually a bunch of reporters waiting outside, following me wherever I go. You got any ideas?"

General X did. "I know that you are giving a speech tomorrow to the American Legion at the Armory. The speech is scheduled for eleven A.M. Arrive at ten-fifteen, and tell your host that you have arranged with a member of your staff to go over the speech with you and that he is meeting you in Room 24A—and you do not wish to be disturbed. Is that satisfactory?" Goldwater had said that yes, that was satisfactory.

The senator looked very tired. It had been a grueling fortnight, never mind his formal convention victory. At San Francisco the attack on him by the candidate around whom the opposition had consolidated had been deeply wounding. It helped that Governor William Scranton had sworn to him over the telephone that he had never laid eyes on the scurrilous letter Scranton's aides had written to Goldwater on Scranton's stationery, addressed "Dear Barry" and signed (by typewriter) "Bill." The letter suggested that the entire Goldwater movement was in the hands of kooks and warmongers. Every delegate found a copy of that letter under his door the next morning; this generated wild rumors, huge resentments, a divided convention, a divided Republican Party, and augured a defeat in November.

The Johnson forces, sensing the possibility of an early knockout, had run a television commercial, the idea of press secretary Bill Moyers on which an inventive, expensive New York advertising agency had put the finishing touches. It showed a little girl in a sunny field of daisies. She began animatedly plucking petals from a daisy. As she plucked away, a male voice in the background began a countdown ". . . ten . . . nine . . . eight . . ." the voice becoming constantly stronger. The screen suddenly exploded and the child disappeared in a mushroom cloud. The voice concluded by urging voters to elect President Johnson. "These are the stakes: to make a world in which all of God's children can live, or go into the dark. We must either love each other, or we must die. Vote for President Johnson on November third. The stakes are too high for you to stay home."

Goldwater had heard about the ad minutes after it was shown over NBC and his indignation reached such furious pitch that he went to the telephone and called President Johnson—who denied any prior knowledge of the ad, and said he would see to it that it did not get shown again. But at that point Barry Goldwater had ceased believing anything Lyndon Johnson said.

"More exactly," Baroody corrected him, "you don't think something is true merely because LBJ *says* it's true. It might just *happen* to be true. That's the way to sum it up, isn't it?" Goldwater agreed. Yes, that was a better way to put it.

As they made their way home, Goldwater and his one bodyguard and his driver in one car, Baroody and White in a second car, Baroody said to White, "I never saw him before exactly in this shape."

"What do you mean?"

"The combination of indignation and despair. Well," he said, unsmiling, as the driver approached his own house before driving White to the hotel, "at least we got him laughing about all the X's and little X's in the general's house."

"Your aide knows exactly where to go?" the American Legion hostess asked the candidate. Goldwater nodded. "Fine. And no one will disturb you, I can assure you of that. You can even lock that door from the inside."

Goldwater opened the door with some curiosity. It was a comfortable room with a large couch and three armchairs, a mirror for makeup and a private bathroom. He locked the door and sat down but immediately rose when he heard the knock. He approached the door:

"Who is it?"

"The general." The voice was high-pitched and soft.

Goldwater opened the door and admitted a man dressed in a seersucker jacket and khaki pants, without a tie, a large American Legion badge pinned to his chest pocket. He was perhaps fifty years old, slender, his hair sandy brown, his face tanned by years of exposure to the sun. His smile was genuine and relaxed. They shook hands; the general sat down and went immediately into his subject.

"I can't tell you this with the finality I have reported other things, Senator, like 34-A and the documents on the Trail. But I think I have pieced together an operation designed to do several things. First, persuade the American people that President Johnson is going to take a stronger stand on Vietnam, and two, get from Congress a blank check on anything he proceeds to do. Which, you ought to know, is a hell of a lot less than what he ought to do."

"Well, General, before we get into that, what exactly do you expect he's going to do?"

"One of the reasons I insisted on seeing you is that I have only pieces of information, and maybe you can put them together better than I can. Maybe between the two of us we can figure it out."

"Well," said Goldwater affably, "we may as well begin. We've got some time, but not all day."

The general leaned forward and said:

"Two destroyers, the *C. Turner Joy* and the *Maddox,* have been instructed to initiate patrols closer to North Vietnamese and Chinese territory by sixteen miles than they ever came before. The *Maddox* has been ordered to cruise right up to *seven miles* from Dong Hoi, and then

within eleven miles of Hainan, the Chinese island northeast.

"Now I can tell you this: There is *nothing*
those two destroyers can accomplish up that
close to enemy territory that they can't accomplish at the conventional thirty miles away. The
34-A fake fishing boats are getting all the close-
in intelligence we need, and there isn't anything
on those destroyers that will accomplish anything seven miles from shore that isn't being
better handled by those little boats with the
South Vietnamese crews."

"What's the point, then?"

"There can't be any other motivation that I
can think of except to provoke the NVA."

"But why would the NVA permit themselves
to be provoked? What's Ho Chi Minh got to gain
by shooting a couple of torpedoes at U.S.
ships?"

"That's what I don't have the answer to, Senator. *I don't know* why the NVA would do that.
It isn't as though they had the resources to do
a Pearl Harbor on us. So what if they hit the
Maddox or the *Turner Joy*? So they have damaged or even sunk a U.S. destroyer, and run the
risk of getting the United States into an all-out
war with their country—"

Goldwater held up his hand. "Wait, wait. Another thing, General: What do the captains of those two destroyers, or for that matter the commander of the Seventh Fleet, what do they think they're accomplishing by going up that close?"

"I *can* answer that one. The CIA station in Danang has reported that intercepts of NVA military radio transmissions indicated that the NVA are on to 34-A, and are thinking of going out after those fake South Vietnamese fishermen. Our idea has got to be that a show of strength by the Seventh Fleet will nail down the freedom of the seas, which includes the right of the 34-A 'fishermen' to go right up there to the three-mile limit. As far as the Navy is concerned, they're there to assert the U.S. three-mile rule."

"Have the North Vietnamese proclaimed a twelve-mile limit?"

"That's something very curious. CIA has intercepted NVA messages in which they refer to a 'twelve-mile limit' but there haven't been *any* public assertions on the subject. *None.* No complaints to the International Control Commission, to the U.N., to the State Department—none."

"Does Admiral Sharp know about those radio intercepts?" Senator Goldwater's reference was to the CINCPAC in Honolulu.

"I don't know. I may be able to find that out. I'm already doing some discreet digging on that point. Right now I just don't know."

Barry Goldwater had a faculty widely remarked by his staff of asking the same question of very nearly anyone he engaged in serious conversation. It didn't have to be a highly placed person close to him. It could be and had been known to be the hotel bellman or cleaning woman. He asked it now:

"What would you do, General, if you were in my shoes?"

The general was surprised, but not taken aback. "I don't know. The fact of the matter is, Senator, the Johnson administration has no *strategy.* They do have the big Igloo project I've told you about, to tie up the Ho Chi Minh Trail, and they're getting more and more data for that big notebook McNamara keeps filling up that results in no action that stops Ho Chi Minh in his tracks. I can guess only this: President Johnson isn't going to take any decisive action before the third of November. And I haven't seen anything to suggest that they have a strategy for *after* the election. But whatever you decide to do, I figured you ought to know what's going on."

Goldwater paused. "Did you see the business

on television night before last? The little girl with the daisies?"

"I didn't see it. I might as well have; it's the talk of the Pentagon. And I'm not the only officer there who was pissed off about it."

"You don't happen to know if LBJ knew about that commercial. I mean ahead of time?"

"Senator, there isn't *anything* relating to his campaign the President doesn't know about ahead of time."

A knock. Goldwater rose, went to the door and said in a voice loud enough to be heard at the other side, *"I'm coming, I'm coming. Joe, take the folder back to the office. See you later."* He turned to the general and whispered; "Thanks, General—" he smiled, "Eggs. You are a good man. I mean, a good general."

"Good luck, Senator."

They shook hands.

★ ★ ★ ★ ★ ★ ★ ★ ★

Chapter Eighteen

For their next meeting in Saigon, Rufus took the precaution of calling Tucker into town one day before Blackford. His message said merely that he was calling him in from Nakhon Phanom one day before their joint meeting "to give you a few hours of leisure in a city where you can order a decent meal." Blackford flew in from Danang on Air America, went directly to the apartment (a different one, of course) to which they had been directed. Tucker had spent several days making tests and his mood was transparently high. He welcomed Blackford warmly, as Rufus did, in his own way.

They drank iced tea. Rufus gave a general

account of the political picture. Not much there, really, that they hadn't picked up on Voice of America and in *Stars & Stripes,* though as Rufus spoke of the political picture it was clear that it was freighted with the suspense that attached to coexisting anomalies that couldn't go on too long without colliding. North Vietnam was technically at peace with South Vietnam. South Vietnam was technically at peace with North Vietnam. The United States was technically at peace with North Vietnam. The Geneva Accords forbade its signatories, including the Soviet Union and North Vietnam, from doing what they were nevertheless blatantly doing. Codicils to the SEATO treaty and to the Geneva Accords pledged the United States to defend a nation being aggressed against. And nothing—nothing decisive—was being done to reify, and then act conclusively on, reality.

"The only thing we are doing that is unambiguously legal," Rufus sighed, an amused-bitter sigh, "is what you are up to, Tucker. Because what we do in Thailand, at Nakhon Phanom, in order to close down the Trail in Laos, is of no theoretical concern to the North Vietnamese, since Laos is a foreign country, pledged to neutrality."

Blackford tilted his iced tea glass, swallowed, then said, "As a matter of curiosity, Rufus, what's legal in respect of North Vietnam isn't necessarily legal in respect of Thailand and Laos, is it? I mean, we're operating out of two independent countries—"

"No, it would not necessarily follow. But in this case it does. We have the permission of Thailand to proceed with Operation Igloo White, and under the 1962 Second Geneva Conference Accord, all parties are not only permitted to take steps to ensure Laotian neutrality, they are *urged* to take such steps."

"Including bombing Laotian territory?" Blackford pressed the point. "After all, when we bomb the Trail with our Thai planes, we're bombing a foreign country."

"We are not now bombing Laotian territory. We are *preparing* to bomb Laotian territory. Our motives in doing so are to put into effect a neutrality that was guaranteed to Laos, and by Laos. You speak like a lawyer, Blackford."

"Rufus, considering what I've done for you in the last thirteen years, if I were a lawyer I would have to, as a matter of honor, disbar myself."

"Now wait a minute, Blacky—" Tucker spoke up. "This business of what's legal and what isn't legal in these modern situations doesn't really work, does it? I mean, you're going to tell me the war I fought in in Korea wasn't a war because Truman called it a police action one year after swearing in a public ceremony to preserve, protect and defend the Constitution that says only Congress can declare war?"

"Declaring war is out of fashion," Rufus said. "The atom bomb did that."

"Yes," Tucker said, his voice dimmed, the aggressiveness suddenly gone. "Hiroshima changed everything . . . didn't it?"

"I don't think so," Rufus said. He was in his contemplative-analytical mode. "What it did change was the appetite to declare war. When a country declares war it is expected to use its maximum resources to win that war. We can't use the bomb in Vietnam—we all grant that. But the general fear of the bomb extends to a failure to use even the next echelon of modern weaponry. Hanoi and Haiphong would cease to exist if we were to drop half the bombs there that we are prepared to drop, so far as I can see, on the Trail. So? We fight with a third echelon—supplies, training, intelligence: support systems, essentially, while the enemy's use of its third echelon is decisive."

"Decisive?" Blackford asked.

Rufus weighed his words even more carefully. "Contingently decisive, I should have said. The NVA are prepared to kill and to torture the entire South Vietnamese clerical class, the whole intellectual, educational, political, and religious infrastructure: that is what the Vietcong are doing right now, in the countryside. How much of that, backed up by conventional North Vietnamese military, will they need to do before winning? They have very nearly succeeded in seizing effective control of the Mekong Delta."

Rufus's reference was to the dumpy southern one third of South Vietnam, sometimes called the rice bowl of Asia, which the NVA were reaching not only through exhaustive long marches down the 400-mile Trail, but also by shipping into the southern port of Sihanoukville in Cambodia. "But we must take such comfort as we can, gentlemen, in knowing that we are following the orders of a constitutionally elected government and that we are pursuing objectives which no one could judge dishonorable."

"Rufus, when we get tried by Bertrand Russell in Sweden, I want you for my lawyer."

"Blackford, if you go to trial in Stockholm, I shall long since have been hanged."

Tucker found himself suddenly prompted to break his long-standing covenant never to refer to his role in creating the overweening dark cloud of the day, surely a capital crime in the statute books of Lord Russell and his assorted committees calling for unilateral disarmament. But he drew back before the words passed his lips. He said only, "I guess that gang would get us all, if they could."

"And they'll need to get us to Stockholm to do so," Rufus said. Had they been younger men, Rufus would have taken the moment to remind them to be alert at all times to security. But he was talking to men experienced in the trade in which they were engaged. So he asked instead, "How is it going, Blackford?"

Blackford spoke for half an hour about operations in Danang. "If you want a head count on the interdiction process we're subsidizing, prepared to be impressed. During the first seven months of this year, the South Vietnamese patrol boats we pay for, supervise, and give instructions to have inspected one hundred and forty-nine thousand junks plying nine hundred miles of coast north and south of Danang, mostly north, obviously. We have, by one reckoning, inspected five hundred and seventy thousand North Vietnamese fishermen. That's a cumulative figure, of course: some of the same persons have been stopped and inspected a half-dozen times. We have amassed an *armory* of Soviet materiel taken from apparently innocent junks. That part of 34-A—interdiction of subversive materiel and personnel—has become routine, and routinely successful in terms of the quantity of stuff we're stopping."

"And of course to the extent that you succeed," Tucker interrupted, "you increase the pressure on my side of the border."

Blackford said, "On the second mission, our own disguised fishing boats are bringing in information I've been feeding you, Rufus, through channels every few days. There isn't any doubt about the latest fact: the Soviets are installing a new generation of SAM missiles stretching right down along the coast from Haiphong to Dong Hoi. All we can tell you is where they are, how numerous we think they are, what kind of radar keeps watch over them. And wait for something to give."

"And wait for something to give," Tucker said.

"That's right." Blackford motioned to him to take over.

"On the western front, we have a hell of a lot of work to do, but the essential thinking is done. The idea of the Spikebuoys has been tested. The product will be 5.5 feet overall. When it's dropped from the plane, stabilizing fins will direct it as they would a bomb. About 30 inches will bury into the ground, with a diameter of six inches. The upright antenna will be 48 inches with four radiating arms at right angles to one another, each about 18 inches long. It will weigh twenty-five pounds, and the batteries will last as long as forty-five days, but almost certainly thirty days. And we've come up with a slightly different design for the acoustic-seismic devices, same family as the Spikebuoys. They're called ACOUSID, for Acoustic and Seismic Intrusion Detector. They weigh 37 pounds and bury themselves almost the whole of their 48 inches into the ground. The antenna is about the same length. Their microphone is on the top of the buried portion, at the base of the antenna, above ground. We can activate that microphone by remote control from the air. It'll pick up the sound of a man pissing. I'm working now on a display, a giant wall map—all electrified—inside the installation at Nakhon. It will plot the Trail through the two passes. The sensor locations will illuminate on our screen. By the end of the year we ought to know better than the gooks just where their caravans are." He looked somehow, for the moment, sad. Then he lifted his hand. "Hey, I'm hungry! And thirsty! Let's avoid the hard part: What Washington will decide to do with all that information we're prepared to give them."

Again they separated for dinner. Tucker had become more outspoken about his "friend." Rufus, ever aware of Blackford's own penchant for sowing wild oats, always made it possible for Blackford to withdraw, to make his own private dining arrangements. But he was always glad when Blackford said, which most of the time he did, that he would prefer to have dinner with Rufus. They dined this night at the Caravelle, Blackford doing most of the chatting, which was how Rufus liked it. At ten they said good night, Rufus departing for his safe house, Blackford for the officers' quarters at the airport.

On impulse he decided to stroll first down Tudo Street toward Cho-lon, the festive area adjacent to Saigon. "Saigon's Bourbon Street," he had heard it called. He turned back to the Hotel

Caravelle and checked his briefcase in one of the steel lockers that had recently been set up near the cloakroom. And he walked out down Tu-do Street, turning left toward Cho-lon.

It wasn't really like Bourbon Street, he reminded himself. More like Paris or, more accurately, Marseilles. By New Orleans standards, the sound was relatively muted. The lights from the restaurants and bars were yellow and enticing. The prostitutes were easily spotted. Some would see them merely as young women out for a stroll. He paused beside one nightclub, wondering whether to enter it and order a drink. A girl, surely less than twenty years old, dressed in tight yellow cotton only just covering her breast line, with large brown eyes and high pink cheekbones, approached him, Did he have a light? Her English was broken, as also one of her teeth. Blackford replied in French, Sorry, he didn't smoke.

Would he like a lesson on how to smoke? she asked, cocking her head.

Not really, thanks. It had taken him ten years to give up smoking.

Would he be interested in having a drink with her? Perhaps even treating her to a drink?

Blackford smiled down at her. *Poor beautiful wretch, he thought.* I don't drink, he said.

Did he not permit himself to take pleasures of any kind? she wanted to know.

I take pleasure, he said, putting a banknote in her hand, gently, in avoiding vice squads.

She left, with a pert little smile. He entered the club and sat down at the bar. At the opposite end were three Americans and a couple of girls. He ordered a Campari and soda and then lifted from his coat pocket the letter he had first read on checking in at the APO post office at the airport. It was so—well, perhaps not typically Sally: distinctively Sally. It began:

My darling Blacky: Now first hear this from the only English teacher, I should hope, you have ever slept with. When you use the phrase "the good ship," as you did in your last letter, the next word you use has got to be *"Lollipop."* Otherwise you are using a quite humdrum cliché, and we agreed when you were a senior at Yale that you and I would try never to exchange clichés. You do remember?

Now, you have, sometimes, a terribly obscure way of expressing yourself, a difficulty you may have noticed (you should have noticed) that never afflicted my mentor, J. Austen, who had no problem in expressing thoughts, no matter how subtle, with unambiguous lucidity. Just for instance:

". . . Elizabeth was called on by her cousin, to give her opinion of all that she had seen at Rosings, which for Charlotte's sake, she made more favourable than it really was. But her commendation, though costing her some trouble, could by no means satisfy Mr. Collins, and he was very soon obliged to take her Ladyship's praise into his own hands." P/Prejudice, Chap 23, last line.

Granted, we would not now tolerate that comma after the word "cousin," but whereas that can be called progress, it cannot be progress to write as you did, "it truly strains me to say what it is that is on my mind, so much of it confused, all of it, I think, comforting, if you see what I mean." My comment: I do not see what you mean. I do not see why it is that you cannot tell me what is on your mind. Even if it confuses you, it does not follow that it would confuse me. Why? Because I have trained myself to focus on ambiguities and to sort them out. You speak of marriage at the end of the year and then you speak about burdens from which you cannot free yourself, and then you say that you are certain (only you make it obvious that in fact you are not certain) you can resolve these difficulties, but you then speak as though those difficulties are creatures of others' makings: from which it is obvious that you are simply trying to say, I would like for us to be married in December but there is no assurance that we can be married in December. So what am I supposed to say?

Oh darling, do you even love me—chastely? I doubt it. It is not one of the disciplines, chastity, in which you are proficient. Who should know this better than I? . . . But this is not a subject you will want to discuss with me. Know then this, that I shan't, as I once did, marry another man. Not because I regret that I did; Tony was as special in his own way as you, and our son promises, at two months, to be—how should I put it?—as priceless, as unique, as his father and his stepfather-elect combined. There now. My news? . . ."

He did not reread the brief account of doings at the Casa Serena. He was interested in doings in a house he might find himself inhabiting one day, but when quotidian experiences were recounted, inevitably his mind turned to his own day-to-day life, on a scene where spectacular historical developments were taking place—which, he had begun to sense, would eventually engulf the entire country in whose capital he was now sitting, drinking a Campari and soda by himself.

He looked up, taking in the general atmosphere at La Tambourine. Over there he saw Tucker Montana seated at a small table with a single candle between him and one of the loveliest women Blackford had ever seen in Asia. Should he?

The decision was taken from him. Tucker stood up and motioned to him. Blackford walked over, drink in hand. "Blacky! You old rake, sitting in this disreputable little place, all by yourself! Please meet Lao Dai." She lowered her head, in diminished oriental manner, the little sign of deference muted by experience with Western informality. Blackford extended his hand. Tucker brought over a chair and signaled to the waiter for another Campari and soda. "That is what you are drinking, isn't it? I think I recognize it. I had a great-aunt who used to order that shellac." Blackford sat down, and Lao Dai gave him, now, a radiant smile.

★ ★ ★ ★ ★ ★ ★ ★ ★

Chapter Nineteen

AUGUST 1, 1964
DONG HOI, NORTH VIETNAM

Le Duc Sy's rage was uncontrolled, and on the evening of August 1 he spit it out.

His vehicle was the squadron leader of the NVA Dong Hoi patrol boat fleet, Captain Thanh-Lang. He found him, as he hoped he would, at the bar near the dock, a favorite of the naval officers. He would approach him with some care, and for that reason paused at the bar to chat with the talkative French owner, who had been permitted to stay on in Dong Hoi because during the war with the French he had been cooperative. The Frenchman had been so not out of any special sympathy for the Vietnamese, but because he thought it of primary importance to save his restaurant and its wine cellar. He liked to tell his customers that in Paris, during the occupation, the restaurants—the "best restaurants"—never missed a meal. "It is bad enough to be occupied and to be at war, but to be occupied or to be at war and to be without a place safely to relax with your friends and have a little spirits or beer—that is too much, do you not agree?" He asked that question of everyone, but Le Duc Sy didn't mind hearing it again. He agreed fully, he said, instructing the barman to pour him another glass of wine.

The Frenchman was still talking when suddenly Le Duc Sy wheeled on him: "Can I use your back room for a few minutes? It is quite important." The Frenchman readily agreed. It was then that Sy went over to Captain Thanh-Lang and asked that he join him for a private conversation back there. He looked down to see what Thanh-Lang was drinking, and asked for a bottle of Tiger beer to be brought in.

"Of course, M. Sy," the Frenchman said, obliging as always. "And I shall see that you are not disturbed. On the desk is a buzzer. If I hear it ring, I will understand that you and the young officer"—he pointed approvingly at Captain

Thanh-Lang—"are ready for a little more re-freshment."

The door closed. Le Duc Sy came right to the point. "On the patrol with you this afternoon I kept checking the radar. It confirmed that you were at all times just inside the three-mile limit."

"Of course, Sy, I am very particular about that. Orders."

"As you know, those orders often flow through me."

"I know that you are a special representative of Colonel Giap."

"Well, this afternoon when I was not looking at your radar I had my binoculars fixed in the direction of the southern fleet." Sy poured himself another drink. "Perhaps you do not know, Captain Thanh-Lang, that I am more familiar than perhaps any of our comrades with the enemy fleet based in Danang. Familiar with the so-called fishing fleet, and familiar with the American warships that come to Danang for fuel and for repairs."

"I did not know you had spent time in Da-nang."

"Well, I did. And let me tell you what. This afternoon I saw it. And *it* was not observing the three-mile limit. There could not have been more than one and one-half miles between us."

"You saw what, Le Duc Sy? I *heard* you shout, and I even started to go to see what was wrong, but you waved me away, remember? What did you see?"

"I saw an American destroyer. Naturally we were too far away for me to see which U.S. destroyer it was, but that it was a destroyer I do not doubt, and that it was as close as 4.5 miles from shore I do not doubt. Possibly as close as 4 miles."

He banged his wrist on the table. "Four miles from *our* shore! Now you know that when we liberated Vietnam from the French we inherited the traditional territorial limit of twelve miles. We have been observing the traditional three-mile limit of the French purely as a matter of—proto-col? And the Americans have been observing eight miles, perhaps as a conciliatory gesture, since they say they formally respect only three miles. But now—now they crash through the eight-mile barrier. Breaking the tradition of ten years."

"Since I did not sight the U.S. destroyer I did not report it. Did you, Le Duc Sy?"

"It is because I intended to report it that I did

not there and then tell you about it. When we came in, I went to the radio room and telephoned to Colonel Giap and spoke to the colonel himself."

Thanh-Lang was much impressed. "What did he say?"

Le Duc Sy raised his glass with theatrical gravity. "What he said, Captain, was that he was grateful to me for this confirmation. That the shore radars had picked up something that seemed too formidable merely to be a big junk or shipping boat and had tracked it for two hours. It traveled along our coastline and then over to Hainan"—Le Duc Sy referred to the Chinese offshore island, 150 miles northeast. "Colonel Giap told me that he had conferred with the general, his uncle, and with President Ho, and that the decision has been made. If the destroyer appears again tomorrow, this side of the eight-mile limit, we"—he looked at Thanh-Lang as if he and Le Duc Sy were chosen centurions guarding the Independence Gate—"will torpedo it."

The captain was struck with excitement. "Do you mean Squadron A? Squadron A, under *my* command?"

"I mean Squadron A under your command,

Captain Thanh-Lang, and I mean an attack under the command of Le Duc Sy."

"But of course, Le Duc Sy, I acknowledge that I am your subordinate. Even so, it is I who will be responsible for the maneuvering, for the firing. I have dreamed of this day. I have gone over it first, of course, at the admiralty school, and then in maneuvers. But I have gone over it in my sleep. I know exactly where and when to let those torpedoes go. I have taken account of the maneuverability of the U.S. destroyer and I know just when to catch it off guard. I am not, Le Duc Sy, a nobleman by rank, like your excellency. My people are fishermen. But I grew up with the sea. The sea is my home. And when you tell me that the imperialists are trespassing on my home, you might as well be telling the farmer that the French are plundering his land. My blood boils, and all my thinking, all my knowledge, rise to my head. Do you wish to hear me out on the maneuvers?"

Le Duc Sy was himself excited, but before leaning over to study the pencil markings Captain Thanh-Lang was making on the pad of paper, he pressed the buzzer. Well before the captain had sunk the destroyer by Tactic A, two bottles were brought in by the Frenchman's fourteen-year-old son, who put them down and left the room discreetly. Le Duc Sy listened one full hour to Captain Thanh-Lang, whose enthusiasm for a possible encounter on the following day in turn fired Le Duc Sy, who talked now about the joy of humiliating the imperialist marauder, and how the Yankees would learn the high cost of poaching on waters indisputably North Vietnamese.

Captain Thanh-Lang suddenly pushed aside his half-dozen sheets of paper, each of them demonstrating a different nautical maneuver. "What will the Americans then do, Le Duc Sy?"

Sy smiled. "What more can they do than they are already doing? They dominate the Gulf of Tonkin today. They arm an entire fleet of the Southern rebels, disguise them, dispatch them to our waters to inspect our defensive resources. On our western border they plot to interrupt our flow of men and materiel to press the war of independence—"

"The Americans have not bombed us."

Le Duc Sy jiggled his fingers dismissively. "They *can* bomb us, of course. And China can bomb Taiwan. And Pyongyang can bomb Seoul. And Moscow can bomb Paris. But the Americans do not *want* a world war, Captain. And do not forget that there is an election being contested in the United States. No, the United States will simply absorb the punishment. Perhaps even the representative of the United States in the United Nations will apologize for its provocative acts within our territorial waters. But we will then emerge, Captain, as the valiant defenders of our little state, not afraid to tell the great dragon of the West when it has gone too far."

Thanh-Lang was so overjoyed he very nearly couldn't bear it. He asked Le Duc Sy whether he thought it appropriate that, together, in muted voice so as not to alert or alarm the company next door, they might hum the opening bars of the national anthem. Le Duc Sy, entering thoroughly into the spirit of martial enthusiasm, thought this a fine idea. "We'll sing to our country," he said, "and then we will drink one more time to our country."

At 11 A.M. the following day, the three patrol boats of Squadron A hid behind the little island of Hon Me. Two nights before, Hon Me had been assaulted by South Vietnamese naval guerrillas. They had attempted to land, intending to sabotage its radar installations. Rebuffed, they settled for strafing it from the sea. Now it served as cover for Squadron A. Just before 1300, radar detected, at a distance of just over six miles, a heavy congestion of junks: South Vietnamese fishing boats. But one mile off, on a course more or less parallel to the junks, was a solid, squat blip. Le Duc Sy measured the speed it was making over the ground. "Just under 25 knots," he called out to Captain Thanh-Lang.

"It has to be what we're looking for, no?" Thanh-Lang asked eagerly.

Le Duc Sy lifted his head from the radar. "Let us find out."

The Soviet-built patrol boats could travel at almost 50 knots, twice the speed of the USS *Maddox* which, spotting the several craft approaching, turned to head out to sea.

It took time for the NVA patrol boat to come within attack range of what Le Duc Sy now knew for a certainty was an American destroyer. The sun was blistering and even at 50 knots Le Duc Sy could not get much relief from it; if he stuck his head out of the cockpit, the vessel's speed exposed him to such a rush of wind speed he had to yank his head back in.

It wasn't until eight minutes past three that the

pursuers and the pursued came within range of each other. Just as Captain Thanh-Lang ordered two torpedoes loosed, the *Maddox* began to fire its big guns. By radio Captain Thanh-Lang instructed Vessel Number 2 to bear down on the destroyer's starboard side, intending to limit the enemy's right-side option to step out of the path of the torpedoes. Vessel Number 2 roared ahead while Captain Thanh-Lang adjusted to a port tack, intending a straitjacket that would lock the *Maddox* into immobility, and a bloody death after the torpedoes struck.

Now Vessel Number 3 was abeam of the *Maddox,* loosing a third torpedo. Captain Thanh-Lang viewed it anxiously as shells from the huge 5-inch gun from the *Maddox* tore into Vessel Number 2. Thanh-Lang shouted into the radio.

He was quickly reconciled: The vessel was lost. Almost simultaneously he knew that his own torpedo had been a dud; either that, or else he had missed his target.

At that moment the strafing began. Neither Le Duc Sy nor Captain Thanh-Lang had spotted the American fighter planes, which now dove down, strafing the two remaining boats. Involuntarily, everyone on the patrol boat dove for cover, sweating now from the heat of the sun and of the rocket fire. The destroyer, in a maneuver that seemed almost casual, had eased its way out of the path of the two torpedoes and was headed now not away from the remaining Vietnamese boats but toward them. Captain Thanh-Lang hesitated an instant. Le Duc Sy, his exuberance spent, spoke. "Head back! Head back! We can't handle the destroyer *and* the airplanes." At that moment—for some reason— the *Maddox,* instead of continuing its pursuit, turned away, out to sea.

The two patrol boats limped back toward land, Captain Thanh-Lang looking up anxiously at the planes overhead. They circled, but evidently satisfied that the engagement was over, flew casually off to the south.

Vessel Number 1, Captain Thanh-Lang reported to shore radio on his painful retreat, would be returning with two wounded aboard and two dead—at that, fewer than the five casualties of Vessel Number 3. The strafing had done severe damage to both vessels. They set out for their shelter traveling at only one-third speed.

It took them two hours, at 15 knots, to make land, a dispirited squadron leader and his political leader having spent the time in silence. When finally they docked at the naval facility behind the island, they found a detachment of six North Vietnamese soldiers waiting. The lieutenant called out the names of Le Duc Sy and Thanh-Lang. The two men descended the gangway. Handcuffs were put on them. They were led to a waiting van.

★ ★ ★ ★ ★ ★ ★ ★ ★

Chapter Twenty

There was no hesitation at the Pentagon when word came in from the Gulf via Honolulu. *Wake the President.*

They rang him at 3:29 in the morning and by 3:30 he had taken command. In his bathrobe and slippers he walked down to the spare, grim Situation Room.

Within half an hour he had what he wanted to know. 1) There was no question that the torpedo boats were North Vietnamese. 2) There had been zero U.S. casualties from the machine-gun fire by the one patrol boat, nor was there any question that the patrol boat had subsequently been sunk. 3) No question that fighter planes from the *Ticonderoga* had coordinated the defense and strafed two of the patrol boats, partially disabling them and causing them to return to port. He learned that Admiral Sharp had given instructions to Captain Herrick aboard the *Maddox* not to give chase. (It would have been altogether feasible to do so, because the two damaged patrol boats were—even now—traveling back toward their base at limited speed.) Admiral Sharp, LBJ noted, had done the prudent thing.

President Johnson dismissed his two aides and gave orders that nothing was to be said to the press until he had given instructions to his press secretary, Bill Moyers.

"Should he be awakened, Mr. President?"

"Naw. But call him at six an' tell him to come on over here at seven. Ah'll be ready for him. An' tell Secretary Rusk and McNamara to be here. Oval Office. Yes. Goonight."

"Well," he began, placing another cube of sugar in his coffee cup, "looks like they begun it."

Dean Rusk spoke. "Looks like it, but it's confused. I had a call from Seaborn, International Control Commission. They just received a blistering note from Hanoi. Complaining about our 34-A raids. 'Acts of war.' 'Violation of all neutrality laws'—the whole bit. Now this is the first official complaint we've had from Hanoi on these raids from the South, even though they've been going on for three months."

"Did our people do anything special that accounts for the protest?"

"Not really *special*," the Defense Secretary broke in. "ARVN did attempt a landing on Hon Me—that's the little island, Mr. President, five or six miles off the coast, about seventy miles south of—"

"Ah know where Hon Me is."

"Yes," McNamara said. "Well, the landing party wasn't able to bring it off, so the ARVN went back to their boat and fired away at the new Soviet radar. But we've been—they've been firing at radar installations along the coast for *ten weeks*. Don't quite see why Hanoi would choose *this* moment to protest."

"Seems pretty obvious to me," said the President. "They wanted something to offset their attack on the *Maddox*. Why isn't that obvious to you, Dean?"

"Well, there is a rough parity, if that's what you mean, Mr. President. You attack me, I attack you. But *why now*? They could have struck out at us any time since we began 34-A, back in March."

McNamara again. "Don't forget, we've been easing the Seventh Fleet closer to their territory."

"But the *Maddox* wasn't close in when they attacked, right?"—the President knew exactly the location of the *Maddox,* but he wanted to shape the conversation.

"Right. But it had been, a few hours before."

The President sat back in his rocking chair, patterned after his predecessor's. "I've made a list, and here it is:

"We're going to send a diplomatic note to Hanoi."

"We've never done that before, Mr. President."

"Ah know we never done it before. That's one of the reasons I want to do it now. That note will say that if there is any further interference with the freedom of the seas, there will be quote grave consequences unquote." The President's voice was grave.

"Ah'll use the hot line to Brezhnev, tell him we have no desire to widen the war being fought illegally by North Vietnam against South Vietnam. Who knows how to work the hot line? I don't; never used it."

All three men raised their hands.

"Admiral Sharp should be told that the Seventh Fleet will continue to patrol the Gulf of Tonkin closing on up to, uh, eight miles, yes, eight miles from the shore. And that it is to return all hostile fire.

"Now, Bob, on the matter of the press release. Bill Moyers here will handle the first release. You should be *ver-ry* calm. Stress: *no* American casualties. Just one of those—accidental encounters, I guess is the best way to put it. No mention, obviously, of our diplomatic traffic with Hanoi or Moscow."

He got up.

McNamara spoke as he too, with the others, got up.

"You should know, Mr. President, that the Joint Chiefs think we should take retaliatory action."

The President put his hand on his forehead and closed his eyes in pain. "The military *always* like to fire their guns, don't they, Bob? Kinda natural. Well, you've passed on their recommendation, as you should. An' you have my answer: No."

"One more thing." It was the Secretary of State. "Do you think we should inform Senator Goldwater? I mean, brief him personally?"

Lyndon Johnson hadn't thought that one through. "Ah'll consider that. Let you know by noon. Since we want to treat this in a—*particular* way, if he gets a call it should be from you, not me." He repeated that he would decide by noon.

They nodded and filed out of the room.

He recalled Moyers. "Call Abe Fortas, brief him on what's happened, then ask him to come over and have a little lunch with me upstairs at twelve o'clock."

"Well," said Abe Fortas, walking into the little dining room opposite the presidential bedrooms, "that was one hell of a coincidence. Have you got what you want?"

"I don' really think so," said Lyndon Johnson, squeezing a whole lemon into his small glass of tomato juice. "You pull it all together, an' I don't think it's quite right. The voters aren't going to want to think that the President takes the very first opportunity, a little chance engagement in the Gulf, no Americans hurt, to go shit on the North Vietnamese, and who knows before you know it at this rate maybe we'll be at war. No, they don't want that; aren't ready for it, it seems to me. An' then there's the Hanoi protest comin' in first, right at the same time, and how do we know how long before it gets out what our 34-A missions are up to?"

"But we've *talked* about that. You have *very good* justification. I mean, your public justification is the same as your private justification. We are simply engaged in hindering an aggressive war by the North Vietnamese, and to do that we are making a variety of ordnance available to the South Vietnamese.

"I mean, the American people know we have seventeen thousand military advisers in the South. What are they *supposed* to be doing?"

"Abe," Lyndon put down his toast and spoke as he chewed a mouthful, "the answer is we just don' want a great big debate in the United Nations or for that matter in Congress about what we been doing. I'm surprised Ho hasn't gone to the U.N. on the 34-A operations, probably because he's got plenty to hide, what he's doing in Laos on the Trail, and that's why he's holding back, ah figger."

"So you don't even think it's time to go to Congress for that special resolution?"

"I don't think so."

Abe Fortas was quiet. *"You told me in July you didn't want to know when our—little business got done. We'd let our man on the field use his own timing. Still feel that way?"*

"No."

"You know when you want them to go?"

"Yes."

"When?"

"Now. One attack, we're calm about it. Accidents happen. Two attacks? That's different."

★ ★ ★ ★ ★ ★ ★ ★ ★ ★ ★

Chapter Twenty-One

AUGUST 3, 1964
WASHINGTON, D.C.

The following forty-eight hours were hectic, mad; to this day, inscrutable.

Sundown at the Gulf of Tonkin, on August 2, is at 7:40 P.M., and in 1964 brought in a moonless night. It soon seemed that everyone in the whole world was trying to find out exactly what happened on that mysterious night in the Gulf of Tonkin. The military to begin with, of course. And then congressmen, in particular the membership of the foreign affairs committees, which had been especially pushed for action, *now.* And of course the press. They bore down in Saigon, in Guam, in Honolulu, and in Washington, trying to find out: *What, exactly, happened?*

It was hard, in the flurry, to get the story line straight.

The Navy acknowledged that after the Sunday afternoon attack of August 2 by the three North Vietnamese patrol boats, Admiral Moorer, the Pacific Fleet Commander, had ordered a fresh patrol: two destroyers, the *C. Turner Joy* joining the *Maddox.* And the Navy acknowledged that their orders were for the destroyers to steam in toward NV shore during the day, and to retire to sea at night.

The Navy did not answer questions having to do with *exactly how close* to North Vietnamese territory the destroyers were permitted to go. "We respect internationally recognized territorial limits," was as far as the naval press spokesman himself would go.

The *New York Times* hadn't been quite ready to run with its exposé of Operation 34-A, but the Gulf of Tonkin crisis accelerated their deadline and in a day and a half the story was everywhere circulated.

"United States military and intelligence advisers," began the lead on the story, "have been equipping a certain number of boats (exactly how many cannot be ascertained at this point) which in the guise of commercial fishing in the

Gulf of Tonkin have been actively engaged in attempting to stop North Vietnamese infiltration of the South. These '34-A' boats have been patrolling the North Vietnamese coast, arresting southbound traffic in an effort to interdict the smuggling of North Vietnamese insurgents and materiel to the South. In addition to the naval campaign to stop traffic and examine it, the South Vietnamese have recently engaged in direct military activity: strafing shore installations along the coast, up to—but not including—the North Vietnamese port of Haiphong."

A Dutch freighter intercepted an order broadcast to the fleet by Captain Herrick of the *Maddox*. It said that Sunday's attack on the Gulf had meant that North Vietnam had "thrown down the gauntlet," and that from this moment on, approaching gunboats from North Vietnam should be "treated as belligerents from first detection and must consider themselves as such." The Navy declined to confirm or deny that such orders had been issued by Captain Herrick.

An unnamed junior officer aboard the *Maddox* was quoted by the Associated Press in a long story on Monday. "We [the *Maddox* and the *C. Turner Joy*] were moving north, up the coast from the 17th parallel [which divides North and

South Vietnam]. We got to within 9.2 miles of the islands of Hon Mat and Hon Me, then we turned east at dusk, heading out to sea.

"Commodore Herrick called his staff up. He'd told us that two hours earlier, he learned that South Vietnamese 34-A boats had left Danang proceeding up the coast, 'right on our tail' was the way he put it. He didn't like that, so he had radioed the U.S. command recommending that they terminate the 34-A patrol. The recommendation went up to Admiral Sharp [Pacific Forces commander]. He overrode the captain, said he wouldn't stop the 34-A South Vietnamese. He told Herrick to keep his two destroyers 10 minutes north of 19 degrees latitude, between two geographical points, Charlie and Delta—that way we would avoid any possibility of interfering with 34-A. And then, the admiral pointed out, there was the further advantage: By removing ourselves from the 34-A patrol, we might succeed in drawing North Vietnamese PGMs [Guided Missile Patrol Boats] away from the area of 34-A operations."

The talkative young officer went on to the following day, August 4. "We learned through intelligence, just after midnight, that the South

Vietnamese 34-A boats had fired on two North Vietnamese targets, Cap Vinh Son where a radar station had been constructed by the Soviets, and Cua Ron, a security post. They exchanged fire, but that finished by 1 A.M. One hour later, Captain Herrick got us together again. He had a translation of radio intercepts. Hanoi had concluded that the 34-A operations against their installations were a part of the same maneuver we [the two U.S. destroyers] were engaged in. Herrick didn't say that any attacks were therefore planned on us, but he gave orders to radio the *Ticonderoga* [U.S. aircraft carrier, Seventh Fleet] to request air cover, just in case. It took a couple of hours for the people on the carrier to react, but at 4 A.M. they did: 'Request denied,' but they said they would stand by in the event anything happened. We continued routine, through dawn, when we turned back to do our regular daytime cruise along the North Vietnamese coast. We were within 13 miles of Hon Me at that point."

The *Times* broke up the story to report that early in the afternoon of August 4 the *Maddox* had reported to headquarters a "material deficiency" in the operation of its sonar devices. But soon after that a report was filed that repairs had been made. That question, of the efficiency of the sonar devices, had become critical.

"At 2:30 P.M.," the naval official of the *Maddox* continued his account, "we got word from our radar that unidentified surface vessels were par-alleling our track and that of *Turner Joy* [the second U.S. destroyer, making the run with the *Maddox* since the attack of August 2]. We flashed over to the *Turner Joy:* Did their radar show the same thing? Negative. Our radar man kept looking, and conceded that the contact was 'intermittent.' "

It was several hours later, after dark, that the situation grew menacing, said the young officer, continuing his story. "We were at that point near the center of the Gulf of Tonkin, 65 miles from the nearest land, and we were headed south-east. That's when Captain Herrick concluded that the maneuvers of the unidentified vessels gave rise to the suspicion that an attack by them was imminent. At about 8 P.M., our radar de-tected two unidentified vessels 36.4 miles away, traveling in our direction at a speed of 33 knots. We flashed over again to the *Turner Joy,* but their radar didn't have equivalent findings. In any case, maximum boiler power was ordered for both destroyers. A few minutes later, our radar reported that the unidentified vessel (we lost the other one) was now 37 miles away. But five minutes later, he reported that two *additional* radar contacts had been made, in the same general area.

"Captain Herrick concluded that a trap was being set up. The *Turner Joy* still had no contacts, but our radar showed the three contacts merging into a single contact, at a range of 32 miles. And then, at 8:15, we got it over the radio through another intercept that an attack on the destroyers was imminent. We proceeded to head south at full speed. At that point we had still another radar contact report: two unidentified surface vessels and three unidentified aircraft. But we learned quickly that these must be the U.S. fighter aircraft launched from the *Ticonderoga* to give us protection.

"We felt the crisis was coming in real soon when at 9:30 our radar reported additional unidentified vessels, all of them now closing in rapidly on us at speeds in excess of 40 knots. Then—suddenly!—our radar man reported that the contacts had—'evaporated' was the word he used.

"So what we did, Captain Herrick asked the

Ticonderoga to instruct one of the aircraft flying over us to investigate one of the unidentified vessels, which we figured were now only 13 miles away. The aircraft went to the indicated location but reported back that it had seen— nothing. But meanwhile, the vessel had reappeared on our radar screen.

"The captain thought it prudent to take preemptive action. Accordingly he ordered fire at one of the unidentified vessels, and the *Turner Joy* began to fire at another one, on the right. Both of the targets were geographical coordinates—based on the projections of the approach when last sighted on the radar of the *Maddox,* only a few minutes earlier.

"At this point, our sonar reported a torpedo in motion. We flashed the news to *Turner Joy.* By 10 o'clock P.M. both of us reported continuous torpedo attacks, and both of us engaged in defensive counterfire. The *Turner Joy* changed course to evade the torpedo we reported. The *Joy* reported sighting wake. But, it's true, the *Turner Joy*'s sonar operator said he never picked up a 'torpedo noise.' Sometime between 9:30 and 10:25, aircraft from *Ticonderoga,* at the request of the *Turner Joy,* began strafing the general area. Meanwhile our sonar reported still another torpedo, and once again we warned *Joy.* And then at 10:15 we reported that we had avoided all torpedoes and had sunk one of the attacking craft. We sank another one at 10:42, and at 10:52 the radar and sonar indicated we were again under attack. It got pretty hot, and a half hour later *Turner Joy* told us they had had five torpedoes fired at them and that she was planning to ram one of the North Vietnamese boats. At midnight, *Joy* was still looking for a patrol boat to ram, but their radio seemed to show that one of the enemy boats had acciden- tally sunk one of its own boats.

"It was hell. It was crazy. The blackest black outside I ever did see, and muggy, hot."

10:50 P.M.

"JUST THAT ONE FLASH! TURN IT OFF NOW! OFF! GODDAMNIT OFF! QUICK!" *The search beam went off and the speedboat swerved quickly to the left at 40 knots and was well away when they saw the tracer bullets firing at the spot where the beam had briefly been flashed. The spotlight operator shouted out:* "Here we go again. Keep your head low." *He zoomed past the destroyer at a speed not much less than a torpedo would run at. The roar of the engine cut through the aimless firing from the destroyers, and through the noise of circling aircraft above. One thousand meters past, the operator turned the boat sharply, the salt spray drenching him and his companion.* "THE RADIO NOW TAPE NUMBER THREE QUICK!" *As he roared back toward the* Maddox *he saw the tiny green electric pulsations: they were transmitting.* "GOOD GOOD ENOUGH. CUT IT NOW! CAAAAARREFUL!" *The operator made a sharp right turn to avoid a probing searchlight from one of the vessels.* "ONE MORE RUN, JUST ONE MORE." *He aimed his racer now obliquely toward the stern of the* Turner Joy. *He caromed toward its starboard flank and then turned to leave, their wakes a mere twenty yards separated. His companion was lying in front of the wheel, his instruments protected from the salt spray by the deck over the little cutty cabin.* "ALL RIGHT NOW. WE HEAD BACK. PREPARE CASSETTE THREE FOR TRANSMISSION AT 1124." *Thank God it's the blackest night of the year, the operator thought as he eased the power down, reducing his speed to 30 knots. Four hours. He fastened the earphones and kept careful view of his tiny compass with the red-light illumination. Steady on that radio signal, 2171 kHz Danang Lightship. Steady as she goes.*

The President convened his National Security Council at noon, which corresponded to midnight Gulf of Tonkin time.

He gave his staff an up-to-date digest on what had happened, and ordered the Chairman of the Joint Chiefs to prepare a list of appropriate targets for a retaliatory strike. At this moment he was interrupted. He read the dispatch his aide had brought in, and then spoke to the assembly:

"Good news from the fighting front, gennelmen. No casualties on our vessels, and our defense aircraft from the *Ticonderoga* are right now illuminating the area and preparing to attack the enemy surface craft. The two destroyers count twenty-two torpedoes that have been fired at them, an' they figure two enemy craft sunk so far in the engagement."

The Chairman of the Joint Chiefs, who had arrived prepared, had the floor.

But a half hour later the President was interrupted again. He read the fresh dispatch, and his face contorted in concentration. His staff looked up eagerly for the latest news.

"A little confusin'. The *Maddox* reported they

saw a flicker of light from enemy searchlight, but there was no enemy fire. But the *Joy* reported fire from automatic weapons while being illuminated by searchlights.

"What's confusin' is the *Turner Joy.* They claim to have sunk three vessels but now they want the Commander, Pacific Operations, to initiate a thorough reconnaissance in daylight by aircraft. Same thing with the *Maddox.* Herrick wants a 'complete revaluation before any further action is taken.' Anyway, the firing is over, far as we can tell. Bob," the President turned to Secretary McNamara, "you better go meet up with the Joints Chiefs and with Cy Vance, go over all this stuff and plan the raids we've ordered."

At 5 P.M., McNamara called to inform the President that Herrick had cabled. "DETAILS OF ACTION PRESENT A CONFUSING PICTURE, ALTHOUGH CERTAIN THAT ORIGINAL AMBUSH WAS BONA FIDE." McNamara then called Admiral Sharp in Hawaii and told him to be "damned sure that the attack had taken place." Admiral Sharp radioed orders to Captain Herrick on the *Maddox* to confirm "absolutely" that the two ships had been attacked. Herrick was ordered to relay his findings

to the *Ticonderoga,* to ensure prompt forward-
ing to Honolulu.

At 5:23 Washington time, Secretary
McNamara received a telephone report form
Admiral Sharp. He was certain that the attack
had actually occurred, citing the radio intercept
intelligence as circumstantial evidence of a con-
clusive character. He was told by McNamara to
collect debris "to substantiate" the attack.

At 6 P.M., August 4, 1964, President Johnson
opened a National Security Council meeting to
advise that he had ordered retaliatory bomb-
ings; that he had issued a press release announcing the second incident in the Gulf of
Tonkin; and that at 6:15 he would meet with the
congressional leaders to inform them that a
strike had been ordered.

At 10:40 P.M. the first planes left off the *Ticonderoga* and *Constellation,* bound on a bombing
mission in North Vietnam. The first U.S. combat
mission in Indochina.

Ten minutes after the bombers took off,
McNamara called the President again. Captain
Herrick had reported to Honolulu that the fighter
aircraft had not located any targets; that the
Maddox had scored no known hits, and had

never positively identified any boat. He had noted that it was "probable" that a torpedo had been detected on the sonar. "The first boat to close on *Maddox* probably fired torpedo at *Maddox* which was heard but not seen. All subsequent *Maddox* torpedo reports are doubtful in that it is suspected that sonarman was hearing ship's own propeller beat." President Johnson told McNamara that in his judgment there was no doubt that there had been an attack, and that in any event, as McNamara knew, the bombing mission was on its way.

At 1:15 P.M. our planes dropped bombs on North Vietnam, smashing a patrol base and support facilities at Quang Khe.

The next day at noon, on Wednesday August 5, President Johnson sent to Congress a resolution requesting congressional advice and consent. It became known as the Gulf of Tonkin Resolution.

The Resolution would authorize him to "take all necessary measures" to repel attacks against U.S. forces and to "prevent further aggression" as well as to determine when "peace and security" in the area had been attained.

The Resolution went to the Armed Services and Foreign Relations committees of the Senate for joint hearing. At this hearing, Senator Wayne Morse announced that an informant had advised him that the *Maddox* was actively coordinating with South Vietnamese 34-A raids, and that that informant doubted whether the second attack had actually taken place at all! Senator Morse demanded to see the ship's logs.

On August 6, the combined committees heard Secretaries Rusk and McNamara for one hour and forty minutes. They denied charges by Senator Morse that the *Maddox* was an accomplice in the 34-A raids, and denied that the *Maddox* had violated North Vietnamese waters.

On August 7, Senator William Fulbright, acting as floor leader in favor of the Gulf of Tonkin Resolution, dissuaded Senator Gaylord Nelson from submitting an amendment that would require congressional approval before the dispatch of a land army to South Vietnam. Senator Fulbright said he did not contemplate such military action, though he agreed that the wording of the Resolution permitted the President to do what he wished.

At 1:15 P.M., EDT, the Senate, culminating eight hours and forty minutes of debate stretching over three days, passed the Resolution by a vote of 88 to 2. The House, earlier in the day, had approved the Resolution by a vote of 416–0.

There was no communication between President Johnson and Abe Fortas during the next week. But Mr. and Mrs. Fortas were guests at a dinner in mid-August for Premier Bjarni Benediktsson of Iceland. As he shook the President's hand on the receiving line, Fortas commented, "Good action you took on the Gulf of Tonkin incident, Mr. President."

"Ah thought you'd approve of that, Abe. Got to tell those people ther're some things they cain't get away with."

"Yes, sir."

★ ★ ★ ★ ★ ★ ★ ★ ★ ★ ★

Chapter Twenty-Two

AUGUST 8, 1964
DANANG, SOUTH VIETNAM

It was 2:10 A.M. in Danang, seventy-two hours after the end of the second engagement. Blackford Oakes snapped off the short-wave radio on the bookshelf of his small round office. From the outside it looked somewhat like one half of a water silo, but with a tufted thatch roof. Inside was strictly G.I. utilitarian. A few chairs, a cot to sleep on if it got too late to trudge back to BOQ. A jangle of electronic machinery. A large safe, a desk, a typewriter, a card table at which Alphonse Juilland sat, and a refrigerator and hot plate.

Blackford looked up. "Well, Alphonse, we did it. The Senate has voted, and the House vote earlier today was unanimous. Nothing like democratic government, no sir. Ye shall know the truth, and the truth shall set you free. *Evidemment.*" He yawned and then said, "We've been on duty all night, but nobody's going to call us at this hour, I'd guess. Go for a drink?"

Alphonse nodded, with his usual rather formal smile. Blackford knew he would nod. Alphonse Juilland almost always nodded, no matter what was proposed. But if a drink was proposed, he always nodded.

"Scotch?"

"Vous avez vodka?"

"Sure. With what?—Why am I asking you? You will say, 'With not too much water.' " Blackford poured out the two drinks and took some ice cubes from the refrigerator.

"Do you mind if I speak frankly, Mr. Oakes?"

Once Blackford had asked Alphonse to call him by his first name. A second time, he had asked him with some emphasis to call him by his first name. Both times Alphonse Juilland had nodded appreciatively, subsequently referring to him as "Mr. Oakes." Blackford would not ask him a third time. If it made Alphonse comfortable this way, Blackford figured he could live with it. "I guess I'd have to answer that question carefully, Alphonse. I'd mind, for instance, if you said that, frankly, you were a North Vietnamese agent."

Again the same smile. "You like to joke, Mr. Oakes. But you know that I am not likely to be an agent of the same people who killed my father and my sister. . . . No, my question has to do with intelligence practices, about which I know very little. I think of myself as a well-read schoolteacher, but of intelligence I am ignorant."

"What are you getting at, Alphonse?" Blackford wasn't impatient. In fact he didn't want to go to sleep. A little badinage with Alphonse, even serious badinage, might be a relaxing little workout after four hours of concentrated listening to the short-wave radio. But he did know that Alphonse had a Gallic disposition for circumlocution, so he thought he'd just help him along . . .

"Well, Mr. Oakes, you and I carried off this operation. Many people helped assemble the necessary artifices, and of course Mr. Montana was—critically instrumental in their design. But the assemblymen, the mechanics, they knew nothing, and know nothing, of the purpose of equipping the Stiletto in the way it was equipped. The impression, after all, was carefully cultivated that the speedboat was going off on some kind of mission with the 34-A's against a mainland target. That means, one: the gentleman, whoever it was, who gave you the orders to do what we did, two: Major Montana, three: you, and four: I—we are the only ones with direct knowledge of the use the boat was put to."

"That's right. And we could have used a fifth." Blackford took a swig of his scotch. "On a few of those passes Sunday we could have done with a third hand. Steering that thing, broadcasting your threatening radio dispatches—good thing you speak Vietnamese like a native—sowing those sound buoys, riding those wakes aren't something I'd want to do again even with your expert help. Thank God for our two dress rehearsals. And for the blackness of August second."

"Yes, Mr. Oakes; there were two or three times when I too felt, well, a bit—overworked?"

"Yes, but not underpaid, I hope you will agree."

Alphonse Juilland bowed his head, in acknowledgment of the very special purse he had received for duty indisputably hazardous. "No, my point is unrelated, Mr. Oakes, to the shortage of extra crew help on Sunday night, and certainly unrelated to the compensation. It has to do, as I began saying, with intelligence practices. The gentleman who gave you orders, whoever he is, is obviously high in government and is secure. Major Montana is a very considerable national asset, I take it, judging from his inventiveness with the instruments we needed to conduct our own mission. And although I do not know the details of his responsibilities at Nakhon Phanom, I deduce that his role is most important."

Blackford said nothing, and now only diddled with his drink.

"As for you, the third of the four insiders, I can only assume that you too are of considerable value to the . . . Agency. And that you are completely trusted, or else this—delicate assignment would not have been given to you, am I correct?"

Blackford now knew where Alphonse Juilland was going, and decided on Operation Compression.

"Dear Alphonse, there is much that I do for my country that I would just as soon not do. For instance, our mission on Sunday night. Much of what I do, I do because I have committed myself to following instructions, and I do follow instructions except when or if—it has not happened to me in thirteen years—such instructions are morally intolerable, which last Sunday's exercise was not. Though it does serve to instruct us on what political ethicists might call 'some of the limitations of democratic government.' But I would not ask you, or anyone else, to serve as a confederate in any enterprise which subsequently required your elimination. That's what you are coming to, isn't it?"

"Well," Alphonse Juilland smiled, a little more broadly than usual, "yes, I was headed in the direction of asking you that question. Not knowing much about what I call intelligence practices, I permitted myself to wonder whether I was now not merely expendable, but . . . dangerous, so long as I was alive? I have to admit that—simply as a precaution—I *did* leave a letter with my cousin in France, who is a solicitor—"

Blackford banged his drink down. "Oh shit, Alphonse. Now let me tell you something. One: Get that letter back. Two: Burn it. Three: Pretend you didn't tell me about its existence. Because we're ready to ride out the whole thing with you as a confederate. But we're not willing to share presidential secrets with you and your cousin and a piece of paper. You could, after all, die of a heart attack tonight. And what then does your cousin do with that letter?"

"Ah, Mr. Oakes, please do not be upset. My cousin has been instructed to burn the letter on receipt of a telegram from me—"

"Saying what?"

Alphonse smiled again. This time he sipped heavily the vodka before answering. "You desire to know the exact code?"

"I desire to know it, and I desire *you*"—he looked at his watch—"to send the correct message as soon as the telegraph office opens. But in the event you do *not* last until six A.M.—I am speaking of an Act of God—I desire you"— Blackford extended a writing pad and pencil to Alphonse—"to write on that pad the name and address of your cousin and the coded message you are supposed to send him."

Alphonse smiled, and bowed his head. "I feel in a bargaining mood, Mr. Oakes."

Blackford looked up sharply, quizzically.

"I will do as you say," said Alphonse, "provided you give me another drink of vodka."

★ ★ ★ ★ ★ ★ ★ ★ ★ ★ ★ ★

Chapter Twenty-Three

Le Duc Sy made a most earnest attempt to persuade the military court that Squadron Captain Thanh-Lang could not have known that Le Duc Sy had completely fabricated his conversations with Colonel Giap, that he never doubted that Hanoi had actually ordered the raid on the American destroyers.

"I lied to him. It is that simple, comrades. He had been taking orders from me for over four weeks and he simply assumed that anything I passed along to him was in effect an order from Hanoi."

Had Captain Thanh-Lang used the verification procedures stipulated?

"No, comrade judges. It is true he did not do this. But these verification orders had to do with military initiatives by Captain Thanh-Lang's squadron, and he never took an initiative, he merely followed orders he thought originated with headquarters. It isn't that he was remiss in regard to a detail to which he was accustomed. Never before having received an order to go on the offensive in the Gulf, he just assumed that my having issued that order, given the authority vested in me on my arrival, was sufficient. And of course I told him in some detail about the order to me from Hanoi. He had no doubts."

The court ordered Thanh-Lang demoted to the rank of private in the infantry, assigned to help to carry supplies south on the Trail, with permission to reapply to serve in the navy in twenty-four months.

At Hoa Lo prison in Hanoi, Bui Tin offered his friend Le Duc Sy a cigarette. Sy took one and joked that now he could avoid worry that smoking would hasten his death. He took from his pocket the letter Bui Tin had promised to accept from him, to be mailed through channels in Singapore to Lao Dai. Bui Tin put it in his briefcase and took out a bottle of brandy and two paper cups. As he poured he said:

"You should be clear on this point. It is that if I had been one of the judges, I'd have passed the same sentence. Your recklessness at school was punished by flogging. In the field it was punished by unnecessary exposure and perhaps even unnecessary deaths, though I do not conceal that what you did was, yes, reckless, but also very courageous. What you did on Sunday in the Gulf was courageous. But you jeopardized not only yourself but the diplomatic timetable of Ho Chi Minh, and on this the Independence Movement depends."

"Did you hear me ask for mercy?"

"No. I doubt you'd have asked for mercy if you *had* been carrying out orders personally given to you by Ho Chi Minh." He raised his cup and drank deeply, as did Le Duc Sy. "I mourn not your removal from the scene—the days and months and years ahead of us are too important to accommodate eccentric misbehavior. I might even say, Le Duc Sy, that what you did was a form of exhibitionism, taking on two U.S. destroyers and precipitating a diplomatic crisis."

"Well, what about the North Vietnamese exhibitionists who did it on Tuesday?"

"There was no attack on Tuesday. That is all U.S. invention."

"You are telling me we made no attacks against the American destroyers on Tuesday? You should know, Bui Tin, that friends who have visited me during the past forty-eight hours do not get *all* their news from Hanoi Radio. They also get it from BBC."

"BBC has no reason to question the official American account."

"Very well. But every time I think of those American hypocrites arming the enemy, interfering with commercial shipping without any thought given to their precious freedom of the seas, and then, on Sunday, attempting a physical invasion of Hon Me! If *only* I had hit one of those fuckers with one of those torpedoes and seen their ship go gurgling down! Ah, let's drink to that!"

Bui Tin raised his cup. "We drink to your last drink, Le Duc Sy." The guards were at the door.

Bui Tin heard the fusillade while sitting at his desk. He closed his eyes for the briefest moment. Then he leaned over and took from his briefcase the letter his late comrade had written to Lao Dai. He could not send it unexamined, and it even crossed his mind that it was surprising that Le Duc Sy thought he would do so. He opened the envelope after exposing it to the steam escaping from the teakettle. He read quickly the opening paragraphs, which were professions of great, ardent, perpetual love. And then:

"My darling, you must know that tomorrow morning I leave on a very hazardous expedition. It is always just possible that I shan't return. If that should be, communications from me will end. If so, remember that you can memorialize me only by making every effort to advance the great cause of independence, even as I am doing. With all my love, my darling Lao Dai."

Bui Tin picked up the telephone.

"Get me Colonel Giap . . . Giap? Bui Tin. I wish to read you from the letter written by Le Du Sy to Lao Dai."

After he had read the passage he said to him, "He was reckless and he paid a price. But he was truly loyal. In a few days you will—of course—inform Lao Dai that Le Duc Sy died an honorable death for his country?"

"Of course, Bui Tin."

Senator Goldwater was always faintly amused by intrigue no matter how serious the matters dealt with. Now it was a new communication from General X, one that had not come in the customary way. First, the telephone had rung. As usual, the telephone request came to be put through to Bill Baroody. But then General X had said to Baroody that he would be sending a personal communication by messenger which must go directly to Senator Goldwater. Baroody asked how the envelope would be identified. It would be on writing paper of Washington's Hay-Adams Hotel. Baroody told the receptionist at headquarters that a messenger coming in with a personal envelope to the senator on Hay-Adams stationery was to be sent up to the inner sanctum.

Now he took the letter into the office next door, where Senator Goldwater was struggling to adjust the digital recall mechanism on a ham radio set. Baroody handed him the envelope. "General X. Says only for you." Goldwater sat down, opened the envelope, and read the letter silently. He handed it to Baroody and went back to his radio set. Baroody read it:

Dear Senator:

The passage of the Tonkin Gulf Resolution means, as far as I am concerned, that the United States is at war with North Vietnam, never mind the waffle. Anything

306 WILLIAM F. BUCKLEY, JR.

the President now does is authorized de jure, authorized by Congress, and what he decides to do is wholly his responsibility. But since I believe that we are at war I can no longer take a political view of my responsibilities. He is now my Commander in Chief *in wartime.* Accordingly, with continuing high regard, I close my final communication to you. With all good wishes,

    X.

"Eggs says we're at war, Bill." The Senator was bent over, observing the effects on the panel of his switching the toggle up front with his right hand.

"Are we, Barry? You ought to know. You voted in favor of the Tonkin Gulf Resolution."

"Yup," Goldwater said. "We're at war. But Lyndon's not going to make any big moves before the election. And I'm not sure he's going to make any decisive moves *after* November. We'll have to lay relatively low on the Vietnam issue from now on. Don't, really, have much choice." For once he didn't end a sentence directed at his chief brain truster with the interrogatory, "Don't you think so?" Baroody made this unnecessary:

"Yes, I agree. We're at war—and maybe at a standstill."

BOOK TWO

★ ★ ★ ★ ★ ★ ★ ★ ★ ★

Chapter Twenty-Four

SEPTEMBER 10, 1964
SAIGON, SOUTH VIETNAM

It was in early September that Blackford, Rufus, and Tucker next met in Saigon. The political scene had considerably changed since what now went in the military-diplomatic trade by the name of Tonkin 2, distinguishing the events of August 4, which brought on the Gulf of Tonkin Resolution, from the patrol boat raid of August 2. Although President Johnson's retaliatory bombing of the installations at Quang Khe hadn't been followed up by more U.S. bombing, there were plentiful signs of accelerated military activity. Most conspicuous was the construction of a massive air base near Saigon. And the Thai jets that under the guidance of the CIA had been furtively harassing illegal traffic from the North down the Ho Chi Minh Trail were now regularly foraging for targets along the Trail, and here and there engaging in direct strikes. These were not greatly productive, granted, given the route's natural camouflage.

Camouflage. That, Tucker Montana, hard at work outside Savannakhet, would hope soon to penetrate, after Operation Igloo White was operative. At Nakhon Phanom the great old barn-like building originally commissioned by the French was being reconstructed by a heavy concentration of U.S. soldiers operating with the engineering corps. A moving-picture camera recording the day-to-day activity in the area of the big square building would have caught an occasional Asiatic face, but mostly it was sweat-soaked young Americans carrying materiel into the barn while others furnished new roofing and labored to beef up the structure. A candid movie of the events would have suggested a great army enterprise going on during the summer in swampy country in Louisiana or Florida.

Tucker Montana unbuttoned a second button on his shirt and rolled its sleeves high on his arm. He was eager to talk about Igloo.

It was the first time the three had met since

Tonkin 2, the historic Tonkin raid against two U.S. destroyers. Conducted by one heavily camouflaged Stiletto 26-footer manufactured by the Sea Ray Company in Florida capable, with its 350-horsepower Mercury, of traveling 45–50 knots.

"I got to say," Tucker laughed heartily, "when I read that the destroyers had 'seen'—'felt'—'heard'—'experienced'?—I forget all the words they used—*twenty-two* torpedoes, I thought, Oh God, Black and that Frenchman are overdoing it! Course, the next day that twenty-two torpedoes they spotted was down to twelve, and then down to four; don't know where it is right now—one attack by a water-skier? Damn, but those sonar-delusion containers did a nice job! Kind of sorry we don't have any more use for those babies; I'm kind of proud of the way they were designed, what you say, Rufus? And I *knew* that conventional mobile amplifier would do the job on the sonars; you weren't all that sure, now, were you, Blackford?"

"Gentlemen."

Rufus did not approve of talk about the mechanics of operations that had been consummated. It was hardly a question of security. They were in a Saigon safe house, and all three of them had been intimately engaged in the operation, and one of them executed it. It was habit. *Habit! habit! habit!* Blackford had once complained; but he was younger then, and now he knew that training the instinct, the reflex, even— the cultivating of correct *habits* was a part of what Alphonse Juilland called "intelligence practices." And the habit of not discussing, even among confederates, a deep covert operation once it had been accomplished was one of those habits intelligence agents were supposed to get into, as if ignoring a covert operation heightened the chances that the enemy would also ignore it. Blackford permitted himself to dwell on the irony that the "enemy," in this case, was the Congress of the United States. The gooks knew *they* hadn't done whatever it was that had been done. . . . .

Blackford softened the apparent reproach by reminding Tucker that he had only been conscripted into formal intelligence duty in June, "just three months ago."

"Yup. Before that I was just a soldier of fortune, Black."

Rufus said nothing about this soldier of fortune's basic training, building the atom bomb.

They spoke of scheduling, and of the nature

and function of several innovative devices being constructed. In the Gulf, 34-A was now, of course, an open operation, and such camouflage as Blackford directed be used was for the purpose of foiling only North Vietnamese artillery, not of fooling the AP or Reuters. The little armed "fishing boats," closely backed by the Seventh Fleet, were on day and night war alert. Rufus summed it up: "There is no difference between how the 34-A-equipped boats are behaving at sea right now and how they would behave at sea if we were in an official shooting war. Scrupulous attention paid to territorial boundaries is a concern of the past. The trouble is, the Viets—our Viets—know that however much of the contraband they succeed in stopping at sea, the stuff is getting through." He looked at Tucker. "Coming in your side door, isn't it?"

"Yup. And there's nothing much we can do about it, unless the President orders a few U.S. divisions to come on in and take those passes and hold them down. No, nothing we can do about it until those Spikebuoys come in and get set up—the sensors, the acoustic numbers. I've already got most of the preliminary model computers set up, and I got an aide who is lining up analysts and rapid-fire interpreters—not all that easy to get, Vietnamese–English. He's having to settle, for the time being, for a couple of shifts of Vietnamese-to-French-to-English. See, two interpreters listen to the radio voices, the gook puts it quickly into French, the second guy, American, puts it into English.

"My goal is"—dramatically, Tucker pulled a stopwatch from his pocket, depressing the lever with a highly exaggerated arm motion, like the starter at an automobile race—"my goal is *three minutes, thirty seconds* from the time the guy *says it,* to the time the pilot gets his instructions.

"The NVA guy, on the Trail, says to the soldiers sitting down eating their lunch, 'Get moving, assholes' "—he looked up at Rufus. "Sorry, Rufus. The NVA officer says, 'Come on, gang, wiggle your tail: We got thirty trucks need getting down before dark.'

"That's translated into French in forty seconds . . .

"Into English in forty seconds . . .

"Typed, thirty seconds.

"Operations officer reads it, decides affirmative for action required, forty-five seconds.

"Gives estimated location of the caravan.

"Sees on the screen which sensor was activated when the message was recorded, forty seconds.

"Radios Air Control target and location.

"Air Control checks location against placement of aircraft, and either gives the attack order to one that's orbiting in the area, or else zips the signal to a bomber pilot on the ready.

"Five minutes, maybe?

"No, Montana, not five minutes—*three minutes, thirty seconds.* Or, you just pick up the sound of trucks going by and the sensors pick up those sounds and the calculations begin: How fast are they traveling? In which direction? How long will it take before they reach Point A? Zap!—They're hit by our planes!"

Tucker Montana looked up triumphantly. "That's what Igloo's going to look like. It will be a few months before it's operational but only a couple of weeks before we test out here the essential parts. We'll have a few dozen each of the ground-piercing and parachute units, drop them, spread them about in a tight area, get a couple of planes up there, connect up with the computers. Igloo White in miniature."

Tucker was exuberant. The whole of his six-foot-one-inch frame seemed to tremble with excitement. He fondled technological terms and used acronyms to the point of eluding Rufus's understanding; even Blackford, an engineer by training, was sometimes left behind. Neither interrupted Tucker even as he dug deeper and deeper into the bowels of the paraphernalia of Igloo White. Strange. Suddenly Blackford understood. He was listening to a soliloquy. Tucker Montana was letting out in a torrential stream what for so many years he had suppressed. It was a fire storm of technical and inventive ingenuity. An opera singer finally recovered from lung cancer, singing in a shower.

Suddenly he stopped. A little embarrassed, Tucker asked, "Did I go on too long on this?"

Rufus replied, "Tucker, I can say only two things. One: You did not go on too long; and two: I did not follow everything you said. But then it isn't so very important that I should know how it is all going to work. It is only important that I know that it will work. And you have certainly convinced me that you are confident on this point."

Tucker turned. "How 'bout you, Black? Follow me?"

"Mostly," Blackford said. "Though I worry. What I'm up to in the Gulf, combined with what you're up to on the Trail. Doesn't it remind you of the Maginot Line?"

Rufus: "Do you forget, Blackford? The Germans did not penetrate the Maginot Line in 1940. They went around it."

"I remember that, Rufus. But Igloo White and Operation 34-A are less even than a Maginot Line. And the question becomes not so much, How many of them do we stop? as, How many of them get through? Right, Tucker?"

"You right, Black. You right. By 1944 we had command of the skies over Europe. But the German rockets got through. You sure as hell right about that. . . . But that doesn't mean they aren't in for one kick-ass surprise when Igloo White gets going. And at some point maybe, who knows, they got to worry about how many reserves are they going to use up. Wouldn't make much sense, would it, to fight to the last man? Till there are no North Vietnamese left?"

Blackford half-smiled—but there was not much humor in it. Rufus stood up. He had a lunch date with the ambassador. He would meet Blackford the following morning and together they would go to Danang to survey the situation there, and meet again here "the day after tomorrow. In forty-eight hours." Spontaneously, both Blackford and Tucker looked down at their watches, as if to begin the forty-eight-hour countdown. They laughed. Rufus smiled, said good night, and left. Tucker walked into the little kitchen and Blackford heard his voice. "Any safe hootch in this-here safe house, Black?"

"The Agency has been known to look after creature comforts." He walked aimlessly, patrolling the parlor. "Besides, how do we know— maybe tomorrow the safe house will set the scene for a seduction of a North Vietnamese lieutenant general?"

Blackford could hear Tucker opening and closing cabinets. "A *he* general?"

"No. A *she* general."

"We got people in the Agency who can seduce a he general? I wouldn't mind meeting that lady. Ah! I found it! We got . . . scotch, looks like rye or something, gin . . . vodka, two-three bottles of wine. You liking?"

"Scotch. And a little water. Ice, of course. I'll get the ice." He walked into the kitchen.

At lunch, around the corner at a little Chinese restaurant, Tucker was talking, relaxed. He sipped his coffee, noisily. Then he went silent for a time, staring at the table. When he looked up, he said, "Rufus ever discuss with you my past history?"

"Not specifically. I know, of course, about the whole Huk business. And I was there when General Taylor said you hadn't quite leveled with the Army when you filled out the forms. He said something about your work at . . . was it Los Alamos? But I don't know what you did there."

"What I did there was to help to build the bomb, Black. In fact—I've never said this to anybody, but I suppose it's sitting there, in some notebook somewhere; I don't care if it is, but it's a fact—I hit on the way to trigger the bomb. That problem had held up the whole operation for over three months. It was just luck, but in fact the engineers went to work on my design. And then I guess this you don't know. I was there."

"You were where?"

"Hiroshima."

"What do you mean, you were there? *At* Hiroshima?"

"No no. I was on the *Enola Gay.* I was nursing our baby until we dropped it. Saw that all the dials were reading right.

"Then there were the big celebrations. You never saw *anybody* celebrate the way those physicists celebrated at Alamos. Looked like University of Texas football coaches the day they win the Conference, after upsetting Oklahoma. Made the crowd at Times Square look like a retirement home. Well, hell, they'd been working on it for two and a half years.

"I celebrated too. Then, beginning the next few days, the reports began coming in. And of course we had a clinical interest in what happened, like a doctor poking around human organs. That's what it was, really—an autopsy."

He looked down into his coffee cup. "But they were all affected by it, and so was I—as the monks would say, *a fortiori.* A lot—because I was twenty years old, not forty, fifty, sixty. Then I started to read—I was stuck at Los Alamos, under Army orders; my military rank was corporal. I didn't have enough points to get out until December. So I read, and saw the literature on Hiroshima and Nagasaki begin to pile up, and after a time I saw myself as what I had been, a little cog, but who knows, maybe an important one, in a people-killing business out of all proportion to anything ever done before."

"And?"

"And inside, I went gray—and panicked."

Somebody had put a coin in the jukebox, and

the machine blared out a sibilant Chinese melody that seemed to amble about without any musical narrative, although the noise was deafening. Blackford hoped it wouldn't abort Tucker's narrative. Finally, the music ended. Tucker picked himself up but spoke, at first, telegraphically. . . .

"Got out, finally, in December, went back to San Antonio, stayed with my mother, talked with Fr. Enrique, Mexican-American priest who sort of looked after me after my father was killed. Why not a monastery? he said. Why not. I tried that, was happy, really, but never was able to talk about Hiroshima, and nobody knew what I had done during the war. Only the abbot, and he talked to me only when I wanted to talk to him, and that was only twice. He told me that the atom bomb was, like everything else, God's design. That to condemn it out of sight was to lose moral perspective. Well, you know the arguments, there'd have been a million U.S. casualties if we'd had to land in Japan, that kind of thing. But even if that's so, it doesn't mean you want to work on the thing that killed a hundred thousand men and women and kids and scarred up as many more. I got involved with a woman, who later got involved with me, and I left the

monastery and decided I'd look around myself,
to find the perspectives. So I went back into the
Army, this time as a simple soldier, and fought
in Korea, killed plenty of people, including a couple with my bayonet. And then, in the Philippines, helped organize a lot of killing, though
nothing on the scale of Hiroshima. I myself killed
forty-one Huks one night—"

"I know about that. It got you the Medal of
Honor."

"Yeah, and when I heard the news I told the
White House guy over the telephone that if there
was any reference in the citation to Los Alamos,
I'd walk out, I didn't care what Ike's reaction
would be. I can understand necessary killing. I
can understand Igloo White and 34-A; I'm no
pacifist, God knows. The bomb is something
else. If I have regained any perspective, it isn't
quite the way the abbot had in mind. Before I'd
use the bomb I'd surrender. Or maybe just kill
myself."

Blackford understood. He was familiar with
the arguments, had run into people (including
defecting Soviets) who took that position. He
simply thought them—it—wrong.

Tucker watched Blackford's face. His col-

league, his companion. He drank down his coffee. "Ever had any of the same problems?"

"No. Not about the bomb. But more and more
I'm feeling them about . . . enterprises that don't
work. Waste. I was involved in the Bay of Pigs.
Result? Confirmed the loss of Cuba, several
hundred men killed, more than that tortured. I
know all about the need to take risks, but I am
less patient with futile enterprises."

"Like this one?"

Blackford was startled. He had reservations
about the policies of the Johnson administration, but hadn't voiced them.

"I don't doubt that the policy of containment
is the correct policy, though if it leaned to liberation, I'd like it better."

"I didn't ask you that. I don't even say we
couldn't keep it"—his pointed finger slashed his
neck like a straight razor—"from happening,
keep the North from taking over South Vietnam.
But I'm wondering whether we *will* keep it from
happening. Goldwater's not going to be our next
President."

Blackford said he'd just as soon not talk about
it. "I haven't come to any conclusions on what
you're going into, frankly. My rule has always

been—based on the assumption that the gang up there probably knows more than I do—Do what you're told to do. Unless it's something you can't do and go on living with yourself, in which case you disobey orders, or you resign. In one case that happened to me. Only I didn't resign, I was canned." He smiled. And, however briefly, he thought back on his decision, and on his friend, the Soviet physicist . . .

They talked more. Tucker spoke of the days, as a boy, when his mother worked overtime so that she could build his own little library, and about his tutor at St. Mary's, and about the time he tried to enlist when he was only sixteen.

"I was sixteen the day of Pearl Harbor," Blackford commented.

"Sixteen the day of Pearl Harbor?" Tucker stood up, glass in hand. "Goddamn! We were born on *the same day*!" They drank to that, also.

Tucker asked about Blackford's youth, and so he told Tucker about the divorce, when he was fifteen, of his mother and father, about his father's life as an airplane gypsy, about his mother's remarriage to a titled Brit, about an unpleasant term at a strict boarding school in England, which he left just before Pearl Harbor, about completing school in Scarsdale and going

from there to the Air Force ("Dad's contacts
didn't exactly slow me down when when I ap-
plied for flight school"), about hot engagements
with Nazi fighter planes in the winter of 1945
before he got sick, and about going to Yale after
that, and meeting . . .

"Her name is Sally Partridge. Correction. Her
name now is Sally Partridge Morales."

"Married? . . . Happily?"

"Was—her husband is dead. The question
now is: Will we get married when the Mexican
mourning period is over. She wants me to quit
the Agency."

"Because it's inconvenient for her?"

"No—though it is that. More. She thinks the
Agency is a kind of Strangelovish organization
that's prolonging the Cold War."

"God. I assume she has *other* virtues." He
chuckled.

Blackford raised his glass to his lips. "Yes.
She is divine."

"In that case, I'll drink to her," Tucker said.

And then, after lowering his glass, "But you
must join me in drinking to Lao Dai. I will be with
her tonight at eleven, in a half hour. She's tutor-
ing until then. You did find her . . . beautiful?"

"Very. And endearing."

Tucker smiled happily as they got up, splitting the restaurant bill.

That night Tucker set out to persuade Lao Dai to take the next day off from her teaching. He had no official engagements until the day following. "All tomorrow, Friday, is free." They could go on a tour in the late morning, after checking in at a suite he had reserved at the Caravelle. Maybe go up to Bien Hoa, fifteen miles north of Saigon, to a nifty restaurant he had heard about, run by the same French family that had started it before the war and somehow kept it going through the Japanese occupation and through the war against the French. Called Le Bon Laboureur, ever heard of it? Good!

Then, after lunch, maybe return for a little relaxation to the suite, where they could have a late dinner brought up.

Lao Dai promised to get permission for the day off.

The discreet waiter at the Caravelle lived up to Tucker's expectations. He served the late dinner expertly and disappeared. The champagne, the Biftek Calé de Paris, the Meringue Glacée, the Bordeaux. It was so very grand.

But then, suddenly, Lao Dai reached her hand

up to her throat. She was trying to control herself. She did not succeed. The tears came from her eyes. And then the sobs, becoming almost hysterical. Tucker was feverishly concerned. He touched her lightly at first, something on the order of a there, there, now caress, but it didn't work. Desperate, he seized her in his strong arms and hugged her close to him. "Dear, darling Lao Dai" (he pronounced it "Laodai"), "you must tell me. Tell me the whole thing. Tell me *everything,* or I can't help you, my darling."

Lao Dai tried to arrest her sobbing. She felt welling within her a desperate desire to tell the truth to this extraordinary American, so big and tender, so brainy and naïve.

She shouldn't, but she would.

"I told you a lie."

"That's all right, my darling. Most people do." Tucker put his big hand behind her neck. "What is it?"

"I told you my husband had been killed with the South Vietnamese Army in May. Well, that was a lie. But now he *has* been killed. Since I last saw you. And"—Lao Dai's voice evened out, and her tears stopped—"he did not die with our army. He died fighting with—the North." Her eyes were now hers to control. She lowered her eyebrows, and then her head. "He—he was a sympathizer with Ho. And he deserted the—the ARVN troops, and went to the North, and joined the North Vietnamese. He wrote to me and told me. But there was nothing to be done. And then . . . I got the news, just three weeks ago. Killed in action." She paused, and her eyes filled up again.

"He was such a lovely man. You would have liked him—I mean, the political problems, never mind them, you would have loved him, and he would have loved you."

Tucker urged her to talk to him about her late husband, but soon, lying with her head on his lap, she was talking instead of the awful conflict that separated her countrymen. Tucker said that perhaps there would be an end to the conflict, but an end could only come when the North became convinced that its enterprise against the South would not prevail. "After all, that is what finally happened in Korea. I was there, you know that, Laodai. Finally, after 1953, the North Koreans discovered that—it wouldn't work. And when they realized *that,* they slowed down; and South Korea went its own way, and the North Koreans went their way. That's what's important, to persuade the North that it won't work."

"But how is it possible, when they are all sworn to make 'it' work?"

Tucker Montana paused, and then said that he was himself engaged in a project which, when fully realized, might in fact persuade the North that it was fruitless to pursue its aggression against the South.

What kind of project, or did Tucker not want to talk about it?

He smiled, and kissed her on the lips. "I wouldn't mind talking about it, but it's too complicated for a mere linguist like you to understand. All I can say is that it is designed to—to stop the killing, to diminish unruly . . . yes, unruly appetites, like Ho Chi Minh's, and the people in the world he admires, Mao Tse-tung, Khrushchev, the whole gang." Wasn't that the most important thing, he asked her, to control unruly appetites? Lao Dai said that of course that was correct, though the subject was indeed complicated. Tucker said that it wasn't fair for her to bring up complicated questions since he, Tucker, had already spoken of his complicated mission. But that since they were both struggling with definitions, what was this about an unruly appetite, and what was so bad about unruly appetites?

He sipped his glass of cognac, and suggested that they take their complications to bed, unravel them there, and meditate on what appetites were unruly, what others were—he lifted her up from the couch, cradled her in his arms, and walked toward the bed—beautiful . . . ennobling . . . inspiring!

Later he said to her that she was the most ardent partner he had ever—"communed" with; he liked that, in fact he found himself reciting to himself a Hail Mary before closing in on her, a little obeisance . . . was it really sacrilegious, or was superstitious the better word? After all, he was unmarried, Lao Dai was truly a widow, a grieving widow; could their liaison really be wrong, as Fr. Enrique had taught the boys back there in San Antonio? Surely two people who love so passionately mustn't deny themselves the comfort they get from each other? He leaned over on strong arms and as he entered her he experienced the perfume he had given her before dinner, now transformed on her skin, overpowering. He expressed his love and excitement with a punishing yet loving vigor and she in turn, in little exclamations, pronounced him unique; his passion, she tried to say, made it all so much so much so much more *more* unique. They were lost in long moments of an irrepressible yet expressive rapture, soon driving to an abandoned, voluptuarian high—except that through it all, deep inside her mind, she felt the ticking sound, however faintly, never closing it off.

Le Duc Sy had given the final act of love, his life for his country. Now she truly was a widow. Was there a drumbeat at the base of her mind? Not a nagging Catholic conscience, like Tucker Montana's, which had brought on the almost silent hasty little prayer to his own God, but insistent, subordinated only in that her passion was genuine and even had she wished to do so, she could not have controlled it. But although she surrendered, she had not capitulated. She felt that her joy, requited, was, finally, a reminder of a transcendent mission. She kept that mission in mind, guarding against any temptation to thrust it out of the way, if only for these holy moments. As she rose toward him again, she harnessed her thinking with merciless determination, even now as the climax was at hand: She was doing this—this sublime thing, for something more sublime, more important, for which her Le Duc Sy had died so heroically.

★ ★ ★ ★ ★ ★ ★ ★ ★ ★ ★

Chapter Twenty-Five

Through room service, Tucker had ordered, indeed invented—the hotel had never had exactly such a request—an American breakfast. A Texas-American breakfast of rolls and orange juice and jam and scrambled eggs and fried potatoes and corn cakes, the nearest he could get to the hominy grits he had unsuccessfully attempted to describe to the chef. Tucker was disappointed that Lao Dai had taken to eat only the roll, with a little jam, and coffee. *"Petit déjeuner, simple,"* she smiled at him, expressing admiration over the cornucopia he had ordered and was proceeding, with such wholesome pleasure, to devour. He was wearing shorts, nothing more, and she told him, as he stuffed a corn cake into his mouth, that even when he was being *disgustingly* greedy, he was very beautiful, and where had he got that scar; she pointed to a line just to the right of his navel, drawing down his shorts a few inches to inspect the length of it.

"In the Philippines?"

He had told her of his experience there with the Huks. "Now," he smiled, reaching over to draw down her negligée, "do *you* have any scars? Let me examine you. . . ." He did so, and she laughed, escaping.

"You have not told me," she insisted. "Where *did* you get that scar?"

"It was a very evil man who did that to me," he said solemnly. "He approached me with a sharp knife. I was knocked out, unconscious, but somehow I saw him. He came at me with that knife. My hands were tied down and I could not see the expression on what I suspected was a sadistic face, and I thought, well, this is the end, tortured to death. I became then fully unconscious, and woke up I don't know how many hours later."

Lao Dai was tense. "Tell me."

"Well, I saw that man again, only now his

334 WILLIAM F. BUCKLEY, JR.

mask was gone and he was—grinning at me, staring down at my lower stomach." He paused. "Dr. Stringfellow had taken out my appendix."

She reached for the cushion on the chair by her and smashed it down over Tucker's head. "You—*you* are the sadist." She laughed, and Tucker laughed, and he told her he had not completed his physical examination, that he could not do so until she was completely un-clothed, lying down in their bed, to which he lifted her in his arms, and there completed his examination, leaving no part of her unexplored.

Driving to Bien Hoa an hour later he asked her, had she ever traveled away from Vietnam? Yes, she said, and lowered her voice.

"Where?"

"To Japan."

"To Japan? A Vietnamese girl traveling to the nation that—that occupied your whole country? Whose soldiers, I have to guess, occupied you . . . too?"

"Yes," Lao Dai said. "Both are—in a sense—true. Though it wasn't me, but my mother, that the Japanese 'occupied.' I was three years old when the Japanese were defeated, but for two years my mother was placed in a Japanese-run brothel. And that, in a way, is why I went to Japan.''

''Explain,'' Tucker said, slowing down the Army jeep he had commandeered, to dodge the potholes as best he could.

''It was four years ago, I was eighteen. The Japanese consul sponsored a 'cultural exchange.' For the first time, a Vietnamese delegation would travel to Japan, and at the expense of the Friendship Association of the emperor, so that we could see how the . . . new Japan was so different from the Japan of our nightmares.

''Our president refused to go. He said he had too many memories of the occupation to make it possible to guarantee 'civil behavior.' So the mayor of Saigon was deputized, and said he would take with him six young people who had not themselves suffered from the occupation, but whose parents were the victims of it— Mother committed suicide one year after the Japanese left. I don't know what the process was of selection, but at the finishing school I was attending, studying English and oriental history, I was told I would be one of the lucky travelers; so I was prepared, and was given a very luxurious wardrobe, three dresses, one of them suitable for very formal occasions: we would have an audience with the emperor."

"Did you?"

"Yes. A wonderful, austere, removed man, Emperor Hirohito. You would not have thought that he had anything at all to do with the Japan that led my mother into a brothel that drove her mad."

"Did he say anything?"

"He recited one of his own poems. We—the two other girls, and the three boys—did not know what it was all about, but we took the signal and applauded."

"And then, besides the emperor?"

"Oh, the usual things. And one unusual thing. One unique thing, I hope." She hesitated.

"What?"

"Hiroshima."

Tucker stiffened, and now he looked only straight ahead at the road. He said nothing.

"If you only *knew.* Have you ever been there?"

"Not exactly," Tucker said.

"What do you mean, 'not exactly'?"

Tucker Montana snapped, "If you don't know idiomatic English enough to know what 'not exactly' means, then you should go back to your finishing school."

She was transparently hurt. She said nothing until, finally, he broke the silence. "All right. Tell me. What did you see . . . in Hiroshima?"

She closed her eyes and said, "I went to the museum. The museum of August 6, 1945. And there I saw the actual table—one of I don't know how many thousands that were *not* preserved in museums—the dining room table of a couple with two children. I do not know how it was accomplished, but the mother and the father and the boy and the girl were still sitting upright at that table. There were no facial features visible, only charred flesh. We knew which was the mother, which the father, only from the swelling at the breast level. There were four plates on the table and a large pot. They were all . . . char. And then there were the photographs, a dozen, a hundred, it seemed like a million of them. After five minutes, I just closed my eyes, but every now and then I open them, and I think: Are we moving in that direction? Toward Hiroshima? In the direction of a global, nuclear war?"

"Why in the hell should we?" Tucker spoke severely.

"Because great wars happen sometimes when little wars do not—give way. You read about Charles de Gaulle's press conference Friday?"

"What press conference?"

"He said that the war in Vietnam would not be settled by military force. That if the Americans insisted on using all of their resources, they would—as he put it—'risk a general war.' So it isn't only little girls who went to the museum in Hiroshima who think of this . . . think of this possibility."

Tucker drove into town and asked a passerby the direction of the restaurant Le Bon Laboureur. But he could not make out what he was being told, and so asked Lao Dai to take over. In Vietnamese she posed the same question and then translated the instructions for Tucker, who drove on, turning right at the indicated street. He pulled up at the restaurant and, wordlessly, opened the door and led her in. Throughout the meal his conversation was distracted, perfunctory. She would not take dessert, she said, or even tea. He went immediately to the counter to pay the bill rather than sit and wait for it to be brought in.

Tucker walked ahead of Lao Dai to the parked

jeep. He helped her aboard and she could see that he was perspiring heavily.

"Are you all right, darling?"

"Yes. No. I mean, I'm all right, but I have a . . . every now and then I get a little . . . giddy. I mean: Would you mind driving?"

"I don't know how to drive."

Tucker sat on the fender of the jeep and leaned down. "Sorry. Just trying to get some blood up into my head, that's usually all I need to do. But it will take a little—" He stopped talking.

"Take all the time you want, my darling."

Tucker did not answer. He was immobile for ten minutes. Lao Dai turned away, to spare him embarrassment. At length he stood up again. "I'm all right now," he said.

He drove back toward Saigon without speaking.

As they reached the outskirts of the city, Tucker said that on reflection he had to prepare for the afternoon conference, so it would not be feasible to return together to the Caravelle. Instead, he drove her to her little apartment on Henri Brevard. She leaned over—he had stayed in the driver's seat—and kissed him.

"Will we be meeting tonight?"

Tucker roused himself. He smiled up at her. "Of course, dear Lao. Of course. I will meet you at La Tambourine. At ten o'clock, unless there are problems, in which case I shall leave word with Toi." He returned her kiss, absently, and drove off.

★ ★ ★ ★ ★ ★ ★ ★ ★ ★ ★

Chapter Twenty-Six

Lyndon Baines Johnson was morose. He sat there in the Cabinet room with his closest aides—McNamara, Bundy, Rusk, Rostow, and also Valenti and Moyers. They had all seen him in such condition, but rarely. When it happened, the vitriol reigned for the initial period, and then, eventually, he would focus his powerful mind on the vexation, the irritant, the goddamn son of a bitch *creating the problem*! His sense of maneuver would then awaken, and he would rise from despondency to a cathartic kind of torrential abuse—after which order imposed itself on his thinking. Then would come the planning. For the time being, all he could say was, "Surely de

Gaulle under*stands*? I mean, what was all that Cross of Lorraine shit if it didn't mean that *he* would fight until *he* won?"

"My guess," Walt Rostow volunteered, "is that de Gaulle is scarred by his own experiences, more recent than those fighting the Germans to reconquer Paris. His country lost Indochina, and he lost Algeria." Johnson turned to him, shaking his sad face ever so slightly, the effect of which was a kind of purring satisfaction: somebody else at the table was doing the talking, relieving him of the pain of doing so in his depressed state, and he hoped this would continue until his energy was reconstituted; meanwhile, who knows, conceivably what was being said would be worth listening to.

"We can't forget that, Mr. President. The defeat of the French in 1954 at Dien Bien Phu was a national devastation. De Gaulle was at Colombey-les-Deux-Eglises, waiting to be called to duty, a call that didn't come until four years later. He was very careful not to blame Dien Bien Phu on bad generalship in Vietnam—because he does not think of it as a national defeat. He thought the odds were, well, ontologically against France."

"Onto-what?"

"Sorry, Mr. President—er, organically, beyond reach, structurally against France. So along comes the United States, ten years later, and decides to save not even the whole country, but half the country. He is bound to feel that if we bring it off people might ask, How come France couldn't bring it off? Not the kind of questions he wants to encourage."

"And then," Bundy chimed in, "there's Algeria. By no means settled, with a great many very determined men turning on de Gaulle himself. What he did there, Mr. President, is really what he is urging us to do. He decided a couple of years ago that the military could not impose a French solution on Algeria. The French call it *force majeure*—"

"Is that the same as ontomonism?"

McGeorge Bundy quickly studied the Commander in Chief. But his face was entirely innocent. He was not being teased, Bundy concluded. He would slide out of the problem deftly. "Yes," he said, evading entirely the question he had been asked, "the idea of an overwhelming force against which one simply doesn't *argue*. Almost as if it were fate." Bundy picked up his notebook. "De Gaulle said at the press conference, 'It does not appear there can be a military solution in South Vietnam—' "

"How the hell does he know?" The President was aroused. "The Vietnamese who beat the French were fighting for independence from France. The South Vietnamese are fighting for independence from North Vietnam. They know goddamn well the United States doesn't want to colonize South Vietnam. Shit, I'd like to think in a year, two years mebbe, the whole Vietnam business will be just a memory, a bad memory. But even if there weren't any more people out there than on Quemoy and Matsu—how many was that, Walt, about fifteen?—even if we weren't talkin' about *fifteen million people we promised we'd keep free,* we have the SEATO alliance, and we have the Containment Doctrine. Are we supposed to repeal all of those simply because *General* de Gaulle, who never won a military battle in his life, that I was ever told about, says there cain't be a military solution?"

Bundy held in there. "Sir, he goes on, he says . . . 'Certain people imagine that the Americans could seek elsewhere this military solution that they could not find on the spot, by extending the war to the North. Surely they have all the means for this, but it is rather too difficult to accept that they could wish to assume the enormous risk of a general war. Then since war cannot bring a solution, one must make peace.' "

McNamara opened his own notebook. "Listen to what's been happening since our raids, Mr. President. Here's our friend Khrushchev. He said your—our—raids (he was talking about the retaliatory raid after Tonkin 2) were 'an attempt to restore the use of violence and piratical methods in relations between states.' And he said the U.S.S.R. would 'stand up for other socialist countries if the imperialists impose war on them.' Since Khrushchev always says the same thing at least two times, he said it again in his next sentence. Retaliatory raids are 'a threat to the security of the people of other countries and can entail dangerous consequences.' " McNamara raised his hand, asking the President to withhold comment for one moment. "And then two days earlier we got this from Peking: 'The so-called second Tonkin Gulf incident on August 4 never occurred. It was a sheer fabrication in order to extend the war in Indochina.' And then, one day later, the Peking Party newspaper writes that we have committed 'armed aggression' against North Vietnam in order 'to gain some political capital for the coming presidential election and to involve the allies of the U.S. in war.' " McNamara raised his hand even higher, pleading to hold back the presidential reaction. He had one more. "So two days after *that,* 100,000 Chinese rally at Tiananmen Square where Lioa Chengchih says it all: 'The Chinese people are determined by practical deeds to volunteer aid to the Vietnamese people in their just struggle against U.S. aggression and in defense of their motherland.'

"There, Mr. President, there it is. As far as de Gaulle is concerned, there are two alternatives. The United States either negotiates or faces a"—McNamara's voice was solemn—"a world war."

Lyndon Johnson took over.

"Well," he said, "and what does de Gaulle propose? He proposes we all go back to the Geneva Accords. Genius! Sheer genius! Give that man a Nobel Prize. What in holy shit does he think we've been sayin' over the last five years? That the Accords have been *violated*! The Geneva Accords *recognized* South Vietnam. There was going to be a vote on unification but Diem said no, because the terror campaign

had begun by the North. One million refugees—
that's the right figure, isn't it Walt?" Rostow nodded—"*One million refugees* and then a terror
campaign," he repeated the word. "What we
have is just what we have said it is, a war of
aggression staffed by Communists supplied by
Communists, one more of their fucking acts of
aggression against the free world."

There was silence.

"Now, Dean, here's what to do. One, get
Bohlen over here from Paris, and you," he
pointed to McNamara, "brief him on the plans
we've got going to seal off that Trail. Tell
Bohlen—what the hell's an ambassador to
France for?—to go and *see* de Gaulle and *tell*
him that goddamnit we are not going to have a
world war but that if every time the Communists
want to take over one more country they say,
Get out of our way or it's going to be a world war,
then they can gobble gobble gobble—Wonder if
Chip Bohlen knows how to say 'gobble' in
French?" The President looked around the
table, willing to give any volunteer the opportunity to come up with the French word. He
resumed. "Tell de Gaulle we have *very* modest,
er, plans but we believe, we damn *well* believe,
we can stop them, because the South Viet-

namese people, including those one million refugees, don't want that *poet* Marxist Ho Chi Minh
to take over their country. Okay?" Dean Rusk
was taking notes.

"Yes, Mr. President."

"And then issue a statement—"

"Yes, we'll need a statement. Over your signature?"

LBJ paused. Then, "No. I don't want to give
General Charles de Gaulle, President et cetera
of France, holy—holy *carrier* of the Cross of
Lorraine, the feeling that every time he says
some dumb thing at a press conference, I'm
going to twitch. Over *your* signature. Give it out
as a State Department reaction. Say what we
all"—he looked around the table, his face one
big interrogatory—"what we *all* think. Right?"

"Right, Mr. President."

Late that afternoon the State Department issued the press release. It said, in part, "The
United States seeks no wider war. If others
would keep the solemn agreements already
signed there would be no problem in South Vietnam. If those who practice terror and murder
and ambush will simply honor their existing
agreements, there can easily be peace in
Southeast Asia immediately. But we do not be-

lieve in conferences called to ratify terror, so our policy is unchanged."

Listening to the six o'clock television news, Lyndon Johnson heard the statement read out by the State Department's press officer. He was much cheered on hearing it. *"That's telling them,"* he muttered to his wife. Lady Bird agreed.

★ ★ ★ ★ ★ ★ ★ ★ ★ ★ ★

Chapter Twenty-Seven

SEPTEMBER 12, 1964
SAIGON, SOUTH VIETNAM

At the safe house, Tucker Montana asked Rufus
what was it exactly that de Gaulle had said.

"I just this afternoon read the cables, after
Blackford and I got back. You heard about it?
The press conference? Where . . . ?"

"From my friend. My girlfriend. Lao Dai—
Black knows her. She's pretty affected by it,
says de Gaulle said we can't win a 'military victory' unless we're prepared for a world war.
Makes a big difference, you bet, hearing this
here from the biggest cheese in France. I guess
a lot of the locals figure, if the same country that
lost in Indochina ten years ago is now saying the
Americans can't win in Indochina unless they

want a world war, that kind of cools their optimism, right, Rufus?"

"I assume it had that effect on your friend, Tucker?"

Tucker nodded. "Right."

"I imagine the State Department or the White House will have a reply in the next few hours. I've left word for it to be brought in, if it's while we're still here; otherwise we can get the news tonight or tomorrow. But you're right. What de Gaulle said is worth a lot of strategic hamlets to the enemy. It's one more burden, but let's hope it won't be decisive. Our problems are more mundane. Blackford, give Tucker the figures you've accumulated—the Agency, Tucker, wanted gross figures on the operations of 34-A, now that it is a—public enterprise."

"After what de Gaulle said"—Blackford looked grim—"I wouldn't be surprised if some of those people we're talking to, yesterday and today, are looking at all those junks out there and thinking, Dunkirk! Only where would they sail to? But that's another question—sorry. Yes, the figures.

"Well, Tucker," Blackford brought out his notebook, "to give you a little perspective: In the last six months of 1961 the South Vietnamese clocked one hundred and forty incidents of infiltration by sea. These included infiltration of bazookas and groups of up to sixty-five men strong, by single junks. The estimate is that fourteen hundred infiltrators passed through the coastal system during those six months. That's a lot of armed men shipped here to kill rural schoolteachers, mayors, and guards, and any women and children who get in the way.

"Back in the fifties, the South had a total of only eighty junks, all of them sailing boats, no motors. Beginning in December 1961, President Kennedy moved in. Five hundred junks were built with U.S. funds, sixty more using South Vietnamese funds. Three kinds of junks: About thirty 'command junks,' each carrying a crew of ten, with automatic weapons and radios. About two hundred and fifty sailing junks, for conducting surveillance as pickets or patrols. These are stationed in specific harbors. A few hundred motorized sailing junks for patrolling extended areas of the sea. By the beginning of this year we had about six hundred and fifty all told."

"What have they accomplished?"

Blackford didn't need his notebook. The figures were logged in his memory. "You've already seen the figures on the number of searches—three hundred and fifty thousand. They fingered one hundred forty VC agents. They're going at it every day, covering eight hundred miles of coastline. Obviously we have no way of knowing how many got through, either because they were detained, examined, and thought innocent, or because they penetrated the naval screen.

"Now, Rufus, this isn't in our Gulf–Trail script, but I just want to make one point. If, after he gets through with his Igloo operation on the Trail, Tucker finds his front as leaky as mine is, what have we accomplished?"

"Don't we have to assume that the number of North Vietnamese is finite, Blackford?"

"Yeah, I guess I'd weigh in with that, if I were a Pentagon planner. But nothing seems to discourage these people. Nothing. Goddamn, three hundred and fifty thousand at-sea searches, and there's no indication, we all know that, of any decrease in the level of guerrilla activity out there. Hell, we're surrounded by it. Now, Tucker, you've got something real fancy coming up here, the Igloo operation. But these bastards are regenerating at one hell of a rate—"

Tucker broke in. "Never *mind.* What do you

do when your junks finger a couple of NVAs with bazookas hiding in a fishing boat? They're brought in. Maybe they're put in prison. Maybe they're shot. But that's small potatoes, and we're always going to lose on the small-potato front, even if the gooks don't succeed in bringing down enough infiltrators to win the war. We *know* what they're *planning* on, they're planning on *twenty thousand troops per month* coming down the Trail, and that's the big artery we're going to choke up. If we can seal that off, then at your end all you've got to do is intensify the search procedures, maybe sink a few more of those buggers out there at sea: then give the South Vietnamese a chance. If ever they stop playing musical chairs with the presidency, they can go out there in the country and sniff out the North Vietnamese guerrillas and their allies in the South—who, we've all agreed, aren't numerous.''

Blackford sighed audibly. "Yes. I know that's the plan. And we're here to set the plan in operation. But I've got to say, Rufus, it doesn't look good.''

Rufus was brisk with him. "Our job is to make the situation better. It is Washington's responsibility to decide whether making it better is not enough."

Rufus resolutely pursued his agenda. But Blackford knew that Rufus's rare display of anger, frustration, disappointment and disagreement wasn't directed at him.

Should he try to sleep? Or should he *not* try to sleep? He had Richard Tregaskis's *Vietnam Diary,* from which he got reconfirmation on the subject of the dogged spirit of the Vietnamese, in particular those in the North, who had borne the brunt of the bitter war against the French.

The book was engrossing, if depressing. He considered turning to the new novel by Harold Robbins, or to Faulkner's *Sanctuary*, which Sally had sent him in paperback. ("If you haven't read this forty-eight hours after receiving it, give up whatever else you're doing. You can't grow *one week older* without reading *Sanctuary*!") Her weekly call came in, generally, between 2 and 3 A.M. Not an incivility of hers, to call at that hour. For some reason 6 to 7 P.M., Mexico time, was the best hour for getting through; she couldn't figure out why, nor could he, and to tell the truth, after a while they didn't try.

As a rule she called the BOQ, because he was usually in Danang; and that meant he had to pull up a cot by the side of the phone at the end of the corridor, so as not to wake other officers housed there. But she knew this week to call the hotel in Saigon. Should he try a quick nap? It would be harder, after they spoke, because her voice put him in high gear. Soon he was dreaming that he was trying to decide whether to dream . . . and the telephone rang.

"Hello, my darling Blacky."

"¿Qué tal, mi querida Sally? ¿Cómo estás? ¿Cómo está el bebito?"

"Not bad. No, not bad. Not terribly taxing, those sentences, granted. But even the Spanish accent sounded good. Great heavens! Is that you, Blackford, or is it some spy brought in from the Mexican cold, pretending to be you?"

"You kech me up, gringa. Fok you!"

Sally laughed. She asked how he was. He was fine, thanks. Had he been to church the preceding Sunday? In fact he had, had she? Yes, she said, Tony was a very faithful Catholic and the little boy would be brought up in the Church so she figured she might as well learn a little more about it. "You've always been more of a Christian than I, darling," she conceded.

"Maybe I can catch up one of these days. On the other hand, it isn't *absolutely* clear, is it, that your profession exemplifies the practice of Christianity?"

"Not if it isn't certain that communism exemplifies the anti-Christ."

"Oh dear, darling, here we go again. We mustn't, of course, and it's my fault, though your retaliation just now was, really, a little massive, don't you think? No, you don't think. I guess I just ought to tell you this, that the majority of the people I talk to among the faculty at the university here in Mexico think that the Vietnam war is simply a matter of an assertive North wanting for the South the same independence the North has achieved—"

"Darling?"

"Yes, darling."

"Why is the average university professor so stupid? I mean—now listen, Sally; just once, listen. We've got a perfect phone connection, so just pretend this is another seminar, without Jane Austen. The North Vietnamese are *totally* dependent on the Soviet Union and China. Without them they couldn't build a tin canoe, let alone a SAM missile. What's *our* record in this part of the world? Sure, we conquered the Philippines. But that was sixty-five years ago and had to do with war against Spain. So, after planting a few democratic seeds there, and fighting a war of liberation against the Japanese, in fifty years we made the Philippines free. We occupied Japan and then left it to run itself. We fought for Korea, then let it fend for itself, with a couple of divisions sitting there in case they were needed. Intellectuals who think the North Vietnam business is only about anticolonialism just don't think, except for that Anti-U.S. Think which most foreign intellectuals go in for, their special brand of masturbation. How do *they account* for the impulse of Communist-driven leaders to expand their power? East Europe, Greece, Berlin, Korea, Vietnam—"

"Blacky, Blacky. Yes, and of course there's a lot of packaged anti-U.S. thought among these people. But on the other hand, *you* can't account for the popular support for Ho's movement in the North—"

"How can you say that, darling? That popular support shows itself, among other ways, in that one million people have left the North since Geneva—"

"Well, you can't tell me all those people coming down to fight for Hanoi are all conscripts, can you?"

Blackford thought: *He did not have an answer to that point.* Sure, he could edge away by saying that most Germans fought for Hitler, and Russians for Stalin, and no doubt their understanding of what they were doing transcended any question of personal loyalty to Hitler, and to Stalin, whom so many of them loathed. But Sally was pressing her point.

"I heard a Spaniard, a journalist," Sally was saying, "just back from Saigon—charming man. If he goes back to Vietnam I will tell him how he can get in touch with you. There were six of us, and he was telling this story after dinner. It goes like this: A North Vietnamese nineteen-year-old soldier starts out from North Vietnam with an eighty-pound pack. He goes down the Trail. He makes out with bread and water as he can. He wades through fetid swamps, climbs icy mountains, gets bitten by snakes and mosquitoes, sweats with malarial fever, but plods on and on and on and on and two months later he has covered four hundred miles and delivers his cargo to the Vietcong unit where the captain meets him, gives him some rice, tells him to rest up for a day, and then to go back to Hanoi and bring another bundle of the same. . . . Kind of gets you, doesn't it?''

Yes, Blackford said, it does kind of get you. By polemical forward inertia he'd have gone on to say that history was full of surprises about the stamina shown by tyranny when colonizing, but he was exhausted. Not physically; it was something else. The awful, demoralizing, subversive plausibility of what Sally was saying. This tired him, he thought, reaching with his right hand to press the flesh on his right thigh so hard as to cause him to start up with the pain of it; *anything* to wake him from the sudden torpor his mind, not his body, had taken him to. He managed to rouse himself, and for a few minutes more they traded small talk and then love talk, and he hung up. He went to the closet and brought out a small bottle of gin, poured a quarter glass, gave it a little water from the jug on the table and drank it down. He sat and thought. And then he knelt down and, as he had done so many times before, but so infrequently in the past year or so, prayed for guidance. Prayed that General de Gaulle was mistaken. Prayed that he, Blackford Oakes, on a mission for his country and, yes, for the free world, would regain his faith in the Vietnamese venture. A faith, he realized, he had—only just tonight—realized he had lost.

★ ★ ★ ★ ★ ★ ★ ★ ★ ★ ★

Chapter Twenty-Eight

When Senator Barry Goldwater stepped out of the White House, escorted to the door by the President himself, the entire West Wing lit up with flashbulbs.

What ground did you go over with the President, Senator?

Did you talk with him about the civil rights bill?

Did Vietnam come up?

Is there any chance, Senator, of a televised debate?

What do you think, Senator, of the President's campaign ads?

Did you have coffee?

Barry Goldwater, groping his way to his limousine, interrupted his smiled silence to bark, "I don't drink coffee." In his car, the glass divider up, his campaign manager Denison Kitchel asked how it had gone.

"All right. He gave me one of those half-Johnsons. You know, hand on my shoulder. I was watching for what in the Senate we call a 'full-Johnson.' That's when his arm stretches all the way to your other shoulder. That's when he *really* wants something. If he had given me one of those, I'd have expected him to tell me I ought to drop out of the race."

"So?"

"Well, it was my meeting, I asked for it, and I told him he ought to get a new Secretary of Defense, that the Vietnam scene was a mess, but that I didn't think we ought to divide the country on that issue during the campaign. Wait till it's over."

"He liked that, I guess."

"Said he did. Said of course we both had to continue to campaign as we've been doing, and I said sure, but maybe it would be good if we agreed none of our people would call him a pinko, and none of his people would call me a Nazi."

"Agreed?"

"Agreed."

They left the car on Connecticut Avenue and went into a staff meeting. Goldwater had in front of him notes assembled during the week. He began by telling his staff that he had told LBJ the Goldwater camp would not make a big issue of Vietnam, but he thought we were losing out there. Look—he pointed to his sheaf of notes— just one week, and look. He adjusted his glasses.

"Casualties: 1,387 U.S. to date—163 killed in combat, more than one thousand wounded. That's men *killed in action.*

"LBJ orders five thousand more military into Vietnam. That was last Tuesday. Thursday, new estimates from the Pentagon say the Vietcong number more like 75,000 than 25,000. How come? How come they are increasing, after six months of our 34-A operation in the Gulf? Did a lot of South Vietnamese just happen to fall in love with communism? With President Ho?" He turned to Baroody.

"I don't know, Bill. You say it isn't a good campaign issue to go out there and just say the whole Vietnam operation is screwed up; maybe you're right, you're probably right. The minute I touch on foreign policy, I'm identified as a warmonger. It's just that simple. We should make a note to tell the Republican candidate in 1968: Don't touch foreign policy. Just pretend it doesn't exist."

"Oh come on, Barry." The voice of Bill Baroody, pacifier.

"What do you mean, come on? They asked me in California what I would do about the Trail, I told them not what I would do, but what *the Pentagon* at one point was *considering*—defoliation by nuclear tactical weapons. And I tell them *I* don't think that's too good an idea—and the press has *me* in favor of nuclear war in Vietnam! I tell 'em defensive tactical nuclear weapons have to be at the disposal of the NATO commander, next day I'm in favor of giving every staff sergeant in NATO a nuclear weapon. So General Partridge, who *was* head of NORAD, pops up and says *he* was authorized by Ike to use tactical nuclear weapons in combat defense, and Ike up at Gettysburg doesn't deny it. Does anybody notice? No. Fuck it." He sank into a chair and said:

"You see what Sulzberger wrote in the *Times*?"

There was silence in the room. They had all seen it. But Goldwater insisted on reading it aloud. He picked the paper on which it was clipped out of his notebook. " 'The possibility exists that, should Goldwater enter the White House, there might not be a day after tomorrow.'

"So, since we all want a day after tomorrow, we'll hit the Vietnam question on the broad front. We'll just say we're in favor of meeting our commitments to SEATO, of observing the Containment Doctrine, of maintaining a strong presence in the Pacific, of helping the South Vietnamese as best we can, that kind of thing. But we aren't going to tell Lyndon Johnson how to *win* that situation out there. Nobody's going to listen, and he'll make us sound like warmongers. He's already done that. So unless he really screws up in the next few weeks we let it alone. And if I do decide to go after him on it, I'll call him up and let him know ahead of time."

"You're not likely to have to do that, Barry." It was Kitchel talking. "They've got a mole in our outfit. Don't know who he/she is, but all those rumors about a mole have got to be right. Every time you give a speech, even speeches we keep from the press till you deliver them, the Democrats have a point-by-point answer ready for distribution to the press in about half an hour."

"Denis," Goldwater spoke with mock gravity, running his hand across the table to include all the eight staff members in the room, "give 'em all lie dectector tests by tomorrow."

The tension broke. Goldwater left the room, and Kitchel took over, going down the agenda. There was the speech tomorrow in Cleveland—

"Deny, does the senator mean we can't use something like this?" Freddy Anderson, the young speechwriter, handed the campaign manager a clip. Kitchel read out loud the AP bulletin. " 'General Maxwell Taylor, U.S. Ambassador to South Vietnam, met yesterday with Premier Nguyen Khanh. He told Premier Khanh that his threats of carrying the war beyond South Vietnam's borders were contrary to U.S. policy . . .' " Kitchel moaned, and finished reading the clip. "It is contrary to U.S. policy to cross over to their side of the fifty-yard line. No, Fred, you heard the candidate. We don't use it."

"Okay," said Anderson. "I'll just write about how we ought to abolish Social Security."

"Yeah," Dean Burch spoke up. "And don't forget to include something about selling off the TVA."

Baroody nodded solemnly. "Sounds like you

got the makings of a good speech. Just don't forget to say something against the poverty program. Something really . . . inspiring."

Freddy Anderson was moving his pencil with feverish haste, as if transcribing carefully his instructions. Didn't want to miss any of it.

Nice tableau, Kitchel thought to himself, as Baroody broke out in laughter. He reached into his coat pocket. "Here's a letter came in from a G.I. in Vietnam. No name, no address. 'Dear Goldwater Headquarters. Thought you'd like this one, maybe you can use it. I was there. McNamara and General Taylor last week on their morale-boosting trip with General Khanh, visiting ARVN units all over. McNamara was given a few words in Vietnamese to memorize, and everywhere he went he stood up and spoke them. The words he was given say, in Vietnamese, 'Vietnam a thousand years!' Only he pronounced it wrong, and what came out was, 'Southern duck wants to lie down.' " More laughter.

"Let's go to work," Kitchel said.

★ ★ ★ ★ ★ ★ ★ ★ ★ ★ ★

Chapter Twenty-Nine

It was as if that afternoon two weeks before at Bien Hoa, in which Hiroshima had come between them like a mushroom cloud, hadn't ever happened. Tucker's exhilaration subordinated any thought given to any other question or distraction. He hadn't known at Nakhon Phanom exactly when or at what hour the test would end, and by the time it did, at noon on Monday, it was too late to telephone, so he went directly from the airport in Saigon to her apartment with a bottle of champagne and a jar of Strasbourg pâté.

She was not yet back from school. For a moment Tucker just stared at the lock, kept looking at it as, slowly, he bent down to deposit his packages on the floor. He emptied the contents of his pockets into his hand. Anything there might do the trick? Hm. No, not really. He stuffed it all back into his pockets and then opened his briefcase, poking about in it. One of his folders was bound together by a large paper clip. There. Was he not, after all, the son of Faraday Montana, who could fix an electric fan by . . . looking at it?

In a few moments the door was open, he had brought in his little goodies, and sat down in the armchair Lao Dai once told him was all that she had salvaged from her father's household because, the day before his arrest by the French, fearing the confiscation of his property, he had asked a neighbor to accept in safekeeping a few articles he especially treasured, the armchair among them.

He did not have long to wait. Whether she was using her lovely hands to carry school papers, or using them to tidy the little bun of her splendid hair, or to knead more and more joy into his adoring body, they were a captivating part of Lao Dai. She dropped her package of papers and flew into his arms.

"It works! It works!" Tucker made her dance

around the room with him. Then stopped: "And now you will see, dear Lao Dai, a gradual contraction of all that killing and terror in the countryside, because the flow from the North will soon be down to a trickle, and then perhaps they will sue for peace!"

He felt her sudden stiffening.

"No no no, you must not be afraid. This will take us in the *opposite* direction of a general war."

Lao Dai took the bottle from him, opened it, brought out two glasses and plates and knives while Tucker told her how lovely she looked, caught by surprise at midafternoon, and how he had hoped to be able to telephone her from "the field" to give her some warning of his arrival, but that in fact he had arrived back just about as expected.

When they were seated, Lao Dai told him how pleased she was that he had got on so well with his work. "And it is especially good news that you think the war will be shortened. But how is that so?"

Tucker said that it is generally a myth that a country is prepared to fight to the last man— "doesn't matter what the cause is. I mean, look at the French. There were lots of live Frenchmen left in June 1940. And it was their own country they were fighting for, not like when they fought here, which was just a colony."

"But the North Vietnamese think of South Vietnam, don't they, as their own country?"

"Well sure. And the North Koreans consider South Korea as a part of their own country. My point is that the North Vietnamese have got to reach a point where they figure: It isn't worth it. Now I have to confess, a couple of weeks ago I was wondering whether they would ever reach that point, but my little doohickeys performed so well, I think I can see the thing differently now, and maybe closing out the possibility of the war going on and on and on until—"

"Until the United States tires of it?"

Tucker was drawn up short. "Well, that could happen, sure. But the U.S. has had just over a thousand casualties, which is something a country ten times as big as North Vietnam can put up with."

"How will your invention work? Or is it so secret you can't tell me?"

Tucker poured another glass and looked at Lao Dai. Did it matter? No, actually.

"Let me think a minute," he said to her.

She smiled. "I'll go to the kitchen and be back in a minute or two."

What was the purpose of this whole enterprise? Tucker asked himself. It was to deter the North Vietnamese. If they became convinced that they would not prevail, then they would stop trying, wouldn't they? Wouldn't *we*? Wouldn't *anybody*? Wasn't there in fact a pretty good argument for calling in the representative of the International Control Commission, explaining to him the technology the Americans had prepared to seal up the Trail, with instructions to report it all to Ho Chi Minh, and maybe he would realize, then, that his great big Trail operation wasn't going to work?

Tucker was inflamed by the idea. And *anyway,* he continued feeding his enthusiasm, it would be just a matter of days, once Igloo was in operation, before the gooks got hold of one of his Spikebuoys. Granted they were designed to explode when the battery inside reached a certain level of weakness, but using five, ten, twenty thousand of his Uggies over a period of time made the probability of their getting one that hadn't exploded, even though the battery was down, or spotting one whose battery was still strong, inevitable. Then the Uggie would be sent to Hanoi and examined there or, more likely, at the weapons lab at Podolsk, just south of Moscow. So, they would find out what the Uggie did. So? How could they keep the U.S.— or Charlie, for that matter—from using them?

He sensed that he was moved also by other motives than merely pleasing Lao Dai and satisfying her curiosity. After a hiatus of almost twenty years he was suddenly *proud* of what he had accomplished. He had been praised during recent weeks for his ingenuity; some had actually used the word genius. Praised by professionals in the physics and weaponry community, by military men and their associates, the likes of Rufus and Blackford. He wished now the praise of someone he truly loved and wanted to make happy. Somebody who leveled with *him,* like when she volunteered that her late husband had gone off to fight with the North.

And anyway—his face broke out in a smile. He had solved his own problem!—and anyway, she would not get any of the technical details, which she wouldn't understand, and if she did, wouldn't remember. What he was bound to do was to reassure her: that the war might be coming to an end—thanks in large part to the work of her . . . lover.

"Okay! I'm ready," he called out.

Lao Dai came in from the kitchen and sat down eagerly.

Tucker went to his briefcase and brought out a sketch of his UGS. "There. That's my little baby. UGS stands for 'Unattended Ground Sensor.' That means pretty much what you would think it would mean. It is unattended by any soldier. It just sits there, or rather stands there. It is designed to go into the ground—see there, the long, needlelike plunger? Here, in the body of the UGS, is a long-lasting battery. Small, but potent. Up here is the electronic wizardry, if you don't mind my being a wizard for just a minute, that picks up sound, any sound. And that unit broadcasts through the antenna over here the character of the sound to a computer receiver in an airplane overhead. That airplane transmits to where we are"—he didn't give the name of Nakhom Phanom—"and we get the sound, we know where it came from because we spot the transmission on a screen that has in it the location of all the Uggies, and after we classify the sound— the noise of a truck, or conversations between soldiers, or a tank or a motorbike, whatever—we give our instructions to the fighter plane, which whoops down on the target, and bang! Pretty soon, no more targets. Because the bad guys have to go through—through a couple of passes."

Tucker poured himself another glass, ate a pâté-covered cracker in one gulp, pulled out a cigar case and lit up.

Lao Dai was examining the sketch, admiring the draftsmanship. "It is quite remarkable, dear Tucker. I am very proud of you."

"Enough details?"

"I'm afraid I would not understand more. But, dear Tucker, would this not simply mean that the gooks, as you call them, would come south in other ways?"

"Well, they'll *try.* But we've got the DMZ pretty well sealed up. And the Navy can do its job on the Gulf, after a while. You know, get more sophisticated about the phonies who creep through. I am not suggesting there isn't a whole lot to be done, just that what Ho was counting on primarily is the Trail. Want to know how many? How many troops they plan to send down here, every month? *Twenty thousand!* And one late estimate raises that to twenty-five

thousand. So obviously they have been counting on the Trail primarily. Well, when they get
there, ole Igloo White pretty soon will be waiting
for them, and there ain't any twenty thousand
soldiers going to come down my Trail, Laodai,
you bet!"

"But what if the Vietcong just grow and grow?
What if—what if Russia says no to your Uggies?
What if they bomb your—facility? Then don't we
have just one more element of increasing the
war?" But she interrupted herself. She was
genuinely happy.

"Darling! Before you answer, let's agree
whatever I say, or you say, this is a night to
celebrate. Now, shall we have another bottle of
champagne? One was not enough." She held
up the empty bottle. "Here, let me pay for it"—
she got up from the chair.

"Whaddayamean, you pay for it! This is *my*
party. Siddown. Where do I go?"

"It is only two blocks. Turn right when you
leave the apartment house, walk two full blocks.
Then on to the corner, where there is a little
wine shop."

Tucker was already standing. "I'll be right
back." He walked to the door, then spun around
and grabbed her by the waist, kissing her ar-

dently. "But that's for later, that's for *after* the champagne!" He went out the apartment door. Lao Dai went to her closet and removed the camera. She took Tucker's notebook to the bathroom and turned on the sun lamp, photographing all thirty-two pages.

When Tucker returned, she was in bed. She smiled at him. "Let's have the champagne," she said, "*after,* not before."

★ ★ ★ ★ ★ ★ ★ ★ ★

Chapter Thirty

OCTOBER 2, 1964
GULF OF TONKIN

Colonel Yen Chi, the head of South Vietnamese Intelligence, complained once more through channels to the Pentagon that there weren't enough junks in the 34-A operation to interdict efficiently all the guerrillas and weapons coming down the coast. While it was true, he said, that thousands upon thousands of personal searches had been made since the operation began, as recently as a week ago an ARVN unit had come upon a cache of enemy weapons not far from Hué, the northernmost South Vietnamese stronghold. The guards were apprehended and after some persuasion divulged that the most recent addition to the cache had come in only the day before. The question was, How had the smugglers got through the 34-A screen? Colonel Yen reminded the Pentagon that stopping a North Vietnamese junk at sea, boarding it and searching it thoroughly was an operation that required as much as two hours. "We do not have enough ships to stop every boat that comes down the coast and to give two hours' time to it."

What Colonel Yen wanted the Pentagon to come up with was some kind of a long-range metal detector or something that could be trained on a passing junk, something sophisticated enough to let pass without wasting time vessels that were not carrying weapons cargo, leaving ARVN patrol boats to concentrate on suspicious or manifestly contraband vessels. And the question was: Could such a device be developed? Or would it be unable to distinguish between the necessary paraphernalia of the professional fisherman, some of which was of iron and steel, and those of guerrilla fighters?

A prototype developed by the CIA's Technical Services Division had arrived, and Blackford and Alphonse Juilland and a technician from Maryland would now try it out. If suitable, it would in due course be mounted and encased in the upper deck section of a 44-foot patrol boat alongside the radar, to which it was similar in size and shape, and more would be made. Rufus did not elect to go out with them into the Gulf. He said, rather more vaguely than usual, Blackford thought, that he had other business to attend to.

The patrol boat, the *Mai Tai,* had an engine that would permit it to speed up to 17 knots. That morning's briefing at the dispatch office had assigned it a sector twenty miles wide, paralleling the coastline for as long as the workday permitted. The *Mai Tai* would go out to sea, then take diagonal courses within the sector, returning at nightfall to Danang. Its job: to scan and stop any non-Vietnamese junk, irrespective of whether it was outside territorial limits; board it; inspect its cargo and personnel; release it if innocently engaged; bring it to Danang if caught smuggling.

These encounters were with increasing frequency leading to combat at sea. *Mai Tai*'s sister ship, the week before, had signaled a junk its intention to board and had been met, moments before throwing over the grapnel, with machine-gun fire. The ship had maneuvered quickly and a 40-mm. projected from its hull, to do duty

along with a .50-caliber machine gun up forward. The smuggler sank, without survivors; but
by then one South Vietnamese naval hand was
dead, another wounded.

New orders had gone out: A boat hailed now
for boarding received instructions by radio and
by megaphone: every member of the crew was
to appear on deck, both hands clasped to the
ship's lifeline, before the boarding actually
began.

When *Mai Tai* came about and began its diagonal course, Blackford could with naked eye
count thirty-two ships on the horizon, clear evidence of the need for the metal scanner to do
its work. He stood by the technician, observing
the dimly lit yellow screen as the scanner
beamed in on their first junk.

"Tell the captain he has to get closer," the
technician called out to Juilland, who relayed
the message in Vietnamese.

"Tell him *much* closer, like 100 meters. Ask
him how far away are we right now."

Juilland relayed the two questions, the first to
the captain, the second to the radar operator,
who answered him:

"Radar says we are at 200 meters."

"Get closer, and then move parallel with him and go at his speed."

Alphonse Juilland relayed the orders. The captain ordered the crew to their stations, one standing by the cannon, a second by the .50-caliber gun. By radio he gave orders to the junk, reiterated by the amplified megaphone.

"Call out distance to target," the technician demanded. Juilland now interpreted . . . 180 . . . 150 . . . 130 . . . 110 . . . 90 . . . 80 . . . 75.

"All right, hold it there." The young technician turned to Blackford. "See that grainy stuff? Metal. But it seems to be scattered along the length of the boat. Probably pails, fishhooks, maybe a rifle or two there. Let's board and have a look."

The fishermen, eight of them, were standing dutifully on the weaving deck, both hands on the lifeline. At 50 meters the technician snapped a Polaroid picture of his screen.

They boarded the boat, the sailors were frisked, and a conventional search began. With his Polaroid print in hand the technician, followed by Blackford and Alphonse, went through the boat stem to stern, attempting to match metal objects they saw with corresponding spots on the facsimile screen. The anchor was definitely there as a bulbous dot, so was a large barrel used for scraping the fish, so was the engine, and here and there little dots, some of which did not appear to correspond to anything.

"What if the bad stuff was parked right alongside the engine?" Blackford asked.

The technician shrugged his shoulders. "No way our little scanner could help you out there. Where it's useful is in finding the big, bulky items. Fifty crates of hand grenades. A hundred rifles. Twenty bazookas. That kind of thing."

The *Mai Tai* spent the balance of a hot and windless day going from junk to junk, the technician making his notes, conducting his searches and consulting with Blackford. They boarded twenty-one vessels, which meant that they did not board another twenty-one, for lack of time. And the question before the house was: Would Operation 34-A be more effective scanning all forty-two with the new devices and boarding only those with a suspicious density of dots or an eye-catching configuration? Sweating heavily from the heat, Blackford, Alphonse, and the American technician walked off the *Mai Tai,* having informed the captain they would go out again the following day and look out only for much more suspicious cargo. Blackford agreed with the technician that the day's run had been inconclusive, but instructive. He would report the results to Rufus, and meet the *Mai Tai* at seven in the morning. Blackford said good night to Juilland and walked the few blocks to his BOQ, grateful for the rise of an onshore wind. There he showered, dressed, and soon arrived five minutes early at the little restaurant. Rufus was exactly on time, of course.

They sat outdoors, at the seaward corner of the second-story veranda, well insulated for private conversation conducted in a low tone of voice. The waitress took their order, iced tea for Rufus, an icy beer for Blackford.

Blackford told him about the ambiguous day aboard *Mai Tai.* He gave him every detail, let him ponder every question. "I know they checked the machine out with various kinds of shipping off the coast of Maryland, but I can see that it isn't easy to duplicate the traffic in junks we got out here. Tomorrow, limiting our boarding to suspicious ships, we can probably scan three or four times the number we did today."

Rufus nodded. "Yes, we will need more sub-

stantial sampling before we equip the entire patrol fleet with the scanner. Let's see what happens tomorrow."

"Okay," Blackford said, draining his glass of
beer in a swallow and signaling for another one.
He knew when Rufus was saying: That is the
end of our conversation on that subject. We can
move to another.

Blackford said, "Any news?"

"The Warren Commission filed its report. The
investigation concludes that Lee Harvey Oswald
did it all by himself."

"You go along?"

"I haven't read the report. I am not surprised
by its findings. There was no mention of Oswald's visit to the Cuban embassy in Mexico."

"Why didn't . . . we give them that?"

"The decision was made."

Blackford laughed, pulling out the front of his
shirt to receive the evening breeze. "You kill me,
Rufus. You're the damnedest combination. The
no-questions-asked, that's-none-of-my-busi-
ness Rufus, your eyes trained on duty. And yet
if there is a moral breeze in the air, I can feel you
rustling."

Rufus did not enjoy personal references, and

few of his associates would have ventured to make any. But he permitted himself a smile.

And then, out of the blue, he said, "Do you know, Blackford, our friend Tucker is not very bright. He is something of a genius, but not, no, not very bright."

Blackford was taken aback. Instinctively he was defensive about his friend—while wondering whether, in their association, he had missed something Rufus hadn't. He found himself forcing a retrospective review of all that he had seen and heard from Tucker during the past weeks, begining when they had met to survey the Trail. Meanwhile:

"What do you mean, Rufus? We're talking about a guy who—I mean, just look at the whole Igloo enterprise—"

"I am not talking about his gifts. I am talking about his judgment."

Blackford thought hard. True, Tucker's fixation with Hiroshima clouded his political judgments—that certainly was so. And, clearly, Tucker was not in sufficient control of his libido, though Blackford, who considered himself "bright," acknowledged that in making that judgment, he was living in a glass house.

Though Blackford hadn't, in fact, let his romance affect his political judgment. . . . Surely if he'd done so, Sally would long ago have been his wife. . . .

Rufus continued. "I have looked very closely into his background, only the general outline of which you are familiar with, I think. When we took him on, we had *only* an outline. His role in Los Alamos turns out to have been much more than merely that of an assistant physicist. Did you know that?"

"Yes. He told me. Just two weeks ago."

"In fact at one stage of the bomb's development Tucker's contribution was evidently critical. It is entirely probable that the bomb would have been delayed weeks, conceivably even months or more if it hadn't been for a breakthrough of his. You also did not know this: he was on board the *Enola Gay*—"

"Yes, he told me that too."

"And after returning from that mission, after a month or two, he had a nervous breakdown. He was discharged, and went into a Benedictine monastery in Rhode Island. Did he tell you that as well?"

"Not quite so—nakedly."

"And then—" Rufus did his half-smile.

"And then?" Blackford asked, gravely.

"The priapic daemon. Our friend is a highly developed—highly obsessed—satyr. It began— at least, I suppose it began, there being no record of his romancing while at Los Alamos—not easy to do, at Los Alamos—at the monastery. Before Alamos he was at the University of Texas, working around the clock. But his stay in the monastery was aborted by—"

"A lady?"

"A woman. He left and took a job as a Spanish teacher in a boys' school in Massachusetts, and seduced the French teacher. He was dismissed—in those days, such behavior was thought incorrect"—Blackford noticed that Rufus was not at this exact moment looking Blackford directly in the eye—"and we next found him back in Texas. El Paso, where he lived with a rich Mexican socialite until Don Husband came in one day with a loaded pistol. He missed. Tucker joined—rejoined, actually—the Army. Personnel, for some reason, never came up with the record of his previous service at Los Alamos, which for reasons having to do, I suppose, with the Hiroshima pathology he had intentionally concealed. He was sent to Fort Benning, got a commission in the infantry, and found himself in Korea, where he seemed to have no psychological problem at all engaging in combat. He won a Silver Star. And then there was the business in the Philippines, which you know about, and the Medal of Honor. I did tell you about the forty-one Huks he over-whelmed?—Yes. He was frequently absent without leave, always because of a . . . romance. But when General Lansdale was consulted about someone to go with you on the Trail, he said he had just the right man, named Montana. Then there was that odd business, his suddenly coming up with that dazzling concatenation of—Well, he is the godfather of Igloo."

"What makes you conclude—what you began by saying?"

"That he's not very bright? Observation, my dear Holmes."

"You mean the business of his girlfriend in Saigon? Lao Dai?"

"In part. At first I thought that his rushing off to see her so often was simply the priapic imper-ative at work, his—"

"Phallus?"

"—Yes, taking over from his brain, one more time."

"It's more than that. He is genuinely nuts about her."

"Yes. Understandably so, I gather from you. But no, it is his—naïveté I had in mind."

"You worried?"

"Yes. Lao Dai is an agent of the North Vietnamese. She has done steady work for them for several years. I have been checking her out since she first came into view. It was confirmed today who she takes orders from."

"Oh *God*! You going to tell him today? Tomorrow?"

"No, not wise at this point. I can't imagine he would give Lao Dai details of Igloo. But we are having him followed. Also the girl. The woman."

"We doing it?"

"No. Colonel Yen. But he is reporting only to me. And now, Blackford, you will need to . . . observe him very carefully. He has a way, both of us have noticed—you have noticed it, I must assume—of talking very frankly about what is on his mind. And often in a contradictory way. Last week he was dizzy with delight over the Spikebuoy and the whole Igloo operation. In more recent conversations he was almost unintelligible, talking, rather distractedly, about

the whole operation, wondering whether, in trying to block those choke points—the two
passes—we weren't engaged, in fact, in maneuvering in such a way as to *require* the inter-
vention of the Chinese army. He is now
invoking the Korean parallel. There, we were
fighting the North Koreans—and suddenly we
were fighting the North Koreans and the Chinese Communists. . . ."

"I'm not all that sure that point is all that
dumb, Rufus."

Rufus looked at Blackford intently. "The
larger geopolitical question is not our *professional* concern, Blackford. Granted, we're
never going to extrude from our own pessimis-
tic strategic analysis factors that bear on our
Indochinese operation. But we aren't here to
write foreign policy. This is done, well and
badly, in Washington. I think it is, currently,
being done badly, as I expect you think it is
being done badly. But we are here to apply our
professional skills to the problem at hand *as
defined in Washington.* And we face a problem."

Blackford found his mind fidgeting. He said
nothing, and Rufus was silent.

"Any ideas?"

Blackford shook his head. "I'm not sure I see the point in not telling him what you know about Lao Dai."

"I was on the phone an hour with the Director on that point. The decision was his, and I understand it. What it comes down to is that Tucker is absolutely essential for about eight weeks more on Igloo White. He sizes up the situation as dangerous if I barge in and shatter him about Lao Dai."

"Thinks he'd quit?"

"Maybe, but also we have to weigh it that, given the record, he might have another nervous breakdown. He also figures the North Vietnamese are going to know pretty soon what it is we're up to and it wouldn't make all that much difference if they found out a day or two earlier. But it would make a great difference if Tucker Montana were not here to stitch the operation together."

Blackford leaned back in his chair. "You know something, Rufus, even though I think you're right, that Tucker isn't sophisticated politically, we mustn't ever let ourselves think that he's— dumb. Or—" Rufus began to say something, but Blackford said, "—Or, that he doesn't have some pretty deep insights."

"You mean, on our risking a nuclear war by being out here?"

"No. Not so much that. But on his occasionally wondering whether we're getting anywhere, or how much we are risking and how much we might be paying eventually trying to get somewhere."

"Do you think we are getting anywhere, Black?"

"No, Rufus. I don't. And I'd bet three stripes of Old Glory that, strapped down on a polygraph, you'd give the same answer."

Rufus rose. "Time to go, Blackford. A lot to do."

★ ★ ★ ★ ★ ★ ★ ★ ★ ★ ★

Chapter Thirty-One

At first, when reached by phone at BOQ Danang, Blackford, in his deepening gloom, tried to beg off. But Tucker was so enthusiastic about the idea, he pressed Blackford. The three of them—Blackford, Lao Dai, and Tucker—would drive to Bien Hoa for lunch at his favorite restaurant. "After all, you've got to come in to Saigon for our five o'clock meeting with Rufus. Just come on a morning flight instead of the afternoon flight."

Blackford quickly reflected and said yes, he would enjoy such an excursion hugely, he would have the pleasure of seeing Lao Dai again and after all, Bien Hoa was only 12 miles away so they could easily be back for whatever Rufus had for them on the agenda that afternoon in Saigon.

"How're things going?" Blackford was more experienced than Tucker in the Aesopian mode by which intelligence agents speak to each other over the telephone, but Tucker managed, haltingly. "They're slow, the . . . construction workers. But the, er, machinery, you know, the *agricultural* machinery that—that does all those wonderful combinations?—that is going *very* well, *extremely* well. Am very anxious to talk to you about it. And on your front?"

"That new . . . razor's going to work out just fine, I think. Shaves you real clean. Knows just about as close as it needs to know where the beard is. Very intelligent little razor."

"Good, good. Well, you're a bright, sharp li'l ol' razor yourself, Black-o. I'll see you on Wednesday, five o'clock, usual place. I mean, not the usual place. The new place. So long, Black."

"So long."

Tucker extended the lunch invitation for the following day to Rufus. Rufus replied that he had another engagement, that he was very sorry, and if the 4:15 he had in mind for their meeting the next day was too early, it would not inconvenience him to move the hour to 5:15, since the agenda as of this moment was not crowded. "No sweat, Rufus," Tucker said, to a man who had never visibly sweated in his life. "We can be back easily by four."

They set out in a jeep, Tucker, dressed in white corduroy slacks, at the wheel; Lao Dai, holding down her straw hat with the flowered white band, beside him; Blackford, in khakis and polo shirt, in the rear. Tucker was taking it all in the spirit of a fall outing in New England, on the way to a football game. And indeed as October closed the temperature was lowering. He had brought along a tape player and as they drove along the roadway, dodging bicyclists and pedestrians, slowing for the army caravans and avoiding such axle-breaking potholes as he could, Tucker slipped on Ella Fitzgerald singing Cole Porter. Tucker, carried away by the melody and the lyrics, at one point broke out with his own raspy baritone voice to underscore his enthusiasm for Porter's injunction, "Let's do it. Let's fall in love." Lao Dai applauded. Blackford said that he thought Ella did better on her own, with her own orchestra, unaccompanied by

Tucker—who was much tickled by it all and asked Lao Dai whether today, at the restaurant, she would choose the pigeon again, as she had on their previous outing. She replied that she would always look the menu over very carefully, to examine the choices.

Le Bon Laboureur was nicely located on a corner. A row of tall cypress trees stretched out along one of the streets, planted by the French to break the monotonous concrete profile of a large penitentiary. There was room, at the tables outside under the awning, for twenty diners or so, and inside, crowded about the picturesque little bar, room for a dozen, at four tables with the traditional checked red-and-white table-cloths. Blackford and Lao Dai stood awkwardly just under the awning. Tucker was making a scene.

He was speaking in not entirely secure, but decidedly emphatic French. "I am telling you, *mon cher monsieur,* that I made reservations over the telephone, *by long distance,* three days ago for an *outside* table."

"Yes," the maître d'hôtel said, looking down at his register, "M. Mohn-tana. But, sir, you made your reservation for 1300 hours, and it is only"—he looked at his watch—"1250. Please

please, go inside and have an apéritif, and certainly within a very few minutes I can seat you here outside."

Tucker had few alternatives, Blackford reasoned, since there was not an empty table outdoors.

Inside, by contrast, on such a day there was only one couple. They took the central table from which they could easily spot the first table vacated outdoors. A few minutes later, as the waiter approached them with their drinks, tray held high to clear the heads of the two diners at the adjacent table, the tray and its contents crashed down on Blackford's lap while a machine gun raked the diners outdoors. A half-dozen men dressed in the anonymous, uniform black pajama suits, armed with weaponry of several kinds, were firing at the entrance to the prison, two of them spraying the intersecting avenues with machine-gun bullets. Tucker had thrown himself across Lao Dai, Blackford was on the floor, a bottle of wine and three broken glasses between his stomach and the old auburn tiles. He looked up. Tucker had a pistol in his hand and was beginning to crawl toward the outdoors. Blackford knotted his fist and with all his strength swung it laterally at Tucker's hand, knocking the pistol loose. It slid across the tiled floor toward a recess of the restaurant.

"Goddamnit, Tucker, you idiot," Blackford hissed. *"They've got machine guns out there!"* He suddenly changed his tactics. "Get Lao Dai out of the way. There—" Blackford pointed in the direction of the pistol. Tucker breathed heavily, said nothing, and began to drag Lao Dai toward the kitchen. With the bar blocking their view of the outside, they stayed in place. It seemed a long time before the firing stopped. It was only eighteen minutes, the papers the next day recorded, though parallel coordinated attacks nearby lasted as much as a half hour. A half hour, and five U.S. soldiers killed, seventy-six wounded, five B-57 jet bombers and fifteen transports damaged, four helicopters and three Skyraider bombers destroyed, and the state prison opened, with over one hundred Vietcong released. There were several hundred casualties among the native population, including over one half of the patrons of Le Bon Laboureur who had been dining outside.

Charlie had made his demonstration. He was everywhere. Nobody was safe from him.

★ ★ ★ ★ ★ ★ ★ ★ ★ ★ ★

Chapter Thirty-Two

Robert Kennedy, having resigned as Attorney General to run for the Senate seat now held by Republican Kenneth Keating, was campaigning before a full house of students at Columbia University. He was everywhere met with a kind of tentative affection—not unexpected, less than one year after the tragedy at Dallas, but different in kind from the visceral delight his brother had engendered among college students. His opponent, Senator Keating, had a good reputation. He was a liberal Republican who, however, had been at the forefront of those who had warned against Fidel Castro. It was Kenneth Keating, more than one week ahead of the event, who

had warned, in October 1962, that nuclear missiles were being introduced into Cuba. Official
Washington had paid no attention to what the
insiders dismissed as attention-getting rodo-
montade by a senator who wanted to stay in the
headlines, his campaign only a couple of years
away.

Keating was at heart a soft-spoken man, but
he had been infuriated by Robert Kennedy's
most recent maneuver, against which, however,
he could not publicly protest. For two years,
every week at noon on Saturday, Kenneth Keating had delivered a five-minute radio address to
the voters. The first minute had become quietly
celebrated among political junkies who tuned in.
It was, quite simply, hilarious: whatever the
week's news, Senator Keating would succeed in
giving it an amusing spin. The cost of the humorist's time, who wrote these lines for the senator—leftovers, for the most part, from the heavy
ration he and his three confederates wrote
every week for Johnny Carson—had been subsidized by a friend of Keating's who had insisted
that a jollier public personality would pay off in
the next election. When Bobby Kennedy became a candidate, he and his staff decided that
Keating needed to be separated from his hu-

morist. A Kennedy deputy traveled to Hollywood, easily established that the writer was himself a Democrat, arranged for a personal call from Bobby, together with the promise of "a more realistic" compensation for his extra work, and the following Friday in Washington, when ordinarily the script from Hollywood arrived at Keating's office, there came instead a letter reporting that the burden of work at the studio would, unfortunately, keep him from continuing to supply Senator Kenneth Keating with the weekly roll, wishing him all the best, had been a pleasure working with him, sincerely.

That was bad news, losing his best writer. But when, one week later, candidate Robert Kennedy announced that he too would make a weekly broadcast, Senator Keating and his staff were there, listening in to the first one. And the first full minute was a series of engaging gags about the week's developments, of exactly the pattern Kenneth Keating had made popular.

Keating rose. "He has stolen my humorist!" But of course no one could contrive a non-humiliating formula for making the protest public.

But since the bad news from Vietnam had broken in the Saturday-morning papers, Keating wondered whether Robert Kennedy would begin his noon broadcast, opposite Kenneth Keating, with a joke about Bien Hoa. And what would he say to the Columbia students on the subject?

Kennedy elected to devote his broadcast to the need for federal health insurance. This left his listeners with the impression that the Vietnam news, which overwhelmed all other concerns, had broken after Mr. Kennedy had recorded his broadcast. But he could not avoid being accosted by Bien Hoa when he met with the students at the McMillin academic theater at one o'clock. What matters, his principal aide had said to him in the late morning, "is your *aspect.* Grave, deliberate, outraged, sad, determined. Got it?"

"Got it."

What I want to know, the first student panelist said, after the brief introductory remarks, *is how can the Vietcong stage a massive raid just twelve miles from Saigon?*

It was an act of sheer adventurism, Mr. Kennedy said pensively. By no means representative of the strength of the Vietcong, which we have every reason to believe is diminishing every month, with our strategic hamlet program.

These were desperadoes. They will undoubtedly be tracked down and be made to pay the penalty for killing civilians, to say nothing of brave United States soldiers.

How does the President intend to respond?

Mr. Kennedy had spoken with him over the telephone just an hour or two earlier, and had been told that all the aircraft destroyed or damaged would be quickly replaced, and that the incident would by no means provoke the Administration into relenting in its determination, so frequently reiterated by his late brother, to stop the Communist aggression, or into thoughtless retaliations.

Did Mr. Kennedy think the President's attitude correct?

Mr. Kennedy turned his head just a little, in that special, affecting way of his, and said that yes, he thought the President's strategy sound, but only in context of the imperative need to press for a negotiated settlement, a return to the Geneva Accords, and that when elected—if elected (smile)—he would do everything he could to continue to fuel enthusiasm for diplomatic initiatives. But meanwhile there was no alternative to standing by our commitments to our ally and to the relevant treaties.

The applause, while not deafening, was substantial, and reassuring.

"How'd I do?" Kennedy asked his aide, back in the car and headed for his new house in Long Island, necessary to his rebirth as a resident of New York.

"Good. *Perfect* line . . . got-to-keep-up-our resolution . . . help-our-allies . . . but look-for-diplomatic-pressures . . . Good. Hang on to it. By the way, *did* you speak to the President?"

"No. But I left word with a pal at the White House to log the call in on the record. LBJ will understand. He *always* understands things like that."

The aide was right. President Johnson did understand it. He was casually advised, later that day, of the imaginary telephone call, and of Bobby's comments at Columbia. They were innocuous, LBJ concluded. And Bobby had been correct in reporting that the President would order immediate replacement of the damaged aircraft. He did wonder how Bobby knew this, since the order had only gone out at about the time Bobby spoke, noon. Goddamn informant on the staff, probably over at the Pentagon. . . . What he couldn't understand, and nobody he had questioned could enlighten him on the point—not McNamara, not Rostow, not Bundy, not McCone—was the ability of the Vietcong to stage so dramatic a raid so close to South Vietnamese headquarters; that, and their *motives* in doing so. Why behave so provocatively at this time, so close to a national election?

McNamara had not really been helpful. McCone had said something to the effect that the eternal South Vietnamese intramural political squabbling, and the recent public protests against General Khanh, in-again, out-again, might have been a reason for the North Vietnamese publicly to challenge any notion that South Vietnam was stabilizing.

The door to the Oval Office opened, after a perfunctory knock. A military aide approached the President, laid a folder down on his desk, turned around and walked out. Johnson opened it.

Hanoi had broadcast that the Bien Hoa incidents had been in retaliation for the U.S. raids following the "fake" Tonkin Gulf incident of August 4, and in further retaliation against more recent disguised raids against North Vietnam on the Laotian frontier, and by naval forces which had shelled the coastal areas of Quang Binh

Province. And that the raid had been further motivated in retaliation against Saigon's execution of Nguyen Can Troi, who had attempted to assassinate Secretary McNamara during his last visit to Vietnam.

LBJ allowed himself to wonder whether attempting to assassinate McNamara ought to be a capital offense.

The President allowed himself to wonder where it would all end, how would it end.

★ ★ ★ ★ ★ ★ ★ ★ ★ ★ ★

Chapter Thirty-Three

NOVEMBER 2, 1964
SAIGON, SOUTH VIETNAM

It was after two in the morning when the telephone rang in the safe house where Blackford was asleep. As usual, he came rather slowly to his senses, his reaction beginning only after the third ring. Sally? But as he switched on the light he knew it couldn't be Sally calling. He hadn't given her this telephone number, and hadn't expected a call from her.

Tucker.

"Sorry 'bout this, Black, but I got to see you. Yes, I know what time it is, but I'm scheduled to go back to Savannakhet tomorrow and you're going to Danang, and I can't wait another couple of weeks for our next meeting."

"Come on around, Tucker."

He arrived in ten minutes. Blackford had on khaki trousers and was barefoot. He led Tucker to the kitchen table, on it fresh coffee and two bottles of beer. Blackford sat down. "Take whatever you want, Tucker."

He poured himself coffee. "You, Black?"

"Same."

"I got to tell you something. But I got to swear you to silence."

"Tucker . . . Look, sometimes it can't work that way."

Tucker paused. "Can't you trust me?"

"Can't you trust *me*?"

"What do you mean? Why do you think I'd be here, if I couldn't trust you?"

"I mean: You tell me what you want to tell me, and I'll have to decide whether I'm obliged to communicate it to someone. Trust me to make the decision."

Tucker hesitated. "All right. But on one condition: that you level with me on whether you intend to—to give it away. My secret."

Blackford nodded his head lightly.

"Okay. Well." Again, Tucker hesitated. "It's this. I found something out tonight." He stared away. Blackford didn't press him. His face still turned, Tucker went on. "Madame Lao Dai works for North Vietnam."

Blackford breathed deeply. Tucker did not go on. After a moment Blackford spoke.

"How did you find out?"

"I went to her apartment after the meeting this afternoon. I had told her I wouldn't be there until ten, that I had to have dinner with you and Rufus. I didn't know you had another engagement. I reached the landing—she's on the fourth floor—just when her door opened, and a young guy, Vietnamese, left, carrying a briefcase. Didn't see me clearly, was in a hurry. I kept walking, as though going on up to the fifth floor, let him get to the staircase and start down. I turned around and followed him.

"I swear I don't know what made me do it, but when he was out on the street and had walked maybe a block, block and a half—street was empty—I ran up. Grabbed him. I asked who he was. He said in French he was a schoolteacher. I said let me see your briefcase. With his left hand he handed me the case, with his right hand he went for a pistol in his pocket. He didn't have a chance: I smashed his face in, plenty of time, pistol fell on the pavement. I dragged him and the case into a side alley. He was out. The case was locked. I found the key in his pocket. I opened it. There were two rolls of film in it, undeveloped. And four packets of U.S. bills, $1,000 stamped on each packet. Then . . . then in the document compartment two folders. The first folder had a receipt for one thousand dollars. Signed: Lao Dai, dated yesterday, November 1. And in the other packet, black-and-white pictures . . ."

Blackford waited. Tucker turned, again, to one side. There was an audible catch in his throat. Blackford said nothing.

"Pictures of me . . . having sex with Lao Dai."

Blackford permitted himself to whistle. But he said only, "What did you do?"

"You guessed it, I went back to the apartment house. Knocked on the door, she answered. I locked it behind me, walked over to the table, opened the briefcase, spread out the stuff, told her she hadn't asked for enough money, here was three thousand dollars more, and I tossed her the money."

"And?"

"I don't feel I can go through it all, Black. But that was at about seven o'clock. And I left her half an hour ago, went to a bar and called you. I guess I can just put it together and say: I forgave her.''

Blackford spoke cautiously. ''Why?''

''Because she convinced me. She convinced me she's trying to avoid a world war, convinced me that she loves me, that she will do anything I want, including turn herself in if I ask her to; that the North Vietnamese are going to win, no matter what, and the sooner they do, the less lives it's going to cost. That she had no idea there was a trick camera in the bedroom, she'd give them hell over that; that the money was to pay several subordinates on her payroll. And convinced me that Ho Chi Minh is very sick, is on the way out, and the younger people coming in aren't the old Stalin types, but independents who have nothing but contempt for the old ways, and that the new Vietnam will be just a socialist state, like Sweden—'' He stopped talking suddenly. ''You think I'm crazy?''

''No, Tucker. I don't think you're crazy. But I think you've got to be real careful. I mean, let's take Lao Dai. Maybe she's on the level with you . . . but then maybe she isn't. If she isn't, she might try to ambush you, get you kidnapped—

you'd be a pretty hot property up at Hanoi, you know."

"That's right, Black. Either she's telling me what she really believes, or she isn't telling me what she really believes. I got to decide, right? Well, I have decided. I have decided she is telling me the truth. So the question is: What do I do?"

"You mean, what do you do—other than tell me what's happened?"

Tucker nodded. "Besides that?"

"Well, you won't be surprised, Tucker, if I tell you you owe it to—to all of us to go back to Savannakhet and finish up on Igloo."

"I figured you'd say that."

"Will you?" Blackford spoke slowly.

"I haven't one hundred percent decided. Will you agree to keep secret on Lao Dai until I decide?"

"I have to—for now. For you."

"Black, can I ask you for another favor?"

"Sure."

"Can we talk for a while about something else? Anything else?" Tucker reached for the bottle of beer. Blackford gave his answer by reaching for the second bottle.

★ ★ ★ ★ ★ ★ ★ ★ ★ ★ ★

Chapter Thirty-Four

NOVEMBER 2, 1964
SAIGON, SOUTH VIETNAM–
SAVANNAKHET, LAOS

Tucker left just after 4 A.M. During their last half hour together Blackford decided what he would do. He could keep his word, of course—it was much easier to do than Tucker expected, given that Rufus and South Vietnamese intelligence knew about Lao Dai. He could bring in ARVN Intelligence or for that matter U.S. Intelligence, bring them into the picture in the sense of advising them that, just possibly, Major Tucker Montana would not be going back to Savannakhet. But if he did that, Tucker would be on a kind of CIA–Judge Advocate General–Pentagon assembly line and any hope of dealing creatively with the Montana problem would be gone. As

Tucker talked, of this and that—of his childhood, of Fr. Enrique, of Los Alamos—Blackford decided that the key was Alphonse Juilland. As far as Alphonse was concerned, Blackford Oakes, and only Blackford Oakes, was his superior. He could instruct Alphonse to do anything, and he would do it. And Alphonse, with his knowledge of Vietnamese, could travel anywhere more inconspicuously than any American, and if Alphonse was ignorant of intelligence practice, as he insisted he was, he was not in the least ignorant of ways to get by in Indochina—whom to bribe, how, with how much, how to get information not readily available.

Five minutes after Tucker left, he had Alphonse on the telephone.

He instructed him to be on the 6 A.M. flight to Saigon, to call the duty officer and arrange to have a naval officer sit in at Oakes's office in Danang. He should be instructed to tell anyone who called in for Mr. Oakes that he was out of the office but would be back "in the afternoon," and could the naval officer take a message for Mr. Oakes? He should call the technician from Aberdeen and tell him to proceed without Oakes on the scanner tests. He gave Juilland the address of the safe house: "I will expect to see you at about seven-thirty." He hung up the phone. Tucker: That poor, wretched, complicated, endearing man. He hoped Rufus would not call in. His own calendar called on him to be in Danang. Perhaps he could still catch the 10 A.M. flight. He hoped desperately that Tucker would telephone him with his decision early. If not, Tucker might call him in Danang, perhaps even leave a message with the naval aide. That message: Either Tucker Montana would be returning to duty in Nakhom Phanom, or—?

That, three hours later he explained to Alphonse, was *his* responsibility: to follow Major Montana and to find out when Major Montana goes if he does go to Savannakhet, and from there to Nakhom Phanom. "I know you never laid eyes on him when he was giving us help with the Tonkin raid, but you talked over the telephone. Probably you would recognize his voice. What I don't have is a picture of him, which would be useful right now. But he doesn't look like many other people. He's as tall as Gregory Peck—you know the American movie star? Good. And in fact he looks a lot like Gregory Peck, and his hair is exactly like Peck's. He is almost always traveling with a large, I mean, a very large"—Blackford spread out his hands—

"briefcase, brown, with a lot of old airplane stickers on it. You have to spot him if he goes to the airport—when he goes to the airport. Whatever flight he goes on, I want you on it. Even if it's a flight to Savannakhet. If he lands there and goes on to his office or to his apartment, call me and come on back. If he goes anywhere else, I want to know where. Here," he was glad he had picked up the Danang payroll from Rufus yesterday, "is all the money you could possibly need. Share some of it with the reservations and ticket people at the airport. Don't let them tell you there's not another seat on any plane Montana gets into."

Nine o'clock, no word from Tucker. No word at nine-thirty. He initiated the call, but Tucker's number didn't answer, and he was not going to call Lao Dai, though he had filed away her number. Too late to get the ten o'clock to Danang. He would wait until ten, then rush out for the eleven o'clock flight. He called and switched his reservations. Ten o'clock, no call. Blackford hurried to the street and got a taxi.

When two hours later he walked into his own office he greeted the sleepy lieutenant (jg) on duty, who had been aroused by Juilland at five that morning. "Messages?"

"Yes, sir." The lieutenant looked down on the desk and read out the message he had taken. "A Mr. Montana. He said to tell you he was taking a couple of days off to hunt boar with an old friend in Laos. He'll give you a buzz when he gets back to his office in—" the lieutenant stumbled over the pronunciation of Nakhon Phanom. "All right, sir?"

Blackford thanked him and dismissed him. No call from Rufus, he noted. And no call from Juilland.

At Savannakhet, on the Thai border and the nearest commercial airport to Nakhon Phanom, Tucker descended with his old labeled briefcase in hand and waited in the baggage room for his suitcase. He looked carefully about the large tin-roofed shelter, lit up by neon bulbs around which the flies and the mosquitoes buzzed. He was familiar with the two ancient men who acted as porters, and with the woman at the dispatch desk. Only three other passengers waited for luggage. They had been seated several rows ahead of him on the DC-3. Two of them had sat together talking in Chinese. The third, a younger man, perhaps in his thirties, was absorbed by a crossword puzzle and by a photograph album which he opened three times on the flight. Tucker could see pictures of a young woman and a baby, the baby only a few months old, photographed in every conceivable pose including seated on the potty. The young man closed the album with palpable reluctance.

Tucker's bag came down the slide. He picked it up and went out toward the roadway. He shook his head kindly at the toothless stick of a man who beckoned him toward his taxi. Seconds later a modern Peugeot sedan, dusty, stopped beside him. The driver said in French, "We have been sent by Madame Lao Dai."

The passenger door was opened by the man in back, and Tucker got in. The driver meanwhile took Tucker's suitcase to put in the trunk. He reached also for Tucker's briefcase, but Tucker declined to relinquish it. The doors now closed, the car started up. The man at his side, wearing a deep blue shirt open at the collar, and cotton pants, leaned over, his hand extended. "I am Bui Tin."

"Tucker Montana."

During the thirty-five-minute drive to the Thai inn whose telephone number Tucker had taken the pains to memorize, and which he had called that morning, by way of establishing its bona fides as a functioning inn, Bui Tin spoke without pausing. (Tucker had asked for an imaginary Mr. Chung Leh, the operator had taken a moment or two, evidently looking through her records, and come back: "Sorry, sir, there is no Mr. Chung Leh staying at the Lao-tse Inn.") Colonel Bui Tin talked about the history of this easternmost part of Thailand, about the many military skirmishes that had taken place here against the Japanese during the war, about the prospects for that year's rice crop.

Tucker hardly listened, thinking back always to the tearful Lao Dai, so shaken by the events of yesterday, so insistent, finally, that at the very least Tucker, whom she loved above all mortal beings, living and dead, should meet with her cousin by marriage, Colonel Bui Tin, who was in charge of developing the Ho Chi Minh Trail. "You would be meeting in neutral territory, my darling Tucker. What can happen there? And what is wrong with meeting and hearing the viewpoint of my cousin? You are two very impor- tant historical people. His job is to construct the Trail, your job is to make the Trail useless. It is what might happen if you succeed that worries me most, so much so that I can think of very little else, just of more Bien Hoas, oh darling."

She fell into his arms, exhausted by their three-hour exchange. She did not try to entice him to her bed. She was too afraid, she said, too obsessed with her thoughts and fears. It was then that he had said, his mind a blur, "All right. I'll see him."

Lao Dai's eyes brightened. "You will!"

Lao Dai said she must immediately make the right contact. She would need to go to the public telephone. She would be back in perhaps fifteen minutes.

She was back in forty minutes, glowing with pleasure and affection. Could he leave the following day on the noon flight to Savannakhet, "where you fly to anyway"? Leave word that he is on a hunting trip with friends? If he could catch that flight, her cousin would be there to pick him up. Tucker told her he was already booked on that flight. Now I must go. He kissed her, and went to the bar to telephone Blackford at Danang.

During the six and a half hours of discussions that began at six in the evening and were uninterrupted by the simple meal brought in at eight, Colonel Bui Tin made not a single unfriendly reference to the United States. Quite the contrary, he paid the United States full tribute for the war of liberation against the Japanese, with maybe the exception (Bui Tin bowed his head) of the atomic bomb, about which he had serious moral misgivings.

But the United States simply did not understand the motives of the North Vietnamese. Granted, they were—the North Vietnamese and the American people—attached to different political philosophies. It would after all be unnatural if that were not the case, given the different history of the two peoples, would it not? The Vietnamese were a proud race, plagued by strangers from abroad and neighbors from the Indochinese peninsula for centuries. Their experience was different from that of the Pilgrims who settled in the Commonwealth of Massachusetts. But one thing that was critical to this discussion, which Major Montana had to accept as a constant, was the North Vietnamese determination.

They see what they call the liberation of the South as a sublime and holy goal, and every last one of them—of us—would die to see it accomplished. To that end, Bui Tin whispered, President Ho had wrested very significant concessions from the governments of the Chinese and the Russian people. Peking and Moscow were not only helping the North Vietnamese in their war of liberation right then as the two gentlemen were speaking, in the most civilized way, but were prepared to go much further—I dare not be too specific about this, Bui Tin said—much, much further, if necessary, to accomplish our goal, which they too hold to be sacred. They are prepared to go right to—the brink.

And who knows, when nations in a nuclear age go to the brink, is it ever certain that they can just—stop? Bui Tin asked a philosophical question: Was there *ever* a war entered into willingly, which one combatant retrospectively would have engaged in if he had known its outcome? Imagine General Tojo authorizing the attack on Pearl Harbor if he could have known that five years later he would be swinging from a gibbet! Imagine Adolf Hitler marching into Russia if he had had a preview of his last days in the bunker! Imagine what prophetic knowledge would have done to quiet the enthusiasm in Athens for the last stage of the Peloponnesian War! What Carthaginian would willingly have provoked Rome if he could have seen the wasteland that was left of the great city its citizens had inhabited and taken such pride in?

In this respect, Colonel Bui Tin and Major Tucker Montana were as one, were they not? Neither wished to contribute to the destruction of their two countries. And what North Vietnam wished was so modest historically, so modest geographically: the end of the false division between North and South.

"Yes, sure. But we don't see that and we're preparing to knock the shit out of your supply line along the Trail, Colonel."

Bui Tin smiled. "We know that you have in your hands the technology to prolong the struggle, to cause many more casualties, in the North and in the South—what a little preview Bien Hoa was of the horrors that lie ahead. And if American troops come there will be many casualties, thousands and thousands, tens of thousands perhaps, but the end will always be the same."

"But wait a minute, Colonel. If we stop you at the Trail, how're you going to keep going?"

Bui Tin told him that they would simply find other means. There was *no way* the Americans could stop the passage of the spirit of liberation from crossing rivers and mountains, oceans and rice paddies, seizing the heart of the people.

"You mean seizing the heart of the people by shooting them and torturing them. Come on, Colonel."

Bui Tin explained that he was as much appalled by the practice of warfare as the major, even though the two were professional soldiers. Bui Tin explained that he had been brought up in a Catholic school in Hué, and knew both by education and by experience how precious human life was. But what matters is the objective. He didn't know, granted, whether, if he, Bui Tin, had the authority to drop an atom bomb, he would exercise that authority by going ahead and dropping it on Saigon. But short of an atom bomb, guerrilla warfare, by whatever it was called—look at Algeria!—had always been the same, throughout recorded time. There wasn't any way to keep people from using force and violence to advance objectives they thought themselves spiritually committed to. . . .

At about eleven, Colonel Bui Tin asked whether Major Montana would join him in a glass of cognac. His father, he said, had been a devoted cognac drinker, back in the Hué days, and even as a young man he had been infected with the habit, and liked every now and then to refresh his recollection of the French—miracle.

After so long a talk and all those questions and debate, Tucker was delighted at the idea. He reached into his briefcase and brought out a package of cigars, offering one to Colonel Bui Tin, who declined with a smile. "I used to. But they are too scarce now. I have put them away until—until Liberation Day."

Cognac in hand, Tucker asked a pointed question. "What would it mean if the Trail were clear to you?"

"Just this: The end of the war after maybe one year, instead of five, six years. That, and much more: Avoiding any possibility of a nuclear war."

Tucker emptied his glass, and put it out absentmindedly to accept a refill. They talked another hour, and Tucker announced he would turn in. They shook hands.

In his bed he tried to sleep, gave it up. He had to think. He thought first about Lao Dai. There could be no mistaking the love she felt for him. That was a given. He thought then of the sacrifices she had been prepared to make. He found himself admiring, in a professional way, what she had done. Who was he, who had machine-

gunned forty-one Huks, to criticize her decep-
tions? And then the points she made, and those
Bui Tin had made, paraded by his mind. And,
there was no way to avoid it, he felt the same
seizure he had felt a week or two after his flight
on the *Enola Gay* after he had seen the pictures—hundreds of pictures, clinically reviewed
by his colleagues: the pictures of the aftermath
of total war.

He began to sweat. He was afraid of that particular sweat. It had hit him at Los Alamos, and
again in one of his conversations with Fr. Enrique, after he had left the hospital where he had
been given something or other that kept him,
those three weeks, only half conscious, trying to
drive those pictures out of his mind. And, of
course, the jeep episode with Lao Dai . . .

It was only after he had come to his solemn
conclusion that he finally slept, just as the dawn
came.

They did not wake him. It was eleven when he
suddenly snapped up from a deep, serene
sleep. He dressed and went down to the dining
room. A waitress was there and he asked for
coffee, and for Colonel Bui Tin.

Back in the colonel's suite, Tucker began.

"Do you know, I think you're right, Colonel. Now, that doesn't mean I like your system of government. I hate it. If I lived there I'd do my best to assassinate Ho." He looked up at Bui Tin. Had he gone too far?

His host smiled, in patient understanding of his guest's position. He said only, "President Ho is mortal, Major Montana."

Tucker resumed. "What makes you think I could clear the Trail for you?"

"I don't think you can, Major. If . . . reports of what you are doing in Nakhon Phanom are accurate about the technology you are amassing, you will make it very difficult. Especially in the two passes. It is very sad, because obviously you cannot persuade the Central Intelligence Agency or the Pentagon to cancel the project."

"You kidding? If you think for one minute that your line of thinking would sell in official Washington, you're crazy. No. They're not going to stop work on the Trail. But . . ." Tucker hesitated. His last hesitation. He put down his glass. "What I can do is teach you how to beat our Spikebuoys."

"Spikebuoys?" Bui Tin feigned ignorance of

the contents of Tucker's thirty-two-page note-book, which he and Vietnamese and Soviet technicians had been studying for two weeks.

"Yuh. They're the pivotal devices of our Igloo operation, as we call it. They're designed to send the signals to our computers, which will relay the information to bombers and fighter planes."

Colonel Tin looked forlorn.

"The thing of it is," Tucker said, "I could de-velop a counterweapon. Something that would make the Spikebuoys useless."

Suddenly Tucker Montana, scientist, was en-grossed again, as he had been years before, searching for a trigger mechanism, now begin-ning the search for a device that might remove a trigger. "It's a matter of getting at their fre-quency and displacing it. High-tech dislocators, but doable in the field. Lead scout comes upon the first Spikebuoy, a truck comes in equipped with the right stuff." Each Spikebuoy has a sep-arate frequency, he thought. "You'd need to en-velop the aboveground portion of the Spikebuoy in a copper flyscreen. At the bottom of the flys-creen you'd need a braided copper wire a few feet long, soldered to the screen on one end and soldered to a copper pointed rod at the other end. You got to then stick a carefully shielded antenna, connected to a portable frequency analyzer in there. A technician slams a big sledgehammer on the ground and the Spikebuoy broadcasts an alarm. But it doesn't go anywhere except into the analyst's frequency analyzer. Do that along the whole Spikebuoy fence and then load the frequencies into a kind of sequencer. You can destroy the Spikebuoys and then set a series of transmitters to those frequencies. The sequencer will activate the transmitters and provide the same sounds the Spikebuoys would have broadcast if trucks or troops were being heard. Only you'd do this at the other edge of the pass. Aircraft would attack where the Spikebuoys had been—and then your trucks and troops go through fast after the attack is over. There are lots of details. For instance, the truck would need to be heavily protected by wet blankets or canvas over its hood, prevent infrared detection. And over its body too, to protect against radiation of heat by the crew and their electronics. But I guess I'm just telling you all this. It can be done. I know how to do it.''

At last, Tucker thought. The elusive trigger. The huge cloud. The charred figures at table.

The blur, the dizziness as he had fought for consciousness. Study the *problem,* solve the engineering question. Yes . . . more. But now he was maybe preventing a nuclear war.

Bui Tin drew a deep breath.

"You would be willing to teach us how?"

"Yes."

"When?"

"Now. Tomorrow. It's all here. In my head. No point in postponing it, is there?"

"No point at all, Major."

★ ★ ★ ★ ★ ★ ★ ★ ★ ★ ★

Chapter Thirty-Five

On Election Eve Barry Goldwater was the star of the biggest rally, his supporters and some newsmen reported, in the history of San Francisco. He was grateful for it, but as a practiced politician with a sensitive ear he knew how to distinguish that special sound that said, "Barry, we love you—*even though you're going to lose*" from "Barry, we love you and rejoice in your forthcoming victory!" He thought back on the acclaim given to Adlai Stevenson at the Democratic Party convention in 1960, which had been a way of saying: "Adlai, we love you truly, but we're going to vote for Jack Kennedy." Everyone knew what was going to happen, Goldwater thought to himself, though it was of course important to keep spirits high; and for that reason, in his speech he stressed what he intended to do after he was sworn in, ha-ha. It was only with Bill Baroody and young Freddy Anderson, from whom nothing was any longer withheld, that he would permit himself to speculate on just which half-dozen states he might actually win. Unlike many candidates, Barry Goldwater had adjusted to the outcome. In fact he had adjusted to it at his last appearance in San Francisco—when he was nominated.

His wife, Peggy, almost always at his side—the exceptions being when she sensed that her presence was an encumbrance—whispered to him on the airplane. "Why Fredonia again, dear?" Barry Goldwater had made it a habit to end his campaigns at that little town of three hundred people, half of them Indians, on the Arizona-Utah border, a habit begun when he first ran for state office. "Superstition?" Freddy asked him.

He shrugged his shoulders. "Not really. If it was superstition, that would mean I thought I was going to win. Hell, I'm not even sure I'll carry Fredonia." There he mingled with ease and pleasure among the cowboys and ranchers, the

Navajo and Paiute Indians—"my people," he referred to them, intending to convey exactly that about people uncontaminated with the disease he thought himself at war with.

And then his final flight as a candidate, to Phoenix, to his house high in the hills, nearby Camelback Mountain.

He'd dearly have loved to be left alone that evening, but he would not do that to his staff. They needed those last hours together. The press insisted on one final meeting, and he interrupted his drink of bourbon long enough to say to the crowded room, without much spirit, that he only regretted that he had not spelled out the issues as well as he had hoped to do. But then he decided he would not assume the entire burden of an unsuccessful campaign. He added, "If only Jack Kennedy were here." Yes, it would have been a genuine national debate on national issues if it had been Jack Kennedy. Kennedy was shrewd, like his successor, but there was a certain wholesomeness there, an appetite for a genuine encounter for which Lyndon Johnson had absolutely none. Everyone in the Congress knew, though they did not dwell on it, that Johnson had stolen the votes necessary to get him his seat in the Senate. By means other than vote theft he would continue to win elections. But the loss tomorrow, Goldwater thought, could not be attributed either to the political craft of Johnson or the premature idealism of Goldwater's causes. The public was fatigued. He had several times made a point of this in private conversation. The voters did not like the prospect of three different Presidents in twelve months. He closed his eyes and determined not to think about it.

He would have an hour or two of relaxation before sitting down with the gang in front of the television set and watching the returns overrun him. He'd spend that time engaged in his highest form of relaxation, tuning in on ham radio. The setup next door was his Elysian Field, and in no time he was standing by, as had become his habit for over a year, to patch calls through from U.S. servicemen in the field to their wives or sweethearts or parents or, in one case, banker. This accommodation cannot be performed without listening in to the conversation; the intermediary needs to know when it is terminated in order to bring in the next call.

He patched through four calls, one from a Signal Service sergeant in Danang, a second

from a major in Hué, a third from a private in
Saigon, and then a lieutenant in Saigon. Every
conversation touched on the Bien Hoa assault.

"Was I hurt? Darling, you know that I am stationed in Hué. The gooks have some pretty effective firepower, but they haven't yet
developed a machine gun that will fire three
hundred and fifty miles."

"Oh, honey, that's the best news I've heard in
months!"

The Army personnel, Goldwater noted, were
on the one hand reassuring about Bien Hoa ("It
was just a stunt, Kate. Like when Jimmy jumped
into the pool from the roof, you remember? He
didn't try it twice"), on the other hand detectably
discouraged. He knew then that the shock conveyed by the headlines in America registered a
shock genuinely felt in the field. He was musing
on the implications of Bien Hoa when Peggy
called him in. She smiled: "For the festivities."

"Yeah." He kissed her, in the privacy of his
radio room, with heartfelt passion.

Goldwater entered the living room. And, unex-
pectedly, the fourteen people in it, his staff and
a few old friends, stood up. As they might have
done if he had entered as President-elect of the
United States. He had to turn his head to con-

ceal the sudden mist. "Hey," he said, addressing himself to nobody in particular, "let's not make the concession speech till tomorrow, when nobody will be listening. I don't want to hear LBJ pay me compliments. Might gag."

Denis Kitchel answered him. "Oh. But that won't make the press outside go away. So, if you change your mind they'll be there."

"I won't change my mind," Senator Goldwater said, a glass of bourbon in his hand, sitting down in the armchair left vacant for him opposite the large television set.

Four hours later, the cheering in the room was limited to cheers for Alabama, Georgia, Louisiana, Mississippi, South Carolina, and Arizona. He had carried Fredonia.

★ ★ ★ ★ ★ ★ ★ ★ ★ ★ ★

Chapter Thirty-Six

Tucker spent two days at the inn with Bui Tin and the two technicians who had flown the 250 miles from Hanoi to Savannakhet on the chartered flight when the word was passed up that Montana was prepared to cooperate. The technicians arrived in the early afternoon of the day following Tucker's long evening with Bui Tin. Tucker had occupied himself during the morning making sketches of the evasive equipment that would substantially nullify the whole of the Igloo White operation except, as he explained to Bui Tin, on those occasions when troops traveling down the Trail failed to spot a Spikebuoy, shield its transmission in time, and penetrate its frequency. "This isn't going to protect everything you've got, Colonel."

"I did not expect that it would, Major." Bui Tin spoke deferentially, as always.

Late in the morning Tucker said he would need some proper drafting paper. This was not readily available at the Lao-tse Inn, so Bui Tin gave careful instructions to the driver, who an hour or so later came back with it. He had found, he said, the small supply store that furnished routine provisions to Nakhon Phanom, forty-two miles away. Tucker found himself sketching on paper on which appeared, in tiny print at the bottom right, "U.S. Government issue." He bit his lip. He would need to get used to the paradoxes. Already had, in a way. Since making up his mind the night before, he had not tortured himself about it. He continued with his work.

The Russian who came in from Hanoi knew only German, so that his questions to Tucker needed to be relayed through his colleague, the North Vietnamese technician, who also spoke German. Within ten minutes Tucker knew that he was dealing, in the case of the gook, with a total naïf. The Russian's background, on the other hand, was considerable—but oh, light-years behind what Tucker Montana was talking about, so that he had to proceed slowly, spelling out every step of the technological machinations by which his powerful offensive system could be cheated of its prey. The last day was devoted to doing detailed sketches, with careful attention given to the three radiating elements that extended about 24 inches, enclosed within the flyscreen, and explicit instruction on how to tap the antenna with the frequency analyzer. These instruments, the Russian said, were available in rudimentary shape in the Soviet Union, but if the major could acquire one from the CIA and slip it to Bui Tin, that would of course make the work of refining it easier. Tucker nodded, making certain, by his detailed designs, that whatever the delay in getting their hands on an American sequencer, the technicians in Moscow could get on with the development of an adequate facsimile.

By dinnertime the job was done. There was nothing left to do until the airplane the next day. The flight to Saigon left at 11:15 A.M.

"With your permission, Major, we will leave on our charter before you, at ten."

"Sure, Colonel." Tucker did not care if they left at ten that night. He would make an excuse to Bui Tin, eat alone, and spend the evening reading. He hadn't let on to anybody that he had yet to read *Gone with the Wind,* and it was only when Lao Dai, who had just finished it, pressed him to help her analyze it that he confessed. Without hesitation, she had stuffed the fat paperback into his briefcase.

And that was only three days ago, Tucker thought. He agreed to have a cognac later in the evening with Bui Tin, and they met in the colonel's suite, without the technicians, at 10:30.

Bui Tin had given much thought to what, exactly, to say at the end. There must not be a hint of gratitude in the sense of favors done—quite wrong: Why should Montana do Bui Tin a favor?—But something, just a trace, of idealism shared. So that when he had poured the two drinks, Bui Tin lifted his hand and said, "Let us drink to a world without nuclear devastation." That sentiment surely ran no risk, and of course he knew, after the careful briefings from Lao Dai, that this theme was the fastest and surest way to Tucker's conscience.

Tucker raised his glass. "That's good enough for me, Colonel."

Something personal was needed, Bui Tin thought. He knew for certain only that Tucker would return to Lao Dai. He did not know whether he would now resign from the service, or continue in his job as if—as if nothing had happened. He eased into the subject carefully.

"Please give my cousin, Lao Dai, my warmest regards."

"Oh, I'll do that, Colonel, don't you worry."

A little probe. "Will she be returning to the United States with you?"

Tucker was startled. He had given the subject no thought, he reminded himself. But why should he have, since up until now he had thought himself as stuck in South Vietnam and Nakhon Phanom into the foreseeable future. "That's for down the line, Colonel."

"Why of course, I forgot. You are obviously needed here, in Nakhon Phanom."

"Actually," Tucker said—he was almost talking to himself—"actually, I'm not really needed. They've got all my ideas, the equipment is tested, it's just a matter of production and coordination. They don't really need me for that, though they think they do. But here I am, and here Lao Dai is, and as long as we're both together in the same place it doesn't matter, I guess."

Bui Tin nodded, as though he had expended his interest in the subject. He began one of his rambling historical disquisitions on the history and culture of the region, as if determined to complete what he had begun in the car. Tucker's mind was on other matters, though he sat there with the fine cognac, puffing on his cigar, producing his perfect smoke rings, and occasionally grunting this or that to suggest that he was following the colonel's anthropological lecture. When his cigar was finished, he took advantage of a cadence in the colonel's thought to rise and say, "That was very interesting, thank you very much."

Bui Tin rose, and bowed his head. There was a moment's pause.

Shake hands? The hell with it—Tucker extended his hand, and Bui Tin took it. There was no pressure exerted by either party. It was a formality.

The following morning, from his window, Tucker saw the three men departing in the same car that had fetched him. He would be following them out to the airport in an hour and a half. He had made his own arrangements with the inn to hire a car and driver.

Colonel Bui Tin let the technicians go through airport procedures ahead of him. They went through Laotian Customs and Immigration and would wait in the boarding area, or perhaps even inside the plane with the pilots, until Bui Tin joined them. This he would do quickly. Except as required, he did not want the pilots and the technicians in each other's company. No loose talk. Having waited ten minutes, he opened the car door. His suitcase had been taken by the Vietnamese technician and loaded onto the charter plane with his own. Bui Tin needed only to complete his passenger manifest card, go out through Customs and Immigration and board the charter.

He bent over the counter, writing out his name, address, birth date, profession, passport number and expiration date—information he had carefully memorized from the passport taken from the manager of a Hanoi state purchasing company. As he wrote out his name, dashing it off as if familiar, there was an explosion. It sounded on his right, outside the main airport shed. Bui Tin threw himself on the floor. So did the dozen other men and women in the shed, whether behind the counters or on the passengers' side. After a brief moment, there was a chorus of shouting and yelling. Two airport guards rushed to the site of the explosion.

In a minute one of them entered and said something in Thai. Bui Tin looked over and saw the passenger agent standing now, brushing off her clothes. He took it to be the all clear, stood up and, showing no emotion, completed his form, handing it to the agent. He leaned down to pick up his briefcase, but it was not there.

Agitated, he calculated: *The chances of its recovery are minimal.* In it were photographic copies of the Spikebuoy manual, taken from Lao Dai's photographs. All the work the major had done on the counter-Igloo operation lay safely with the technicians, who were on board the airplane or in the boarding area. His face pale, he turned to the agent. "Are we all right?"

"I do not know, sir, when Security will give us clearance to proceed." Security did so only after the arrival of central police who inspected the bomb that had sat under a bush alongside the terminal building, evidently detonated by radio signal. It had caused no damage. A search of everyone in the area revealed nothing incriminating. One hour later, Bui Tin and the two technicians were airborne on their chartered DC-3.

A few minutes later, Tucker Montana arrived. He inquired into the causes of the excitement and was told.

One more bomb, more or less, he said to himself without concern as he filled out his passenger form. He waited, seated on a single chair behind the little newsstand. He would prefer not to spot one of his colleagues from Nakhon Phanom coincidentally bound on the same flight to Saigon. He would of course tell any such person that he had been on a hunting vacation, though probably his colleague would wonder why he had not bothered to drop in at their facility while in the area. Tucker planned to return to Nakhon Phanom, but only after a day or two with Lao Dai, decompressing. He would deceive Blackford, talk only about the hunt, and say, Yes, he planned to return to work. He would try to persuade Blackford to keep his mouth shut about Lao Dai, promising in return to try to get her to defect to the South.

But no one came that he had ever seen before, with the exception of the young man who did the crossword puzzles and oohed over the family album. He was evidently bound back to Saigon, having done whatever business he was here to do.

In a piston plane, not a jet, it was a substantial flight, two hours and a half to fly the 360 miles across southern Laos and eastern Cambodia into Saigon, perched there on top of the Mekong Delta. Tucker was drained of strength, just as he remembered finding himself at the end of those sixteen-hour workdays at Los Alamos. He was stirred quietly by the thought of a warm, relaxed evening with Lao Dai. He would of course not tell her what he had done—Bui Tin had reassured him that no one would learn of his complicity from Hanoi—merely that he had listened to Bui Tin's line of argument, that he had found it persuasive, and that he would do his best to introduce her cousin's arguments in the circles he moved in. After all, she had said time and time again that all she wanted was for Tucker to *listen;* now he could safely say that, after all, he had spent two and one-half days with her cousin. Could anyone beat that for listening? He smiled as he reflected on the satisfied expression on her face when he especially pleased her.

At the safe house Blackford tore the receiver off the hook seconds after it had begun its ring.

"Yes. Alphonse?"

"Confirmed. He is on the eleven-fifteen to Saigon."

"Okay. Now listen, when he gets off the

plane, you stick close to him. If he waits for a bag, you wait for a bag. Come out of the airport right behind him. As soon as he gets outside, I'll collar him and tell him to come on in with you and me to the Citroën. I'll have it parked close. He trusts me, but I don't want to approach him while he's still in the airport waiting for a bag. Don't want to give him time to think. You got it?"

"*Entendu.*"

They were coming down. Tucker Montana held his nose and blew through it, easing the strain on his ears. Saigon looked awfully hot, compared to life on those nice hills in Thailand–Laos.

He walked down the narrow gangway and into the familiar airport, which seemed to grow in size every time he landed. He grabbed a copy of *Stars & Stripes,* which he scanned as he waited for his bag. Well whaddayaknow, Lyndon Johnson had been elected for a full term as President! There was a front-page picture of Goldwater, with the caption: "The Candidate who refused to concede until the next day." Probably had a hangover from celebrating, Tucker thought. Celebrating that he wouldn't have to handle this mess. But it was a good thing Goldwater was beaten. He was sure as hell likelier than Lyndon to bring on a world war.

He spotted his bag, picked it up, shoved the stub into the hands of the guard at the gate, and went out in the relentless sun to hail a cab.

He spotted Blackford walking toward him. He caught just the words, "Tuck, come on . . ."

A uniformed man with a rifle shoved Blackford to one side, hard. Another bore down on Tucker from the right, another from the left, a third behind him. "Major Montana, you are under arrest. Extend your hands behind your back."

Montana felt the steel press of the pistol on the small of his back.

He complied. A van drove up. The back door opened. The officer in charge, a South Vietnamese who wore a colonel's insignia, gave orders in Vietnamese to the driver. Twenty minutes later the van stopped. Tucker could hear gates being opened. He looked through the barred window at the back of the van and saw soldiers closing the gates. The van stopped. Tucker was led out and registered at the desk. Then to a bare wall where his two escorts left him, the officer in charge having said in English, "Stand still. Photograph." Tucker's eyes closed when the flash bulb popped. The guards were back. He was led to a cell guarded by a massive door. Inside there was a bench, and light only from a narrow slit, eight feet up. After he was unshackled, the guards left him, slamming the door shut.

Tucker Montana looked up at the narrow light, lay down on the bench and wept, and prayed for strength.

When the van came to the prison gates, Blackford told Alphonse to slow the Citroën in which they were trailing the military van.

"No point in getting any closer," he said wearily, bitterly. "They were one step ahead of us."

"We tried, Mr. Oakes. Wasn't anything more we could do. Didn't know they were also on the trail."

Blackford cursed himself. Hadn't Rufus *told* him that Tucker—and Lao Dai—would be tailed? There was nothing to be done at this point. Later.

Meanwhile, he had to be in Danang for the final, critical Tracer test. From there he would contact Rufus in Washington.

He didn't know that Rufus had been reached at the airport in Honolulu by the Director. Over the telephone he had been told to return immediately to Saigon. Ambassador Maxwell Taylor had called the Director a half hour earlier to report that South Vietnam Intelligence had picked up the chief architect of Operation Igloo and was holding him, incommunicado, in Kham Chi Hoa prison.

★ ★ ★ ★ ★ ★ ★ ★ ★ ★ ★

Chapter Thirty-Seven

Colonel Yen Chi, the head of the Army of the Republic of Vietnam Intelligence, was not himself able to understand the complexities detailed in the photographs that had been seized from the North Vietnamese colonel at the airport. That the plans had been done by Americans was obvious: all the writing—the specifications, the footnotes, the text—was in English. That it was information given to the enemy by Major Montana, while not yet absolutely established, seemed all but certain. Captain Minh-Lao Hoang had traveled on the Savannakhet flight with him, and had tracked him to the Lao-tse. At the inn he was in the company, continuously, of a Vietnamese who traveled under the name of Choi. A careful check on all incoming flights ended with the tailing, by one of Captain Minh-Lao's associates, of two men, one of them an Asiatic, the second a Russian, also to the Lao-tse Inn. . . . Silver had crossed hands and got from the dispatcher the information that the chartered airplane in which they came had flown in from Hanoi.

At the inn, close observation revealed that the two new arrivals, together with Major Montana and a fourth man, had spent hours together, on Tuesday and again Wednesday, in the fourth man's suite. Instructions had been given to the driver, who stayed by the Peugeot day and night. He was followed, on the second day, into Savannakhet. There he went to a little stationery store stocked with foreign newspapers and supplies specially purchased for American personnel at Nakhon Phanom. At that store the driver purchased several large pads of what appeared to be sketching paper. These had been taken to the inn.

Captain Minh-Lao and his three men, conferring on Wednesday night and ascertaining from the dispatcher that orders had gone out to have the chartered plane ready for takeoff at ten the next morning, concluded that the man at whose suite the meetings had taken place was probably the senior member of the North Vietnamese delegation and that the sketching paper would almost certainly yield important material.

The diversion was planned. Two pounds of explosive were lodged at night, far enough away from the main airport shed to avoid ruining it, but close enough to make a noise deafening to everyone inside the shed. A battery-powered remote detonator was emplaced so that Captain Minh-Lao could set off the explosion with his tiny transmitter, carried in his pocket inside a cigar case. Minh-Lao was slightly puzzled to see only the Russian and the North Vietnamese enter the airport, without their companion, pausing at the counter to fill out their manifests. For a moment he considered detonating the bomb and grabbing one of *their* suitcases. But he peered out the entrance and saw his target sitting in the car, its engine running. So: They were boarding their flight in relays.

He dallied at the newsstand. Moments later, his mark walked into the building and, leaning over the counter, began to fill out the form. Minh-Lao pressed the switch on the transmitter, dove down on his belly behind his target and, while everyone else was prostrate, lifted himself on his knees and slid the target's briefcase into his empty suitcase, just large enough for the briefcase, a few crossword puzzles, and a family album.

Colonel Yen was disappointed that he had not got hold of the sketch pads. "Obviously the two gentlemen from North Vietnam who boarded the plane ahead of your target had those sketches in their own briefcases. So that what we are left with is—this." He pointed at the photographs. "Dr. Fwang-tse from Special Forces will be here any minute. He will surely be able to give us the meaning of the photographs."

Dr. Fwang-tse was there for several hours. He was a trained physicist of some ingenuity, but the transcription was slow because there were many words on the photographed material that were unfamiliar to him, so that they had had to bring in a South Vietnamese student, just returned from M.I.T., to help.

It was almost eight o'clock at night before Colonel Yen was told that Dr. Fwang-tse was ready with his report.

"What you have here," said Dr. Fwang-tse, lowering the intensity of the light he had trained

on the photographs, "is a complicated but com-
prehensive plan based on something the Americans are calling a 'Spikebuoy,' defined as an
'Unattended Ground Sensor.' It is, in simple
terms, a noise detector. It is designed to pick up
any noise, no matter how faint; to transmit that
sound, through its own frequency, to a recorder,
probably airborne, which in turn feeds it into a
computer which in turn records and analyzes
what was heard. Its purpose, I would guess, is
very clear: to use on the Trail in order to detect
enemy transit."

That was enough—all that Colonel Yen
needed.

But he was a cautious man and he decided,
after consulting with his two most trusted aides,
to spend the evening considering alternatives,
of which there were several.

He called the U.S. embassy.

The ambassador was at dinner. Should he be
interrupted?

Colonel Yen was relieved that he had not
needed to speak directly to General Taylor.
"No. But be good enough to pass along this
message to him, that Colonel Yen Chi will need
to see him most urgently at ten A.M. I shall be at
his office."

"Should I write down your telephone, Colonel?"

"The ambassador will not be able to reach me. But you can confirm the authenticity of this call by telephoning ARVN Headquarters. Ask for Intelligence. My office will know about the ten o'clock meeting."

"Very well, Colonel."

And now . . . Should he report immediately to General Khanh? After all, however shaky his hold on the government, he was still the actual head of the Republic of South Vietnam.

No. He would wait. He could always say he had spent the time reconfirming the contents of the photographic material.

The time had come, he told his aides, to visit the prisoner.

Major Tucker Montana, the handcuffs back on, his beard a day old, was brought into the meeting room.

Colonel Yen gave orders to the guards. They removed the shackles and receded to the corners of the room. Colonel Yen now spoke in English.

"*You* may sit down."

Tucker did so.

"Why did you give secrets to the enemy?"

"What secrets?"

Colonel Yen got up from behind the desk and, the photographs in hand, walked around and thrust them under Tucker's chin.

Tucker Montana was visibly amazed.

"Where did you get these?"

"From the briefcase of a gentleman with whom you spent almost three days, who a few minutes later departed, with two companions, on a chartered plane to Hanoi."

Tucker's mind was racing. *How had Bui Tin got hold of the photographs of the Spikebuoy development?* He had not traveled with the portfolio from which these photographs had obviously been taken. And then . . . then he remembered clearly that when he had first mentioned the word "Spikebuoy," Bui Tin had said he knew nothing about a Spikebuoy. Yet in his briefcase all along, Tucker now knew, was a duplicate of his own top-secret Spikebuoy folder. Granted, there were copies of that folder floating about, but every one of them was numbered, and except for copies used every day at Nakhon Phanom and at Aberdeen, there was only his one set, locked in the big vault at the Caravelle.

He said wearily, "I can tell you one thing, Colonel Yen. *I did not give those photographs to—* to the man you took them from."

Colonel Yen sighed. "Ah then, so you are going to be one of those."

"One of those what?"

"One of those who proclaim their innocence, even when there is overwhelming evidence of guilt."

"I'm just telling you: I *did not* give those photographs to the North Vietnamese."

"Ah then. You *knew* he was a North Vietnamese?"

Tucker said nothing.

"What were you talking to the Vietnamese about, him and his two friends, including the Russian, for two days and two nights?"

"About how to end the war." Why not be truthful? he thought. When possible.

Colonel Yen yearned to submit his prisoner to physical pressure. The two guards had been especially selected: they were well trained in the arts of persuasion. He thought about it.

No. He had better not mangle the prisoner before his meeting with the ambassador the next morning. And with General Khanh. He drew slowly on his cigarette. Then said sharply, "We will continue this tomorrow.'' He spoke to the guards in Vietnamese.

Tucker said, ''Colonel, would you pay a fellow officer the respect of putting a reading light in my cell? And could I see a newspaper? And maybe you have a book or two in English here?''

Colonel Yen lifted the telephone and spoke to the chief warder. Tucker didn't understand it all, but got a few words. ''No lights for prisoner.''

He looked up at Colonel Yen and spat on the floor.

★ ★ ★ ★ ★ ★ ★ ★ ★ ★ ★

Chapter Thirty-Eight

At 2:30 the next afternoon Blackford, somber, intent, was on the lead patrol boat in the Gulf, on the final test run with the metal scanner. To be tested was a second South Vietnamese patrol boat in which the U.S. technician had carefully stored, in shipboard compartments variously shielded with silver oxide paper, wet blankets, and other materials designed to deflect inquisitive beams on the prowl for metals, several kinds of weapons. The question was: Might the North Vietnamese, once they became aware of the Tracer, easily package their contraband in such a way as to escape detection at sea? The American technician was most anxious to be done with this, the concluding test, and to get back to Washington with his notebooks. When the mate called Blackford to the radio, he waited impatiently by the screen of his device. To the technician's surprise, the *Mai Tai* suddenly turned, not toward the patrol boat its mission was to scan, but back toward Danang. At full speed.

He rushed up to the noisy cockpit. "What goes on?" he asked Blackford.

"I've been called back. Emergency."

"But—but we could have done our test in just over an hour!"

"You can go back and make the test."

"That will take us another two hours round trip!"

"So, Lieutenant, what do you want me to do? Radio back to cancel the emergency?"

Rufus's voice was tense. Could Blackford make the four o'clock scheduled flight to Saigon? If not, Rufus would arrange for an Air America transport.

"No, I can make it. If I miss, I'll call from the airport and tell you. Do I need to bring anything special with me?"

Rufus paused. "Bring your gear."

Blackford supposed he was being sent to America. Perhaps with Tucker? If so, would Tucker wear handcuffs? If only he knew exactly what Tucker had done, closeted at that inn with the North Vietnamese.

He called Juilland. "Alphonse. Meet me with the car at BOQ. You'll be running me to the airport."

He emptied the contents of his chest of drawers into a large bag and, into another, his reading and writing materials. In less than fifteen minutes he was in the car, in less than two hours at Rufus's safe house.

The door latch responded instantly to his knock. He left his baggage on the landing and rushed upstairs. Flinging open the door, he collapsed, sweating, in the armchair. "What's up, Rufus?"

Rufus told him about Tucker.

And Blackford told Rufus about Tucker. When he was through he said simply, "Since you already knew about Lao Dai, it was easy for me to promise not to tell you about her until he made his plans. You should know, Rufus, that my plan was to pick him up at the airport and get him the hell back to Washington. I don't know what he did at that inn with the gooks."

Rufus made no comment. He told of the events of that morning.

It had been one hell of a meeting, Rufus said, using an expletive he used perhaps once a year, and never during Lent. "General Khanh, Colonel Yen, Maxwell Taylor, and me. General Khanh is being his most obnoxious self. His slippery hold on the government has prompted him to exhibitions of great assertiveness. He is taking the position that what happens to Tucker is the business of the government of South Vietnam, that the government of South Vietnam, 'please remember, Mr. Ambassador,' is an independent state. That the government of South Vietnam is of course very grateful for the critically important aid being given by the United States, but is also aware that the United States is giving this aid to the government of South Vietnam to further United States interests, and United States interests are currently being served primarily by the sacrifice of South Vietnamese lives because the government of the United States, while acknowledging theoretical responsibility for guarding its allies against aggression, is not willing to do what the government of South Vietnam has been urging it to do, what the government of South Vietnam itself wishes to do, namely to declare war against the aggressor and carry the war to the aggressor's hearth. Et cetera, et cetera."

"I get the picture, Rufus. So what does Khanh want to do with Tucker?"

"What he *wants* to do is to torture him for information on exactly what went on in Savannakhet. That is what he truly wants to do, to say nothing of Colonel Yen."

"How'd you handle that?"

"I didn't. But Max Taylor did. Pretty impressively. He said, 'General, the answer is: One, no. You may not manhandle an American official here on military duty. And my second comment is, two, are you aware that you would be attempting to get information from an American who has won the Congressional Medal of Honor for conspicuous bravery?' "

"Did it work?"

"I'm not absolutely sure, to tell you the truth. Because General Khanh went back to a point which is not altogether frivolous. Namely that Tucker has committed treason against the government of South Vietnam. And that it is exclusively the right of the government of South Vietnam to decide how to handle traitors no matter what their nationality."

"I hate to say it, but legally I think he's right, isn't he?"

"Yes. He is right. We will need to lean on the dependence of the South Vietnamese government on the United States. The argument went on more than two hours."

"What was General Taylor pressing for?"

"He wants Tucker taken by the South Vietnamese to the airfield—in shackles; Max Taylor said that would be all right—and placed in one of our military planes, which will take him to Hawaii, and from then on he's our problem."

"Reaction?"

"Out of the question, et cetera, et cetera. And then heavy emphasis on their right to be briefed about the probable military damage done by acquainting the enemy with the secrets of Igloo White.

"They reached a point where there simply wasn't anything to be said that hadn't already been said, so they agreed to meet again tonight at ten P.M. But—but, we got one small concession from them. You will be permitted to talk to him. I told the general, and Colonel Yen, that you were an important influence on him, that you might get from him cooperation of the kind he isn't willing to give us . . . the whole line. They have nothing to lose by giving this one indication that they are being reasonable. So—you are to be at the Kham Chi Hoa prison at exactly nine P.M.."

"I know what I have to do before then." Blackford looked at his watch. "Rufus, I've got to find Lao Dai but I don't have her address. Your people have been tailing her—"

"Blackford. She has left the city. While waiting for you I went myself to her apartment. She was not there. I went to her school. She hadn't shown up this morning. Back to the apartment, and dug up a neighbor who said she had left in an automobile with three bags at eleven this morning. She's flown."

"Goddamn." He thought for a moment. "But Tucker has no reason to know anything on this score, does he? He doesn't even know that you spotted her as a spy before he did. He doesn't know that you've been onto her for a week."

"I've thought about it. I don't know whether Colonel Yen threw Lao Dai at him. We don't even know how the North Vietnamese agent who met with Tucker at Savannakhet got those photographs. Tucker told Colonel Yen he didn't give away the photographs, that he didn't even have his Igloo folder with him. He may have been lying, but we opened up the hotel safe and got out Tucker's briefcase, broke into it, and his folder is sitting there. Of course, he could have photographed the folder and taken the photographs with him and simply lied to us. I just don't think so."

"You think—?"

"I think probably Lao Dai photographed them at some moment of opportunity. Of which," Rufus looked down, his lips in that fatalistic configuration Blackford knew well, "I am sure she had many."

Blackford did not eat dinner. Instead he walked toward the prison, a half hour away. He arrived early, at 8:30, and entered a Vietnamese restaurant on the corner of the street opposite. He then ordered a bowl of rice and soup. He fiddled with it. His mind was reeling, and he knew that he must do his best to be persuasive. To *persuade* Tucker. He feared for his arsenal of arguments.

At 8:55 he was at the gate. He had carefully straightened his tie. He was wearing a light gabardine suit. He must be the essence of formality with the prison officials.

Inside, he was beckoned into a private room,

and there rubbed down so thoroughly he wondered for a moment whether they would next
demand a strip search.

He had six cigars in a pouch. "Why so many?"
the captain asked.

"I work best when I am smoking. And as Colonel Yen no doubt has told you, I am here to do
very important work on his behalf and on behalf
of General Khanh." The captain gave him back
his matches.

He was taken to the meeting room and told to
sit down. Instead, Blackford turned and walked
back toward the corridor.

"What is the matter?" the captain asked,
clearly alarmed.

"I have been authorized to talk privately with
Major Montana. I am a representative of the
government of the United States, and I decline
to carry out my instructions in a room"—he
pointed to the meeting room, traversing his finger from one end of it to another—"that is obviously wired for sound. I shall return to my
quarters and wait until I hear again from Colonel
Yen."

There was a hurried consultation between the
captain and an adjutant who had said nothing

during the proceedings. They spoke hastily in Vietnamese. The captain turned to Blackford: "Where would you consent to meet with the prisoner?"

"In your office," Blackford said.

There was a pause. "Very well. Follow me."

It was a pleasant, workmanlike office, with a large desk, a small conference table, and two armchairs. The captain walked over to his desk, picked up a few loose papers, tinkered with the telephone, and went out. Blackford was left alone. He looked at his watch. It was 9:15. In five minutes the door opened. Tucker came in. He was shackled, but the guards shut the door behind him, and they were alone.

The two men stared at each other. Tucker breathed heavily, but said nothing. Blackford's voice was hoarse when he said, motioning to an armchair, "We may as well sit down."

Tucker did so.

"I did manage to get you this." He drew out the packet of cigars.

Tucker's face softened. He cleared his throat. "Don't mind if I do. You didn't bring an electric razor, I suppose? Funny, all the fieldwork I've done, I still don't like to go without shaving." He leaned over to draw in the flame Blackford held out. It was awkward, having to lift both hands to hold his cigar to his lips. Finally he had it lit.

"No. Sorry, no razor. Maybe next time. I wasn't sure I could get away with the cigars."

"They've fed me. But goddamn, Black, there's almost no daylight in that cell. And none at night. Not one fucking watt of light. You know something, remember I told you I was on the *Enola Gay* on the Hiroshima run, my job to keep my eyes on the bomb's metabolism? I had to lie down a total of five and a half hours each way, half of it with the bomb as my bedmate, half the time by myself, on the return leg, in the dark, except for those little red lights for reading the gauges. That was the only other time I was where I couldn't read a book, unless you count some of those foxholes in Korea."

He smiled as he drew on his cigar, and without hesitating went on, "I know why you're here, Black. I mean, I knew you'd come and visit me just to be a nice guy, but you're obviously here 'cause you were sent here, and that would be to find out what I was doing with the North Vietnamese guys, and you know something, Black, pal, you're not going to find out. Because nobody's going to find out. What I did would be undone if anybody found out. So that's it, and I hope we can talk about other things. Because . . . otherwise, there's nothing to talk about."

Blackford knew that was it. He said nothing.

And then, exhaling evenly, Tucker said, "What time is it exactly, Black? They took away my watch."

"It's twenty to ten."

"The warder tipped me off an hour ago. You see, he's a Catholic, and saw the bio on me they must have got from the embassy, shows I went to a Catholic school as a boy. What he told me, in case I wanted to say some prayers before then, was: They're going to shoot me at ten P.M."

Blackford shot up. His eyes narrowed. He turned and lunged for the telephone on the captain's desk.

The dial had been padlocked.

He went across the room to the door. It would not open. He banged on it. There was no answer. He was white with rage. In desperation he turned to Tucker.

"It's a scare tactic! Hell, at ten they're meeting, the big cheeses. General Khanh, Colonel Yen, Maxwell Taylor, Rufus—to talk about you! We're trying to get you on a transport to Hawaii!"

"Maybe. Maybe a fake execution. Though something tells me it ain't that, ol' buddy. But you know, Black, what I want, don't you? And I just hope, I just pray—yes, I prayed about it— that you've been to see Lao Dai. I just had a feeling you would. Did you?"

Blackford said. "Yes, Tucker, I did, went there late this afternoon. Of course I didn't tell her where you were. All I said was that I was a little surprised you weren't back from your hunting trip and I wondered whether she had heard from you."

"She was really worried?"

"Yes, she was. She said she guessed you had decided to stay on another couple of days. She . . . she said how much she loves you."

"She was *really* worried about my still being in Thailand?"

"Terribly worried."

Tucker Montana got up and smashed his manacled wrists against the desk lamp, breaking it into fragments. The glass brought blood on his right wrist. He closed his eyes, and a single tear appeared. He spoke in a whisper. . . .

"You didn't see her, Black. And she knows I left the inn, because I telephoned her before leaving the airport. She said she would meet my flight. I been thinking, thinking about . . . the photographs. I'm a goddamned genius in some ways but not too smart in others. I put it all together, one possible explanation. And now I know." The tears were streaming down his cheeks. Blackford embraced him.

The door was pulled wide. Four men with rifles. A fifth with pistol in hand, which he pointed at Blackford.

"Do not move, Mr. Oakes."

The four men went to Tucker Montana and led him out. The captain, his pistol still pointed, backed out of the room. The door slammed shut. Blackford could hear the heavy lock being closed.

Blackford closed his eyes. Minutes later he heard the fusillade. And, after a short silence, the final pistol shot.

★ ★ ★ ★ ★ ★ ★ ★ ★ ★ ★

Chapter Thirty-Nine

NOVEMBER 8, 1964
SAIGON, SOUTH VIETNAM

The dignitaries were served tea. They occupied the elaborately appointed office of the Prime Minister, at Gia Long Palace. There was five minutes of small talk. The atmosphere had calmed down. Then General Khanh addressed his guests.

"Gentlemen, perhaps we have other business than what—divided us this morning? I hope so, because on the matter of Major Montana, the necessary judicial formalities having been attended to"—he looked down at his watch—"the traitor was executed five minutes ago."

Maxwell Taylor stood up, his eyes flashing. He looked witheringly at General Khanh, and at Colonel Yen. Yen was smiling. General Taylor walked without a word to the door. Rufus followed him out.

★ ★ ★ ★ ★ ★ ★ ★

Chapter Forty

Rufus reached the safe house just before midnight. He was not surprised to find Blackford sitting there. The apartment was appropriately utilitarian, as though quickly furnished for a transient client: service-duty furniture, desk, coffee table, prints of pretty young Vietnamese girls with parasols walking down the beach. There was a whiskey glass on the table, but it was still filled.

Rufus turned away, looking absentmindedly at the bookshelf. Blackford heard the quiet voice.

"There isn't anything to say, Blackford. Nothing."

"No, Rufus, nothing. That shit. Those shits."

"It's their country."

"Yes. And—as the saying goes—they can keep it."

"I'm sure I know what you are thinking." Rufus sat down in the armchair opposite. "Is your mind made up?"

"Yes. I'm checking out. I'll be leaving tomorrow."

Rufus spoke very softly. "Tucker was wrong, you know."

"He was wrong, Rufus, about letting the girl get those pictures, yes. About talking to her— and to them. The pictures were only valuable because he had invented what was in them. But, Rufus, I don't think he was wrong on the big point."

"Our presence here?"

"No. I think we have a right to be here, and I think the Vietnamese want us here. But Tucker didn't think we'd stick it out, match will against their will. And I think he was right. Told him so, in fact. I'm not against fighting apparently lost causes if there is at least the possibility of righting a wrong, of winning, but I don't see that there is, in Vietnam—in this climate, in this way. . . .

So—it's time to go, after thirteen years. The best of it has been—you, Rufus."

Rufus got up. For a moment Blackford thought he was coming over to him. But he stopped.

"Where are you going?" He paused. "Mexico?"

"Yes," Blackford said. He picked up his glass, and looked at it. "Mexico." He took the drink and sipped at it, then put it down again.

Blackford stood up, reached for his briefcase, and extended his hand.

"Goodbye, Rufus."

"Goodbye, Blackford."

"I hope you will visit us there."

"I will visit you, Blackford."

"You will always be welcome."

Blackford lowered his head, turned to the door, and let himself out.

This is a work of fiction.

The most conspicuous historical characters are, obviously, characters in history, and some of the episodes are drawn from official and nonofficial, but creditable, sources.

Among the books and materials I have relied upon are the *Facts on File Yearbook* for 1964; *Tonkin Gulf* by Eugene G. Windchy (Doubleday, 1971); *Truth is the First Casualty* by Joseph C. Goulden (Rand McNally, 1969); *Vietnam* by Stanley Karnow (Viking, 1983); and *Goldwater* by Barry M. Goldwater with Jack Casserly (Doubleday, 1988). I shouldn't need to say that constructions of events, as distilled by me, are not necessarily those as seen by the authors cited; but I shall.

Operation 34-A is accurately described, as is Operation Igloo White.

The second Gulf of Tonkin episode remains something of a mystery, though it is, I think, correct to say that the historical consensus is that there was no attack, merely confusion caused by defective sonar work, addled radar readings, and sights and sounds resulting from eccentric meteorological conditions. The sequence of reported events is accurately reproduced.

Colonel Bui Tin was the principal architect of the Ho Chi Minh Trail, and was interviewed by Morley Safer in his book *Flashbacks* (Random House, 1990).

ACKNOWLEDGMENTS

I am grateful to friends who read the first draft and made many useful suggestions, including my wife, Pat, my siblings, Reid and Priscilla Buckley, and my obliging friends Charles Wallen, Jr., Professor Thomas Wendel, and Richard Clurman, and Lois Wallace.

Tony Savage not only typed all the drafts, but encouraged the whole enterprise and also made valuable suggestions.

Dorothy McCartney, as ever, was invaluable in research matters, and I am ever so grateful to her for the pains she took.

Frances Bronson provided the usual editorial coordination, irreplaceable.

Mrs. Chaucy Bennetts, the superb copy editor, rescued me yet again.

Joseph Isola (he keeps count) has, with this book, proofread twenty-five of my books, with diligence and flair and patience.

Alfred Aya, Jr., who in many ways reminds me of Tucker Montana, gave me all the technical data I used: not only a technical description of the paraphernalia that went into our Igloo White operation, which he got from research; but also the counterweapons, which he invented; as also such details as I used in describing the mission of Blackford Oakes on August 4, 1964, in the Gulf of Tonkin. I have all along suspected that an unpublished feature of the ABM Treaty forbids the United States Government from availing itself of the resources of Alfred Aya, Jr.

I have previously recorded my indebtedness to Samuel S. Vaughan of Random House for his prodigious contributions. But this time around he read my manuscript, in line-by-line detail, twice, contributing much of the best that is there. I am obliged to him as an editor, and as a friend.

W.F.B.
Stamford, Connecticut
August 11, 1990

ABOUT THE AUTHOR

WILLIAM F. BUCKLEY, JR., gifted with vitality, vision, style, integrity, and one of the most interesting minds of our time, recently decided to give over the reins to *National Review*, "the most influential journal of opinion of the half-century" (George F. Will). Having helped reconstitute the modern conservative movement in the United States and having had a critical hand in events that made possible the ascendancy of a popular Republican President, Buckley's retirement leaves him with only a half-dozen other careers and enthusiasms to pursue. His syndicated columns continue; as do his occasional harpsichord concerts; the long-running *Firing Line* television program, which offers an airing to myriad political and philosophical viewpoints; as well as his lectures, and sailing and skiing adventures.

The next mystery is whether Buckley will continue sowing his Oakes with a tenth novel.

. . . (A forthcoming *Paris Review* interview will illuminate the novels' origins and inventions.) Also on his agenda: a fresh transatlantic sail— with a twist—and his first collection of essays since *Right Reason*.